EX LIBRIS

VINTAGE CLASSICS

A BUNCH OF FIVES

Helen Simpson is the author of *Four Bare Legs in a Bed*, *Dear George*, *Hey Yeah Right Get a Life*, *Constitutional* and *In-Flight Entertainment*. In 1991 she was chosen as the *Sunday Times* Young Writer of the Year and won the Somerset Maugham Award. In 1993 she was chosen as one of *Granta*'s twenty Best of Young British Novelists. She has also received the Hawthornden Prize, and the American Academy of Arts and Letters' E.M. Forster Award. She lives in London.

REVIEWS FOR *FOUR BARE LEGS IN A BED*, 1990

'This is an outstanding collection of stories – the product of a new, original voice'
Hilary Mantel

'An outstanding collection'
Nick Hornby, *Sunday Times*

'*Four Bare Legs in a Bed* is a collection of short stories that I regard as outstanding . . . You should read her'
John Nicholson, *The Times*

'Sidling on stage as jester at the court of male pomp, kicking off belly-laughs or melting you with an apt phrase, Helen Simpson makes a delectable debut'
David Hughes, *Mail on Sunday*

'These stories display a wonderful, roaming imagination and are told in such succulent prose that you wince at their brevity. This is a most exceptional debut'
Patricia Miller, *Evening Standard*

'This is an inspired debut – her prose positively sparkles'
Trevor Royle, *Scotland on Sunday*

'So true, so funny, so dazzlingly written that they seem to glitter like a heap of jewels in a box'
Jane Shilling, *'The' Magazine*

'She seems to do it all effortlessly: always with style and seemingly without tricks. Gone are the usual, all-too-discernible hallmarks of the "serious" short story'
Sue Roe, *Times Literary Supplement*

'The prose seems polished by years of experience. At the same time it is informed with the freshness of an absolute here and now. She writes about women as for years men have written about men, giving them status, talent, presence, reality. She can be sparingly tragic and unsparingly funny'
Ruth Rendell

'The most sensuous writer in the land – a cross between Chekhov and Colette'
Fay Weldon, *Mail on Sunday*

'Absolutely brilliant . . . I never knew what the phrase "she can write like an angel" meant until I read this babe's book. Because you don't really think of angels writing, do you? You think of them playing harps, and flying about, and grooving en masse on the head of a pin . . . But there is something other-worldly, something seraphically savage about Helen Simpson's work'
Julie Burchill, *New Review*

REVIEWS FOR *DEAR GEORGE*, 1995

'Of all contemporary writers, Simpson has the most honest, the most authentic voice . . . [Her] unfooled but kind eye is matched by her ear for the ebb and flow of everyday talk. But she does more than just record: every word rings true. *Dear George* shimmers with grace and savagery and wit'
Nigella Lawson, *The Times*

'Helen Simpson is a writer with such a gift for sweet tenderness that one could almost overlook the glittering sharpness of the insights . . . [Her stories] have a paradoxical, satisfying quality; they are both deeply pleasurable, and – particularly for male readers – deeply uncomfortable. Not many writers manage to be as funny as Helen Simpson without sacrificing the honesty that her writing unmistakably has'
Philip Hensher, *Mail on Sunday*

'She should be read by men, wishing to understand the women they live with and without. This will be no chore: her stories can be read quickly, knocked back in a single grateful gulp like an aperitif, or savoured with a slow, cool intoxication . . . She is Katherine Mansfield's natural successor'
Kate Kellaway, *Observer*

'This is Simpson's real charm – that she believes in love . . . Like Katherine Mansfield, she both satirises and understands our unfounded trust in sunlight and embraces. She is the heir to Mansfield's sharp combinations; a knowing idealism, a hopeful cynicism. This joie de vivre is a glorious thing for a short-story writer to have'
Natasha Walter, *Guardian*

REVIEWS FOR *CONSTITUTIONAL*, 2005

REVIEWS FOR *IN-FLIGHT ENTERTAINMENT*, 2010

'Acclaimed by Jonathan Franzen and many others, but still not as well known as she deserves to be, Simpson is, to my mind, the best short story writer now working in English'
Ed Crooks, *Financial Times*

'When it comes to contemporary maestros of the short story form, Helen Simpson is up there with Alice Munro'
Lucy Atkins, *Sunday Times*

'*In-Flight Entertainment* is quite delectable, confirming her as the queen of the comic short story'
David Robson, *Sunday Telegraph*

'It is all packaged with Simpson's deadpan wit – she is one of the most sharply funny writers in England today'
Kate Webb, *Times Literary Supplement*

'Very black comedy . . . She is a wry, humane and brilliant observer of our peculiar condition'
William Palmer, *Independent*

'Simpson's gifts are a lyrical vocabulary, an authoritative form, a special funny-sad quality and a subtlety of understanding. Add in political argument, and she is a key voice for our time'
Margaret Reynolds, *The Times*

'These stories are dark and bitter but also at times laugh-out-loud funny. Less furious polemic then, more peerless fiction'
Teddy Jamieson, *Herald*

HELEN SIMPSON

A Bunch of Fives

Selected Stories

VINTAGE BOOKS
London

Published by Vintage Classics 2012

2 4 6 8 10 9 7 5 3 1

Vintage
Random House, 20 Vauxhall Bridge Road,
London SW1V 2SA

www.vintage-classics.info

Addresses for companies within The Random House Group
Limited can be found at: www.randomhouse.co.uk/offices.htm

The Random House Group Limited Reg. No. 954009

A CIP catalogue record for this book
is available from the British Library

ISBN 9780099561576

The Random House Group Limited supports The Forest
Stewardship Council (FSC®), the leading international forest
certification organisation. Our books carrying the FSC
label are printed on FSC® certified paper. FSC is the only
forest certification scheme endorsed by the leading environmental
organisations, including Greenpeace. Our paper
procurement policy can be found at:
www.randomhouse.co.uk/environment

Typeset in Bembo by Palimpsest Book Production Limited,
Falkirk, Stirlingshire
Printed and bound by Clays Ltd, St Ives plc

Contents

From *Constitutional*

From *In-Flight Entertainment*

Introduction

Why *A Bunch of Fives*?
Because there are five stories here from each of my five short story collections so far; and also because, starting in 1990, these collections have been published at five-year intervals.

What was it like to read through twenty-five years' worth of stories at a go?
My first reaction, which I wasn't expecting, was – 'Oh they're good! They're really good!' I felt extremely happy.

Huh! You would say that, wouldn't you.
Well no, actually.

Of course you would!
No, really. I've kicked and berated myself for years – decades – for not being more prolific. 'Lazy', 'Stupid', 'Waste of space', etc. And I was relieved to see none of that showed. They may have taken a long time to write, but they're good.

Five years per collection, though!—Why so slow?
I don't know.

It's a very wasteful way of writing, the way I do it. I spend a lot of preliminary time thinking and reading round it; it's like spending hours cooking a meal only to see it gobbled down in a few minutes. But the way I think of it is – reader, I save you time! I cut to the chase! And of course it means starting a new hare every time you start a story.

There's been a lot of Life, too.

Everybody has that.
True.

OK, no excuses. I will say though that at a certain point I found it useful to adopt the writing motto, 'You can slow down but you can't stop.'

You slowed down alright.
I've kept at it though. Quality not quantity! They're all in print and they're built to last. They earn their living too – they'll often sell more than once (to newspapers, magazines, radio, anthologies, in translation etc.) before being published in a collection, and sometimes they continue to sell afterwards (for example, 'Burns and the Bankers' has just been adapted as a radio play a decade on from when it was written; 'Diary of an Interesting Year', which I wrote just over two years ago, has appeared in eight different publications so far).

Five years, though! That's ridiculous . . .
They take as long as they take.

What I'm hoping is that I'll be given extra time on account of being slower than average – an extra fifty years perhaps?

How did you decide which stories to include?

I chose five from each collection, for fairness. If I'd allowed myself five more, I'd have included 'Every Third Thought' (a cancer farce),[1] 'Opera' (a reworking of the Orpheus myth),[2] 'Millennium Blues' (with its 1999 mass-devastation-by-aeroplane),[3] 'Homework' (larking around with auto-biographical–writing clichés),[4] and 'Scan' (which would have added a soupçon too much death to the mix – I did take advice from my wise young editors here).[5]

Yes, funny how these stories start with sex then move on to babies and finish up with cancer . . .

Well, what do you *expect* over twenty-five years?

Having said which, I've got the full range now – I can reach forwards and backwards, and I'm full of ideas. I can do the whole lot from birth to death and everything in between. I'm in my prime!

So are your stories autobiographical?

Oh yawn.

Sorry. That was rude of me.

Yes I do draw on life, but in the sense of, 'Oh, that's useful, I'll have that.' More than a decade ago a stranger died near me on an aeroplane; it was distressing and sad at the time, but the writer in me stored it away for later. Years on it became the central incident in the title story

---

1 From *Constitutional*
2 From *Hey Yeah Right Get a Life*
3 From *Hey Yeah Right Get a Life*
4 From *In-Flight Entertainment*
5 From *In-Flight Entertainment*

of my fifth collection. But this sort of useful event or scene can equally well appear in a dream – a fair number have to me. So, yes.

If you write a story in the first person and it appears to be thinly disguised confessional or memoir many readers will assume that it's 'really' you. In my first-person story 'Constitutional' there is a detailed portrait of the narrator's grandfather unravelling through Alzheimer's in his final decade. When I rang in with proof corrections to the sympathetic well-read editor of the magazine where it was to be published, he asked me whether I had been very close to my grandfather. But both my grandfathers were dead before I was old enough to remember them, and I've never known anybody with Alzheimer's. That's not to say I made it all up out of thin air, though.

In a way I imagine stories are less likely to be autobiographical than novels – by their very nature they are likely to draw more heavily on generic experience and less on the idiosyncrasies of individual characters. (More than a very little character exploration in a short story and you're edging towards a grotesque.) The stories I've been interested in writing recently have been those where the experience is common or typical – as in a song; that way you can cut down on names and status details, particularly if the story is very short. Although of course the minute I say that I think of other sorts of story where the interest lives in precisely those details.

Perhaps the most that can be said here is: fiction is self-revealing in that it would be a very odd writer who chose to write about things that didn't interest him or her.

Does this question irritate you?

It makes me want to shrug and answer, 'Who cares?' When I read a piece of fiction, I'm not interested in whether it really happened to the writer or not. I'm only interested in it as a piece of writing. Is it a good piece of writing? Does it have the ring of emotional truth? Is it convincing? It's none of my business whether it actually happened to the writer.

Alright though, yes, I admit it. I do feel it myself sometimes, the gossip-fascination; but when I do I tell myself to back off. It's just nosiness and prurience, generally – that good word curiosity is too dignified for it.

Let me ask you a question in return. Do you think women writers get asked this question more often than men?

Why do you ask?

Is it because you think women are less imaginative? That they can only write about what's under their own noses?

Which reminds me – quite a lot of your stories are domestic. Shouldn't you get out more?

Ah, the D word; I was wondering when that would come up. Very often it's a political objection rather than a literary one, this; it's an objection to the lives described, not to the writing itself. This has led to a ridiculous situation where if a woman writer describes domestic work and life (the daily reality of most women in the world), she's seen as letting the side down . . .

Yawn! So are you a man-hating feminist? Because the men in your stories are awful, aren't they?
Blimey, you aren't half sensitive. Did nobody ever tease you when you were young? There are just as many lovely men as stinkers in my stories – more, in fact! Just as there are nasty women as well as nice ones. So what? I'm neither a misandrist nor a misogynist. What I am interested in – among other things – is how men and women (and children) live together. Or don't.

There's far too much baby stuff, though, on the whole.
You think so? Maybe I was redressing the balance a bit. There seemed to be very little in print about it at the time *Hey Yeah Right Get a Life* was published (in 2000), in proportion to how much of it there was in life.

Still, you risk being labelled a baby bore.
Really? Yeah. Who cares.
    It's oddly contentious subject matter; intensely intimate; not exactly marginal but generally avoided.
    Apart from anything else, even the blindest of bats must eventually realise it's parenthood that gender-politicises relationships – which is an interesting fact of life, whether you have children or not (you'll have had parents yourself, after all) . . .

Yawn! Yawn!
Are you suggesting I should be cannier in how I choose my subject matter? That doesn't seem to be how it works; I wait for my subject matter to choose me. It wouldn't work the other way round.

And with the latest book, *In-Flight Entertainment*, you risk being labelled a global warming bore too. What's all that about?

How rude you are!

I'm not writing agitprop. Why would anyone want to know my views on climate change? What do *I* know?

But I am drawn to what's currently uncomfortable, and one such usefully touchy subject now is whether we ought to cut back on air travel for the sake of the future. This suggestion never fails to provoke a silence. That's what started me off, I think.

Interestingly enough, the short story form is particularly good for uncomfortable or edgy subjects because it doesn't allow you to sink down or lose yourself. When you read a novel, it feels natural to hand yourself over and suspend your critical faculties – you're lulled and dulled as (on the whole) less is demanded of you. Whereas reading a short story you have to stay alert; it's more of a performance.

Ideal for an awkward subject like climate change . . .

Talk about doom and gloom! Which leads to the next question – why so many stories about death?

Not that many, surely? Oh yes, there are a few I suppose, if you count the ones about time. Time, death, same difference. So what? All stories lead to you-know-what in the end. But I don't want to be a funsucker, you're obviously sensitive . . .

You'd agree though that the short story is a narrow genre best kept for little subjects?

That is such rubbish. Short doesn't have to mean small or

slight, any more than long means big or profound. The challenge is, maximum power for minimum length.

But it simply hasn't got the breadth of a novel – surely you find it limiting?
I think a good short story can be like a core sample. Think how much a geologist can learn from a core sample – it's the same! If it's a good one, you've got absolutely everything you need to know about the history and geography and inhabitants and social conditions of the area, in wonderfully concise form.

That's all very well but short stories don't sell.
They do sell if they're good. If they're good they sell. But no, they don't sell in anything like the same numbers as novels.

With a short story collection, place this story against that and it throws a certain light; add a third, and the light shifts again. You're allowed ambivalence, and you aren't coerced by the form into resolving everything or making judgements. The novel is by comparison too often a big bully.

But this is also why story collections are so hard to sell – because of their very variousness, they're far more difficult to describe or review than novels. With a collection of stories of varied tone and voices and different subject areas, how is it possible to sum it up in a few words? And of course, when you're selling that's important.

Why don't you have a go at a novel? That's what people want to read, that's where the money is. Surely you could just take one of your stories and . . .
What? Spin it out?

Yes, that's what I was going to say.
I thought so.

One of Katherine Mansfield's most anthologised stories is 'The Daughters of the Late Colonel', and at one point she commented, 'Even dear old Hardy told me to write more about those sisters. As if there was any more to say!' It's lightness of touch you're after as well as power.

In novels you expand, you elaborate; you explain when, where, how things are happening; you go on and on. You don't need to do any of that, really, with a short story. You can just skip all the gossipy stuff and go for the jugular. It's direct and intimate and it doesn't waste time.

Maybe the short story writer lacks the novelist's courage to be boring.

I still find the form as flexible and satisfyingly anti-boredom (from the point of view of both writer and reader) as I ever have. It's quick and light and adrenalised; it can turn on a sixpence. It means I can do something new every time. I like to do something different, formally – shape them differently from each other.

Sometimes you get novels so full of padding you want to say, 'C'mon, c'mon, *move* it.' Usually at the end of a novel I think, I liked that, I enjoyed that, but I wish it had been shorter . . . Writing stories rather than novels, though, the obvious loss is that you don't hold your reader over hours and hours of real time. Reading a novel is a longer, more involving experience. Not necessarily better, though. Often far less memorable. I keep talking to myself about this . . .

But you've never written a novel and you never will . . .
Who says?

One thing the novel can do that the short story struggles with is to show character developing in time. For me, that would be the main temptation offered by the longer form. And as I'm older now it stands to reason I might also now be better at this now than I would have been at twenty.

And you might not.
True. But one day, if I feel like writing a novel, I will.

Meanwhile I've got a really good idea for a story . . .

© Helen Simpson, 2012

From

Four Bare Legs in a Bed

Four Bare Legs in a Bed

When you draw the curtains in the morning you stand in front of the window like a black dog. I am brought down to earth with a bump. It isn't fair.

'Where were *you* last night?'

You ask, even though you *know* we were sitting side by side over a shepherd's pie in front of *World in Action*. I sip my tea and blink at the little azure Chinaman fishing from his pagoda.

'*Well*?' you insist.

I channel vertically under the sheet to hide my blushing neck, muttering demulcent nothings. Goats and monkeys.

What can I say, after all? I can hardly admit that I had a most colourful and stimulating night, thank you, lying bear-hugged with your squash partner skin to skin, dissolving in an exchange of slow damp kisses.

Don't let on to the Old Man, but I think I can safely say I have slept with all the men and boys of my acquaintance, including the grey-beards and one-way homosexuals and those towards whom I had not thought I felt an iota of oestrus.

Only two nights ago I was lying on a riverbank with the other girls, and beside me knelt a boy of about fourteen or fifteen, a childish little chap. A boatload of his school-friends in their uniforms drifted past. They wore straw hats, but the sun beat up from the river to make crescents of light flick like sticklebacks over their faces. As they floated by, their smarmy teacher unleashed on us a particularly obsequious grin. His teeth were snaggled and tarnished. Ooh, we all giggled, revolted, and my little boy showed himself in sympathy. I gave him a kiss and a hug; there was a beam of envy from the schoolmaster. I gave him more hugs and kisses, and a generous warmth spread through me, tantalising and lovely.

'You're only fourteen, aren't you, darling,' I teased, pressing his head to my bosom, pretending to be motherly. I woke describing circles, and I was laughing.

When we were first married, all of six months ago, he used to bring home large men in suits who laughed loudly, drank beer from tins and said outlandish things in suddenly solemn voices: for example, 'It's time to put your cock on the block,' and, 'We are talking serious megabucks.' After a couple of months he stopped inviting them. I missed the flick of their eyes, but by then of course we were talking serious monogamy.

A couple of nights before the wedding we met for a drink on Eel Pie Island. We stood in the long grass staring upstream, watching the Thames flow by on either side, dividing just before it reached us and meeting again behind us. I looked back down half-a-dozen years and saw my secret self at thirteen or fourteen. I had never felt incomplete alone, nor had I ever trembled for security. Now I had a premonition that my privacy and self-possession, which harmed nobody and were my only important treasures, would be things of the past the day after tomorrow. My saying yes to a wedding appeared in this illuminated instant as self-betrayal. A tide of shame and terror crept over my skin, moving fast like spilt wine. I stammered some thin wedge of these thoughts to my future husband, thinking (with an early marital shudder at the predictability), he will say no man is an island.

'No man is an island,' he said.

Incidentally, marriage gave his words the lie, since it made an island of every man except himself. Conjugal life correctly conjugated reads: libido libidas libidat libidamus libidatis libiDON'T. Goodbye to the pure uncomplicated glee which can spring up between strangers, leading them out of their clothes and towards each other in a spirit of, among other things, sunny friendship.

The girls at school had a quasi-religious conviction that once you felt the right way about a man, that was *it*. He was the other half who would make you whole, he was the only possible father of your children. I meet Rhoda every once in a while for a slice of cauliflower quiche, and she still subscribes to all that.

'Either it's Animal Lust, which doesn't last,' says Rhoda, 'or it's the Real Thing, which means Marriage.' Rhoda likes things cut and dried. Recently she became engaged to the only possible father of her children. She took him shopping for a ring, hauled him past the windows of Hatton Garden, and he expressed nothing but ridicule at the prices. Next time he went to tea with Rhoda's parents, he was sitting on the edge of the sofa balancing a plate of flapjacks on his knee when his prospective mother-in-law produced a tray of unpriced rings and demanded that he choose one. She said her daughter Rhoda was not to be shamed by a naked finger. He chose, and of course it turned out to be the second most expensive, over a thousand. There is a moral in that somewhere.

Sometimes I slide my ring off before we go to a party, but he makes me put it on again. That left-handed ring finger is the weakest of the ten, always the first to let you down during a vigorous scherzando; there are sets of arpeggios based exclusively round strengthening its feebleness. It is also the most sensitive, the one women use when following such instructions as, Pat this feather-weight creme lightly into the fragile skin tissue which surrounds the eye area.

Lily-livered, swathed in white from head to foot, I said, 'I will.' Willing and waking may come to the same thing, but sleep is another matter. I am only properly alone now when I'm asleep, such is the encroachment. Well, sleep is a third part of life so I suppose I mustn't grumble.

You don't even have a right to your own bed when you're married. There is no escaping the mildmint breath toothpasting its way across the pillows. I am lying cool and straight in my bed when *he* climbs in with a proprietorial air, and I catch myself thinking, 'How dare you.' I never achieve the old full secrecy now, I never properly escape him, not until I've lost consciousness altogether. And even then . . . The other night as I lay waiting for sleep – almost there – I felt his fingertips on my eyelids, and I knew he was testing whether the eyeballs were moving in order to tell whether I was dreaming or not.

My husband is older than me; not so much older that he thanks his lucky stars for me, but sufficiently older to create the distance of a demi-generation gap between us. He is a Management Consultant and he thinks he's got me taped. He probably has, except for my nocturnal life. He has a square leonine head with icy blue-green eyes. I don't know what he thinks about – 'If only he could talk,' as old people say of their pets.

You could say we rushed into it, but then, why *not* repent at leisure. How dismal are those long-term liaisons where, the seven years and a day being up, no nerve is left to take the plunge. On our honeymoon near St Ives, there was one late wordless picnic down on the beach when I stared at his cleanly minted profile against the night sky and worshipped the silence. Out last week at some busy new restaurant, however, we sat dumbly over plates of chilli-spiced pomfret fish until in the end, to stop the water-drops leaping, I lowered my eyes, staring hard at his tee-shirt, on which was traced a detailed map of half a square mile of the Outer Hebrides, and savagely wished myself there.

His worst failing so far is jealousy. The last time I rang him at the office, his secretary said earnestly, 'I haven't seen hare nor hound of him.' But if *he* rings *me* and I don't answer, there is likely to be an inquisition. Last week it got beyond a joke. I had taken the phone off the hook because Mr Pembleton had come round to give me my clarinet lesson and at nine pounds an hour I don't like to take any chances on being interrupted. Anyway, towards the end of the lesson we were deep into a passage of Albinoni, quite transported by its bosky rills, and Mr Pembleton's eyebrows were leaping in time to the rhythm as always, when in burst my bellowing pinstriped husband.

It was very embarrassing. I was furious. Mr Pembleton was almost crying as he slunk off, not even given enough time to pack away his clarinet properly.

I shall have to be more careful in future.

Sometimes I have a dream that tears through me like a hurricane and leaves me shaking, the sort of dream that used to be explained away as the work of devils. There were sleepy female demons who gave out such heat that even in midwinter the soporific lettuce seeds sprouted when they walked by, the mere rustle of their skirts made frosty rosebushes blossom into full-blown crimson. Such a succuba would descend in a hot dream upon a sleeping man with an appetite so violent that by the time she had finished with him even the densest-bearded would wake quite exhausted and feeling as though his bones had been dislocated. My own hurricanes would no doubt have been described as the work of that cocky male devil the incubus, whose nocturnal interference was held responsible for the births of mutants and monsters.

Occasionally, at the end of some mad sparkling quarrel, he clubs me down at last with that spiteful threat: 'What *you* need is a baby. *That* would sort you out.' Oh yes, that would be the end of this road and no mistake. They're all on his side, of course: First, It was ordained for the procreation of children, etc.

Do you think it possible that a dream confluence – put it more bluntly, fusion with a chimera – might result in a phantom pregnancy? Or does the waking self give up the ghost?

My dreams have been with me from the edge of childhood, mostly the sort of dream in which every courtesy is maintained and every permission given; but I never knew before I married what it was to be a quarreller. Our rows are like the weather, there is no control over them and very little warning, sometimes none at all. We might be basking in the sunshine when a squall appears from nowhere and within seconds develops into a howling tornado. At the same time and with equal speed we hurtle back down the decades, transformed into giant infants stamping and frowning and spouting tears of rage.

'*Don't* talk to me then! See if I care!' rings out with playground simplicity.

I slap his arm and burst into tears of rage and disappointment. I follow him into the next room. 'What about the time you left me stranded by the Albert Memorial,' I yell.

'You sound just like a scratched old record,' he hisses. He follows me upstairs. Insults cramp my throat. I find the best one and aim it carefully like a dart. I watch the pupils disappear to pin-points in the great excited aquamarine irises of his eyes.

'Go away! Go away!' I shout, turning to the wall as he approaches and whamming my forehead against it.

Every time this happens I am astonished at the pack of devils let loose.

We fall into bed like two nasty children. He says things so hard that I feel little shooting spasms in sexual places, so then I feel they *must* be true. I am quiet. I think about them. Then I slap out at him and he thumps me, so I scratch and bite. He says my name after I've turned out the light but I don't answer. We lie awake in that sort of long dead silence when all future life is Arabia Deserta.

We still behave fairly normally in public, avoiding the little bitternesses which longer-established married couples automatically bat to and fro without self-consciousness. Recently we had to go to a dinner party given by one of my husband's grateful clients. Towards the end of the meal, the client's wife ran in from her kitchen bearing a Baked Alaska alight with blue rum-based flames. In case you don't know about Baked Alaska, it is a nightmare of a pudding which only a fool would try to make, a large lump of ice cream covered with heavily whipped sugar-stiffened raw egg-whites sitting on a sponge cake. This structure is cauterised in a scorching oven for three minutes, during which time the ice cream is supposed to stay frozen while the meringue bakes to brown peaks. It is what you might call the Ur-recipe for disaster.

The client and his wife were a fairly tense couple anyway, but the stealthy sniping with which they had seasoned the early part of the meal was now given culinary fulfilment.

'Knife, darling.' His voice rose to shrillness. '*Sharp* knife.'

'I *know*, darling, but cut it faster than you did last time,' she urged. 'You remember what happened *then*.'

'It's *melting*, darling,' he barked.

'You're not cutting it *fast* enough,' she said. A slice shot across the waiting tea-plate, and ice cream slopped onto the tablecloth.

'Come on, come *on*!' Her brows were knitting furiously, and she was dancing a little jig at his side.

'It's been in too long,' he said as the second slice collapsed.

'Three minutes and not a second more, on my mother's grave,' she said with hatred. 'It's *you*. You're so *slow*.'

The table had fallen silent, no chit-chat being possible at the borders of such a scene. I looked on with what I thought of as a sort of Olympian compassion at first, until, like a tuning fork, I shuddered, catching certain unmistakably *married* reverberations.

This morning when I wolf-whistled him as he emerged shaggy and glistening from the shower, he clapped his hands over himself and said, 'That's not exactly very feminine, is it.' He has beautiful hands, fine as earth, rough and warm like brown sand. Sometimes he lets me wash his back and shoulders, which is when I get the *marvelling* feeling most strongly. I have never told him about this.

I first felt helpless admiration when I watched him come off the court after a game of tennis, pulling off his shirt as roughly as a child would, his sweat drops white and pearly in the sun. His face was brighter than silver, sunburnt to coppery patches on the cheekbones, his florid shoulders weathered almost to the colour of claret. Let me love you, I said silently as we went to bed that night for the first time, let me stroke your shadows with my fingers and inhale your skin's smell of honey and air; let me love you before you heave ho my hearty.

At night, in pyjamas (which did not appear until after the wedding), he curled to me like a striped mollusc, with the long curving back of a prawn. My little crocodile, I said maliciously as he draped his length against me in bed. When he whispered in my ears (which he still does sometimes) then he caused trembling while my fingers and toes turned to sparklers. It made him groan like a wood-pigeon before falling asleep, though usually I was chortling away for some time afterwards.

Then, my mind was a sunny prairie of contentment; my body was quick, god-like, with a central line of stars. There was the scarcely-dare-believe-it hope that marriage might even mean years of this ahead, safeguarding a life of such subterranean holiday in perpetuity. Yes, yes, there is more to marriage than *that*, I know that now; but surely there is nothing as good.

About six months ago, a week or two after the marrying event, we were walking along the edges of some stubbled corn-fields when we came to a solitary house in a field of its own. We looked through the windows – some of which were broken – and there was no furniture inside, so we didn't feel like intruders when we lifted the latch of the garden gate. Concealed by its hedge from the gaze of idle ramblers was a menagerie of topiary, wild-looking peacocks, boars sprouting long leafy green bristles, one or two blurred heraldic hounds. It was hot, late in the afternoon, and we lay down on a bed of box clippings at the end of the garden. I could see horse-chestnut trees nodding beyond the hedge. The densely knit noise of bees came from a nearby tangle of blackberries. I slipped out of my clothes, we lay together on his shirt, we concentrated suddenly for a while on a time of intense and escalating delight. Afterwards I was wicked with pleasure, and we shared the bread roll and apples saved from our pub lunch. I remember noticing the red and green striations on the apples' skins and the miraculous honey-combed structure of the bread. Then we fell asleep.

I dreamed an urgent heated dream of the sort which sometimes follows hard on the heels of satisfaction.

I was walking down the High Street in Bakewell with

a modest strong young man. He was quite tall; as he talked to me, he turned his head slightly and tipped his glance down to shoulder level. He was telling me how he made all his own bread, how easy it was, just two or three loaves a week, or four when he felt unusually hungry.

'How on earth do you find the time,' I said. 'All that kneading and proving.'

'Oh, you can fit that in round other things in the odd few minutes here and there,' he assured me.

He showed me his current mass of dough, throwing it lightly from hand to hand like a goal-keeper. Then he wore it as a vast damp pliable boxing glove, deftly pulling at it and pummelling it with his other hand.

'You try,' he said. I found the glove-trick manipulation too difficult, so instead I kneaded away enthusiastically. It grew and grew, elastic and cirrus-streaked, until I felt worried.

'Have I spoiled the loaf?' I asked anxiously.

'Not at all,' he said. 'It'll be even better than usual.' We continued our walk, his arm round my shoulder as friendly as could be.

When I woke up it was almost evening, warm and still. I watched his crumpled face a foot away coming out of sleep, the lids flickering, light clearing the eyes and then a wreath of smiles.

We used to be *friends* then.

He upends me, he takes no notice of anything above the waist. How would *he* like it, that's what *I'd* like to know. And after some farmyard activity, while *I'm* still inside my nightdress, very often, he cages me in his big arms and legs and disappears with a snore.

'How did you sleep?' My husband has started to make casual enquiries. 'Did you have any interesting dreams?' I found a rubbishy paperback calling itself a Dictionary of Oneirology in his briefcase the other night when I was looking for *The Times*. How fascinating to learn that in Islam dreams of shrews are always related to faithless wives; I wonder if that works the other way around. And dreams of being infected with vermin are often the equivalent for pregnancy, it says here. No flies on *me*. Soon he will be cross-questioning me about the possible appearance of daggers, snakes, nail-files and umbrellas in my night pictures.

What does worry me is that I am finding it increasingly difficult to tell the difference between dreaming and awake. I often feel quite astonished when I turn out of a dream into the morning. I shout or laugh in dreams and wake my husband. I dream I am dreaming; or I dream I have woken up. I try to test whether a dream is a dream by cutting a plate of sardine sandwiches; I scoff the lot and am none the wiser. Recently I tried biting my hand in a dream to see if I was awake. Next morning there were toothmarks, so where does that leave me?

I was very late back one night last week, and crept up the stairs hoping he would have fallen asleep. No such luck. He was propped up against the pillows, and closed *Anna Karenina* with a bang as I came into the room.

'It took ages to find a taxi,' I said. 'They seem to dry up after eleven.'

'Why didn't you catch the train? The last one doesn't go until eleven-thirty.'

'I know, but Rhoda and I were having such an

interesting discussion in the wine bar. The film was very thought-provoking.'

'What was it again?'

'*Battleship Potemkin.*' Surely he wouldn't have seen that. *I* certainly hadn't.

'Ah. What was it about?'

'Oh, you know, the nature of war, particularly at sea.'

'And you and Rhoda sat till past midnight discussing naval tactics over the Liebfraumilch.'

'Along with related matters. Look, you can just stop being so suspicious. I'm sick of your bullying. I'm going to get changed.' I stormed off to the bathroom with my nightdress.

'Stay here,' he called. No fear, I thought as I bolted the bathroom door. That way he would see that, at the particular request of Mr Pembleton, I had uncharacteristically left off my bra. I took a quick cold shower using Coal Tar soap, and went back into the bedroom with an innocent smile.

'Where did you find a taxi,' he said.

'Oh, don't start again.'

'I want to know.'

'Waterloo Bridge.'

'But you say you met Rhoda at the Barbican.'

'Yes, I did, but the wine bar was a little way off, and then there are no taxis in the City late at night. So we carried on walking because we knew there are always taxis on Waterloo Bridge.'

'It's miles to Waterloo from the Barbican.'

'I *know*, and that's why I'm so tired and cross and longing for bed. And if that's all the sympathy you can show, I wish I'd never married you.' I burst into tears at last, and finally convinced him of my blamelessness, so much so that he apologised and kissed me goodnight.

Then I woke up, and the crocodile tears were still trickling down my cheeks. I looked at the clock – five a.m. – and at the sleeping bulk beside me, remembering how we had spent the previous evening in front of the fire playing chess. You see how confusing it can be.

He beat me at that game of chess as he usually (though not invariably) does. When I was putting the pieces away, thinking about them one by one, I said, 'I like the knight best. I like his L-shaped hopping.'

'You would,' said my husband, *bitterly*. The funny thing was, I understood exactly how he felt.

When I catch him in some detail of his body, whirling his little finger round an ear rim or squeezing a pore on the wing of his nose, our eyes meet coldly and he looks away. These fugitive glimpses of hatred between us are frighteningly hearty.

Yesterday, on my way to the shops, I was standing waiting to cross at the busy corner by Marchmont Drive, when a blue plumber's van flew by. The driver's window was open and, although he must have been doing fifty, I caught a long moment of his burnished shoulder and beautiful naked arm with the underarm tuft like the beard of a mussel. There was a blast of music – 'Get Out of My Dream and Into My Car' – as potent as a rogue whiff of jasmine, then it was all gone. I almost cried; I still had a lump in my throat by the time I reached the dry-cleaners. You're not saying that means nothing.

Recently I have noticed a disturbing change. Disapproving of my keeping any secrets from him, my husband has started appearing at precisely the wrong moment in places where he doesn't belong. Last night I was lying in a tipped-back chair while the dentist puffed some sort of dizziness around me until I was only half-conscious. He approached and stroked me, removing his white coat, holding me, pressing me to him; and then my husband appeared in the doorway and said, 'Excuse me, I'll take over now.'

I woke furious to his unconscious weight at my side. I felt like hitting him, but subsided, snarling. When I got back again I was by the sea and it was warm luminous evening. The light was so rare, the sky and sea of such a strange icy blue-green, that I knew I was further north than usual. I walked a few steps along sibilant shingle and quietly plosive bladderwrack, noticing that both a red sun and a yellow moon were in the sky, though the sun was very low. Now, running lightly down the dunes of marram grass appeared some sort of fisherman or sea-gypsy; I was only able to take in the black eyes with their oblique gleam.

He was beside me and the sides of our faces touched; his felt like the skin of a starfish and mine like the lining of a shell. I was both aware of existing in my own body – the mild drumming of my pulses, the gentle maritime roar in my ears – and of being able to see myself and this other figure standing on the shore.

He took a small mother-of-pearl box from his trouser pocket and gave it to me, watching intently as I nodded my thanks. Then his arm lifted at the elbow and he slid his finger under a strand of hair which had stuck to my forehead. I saw my face and neck flood with colour just as the disappearing sun set fire to a stripe of sea. He slid his hand suddenly through the deep armhole of my dress and his fingers curled to the shape of my breast. I lost all power and was beached onto his shoulder.

Time makes a little leap. We are in a house built of driftwood and pine branches. The windows show oblongs of brine-blanched aquamarine; there are bubbles and knots in the glass. He is stoking the sea-coal fire. I stand waiting and hot salt tears brim up. He draws me gently into him again. I feel the extreme heat of his body; it radiates through his clothes like the sun. The middle of my own body bucks softly, gratefully. We stare at each other with reluctant half-smiles, and from our stiff breathing you might think we are about to fight.

We lie down together on the bed by the wall. I close my eyes, curiously at rest now, floating. His violent hand plucks me from my suspension in the middle air and I hug him with equal violence. We rock together as though it seems our ribs must crack.

But when at last it comes to it, clipped in the warm frame of his arms, thighs enfolded in his tangle, at this moment I happen to glance across his shoulder and so spoil everything. It has been going swimmingly but now there will be no conclusion. I sit up, spit words of refusal, glare across the room.

He has done it again. This second invasion *proves* he has broken my cover. Now I will never more be private, even in the slumbering third part of my time. There at the window, his face like a censorious turnip, my husband is staring in.

Good Friday, 1663

> We have a winding sheet in our mother's womb,
> which grows with us from our conception, and
> we come into the world, wound up in that winding
> sheet, for we come to seek a grave.

My rustic husband, preferring to be fifty years behind
the times in church matters as in all else, has ordered
Parson Snakepeace to preach only sermons from the old
dead Divines, and to read them aloud without comment.
This being Good Friday, he has chosen the horridest
sermon he could find, all to do with death and
earthworms.

Lord, I'm sure I am grown quite melancholy at that
old barbarous tale of the thorn crown and the sponge in
vinegar. Ha, ha, ha!

This church is as cold as the grave. You would not know
the air was so gentle outside, all the daffodils kissing the
air and the apple trees like brides.

Here, by my pew, lies my husband's mother, Myrtilla
Fanshawe, 26 years old, d. 1634, boxed up in fine Carrara:

God's goodness made her wise and well-beseeming
Her wifely virtues won her much esteeming,
Earth would not yield more pleasing earthly bliss
Blest w'two babes, though Death brought her to this.

That shallow space over there, beneath the window showing St Catherine, is reserved for *my* tomb. I insist on a chaste design. None of your beastly seraphim, mind; I never could endure your marble flittermice.

Myrtilla died in childbed, bearing that blockhead my husband. He sits beside me now pretending to listen to the sermon, his mouth catching flies, a pure clown, mere elementary earth, without the least spark of soul in him. That he should have claimed *me* for his wife! He would be more fitly mated with some silly, simple, peaking, sneaking country girl, one that goes with her toes in, and can't say boo to a goose.

I cannot endure him near me, with his sweating, snoring, scratching, snap-finger ways. He'll sit and yawn, and stretch like a greyhound by the fireside, till he does some nasty thing or other and so gives me an excuse to leave the room. When he has blown his nose into his handkerchief, he looks into it as if there were a diamond dropped out of his head.

There in the womb we are fitted for works of darkness, all the while deprived of light: and there in the womb we are taught cruelty, by being fed with blood, and may be damned, though we be never born.

To confine a woman just at her rambling age! take away her liberty at the very time she should use it! O barbarous aunt! O unnatural father!

My aunt Champflower is a very violent lady. She will fall into a fit or fly at you for the least piddling insignificant thing. In her day she was a beauty, but now she washes her face and hands in lead varnish to hide the dismal hollows of eight and thirty years.

Lord, what a difference there is between me and her. How I should despise such a thing if I were a man. What a nose she has! what a chin! what a neck! She desired my ruin with all her little heart. She danced for pure joy at my wedding.

My father never would have heard Scandal's buzz had she only kept it from him. He would have let me look where I pleased for a husband. I have a tidy fortune. But, no, I must be thrown away in haste to this clodpoll squire.

My aunt calls me to her room and talks of Honour and Reputation with a long face like the beast of the Nile.

'Aye, aye,' says I, 'but what has such talk to do with me?'

'What indeed!' cries she in a passion.

She pauses. She trifles with a lace some time before she speaks next, making play with a certain letter, reading it to herself with a careless dropping lip and an erected brow, humming it hastily over.

I recognise the hand. It is from my Celadon.

'Well, niece, this galloping abroad and allowing young fellows to fool with you has given your reputation no very good complexion.'

'Madam, I seek only to follow your example. Besides, I have heard it said often and often when I was with you in London, that a lady's reputation ought to be a sort of brunette; then it has an attraction in it, like amber. A white reputation is as disagreeable to men, I am sure I have heard you say twenty times or more, as white eyebrows or white eyelashes.'

'Pooh pooh,' says she with a sort of snarling smile. 'You can talk in that airy impertinent way until Domesday but it will not save you. I have other letters. Your fop delights in nothing but rapes and riots, as all the world well knows. I have heard certain tales. I have ocular proof.'

'Madam,' says I, though I start to feel a little uneasy now, 'there are some persons who make it their business to tell stories, and say this and that of one and t'other, and everything in the world; and,' says I . . .

'And your father shall know all,' she finishes.

Our birth dies in infancy, and our infancy dies in youth, and youth and the rest die in age, and age also dies, and determines all. O, huzza, Parson Snakepeace; cheerful matter for an April morning! **Our youth is hungry and thirsty, after those sins, which our infancy knew not; and our age is sorry and angry, that it cannot pursue those sins which our youth did.**

I shall never more see the playhouse, nor go to Ponchinello nor Paradise, nor take a ramble to the Park nor Mulberry Garden. I could as soon persuade my husband to share a sillybub in New Spring Garden or to drink a pint of wine with friends at the Prince in the Sun as I could fly.

My aunt Champflower took me with her to London

last year for a spring holiday. We lodged near by St James's, and I never was so happy in all my life.

I dote upon assemblies, adore masquerades, my heart bounds at a ball; I love a play to distraction, cards enchant me, and dice put me out of my little wits.

On our third evening, then, we saunter to the pleasure gardens at Vauxhall for the sake of the Chinese lanterns and to taste a dish of oysters.

There we happen to meet again with a certain merry sharking fellow about the town, who has pursued us diligently from chocolate house to milliner to the Haymarket since our arrival. He has with him a friend; and this friend is Celadon.

'I came up, sir, as we country-gentlewomen use, at an Easter Term,' explains my aunt demurely, 'to the destruction of tarts and cheesecakes, to see a new play, buy a new gown, take a turn in the Park, and so down again to sleep with my forefathers.'

'We see you have brought your sister with you in kindness,' says Celadon, giving me a mighty wink.

The two fine gallants pay her gross and lavish compliments, ogling and glancing and watching any occasion to do forty officious things. They have all the appearance of gentlemen about them. I notice that Celadon's eyes look sideways on me like an Egyptian drawing. He wears a fine long periwig tied up in a bag.

My aunt curtseys at last. Down goes her diving body to the ground, as if she were sinking under the conscious load of her own attractions; then launches into a flood of fine language, still playing her chest forward in fifty falls and risings, like a swan upon waving water.

Hang me if she has not conceived a violent passion for the fellow.

> . . . when my mouth shall be filled with dust, and the worm shall feed, and feed sweetly upon me, when the ambitious man shall have no satisfaction, if the poorest alive tread upon him, nor the poorest receive any contentment in being made equal to Princes, for they shall be equal but in dust.

I look down now at my arms and see the fine eggshell skin with a pretty sparkle from the sun, and the violet-coloured veins at my wrist. I cannot think I am dust and worms' meat.

The carnation dew, the pouting ripeness of my honeycomb mouth, he said; and that my face was a swarm of cupids.

I do love Love, I would have all the Love in the world. What should I mind else, while I have any share of youth and beauty? When I went to Court all eyes were upon me, all tongues were whispering that's my Lord Spatchcock's fine daughter; all pressed towards me and bowed, only to get half a glance from me. When I went to the playhouse, some stood gazing on me, with their arms across their heads languishing as oppressed by beauty. The brisker fellows combed their wigs and prepared their eyes to tilt with mine. Ah, flattery was my daily bread.

Celadon is so agreeable a man, so eloquent, so unaffected, so particular, so easy, so free. All his finery is from the best in Paris, his shoes from Piccar and his gloves from Orangerie.

He wears his clothes with so becoming a negligence that I can barely wish him out of them.

He had the greatest skill in arranging assignations that ever I saw; and all the while he flattered my aunt with a thousand honeyed words and promises, until I was ready to burst with laughing.

My hair was dressed in flaunting little ringlets and crimped serpentaux puffs. I wore my new under-petticoats of white dimity, embroidered like a turkey-work chair with red, green, blue and yellow, with a pin-up coat of Scotch plaid adorned with bugle lace and my gown of printed calico.

I carried my claret-coloured velvet coat with gold fringes to protect me from the dangers of the night air. Even in spring, jaunting abroad at four in the morning strikes a chill into the bones.

Parson Snakepeace has conceived the pretty notion of keeping a skull upon his desk.

I can never persuade myself that religion consists in scurvy out-of-fashion clothes and sour countenances, and when one walks abroad, not to turn one's head to the right or left, but hold it straight forward like an old blind mare.

O that I were your lover for a month or two, he murmured in my ear like a bumble bee.

— What then?

— I would make that pretty heart's blood of yours ache in a fortnight.

**That God, this Lord, the Lord of life could die,
is a strange contemplation; that the Red Sea could**

be dry, that the sun could stand still, that an oven could be seven times heat and not burn, that lions could be hungry and not bite, is strange, miraculously strange, but super-miraculous that God could die.

The most unnatural spectacle to be seen in Somerset since the Flood was surely my union with Squire Clodpoll here. A dainty girl of seventeen yoked to a greasy, untoward, ill-natured, slovenly wretch! We were the laughing stock of five counties.

Now it is five months since our wedding, which I should rather call a show of Merry-Andrews, with nothing pleasant about it at all but the foolery of a farce.

The nuptial banquet was crammed with baskets of plum-cake, Dutch gingerbread, Cheshire cheese, Naples biscuits, macaroons, neats' tongues and cold boiled beef.

My new husband had drunk heartily. The guests cried out for a speech. He staggered to his feet.

My head aches consumedly, said he; I am not well.

He raised his glass to me, then toppled over behind the table.

There was such a laughing, they roared out again. The ladies teehee'd under their napkins. The teehee took a reverend old gentlewoman as she was drinking, and she squirted the beer out of her nose, as an Indian does tobacco.

By the time the bashful bride, meaning myself, was brought to bed, this numbskull had in some wise recovered his wits. He called for a mouthful of something to stay his stomach, a tankard of usquebaugh with nutmeg and sugar, if you please, and also a toast and some cheese.

'Supper, sir!' said I. 'Why, your dinner is not out of your mouth yet; at least 'tis all about the brims of it.'

That sharp comment confounded him, so that he cursed, and rolled about the bedchamber like a sick passenger in a storm; then he comes flounce into bed, dead as a salmon in a fishmonger's basket, his feet cold as ice and his breath hot as a furnace.

His head is a fool's egg which lies hid in a nest of hair. He hangs his nose in my neck and talks to me whether I will or no. What a poor sordid slavery there is in the state of marriage.

During our brief courtship, he wailed out some songs of love.

> *I have a mistress that is fair*
> *And as sweet as sugar candy,*
> *Had I ten thousand pounds a year*
> *I'd give her half a pint of brandy.*

And all the while he gazes on me like a sick monster, with languishing eyes.

I burst into laughter: 'Lord, sir, you have such a way with you, ha, ha, ha!'

At night He went into the garden to pray, and He spent much time in prayer. I dare scarce ask thee whither *thou* wentest, or how *thou* disposedst of thy self, when it grew dark and after last night. That has set my husband a-tittering. Now he nudges me with his elbow, the filthy fellow. I have no stomach for him. **About midnight He was taken and bound**

with a kiss, art thou not too conformable to Him in that? Is not that too literally, too exactly thy case? at midnight to have been taken and bound with a kiss?

Yes, yes, Parson Snakepeace, I was taken captive in a garden, at my Lady Wildsapte's last summer *fête champestre*, though I cannot see why you should make a sermon of it, for it had nothing to do with you or your talk of the grave.

We went chasing off by the light of torches down an alley of trees, shamming to fight each other with long hazel twigs.

My lady's grounds are full of little pagan temples and other fancies, and at last we fell down breathless at the foot of a pretty Egyptian obelisk brought back by her son from his late stay in Rome. Screened by the friendly shade of some low bushes, we fell upon the ground together; the leaves around us were of the crimson flowering currant for I can still recall the sharp smell when we bruised 'em by lying upon 'em.

'Cherubimical lass,' he called me, and gazed on me devouringly. Our eye beams were in that moment tangled beyond redemption, and I could not bring myself to draw away when he caught me by the hand, wringing and squeezing at it as if he were mad.

He offered me no other rudeness at first, but we only gazed on each other with half smiles; and our breathing grew laboured when we twisted and knotted our fingers together as if in combat. Then indeed my bounding blood beat quick and high alarms.

He swore that he would come down from London in a fortnight, and marry me.

And so we progressed until, with broken murmurs and heart-fetched sighs, he so mousled and tousled me that I cried, 'Sweetheart!' and he clapped a hand over my mouth to save us from discovery.

Good gods! What a pleasure there is in doing what we should not do.

Then were we animated by the strongest powers of love, and every vein of my body circulated liquid fires; until we came at last to that tumultuous momentary rage of which so much has been whispered since the world began.

O Jesu, when I think back to the heat of his sweet mouth and the smell of his skin, I could weep for weeks together.

Hang him, let him alone. He's gone.

Hast thou gone about to redeem thy sin, by fasting, by Alms, by disciplines and mortifications, in the way of satisfaction to the Justice of God? that will not serve, that's not the right way, we press an utter crucifying of that sin that governs thee; and that conforms thee to Christ.

Well, I am eight months gone with child. I may follow Mrs Myrtilla's example more speedily than expected. That would indeed be a convenient conclusion, to be dispatched by my own sin. That would provide matter enough for a month of fine long thundering sermons.

This husband sits beside me like a ball and chain. A pack of squalling infants will do the rest, forging my bonds link by link, and soon I shall inhabit as heavy a carcass as my sister Sarah's. Then will I keep company with the midwife, dry-nurse, wet-nurse, and all the rest of their accomplices, with cradle, baby-clouts and bearing clothes – possetts, caudles, broth, jellies and gravies. I grow nauseous when I think of them.

I may build castles in the air, and fume and fret, and grow pale and ugly, if I please; but nothing will bring back my free and airy time.

Outside this church it is almost summer; see how the sun struggles through these coloured glass saints to fall in jewels onto my gown.

I will not die of the pip, so I will not.

O merciful God, who hast made all men, and hatest nothing that thou hast made, nor wouldest the death of a sinner, but rather that he should be converted and live; have mercy upon all Jews, Turks, infidels, and Hereticks, and take from them all ignorance, hardness of heart, and contempt of thy Word; and so fetch them home, blessed Lord, to thy flock, that they may be saved among the remnant of the true Israelites, and be made one fold under one shepherd, Jesus Christ our Lord, who liveth and reigneth with thee and the Holy Spirit, one God, world without end. Amen.

Give Me Daughters Any Day

'D oes he *have* to be here?' said her grandmother. 'It's not right, having a man in the house when I'm ill.'

'He does live here,' said Ruth. 'We're married, you see.'

'Call that a man,' said her grandmother. 'He's back by five o'clock. He doesn't even teach a proper subject. We all know *English!* He's no use. Look at the handle on that door, it's hanging half off. Why doesn't he fix it?'

'We haven't been here long,' said Ruth. 'We're doing things gradually.'

'Gradually!' jeered her grandmother.

'Can I make you some more tea?' asked Ruth coldly. 'Only I've got to get on otherwise.'

'Oh yes, your *job*. Why don't you make that husband of yours get a *proper* job, a *man's* job. He's *limp*.'

'Women don't like only doing housework and having babies these days,' said Ruth. 'We want to be independent and fulfilled too.'

'You do talk a lot of rubbish,' said her grandmother. 'Just like your mother. She made a fool of that man, cooking him casseroles and buying him Shetland jumpers. Didn't stop him leaving though, did it. *You'd* better watch out for that.'

'I'm not staying in this room if you won't be polite.'

'Suit yourself. You're not doing *me* any favours. I don't *want* to be here, I was made to come. I wish I'd never agreed. I want my own things. I *hate* this house.'

'I know, I know,' said Ruth. 'I don't blame you. But you know what Dr Singh said. The alternative is hospital.'

'Oh, doctors,' said her grandmother, and lapsed back onto the sofa-bed, grey-yellow hair awry on the candy-striped pillows. 'Your ceiling looks like the icing on a wedding cake,' she continued, gazing upwards with goose-berry-coloured eyes.

'She wants you to stay out of her room,' said Ruth to Denzil.

'But all my clothes are in there!'

'Well, I'll have to bloody well get them out,' said Ruth.

'There's a strong Anglo-Saxon element in your family,' said Denzil. 'Your language. Your grandmother's gnomic utterances. "We all have dustbins for minds, but some of us prefer to keep the lids on." "You've got a son until he marries but you keep a daughter for life." As for that spare room now . . . Did you ever hear of Grendel's cave?'

'No. And don't do that. I'm too tired.'

Denzil let her go.

'Do you know what she said to me this evening when I asked her how she was?' he said after a while. 'She said, "I'm feeling a little queer but I suppose I mustn't grouse."'

'Why did I get married?' said Ruth.

'Not that again,' said Denzil, leafing through his Dictionary of Historical Slang. 'Queer, adjective. Base; criminal, from sixteenth century. Derivative senses, drunk, 1800, hence unwell, giddy, from 1810.'

'She says *you're* queer because you're called Denzil,' said Ruth.

'Does she,' said Denzil. 'That's rich, coming from someone called Vesta. Grouse. Cognate with the old French groucier. From 1850, dialect, to grumble.'

'She said there was nothing she could fancy except boiled tongue,' continued Ruth with a bitter laugh. 'So I found a tongue in that smelly old butcher's down by the station but when I got it back and read the recipe it said I had to skin it and put it under heavy weights for hours and hours. It was very expensive too.'

'Tongue,' said Denzil. 'Can't you buy it by the pound at Cullens?'

'I *tried* that. She said it tasted wrong.'

'What do you want me to do, then? Have a go at skinning it?'

'Don't bother. She's had pints of Slippery Elm so she won't starve. Wrap the damn thing up in newspaper and take it out to the dustbin.'

'Couldn't we give it to someone?' asked Denzil uneasily. 'Seems a waste.'

'You bloody well cook it then!' yelled Ruth, tears spurting from the corners of her eyes in jets. 'I haven't been able to do any of *my* work. You're all right, colouring in your third-year charts with pretty crayons, but my agency is grinding to a standstill before it's even got off the ground and much *you* care.'

'Modern men,' croaked Denzil. 'They're all the same. Dirty rotten lot.'

'And don't sneer,' wept Ruth. 'You patronising git.'

Ruth was in the process of setting up the Little Bo Peep Agency for baby-minders and nannies. She had allowed this month to check up on local council regulations and to write an emergency information sheet to distribute among the less experienced of her team.

'Projectile vomiting,' she copied out from a baby manual. 'Do not be alarmed. This is not too serious. Clear up the wall, and inform the mother on her return.'

She took up a tray of tea.

'What have you been up to?' said Vesta.

'I've been trying to write a leaflet but I don't think it's any good.'

'You've been wasting your time, then, haven't you,' Vesta said, incontrovertibly.

'I think I'll try and work here for a bit,' said Ruth, and brought out her book.

'Always bloody well reading,' said Vesta, glaring at the wardrobe. 'First your mother, now you. And if it's not the books, it's some mad scheme or other. *Never* any money, either. Your mother's never had two pennies to rub together. Look at the state of her flat. I wouldn't be seen dead in it. At least you live in a house. Of sorts.'

Ruth tried to concentrate on the print in front of her eyes. 'It is important to teach the child basic principles of "do as you would be done by". It may seem obvious to you that it is wrong to scream your head off when thwarted. It is not obvious to a very young child.'

'What are you reading?' asked Vesta.

'A book on babies so I can write a leaflet for my Bo Peep Agency.'

'What a damnfool name that is,' said Vesta. 'And a damnfool idea too. What do *you* know about babies? You've never had any.'

'You don't always have to experience things personally to know about them.'

'You've left it a bit late in the day if you're thinking of having one now. Even if you did, you'd have *old* babies. Wizened little things with all sorts of problems.'

'I'm only thirty and I'm *not* thinking of having one now,' said Ruth. 'Time enough when I've got some money coming in from Little Bo Peep.'

'I wouldn't bother if I were you,' said Vesta. 'They're more trouble than they're worth. I never had anything but trouble from Janet.'

'But mum's been visiting you every fortnight since grandad died,' said Ruth. 'And that was over twenty-five years ago.'

'Only because she's a social worker,' spat Vesta.

'She says we'll have old babies,' fretted Ruth that night in bed.

'We won't have *any* babies if you carry on setting your cap at me,' said Denzil.

'Don't try to make jokes,' said Ruth. 'Anyway, you agreed it's more sensible like this until you get a Scale Two.'

'Oh yes,' he said. 'More sensible.'

'Why do you make me out to be such a killjoy?' asked Ruth.

'Sweetheart, nothing could be further from my mind,' said Denzil. 'But, if the cap fits.'

'You could always bugger off,' said Ruth. 'See if I care.'

'How are you feeling?' asked Ruth.

'Need you ask?' croaked Vesta.

'Here's the *Mail*,' said Ruth, 'And here are your glasses.'

'Have a cup of tea with me,' said Vesta. 'Look, you've made a ridiculous big pot, I can't drink all that by myself. When I see the waste that goes on in this house I don't wonder you're as poor as church-mice.'

'All right, I'll have a cup,' said Ruth. 'But I've got to make some phone calls this morning.'

'I'm not stopping you,' said Vesta. 'Did you go out for my *Mail* again? You shouldn't have to do that. Why can't you get it delivered? You must live in a very poor area. You should see my paper girl. She's the sexiest little devil you ever saw. It's disgusting really. Ginger hair, too. I wonder why it always goes with ginger?'

'*I've* got auburn hair,' said Ruth.

'You've let yourself go,' said Vesta dismissively. 'No make-up. Just scraping your hair back. Tell me when you get divorced, won't you. Not that *he's* much to write home about either.'

'Why don't you read your paper,' said Ruth, picking up her copy of *Baby Management*. Her grandmother glared at her through her sharp-cornered reading glasses, then studied the headlines.

'Students again,' she muttered. 'Education's a dirty word. Look at the Communists, they've all been to University.

That's why your husband won't get a proper job. All those ideas he got at University *sapped* him.'

'Oh, *shut* up,' said Ruth.

'You've got no control over him,' shouted Vesta. 'You can't even get him to put on a bloody door-handle.'

'Have a betablocker,' said Ruth coldly. 'If you've finished your breakfast.'

In the old days, Ruth had been sent by her mother during the school holidays to be company for her widowed grandmother.

Every morning they went shopping locally in Mortlake, with Ruth carrying the zip-up vinyl bag, for half a pound of this and a quarter of that. On the way they might meet one of Vesta's neighbours, and there would be a formal five-minute exchange on the subject of physical deterioration, while Ruth stood to one side, staring at the pavement. The conversation over, she followed her grandmother off again with mortified canine obedience. Their main meal, at midday, of chops or offal or stew, was followed by Vesta's Rest.

Ruth sat on the rug in the sun and filled in her diary. '*Je suis avec ma grandmère,*' she wrote. '*Ce soir nous donnerons le poisson au chat de Mme Grayling, qui est au Minorca en vacances. Hier soir nous avons entendu Radio 2 depuis deux heures et joué aux cartes. Je suis absolument . . .*' She paused and bit her biro. What was she, absolutely?

She gave up and started to read, alternating chapters of *Mansfield Park* with *Forever Amber*. At about four, she went back to the kitchen and laid the tea things. She was in a hot trance of reading and wanted never to speak again.

At ten past four her grandmother came downstairs.

'Always got your nose in some damn book,' she said. 'What are you reading *now*?'

'At Mansfield,' Ruth read aloud, 'no sounds of contention, no raised voice, no abrupt bursts, no tread of violence was ever heard; all proceeded in a regular course of cheerful orderliness.'

'How boring,' said Vesta. 'I like a bit of life. Why can't you put that down and be *company*.'

'I've got to revise,' said Ruth.

'Don't think exams will get you anywhere,' laughed Vesta. 'Look where they got your mother. Spending her time with drug addicts and sex maniacs and the scum of the earth. No wonder that rotten husband of hers upped and offed.'

'You mustn't talk like that about my father,' said Ruth.

'I'll say what I want in my own house,' huffed Vesta. 'He was a lazy, dirty good-for-nothing. It's no surprise *he* ended up in the gutter.'

'I won't listen!' shrieked Ruth.

'You're getting absolutely neurotic,' said Vesta with distaste.

From the top of the kitchen dresser she pulled down her own favourite book. *The Pageant of Life* by Dr Ethel Tensing, 1931.

'You listen to this and you'll learn a thing or two,' said Vesta, looking at Ruth severely over her reading glasses.

'Oh, no, please,' said Ruth.

'Don't be so ignorant,' said Vesta. 'Now this is her chapter on Adolescence.' She proceeded to read aloud the opinions of half a century ago on subjects as various as menstruation and the advisability of excess energy being channelled into a hobby.

'You could try stamp collecting,' chuckled Vesta.

'I don't need a hobby,' said Ruth. 'I've got reading. And as far as I can see everything's just the same now I'm fifteen as when I was seven. I still go to school. I still come here every holiday.'

'Don't be so stupid,' said Vesta. 'You have your periods now, don't you.'

'Shut up, shut up, shut up,' said Ruth.

'The young adult, or adolescent, is particularly susceptible to unreasonable emotional swings,' Vesta read aloud.

'I'm going to be sick,' said Ruth, 'If you don't shut up. And you can't pronounce menstruation or comparable.'

'When are you going to get a boyfriend,' said Vesta.

'When am I going to meet any boys,' said Ruth.

'It's not natural,' said Vesta. 'Maybe it's because of your weight. But don't think you're going to help matters by trying to wear lipstick. That cheap stuff you put on yesterday made your lips look like two pieces of liver.'

'Shut up, shut up, shut up,' said Ruth, her voice higher this time.

'Calming breathing exercises for adolescents,' read Vesta. 'Come on, now. Inhale deeply, filling the diaphragm with air.'

'You don't sound the *g*,' snivelled Ruth.

Fifteen years later Ruth was saying, 'No. Leave me alone.'

'Why?' said Denzil, breathing hard. 'It's her, isn't it.'

'Oh, go to sleep,' said Ruth. 'It's gone midnight. We're both tired.'

'Don't talk to me like that.'

'Like *what*.'

'Like I'm nothing.'

'You're not nothing,' said Ruth. 'Anyway, you can't. I've started.'

'I don't mind, if you don't,' said Denzil.

'I do mind,' said Ruth.

'Actually, I couldn't give a toss whether you do or not,' said Denzil, pushing his face into hers so that their teeth clashed.

'You're just selfish,' she hissed as they wrestled around on the bed. 'You come in at five o'clock, miles earlier than other men, and you sit around with your bits of paper while I'm up and down stairs with her bloody lemon barley water and rice pudding and pots of tea . . .'

'She won't *let* me go into her room,' interrupted Denzil.

'. . . And it's all very comfortable for you but I have to do everything and now my agency will be late starting if it ever starts and we'll never have enough money to carry on with the mortgage on this horrible house.'

'It's not a horrible house. You only say that because *she* said so.'

'I know,' she said. 'I know, I know.'

Back in the past, Ruth and her mother had visited Mortlake every other Saturday during term-time. Vesta was always spoiling for a fight after a fortnight on her own.

First, there was tea in the kitchen, the kettle smoking like the muzzle of a gun.

'Heard from that husband of yours lately?' said Vesta. This was her favourite opening gambit.

'Not for a while, no,' said Janet, bristling. 'Why?'

'Ha,' grunted Vesta with a merry look.

'What's *that* supposed to mean?' said Janet, humiliation transforming her features.

'Don't quarrel about Dad,' said Ruth. 'We've only just got here.'

'And *you* can shut up,' said Vesta equably, while Janet pulled out a crossword puzzle with a pitiable show of indifference.

The talk trundled off down the same old tracks, stale grudges revived and gathering impetus with the freshening of vicious memories. Soon it was rocketing along. Vesta's blood was up, her face was red. Janet was shouting hoarsely. Vesta was giving her best scornful laugh. Janet, panting, was in retreat, trying to recall her Mrs-Miniver-under-pressure face. Ruth was half-way through the packet of Digestives, making a bet with herself about not grizzling before lunch.

'What are *you* looking like that for?' called her mother, with deflected bellicosity.

'I wish you two wouldn't fight,' mumbled Ruth.

There was a pause.

'You ought to speak to that girl,' said Vesta.

'I'll thank you not to interfere,' said Janet to Ruth.

'Why can't you be *nice* to each other,' whined Ruth.

'Your mother and I are very close,' said Vesta with dignity. 'We just rub each other up the wrong way sometimes.'

'Take no notice of her,' said Janet. 'She gets like this.'

'Ginger, too. Shame she takes after her father,' said Vesta, starting the ball rolling again.

*   *   *

By the end of her second week on the sofa-bed, Vesta had improved enough to dress and come down for her evening meal.

Janet had driven over after work and now crouched, flinching nervously like a horse attacked by flies, on a kitchen stool. Ruth, remorselessly silent, prepared the greens.

'What a day I've had,' said Janet brightly. 'First a school-girl mum, trying to persuade her to go back to school. Then a ten-year-old who put his mother in hospital last week. And a really sad case this afternoon, a nice old boy who can't cope on his own any more. A nasty fall he'd had this time, lying on his own there for two days. Incontinent too. We've done what we can but he'll have to go into a home.'

'Do shut up, mum,' said Ruth.

Looking wounded, Janet took out her cigarettes.

'Oh yes, your daughter's bossy all right,' said Vesta with an angry smile. 'You're looking dreadful, Janet. Your face is all drawn and haggard, and your mouth looks sunk in. That haircut does nothing for you. As for the dye, it makes you look like an old prostitute.'

'Well, thanks very much,' said Janet, turning a gaze of dog-like appeal on her daughter.

'It's the menopause, of course,' said Vesta with relish. 'When you stop being able to have children, your body gives up. You're no use any more. Your hair gets thin. Your skin goes dull. And then, you abuse your health, Janet, you always have. You live out of tins.'

Ruth caught herself glancing appraisingly, almost assess-ingly, at her mother. She turned to Vesta and said, 'You don't look so hot yourself.'

'What do you expect when you get to eighty-five,' said Vesta. In the last week her skin had acquired a translucent mulberry-coloured glaze, and her hands and arms had begun to look pollarded.

Ruth saw that her meal would be ready in a couple of minutes.

'Mum, I think you'd better go soon,' she said briskly. 'You're not doing much good here, and I'm just about to serve up.'

Vesta's eyes reddened and filled with tears. Janet stared at her daughter reproachfully.

Ruth watched them in disbelief. She put the frying pan down and walked out of the kitchen. When she came back, Janet had left.

'What was the matter then?' she asked.

'You were rude to your mother,' said Vesta tremulously. 'She thinks the world of you, and I didn't like it.'

'Phew,' said Denzil, twisting Ruth's left arm behind her back. 'You've become very aggressive in the last couple of weeks.'

They continued to grapple on the moonlit bed, growing increasingly hot and violent.

'Call yourself a man,' hissed Ruth. 'When are you going to get round to fixing that bloody door-handle.' She banged him on the ear. 'Limp, that's what you are,' she continued. 'University *sapped* you. Why don't you get yourself a proper job.'

'Right,' said Denzil, 'If you must.' He kicked her lightly but strategically, and they fell like trees onto the mattress.

'Limp, am I,' muttered Denzil.

'Very funny,' hissed Ruth.

Some while afterwards, Ruth said, 'Of course, you know what I forgot to do before we did that.'

Denzil smirked, his hot face inches from hers.

'Which do you think it'll be?' he muttered.

'Shut up, shut up, shut up,' said Ruth.

'Let's hope it's not a girl,' he continued. 'You can have too much of a good thing.'

Ruth pulled away from him. She knelt naked on the bed. The moon shone in.

'That's what I like,' said Denzil. 'Good child-bearing hips, too.'

Hands clenched, knuckles silver against her belly, Ruth began to knead inwards and downwards.

'No,' she said. 'No. No. *No.*'

The Bed

Let me tell you how a piece of furniture changed my life. I had just moved into a flat with Tom, but things were not going so well. We were poor and over-tired, the flat was dark, dirty and sparsely furnished. I could not see how it might get any better.

I had taken to wandering round department stores in my lunch hour, soothed by the acquisitive absorption of other women and by the somnambulistic glide of the escalators. One day I found myself in the bedding department, a hushed and unpopulated area. I stood surrounded by beds like Ruth waist-high amid the corn, and was filled with a longing more poignant even than homesickness. A rich meadow of sprigged brocade and velvet padding stretched as far as the eye could see. The beautiful mattresses absorbed all sound on this, the fifth floor, and so I did not hear the footsteps of the Bedding Manager.

'Can I help you, madam?' said the voice at my ear. I turned and smiled. I did not need to think before I spoke. Consideration did not enter into it. It was an act of pure instinct.

'Yes, please. I want the best bed money can buy.'

Without worrying, which is unusual for me, I had taken

the day off work to wait in for the bed. It was dark November, and the rain drummed tirelessly on the windows all day. I waited quietly, marvelling at how gloomy the light was in every room, without, however, minding about it. The colour of the air suited the portentous nature of this particular day. The bed arrived late in the afternoon, and I watched with jealous eyes as the men unloaded it, noticing immediately the wet corner frame where they had allowed its plastic covering to fall open. Rainwater does not stain, I told myself, and the mattress itself is dry as a bone, which is the important thing.

I followed the men upstairs as they lugged the folded bed-frame, crackling in its plastic bag. We reached the low-ceilinged part at last, the crooked approach to the bedroom door. The older man heaved and juggled for a few seconds, then turned his rain-streaked face to me.

'It won't go,' he said flatly.

'No. I don't believe you,' I replied.

'Nah, we'll have to take it back,' he persisted. 'Unless you've got a saw?'

I gaped at him, then realised this was his idea of a joke.

Together we assembled the bed. It stood as high as a horse, in layers like a mille-feuille slice, an enormous square of magnificence covered in creamy flowered satin. The little room looked shame-faced around it, like a flimsy shoe box. Next door's radio chattered on, clearly audible through the party wall.

'Nice bed,' commented the younger of the two, gazing at it, smiling with innocent pleasure.

Tom was not so happy. He grew white-hot and enraged, unable to believe that I had done this, furious, incoherent, his tie crooked and his suit steaming damply as we stood by the gas fire. I kept quiet while he let rip and hurled himself around the room.

'How the hell did you pay for it?' he snarled.

'Interest-free credit over ten months,' I mumbled. He smacked his forehead and gave a howl.

'£1,000!' he shouted. 'That's £100 a month, you realise! I suppose you think I should chip in?'

'Don't bother,' I said. 'I'll manage the money somehow.'

'Sponging off me!' he sneered. 'That's what it comes down to, isn't it? All your wonderful talk of independence.'

'You'll like sleeping in that bed too,' I said. I started to cry.

'You make me sick. It's the most irresponsible thing I ever heard of,' he said, and slammed the door behind him.

The flat wasn't really big enough for such scenes. If you left the sitting-room in this fine style, there was only the little bedroom or bathroom in which to cool down. Tom scorned these and stormed out into the rain, still in his suit. I thought of following him as he had had nothing to eat and was soaked through and tired out, but instead I went to have another look at the bed.

We had been sleeping on one of those hard, cheap, Japanese-style mattresses called futons, stuffed with cotton wadding, claimed by the men who sold them to be good for your back. I hated it. It was so hard and ungiving that I felt bruised every morning when I woke up. The softer roundnesses of my body felt snubbed by it. Those futons might be all right for lean male athletes and ascetics, but I could never come to friendly sleeping terms with one of them.

I sat on the edge of my new, hand-upholstered, foot-deep, sprung-edge mattress, and realised how tired I was too. I rolled my head gently, easing the neck muscles, hearing the interior crunch of vertebrae. We had had another quarrel the night before. Tom had humped his back into a foetal arch and prepared, breathing slow and stertorous, to fall asleep with his usual ease. My mind had been alight and leaping with grievances. I could not rest. All issues of grief were sharp-edged and clamorous, jumping up in turn like rows of jack-in-the-boxes. I had wanted him to browse the pastures of insomnia with me, and was pleased when my restlessness prevented him from sleeping. The intensity of my sadness had been out of all proportion to its causes, which after all had only had their nourishment from everyday behaviour in its less attractive aspect. I had been forced up by a spasm of sleeplessness, running through the dark to the door, thudding in bare feet along the black alley to the front room. There I had fallen on the carpet and wept the sort of tears which leave the eyelids speckled with red to the brow next morning. Some time in the early hours I had returned to his side, thoroughly defeated, for some warm touch to banish the energetic mental banshees. And when the morning came, four hours later, every contentious issue was there clear as daylight as soon as I opened my eyes, not ameliorated but no longer appalling.

When Tom returned, I did not rush out from the bedroom for the further effort involved in any sort of exchange between us. I tucked some clean sheets where I could on the bed – they seemed ridiculously small suddenly against the glossy acreage of the mattress – and curled naked there under an eiderdown. I could hear Tom moving angrily from room to room, but tonight it was I who was the indifferent slumbering monarch. I sank gratefully into an unbounded cradle of sleep. He did not join me but I did not know that until eleven the next morning, when I woke, fresh and sound and dreamless, after an unbroken dozen hours of oblivion.

I glimpsed the clock and saw the broad light of late morning, but felt none of the panic I would normally experience on oversleeping on so grand a scale. I stretched slowly until I tingled to the tips of my fingers and toes. I felt well and strong and placid. I padded to the kitchen and made a jug of coffee before ringing the office to say that I was ill and would not be in. I took my coffee back to bed with me, and lay there all day, smiling and drowsing, stretching and smiling, without a practical thought in my head. Tom was right, the bed and I were in a happy alliance of irresponsibility.

He returned at seven that evening with some late anemones and a bottle of wine.

'You shouldn't be looking so well and cheerful,' he said, standing at the foot of the bed, grinning in spite of himself, shrugging himself out of his suit.

'Come and get warm in here,' I said, and held out my new sleep-strong arms to him. Legs wound together, arms straining tight, we made love with violent ease. Our bed bore us up like boats on water, buoyant, pliant and entirely silent.

Hot and happy, he turned his sly-smiling face to me.

'Well, it's a damn good bed for one thing, anyway,' he said.

We had slept in a fair number of beds during the two years we had been together, and each had presented its own unique difficulties. The one in Camberwell had been a worn-out shadow of a bed, rolling us down every night like rain water into a gutter. It had also been mounted on spitefully efficient castors, which meant that any movement more vigorous than turning one's head on the pillow would send it careering towards the wardrobe with prudish vehemence. In the house in Wood Green our room had had two single iron bedsteads which clanked in desolation. The landlady was an ex-matron, and these were ex-hospital beds. We lay side by side at night holding hands across the divide like characters in some terrible play by Samuel Beckett.

Beds are no fit matter for ridicule, no more than sleep or love. I have always liked the fairy-tale about the princess who proves the blueness of her blood by displaying the most exquisite sensitivity in her sleep.

'I trust you slept well, my dear?' enquires the cunning old Queen, laughing up her sleeve; under the twenty mattresses and twenty eiderdown quilts she has planted a pea.

'Oh, miserably!' replies the exhausted princess. 'I scarcely closed my eyes all night long. I lay upon something hard, so that I am black and blue all over.'

What can the sleep-depriving Queen do but allow her son to marry this girl who has shown such entirely proper delicacy over sleep?

Within a month of the bed's arrival, Tom acknowledged its worth and apologised for his initial hostility. Our quarrels dwindled away. Tom showed signs of new energy, left early for work, and looked marvellously well. I felt better, too, but found the opposite about work.

Large doses of sleep had made me invulnerable to worry. From being one of the most conscientious secretaries at the firm of accountants which employed me, always reliable, hard-working and careful, I soon became the laziest and most slapdash. I reasoned with myself as I picked up the phone to report yet another chimerical stomach upset that I had given the firm a year's tense good behaviour and they now owed me some leniency. Besides, it was difficult to sack people these days, and anyway it was nearly Christmas.

I loved the beginning and end of each day. Falling asleep became a swooning pleasure. Sometimes it was like falling slowly down a well, but on other nights it was leaping off the cliff of my pillow into gorgeous spinning blackness. Waking was a warm climb from absolute ease into a state where I lay, half-stunned and splendid, protected for some minutes from the day by the heat-shivering vividness of dreams. The best dream was of the sea, surfy and crystalline, where men raced naked and white as dolphins and I was carried up effortlessly to the point of laughter on great glassy waves.

My new way of life was turning me into an odalisque. I had never before appreciated the pleasures of indolence. I spent hours in the bath, or polishing my fingernails. My face grew sleek and smooth with all this sleep and idleness. At work I was surprised to notice how few people were affected by my new-found langour. One man complained that I was not completing my usual work-load but I merely shrugged my shoulders and made up some story about a broken typewriter. I have shed the load of worry I was born with. I shall never do more for money than I have to again.

One morning just before Christmas, Tom sat with me opening our cards. He was spruce and ready for the office. I was still in my nightdress and had not even combed my hair. We drank tea and slit envelopes with teaspoons. A great batch of cards had arrived, more than a dozen, and soon the coverlet was spread with angels and madonnas and nativity scenes.

'Aren't the stamps pretty this year,' I said, showing Tom the little picture of Joseph with his arm round Mary's shoulder and her hand smoothing the head of the infant Jesus.

Tom's arms held me in a hug.

'You're not too worried about anything much these days, are you?' he commented. He went to the door and stood there, briefcase in hand. 'Lazy girl. I must be off. I'll try not to be late back.'

On Christmas Eve we went to bed early again, and turned to each other. I cannot describe the closeness, the warmth of breath and ideal delight of movement. Ah, he said softly, and fell from me, curved round me, fell soundly asleep with his arms round my neck while I breathed in and out, watching his face in the dusky air. I turned my head and observed my relaxed fingers, the whorls on the palms, the oriental criss-cross patterns on the surface of the skin between the fingers. I saw the early stars, over his head, at the window, and felt I was almost near to understanding about them. I fell asleep.

Flares of gold disturbed the dreamlessness. I became

aware of the sun on my eyelids. My eyelashes fringed a private pavilion of hot pale colour. Beneath my cheek the warmth of the pillow was delicious, and I moved my face slightly once or twice to receive the full vellum softness of the linen.

When I opened my eyes, I saw his face asleep on the pillow beside me, one hand cupped under it, fine and serious. Each feature was fine, attenuated, carven, the eyelids solemn and the mouth curved and cut like a fruit. It was cold outside, I could feel the snap of frost in the air on my face, and there was a distant clamour of bells from St Christopher's two roads away. We were warm under our covers.

It was Christmas morning, of course, I thought, taking this as an explanation for the ecstatic complacence which filled me. I leaned across and kissed his curving mouth awake.

Labour

A Dramatic Story
observing not only the Aristotelian Unity of Time
(taking place within twenty-four hours)
but also the later stricter Unities of Place and Action

Dramatis Personae

WOMAN

1st CHORUS OF MIDWIVES

2nd CHORUS OF MIDWIVES

UTERUS   Before impregnation, a small central
female organ shaped like an inverted pear;
by the end of pregnancy, a large bag of
spiral muscle bundles housing the baby;
otherwise known as the womb

CERVIX   Inch-long passage at the low narrow neck
of the uterus; generally closed

PLACENTA   A liverish circular organ grown solely for
the nurture of the baby inside the uterus

VAGINA   Four-inch tube of muscle leading from
cervix to outside world; among other of
its sobriquets: the birth canal

PERINEUM   Area of muscle fibre and blood vessels
            between vagina and rectum

BABY

LUCINA   Goddess of Childbirth

ACT I

Scene *A hospital room, with a discreetly glittering and flashing battery of equipment. On a high bed lies the woman, a metal belt monitor girdling her thirty-nine-inch forty-week globe. Beside the bed is a carpet bag from which spills: a plant spray; a Japanese fan; a large stop-watch; a thermos of ice cubes; a wooden back roller. The midwives are checking the monitor's screen, making entries on the partogram chart at the bottom of the bed. A cassette-player by the bed plays Edith Piaf's 'Non, Je Ne Regrette Rien'. The wall clock shows 8 p.m.*

CHORUS
            The baby's heartbeat's strong. Unstrap her now.
            Let's check her notes again. Ah yes. We guessed.
            Another fan of Nature's ancient wisdom,
            Not wanting pain relief nor intervention,
            No forceps, see, nor oxytocin drips
            To speed things up. OK, that's fine by us.
            Whether she thinks the same in six hours' time
            Need not concern us since that's not our shift.

WOMAN   The last couple of weeks have been
            spellbindingly hot and still. I confined myself to the
            garden, granted temporary immunity from duty,
            sympathy, even normal politeness towards other

people by reason of being impregnably pregnant. The steady, almost solid, golden air along with the damp clean smell of my own skin were all I cared about. I felt powerful, magnificent, and perversely *free*. My liberator rested too, biding its time, making the occasional dolphin movement when the sun was strongest on my belly (unborn nine-month eyes perceive sunshine on the other side as a warm geranium-shaded lamplight). Then this afternoon the weather broke. There was a new agitation in the air. The neighbourhood cats were slinking around, birds chirred, the trees shook their tops even though there was no wind. The air turned grey, a milky blue-grey, and its temperature dropped suddenly though it was still thick to breathe. Flies buzzed in the kitchen. Then came the first casual thunder and I was grinning like a warrior, suddenly savage and excited. The rain came in isolated splashy drops at first, then soughed into the flowerbeds releasing passionate garden smells, purling down the windows, pattering across limp green leaves and my own still-warm powdery skin.

I went inside and finished packing my bags, swapping my chosen tapes at the last minute, exchanging Dire Straits for *Carmen, Spem in Alium* for Eekamouse. How on earth do you choose music by which to give birth? The National Childbirth Trust recommends whale music, those sweet mournful subaquatic sea lullabies sung by toothless baleen whales. Only the males (and then generally only the hump-backed sort) sing these intricately phrased

half-hour songs, and then exclusively during the
mating season. But in my current incarnation of flesh,
whale music sounded almost *too* much of a creature
comfort.

CHORUS

> The baby sucks its thumb and bides its time
> Buoyant inside its water-bottle world
> Of amniotic fluid. But nine months on
> The reckoning arrives. Placenta's tired.
> The food's less good. Time to move on. So long.
> Sometimes the cervix's cork provides a sign,
> A show, to free the geni from his jar.
> Sometimes the waters break, which happened here,
> A rush of straw-pale almond-smelling sap,
> So, high and dry, the baby *must* descend.

WOMAN When the storm took hold of the afternoon
and shook the house until its windows rattled, that
was the beginning of the end of our time together. I
was sad when I realised that this baby will not be one
of the rarities born in a caul, delivered with the
unruptured membranes covering its face, because *that*
would have meant the impossibility of its death by
drowning. Now it has lost its own individual ocean
and must take its chance along with the rest of us.
Soon afterwards, at groin-level or just above, arrived
certain dull central pangs. I ignored them for a few
hours, dealt with some bedding plants, trailing lobelia
and a batch of yellow-eyed heartsease – easy to do,
since these pangs were unalarming through familiarity,

the usual monthly dullards. But when they grew
uglier, pestering me every five or six minutes and
hanging around for a minute at a time, so that I was
having to stop and grip the garden trowel and
concentrate, then, after a final pot of raspberry-leaf
tea*, I came here.

ACT II

*The wall clock shows 9 p.m.; from the cassette-player comes the
Toreador's Song. The woman moves slowly round the room
changing positions at intervals, leaning against a wall with forehead on folded forearms, sitting backwards astride a chair, kneeling
on all fours, etc.*

CHORUS

Carmen *again*. She's keen on opera.
Six centimetres dilatation. Good.
In four more hours perhaps – or even less –
The baby will be set to disembark;
Then, Steady as She Goes, and, Land Ahoy!
But now it waits, head down, in its old home
The uterus, that muscled bag of tricks,
Which pulls and squeezes with increasing force
Tugging the cervix up over its head

---

* 'The ordinary leaves of the raspberry canes from late spring to full
summer should be gathered and used (fresh, if possible). Infuse in
boiling water and drink freely with milk and sugar. It also makes a
good drink with lemon and sugar. It is well-known as particularly
good during the later months of pregnancy.' *Food in England,* Dorothy
Hartley.

A little more with every strong contraction
On average one centimetre an hour,
Until there is no length but only width.
(In the same way, Caruso's head was perched
Neckless upon his shoulders – that great voice
A direct product of its shortened passage.)
Eight score contractions for a first-time child
And half that count for each one after that;
Slow work, irksome, and most laborious.

WOMAN   Come home with your shield or on it, said
the Spartan mother to her son. When we were
children we used to play dares, stay silent through a
two-minute Chinese burn, grip a stinging nettle and
not cry. I don't know what we thought would come
from this, but something did, some sort of safety. I
knew before I was eleven that I wasn't a scaredy cat
and I still know it. What's about to happen may well
be another less childish sort of mettle detector.
Excuse me for a minute . . .

*(Woman falls silent, concentrates on the clock, fetches quick shallow
breaths like a cat in hot weather.)*

CHORUS
That's right, relax your jaw and shoulders now;
Keep your eyes open, focus on that clock
And concentrate, still while your body works.
We only shut our eyes for pleasant things,
Kissing, and other stuff that leads to this.

WOMAN The approach of labour is unnerving because nobody seems to agree on the *nature* of the pain involved. Susan told me, think of the worst possible pain you can imagine and it's a hundred times worse than that. Her labour lasted twenty-four hours, during the course of which she progressed from deep breaths of laughing gas, which made her dopey but did not take away the pain, to injections of pethidine, which made her sick and vague but did not take away the pain, to an epidural (the plastic tube of numbing liquid inserted through a hollow needle between two vertebrae in your spine), which took away the pain but also removed her capacity to work with her body's pushing urges and so necessitated the baby's forcible forceps removal, which, what with tearing and bruising and stitches both internal and external, meant several more weeks' pain afterwards.

On the other hand, Nicola said that most of her first birth had been no worse than very bad period pains, except at the end, when it felt like an extremely constipated bowel movement involving a coconut.

CHORUS
This talk of pain relief and active birth's
All very well, but what they really need
Are more midwives with more experience.
We have more patience and more creature feeling
For our own sex; know to leave well alone,
Don't crave control or intervene through pride

Like certain doctors we could mention. No.
We watch, wait, check, cheer, wait, and give
    advice.
Before, we'd see each drama to its close,
Before, that is, shift-work became the rule.
Now, though, our drop-out rate's eighty per cent.
Long training with no money at the end,
This no-strike policy and powerlessness
Do not encourage us to persevere.
Good luck, dear, we're off now to Burgerland.
Here comes the next shift ready to take over.
Remember us. Women should help each other.
And *this*, if nothing else, is women's work.

*(Second chorus of midwives enters room, checks charts, exchanges
pleasantries, yawns; woman carries on alone, practising her positions
and concentrating.)*

WOMAN All the pain so far has been well below the
    belt and I imagine it will remain that way. So I shall
    stay upright, whether standing, sitting or kneeling, for
    as long as I can, right to the end if possible. That
    way I'll be on top of it. Whenever I've heard
    contractions described with any attempt at vividness
    it's always been in melodramatic terms: 'great
    breakers surging in the black sea of the body,' and so
    on. I will try to avoid such clichés. Still, to be fair,
    now I'm actually in the middle of it, I can appreciate
    the maritime imagery. Contractions *do* come in
    waves, each building to a crest and leaving a
    respectable breathing space in between. Otherwise I

wouldn't be able to talk to you like this, even if I *am* speaking rather fast.

Last year I had a violent fortnight down on the French south Atlantic, where the coast follows a pencil-straight line for hundreds of kilometres. I have never known bathing like it. It tugged off swimming costumes and teased out mad laughter and screaming. This sea was not to play with but to play dares against. Cross-currents and the suction of incoming waves kept up a continual state of tension only just this side of pleasure. Sometimes, watching the water rear up a few yards from you, towering in a curved wall to block the light, you quailed and forgot to swim into it; then it would break over your head, sweep you off down underneath, nose and mouth filled with brine in a dark, stinging thuddingly silent world. Sometimes, best of all, you steered into and on top of a great boiling wave which had not quite broken, and then you were riding blithely on its crash and roar. You have to keep your spirits up against that sort of sea, shout and sing and concentrate hard on anticipating the violence while holding your body quiet and prepared.

ACT III

The clock shows 4 a.m. The woman is sitting restlessly astride a chair, head on hands on chairback, making an assortment of noises – muttering, grunting, singing disjointed phrases.

2nd CHORUS
    She's reached the state which marks transition
    From waiting into thrustful energy.
    Contractions double up and lose their rhythm,
    Heavy to ride, intractable, austere.
    The baby's almost ready — but not quite —
    Must wait until the cervix's front edge
    (Otherwise known as the anterior lip)
    Withdraws in self-effacement round the skull
    At last allowing space for exodus.

WOMAN   What I forgot to take into account about pain
    at the start of all this was the way it wears you down
    when it goes on and on. I've been at it now for nine
    hours. Excuse me.
        Mmmmarrh. Mmmmarrh. I'll give you one-O.
    Green grown the rushes-O.
        When I time a contraction by the second hand
    of my watch, I now find it's lasting almost two
    minutes, while the rests in between are getting so
    short that sometimes there's no breathing space at
    all. Then just when I think I'm managing, it turns
    into something else so that I'm wrestling with
    unknown quantities like the strong man in the
    myth. It's not fair.
        Mmmmarrh. Mmmarrh. What is your one-O?
    Mmmarrh. One is one and all alone — lalalalaLA
    — and evermore shall be so.
        And that's a lie as well. One *isn't* one. One isn't
    quite oneself at all today. One is, in fact, almost
    two.

And ANOTHER. Come on you Spu-urs. Come
on you Spu-urs. You'll nev-er walk alone.

(Shouts colourfully.)

I've had enough of this. It's got beyond a joke. They
told me at the classes to do without pain relief if
possible. 'Better for the mother.' RUBBISH! 'Better
for Baby.' B***** Baby! I should have had that
injection in the spine at the start of all this, the one
that paralyses you from the waist down, the one
where you can play scrabble during it. It was all the
talk of scrabble that put me off. Every time the word
epidural was mentioned, scrabble came up too. I hate
scrabble. GIVE ME AN EPIDURAL *NOW*!

2nd CHORUS
Too late, dear, sorry, much too late for *that*.
You're nearly there. An epidural now
Would take too long to work, would slow you
    down.
Nor can we give you pethidine – too late!
It might slow down the baby's breathing speed.
Why don't you try a little laughing gas?

*(They hand her a mask, show her how to put it over her face;
she sucks in deep breaths.)*

They all do this, the nature's–children set,
Leave it too late then yell for pain relief.

(To woman)

Not long now dear. Be patient. Don't push yet.
Try lighter breathing – Hoo Hoo Ha Ha Ha.

WOMAN Who? Who? Ha! Haha!

ACT IV

*The clock shows 5 a.m. The woman is sitting propped against
pillows, high on the delivery bed, sideways on to the audience.
The midwives stand around her, showing more animation than
they have done up till now. From the cassette-player comes Lone
Ranger's 'Push, lady, push', the reggae song whose chorus runs,
'Push, lady, push, lady, push; Push and make a youth-man
born'.*

2nd CHORUS
    Strongly embraced by each contraction
    The baby, hugged and squeezed, waits upside
        down
    Until the lock's enlarged before it's launched
    Headfirst, chin tucked to chest, in slow motion
    Through vaults of bone, branched pelvic
        arabesques,
    And down along the elastic boulevards.

WOMAN Ah, the relief! No more forcible dawdling, no
    more long-suffering waiting in the wings! Now I can
    get some *work* done.
        Hgnagggh! Hgnagggh!

(Makes other serving-for-match-point noises.)

And here's my whole body working away like a pair
of bellows, sweating with aspiration, intent on
exhaling a brand-new bellowing homunculus.

(Roars.)

See these women staring so avidly between my legs?
These are my trusty accoucheuses who have whiled
away much of this drama's time with hypothetical
knitting, but who now wait, breath bated, for the first
gasp.

(Roars again.)

2nd CHORUS
    The baby's nearly here — we see its head,
    We glimpse the unfused soft-skulled fontanelle.
    Now it draws back again. Stop pushing, dear,
    Or else you might get torn. You don't want *that*.
    Breathe very lightly, puff from West Wind cheeks,
    Hold baby back with candle-flickering breaths.
    Keep your mouth soft and you'll be wide down
        there.

WOMAN So *that* accounts for all the pouting that
goes on. I wondered what was behind it. Well,
prunes and prisms, prunes and prisms, prunes and
prisms.

(Takes shallow panting breaths.)

Gently they receive its head; they lead out each
shoulder in turn. And now – it – glides – into – the
– world . . . away from me.

*(The midwives crowd in, obscuring the woman from sight. A thin
infantile wail rises, gathering strength.)*

ACT V

*The wall clock shows 6 a.m. The woman lies on the bed. The
baby is at her breast. The midwives are still grouped round her
lower half, obscuring the view.*

2nd CHORUS
 After the birth must come the afterbirth.
 A shot of syntometrine in her thigh
 Will speed things up. Contractions start again;
 We tug the rainbow cord still linking them,
 Its two-foot length still beating with their blood,
 And out slides the placenta. Animals
 Gulp down this liverish morsel routinely –
 Its succulence keeps up the mother's strength –
 And even among certain human tribes
 It's called the midwife's perk. Once in a while
 Some earthy type who's read too much insists
 We pack it up for her to cook at home.
 Not this one. Quite the opposite in fact;
 She hasn't even noticed what's gone on.

WOMAN You were storm-blue at first, covered with
white curds of vernix. Next you turned pink like a
piece of litmus paper. They gave you a lick and a
promise, then handed you back to me, your limbs
lashing, your face a mask of anger. I felt like a
shipwreck, but you fell silent, little Caliban, and
latched on. After that spread-eagling storm we were
washed up onto the beach together. Now you're
quiet as a limpet on a piece of driftwood.

How can I ever think of love again?

*(Midwives still grouped staring between her legs. A hand is seen,
rising and falling, wielding needle and thread.)*

2nd CHORUS
Congratulations, dear. Only one stitch.
You hardly tore at all, you lucky girl.
If Doctor had been here you would need more.
The commonest operation in the West,
Top favourite, is episiotomy,
With one hour's careful stitching afterwards.
They cut the perineum – to make space
For baby's head, they say – unkindest cut
Of all, through muscle layers. Less haste, we say,
Less eagerness to hurry things along,
More willingness to wait, more gentleness,
Would favour women's future love lives more.
Remember, love makes babies after all.

*(Enter Lucina, strong, broad-hipped, big-bosomed, carrying a bundle
of wheat in one hand and a silver kidney dish in the other.)*

LUCINA   As Goddess of Childbirth, it behoves me to point out that such trivial complaints about the possibly diminished quality of her future sex life are light-minded in the extreme. The fact is, *she's* alive and the *baby's* alive. You seem to take that for granted, and yet a hundred years ago – no, even *fifty* years ago – her friends and family would have been sending up heart-felt thanks to me for her safe delivery. It's no tea party, you know, even now, and it's not meant to be. You'll recall how Eve was told, 'In sorrow thou shalt bring forth children,' as the bishops quoted at Queen Victoria when they heard she'd accepted sniffs of the new-fangled anaesthetic chloroform (although *that* didn't stop her using it the next time, and the next). My goodness, women are so *spoilt* these days.

I even hear them complaining if they have to have a Caesarean. They'd have had a sight more to complain about during *my* heyday, when the Roman Lex Caesarea forbade the burial of a dead pregnant woman before the baby had been cut from her womb. A certain number of babies have always got stuck on their way out, but at least now you've got forceps and ventouse suction and other such gadgets to help things along. Not so long ago they were still having to hack awkward infants out piecemeal, cutting off protruding limbs, coaxing out what remained with pot-hooks, spoons, forks and thatchers' hooks. Many's the time I've seen one midwife take hold of the mother and the other seize the emerging baby, both pulling and tugging for all they're worth. And of course, with your short memories, you'll have forgotten puerperal fever? *That* was caused after the birth of the child by bacteria creeping up through the still-open cervix and infecting the womb. Women died raving. Oh yes, puerperal fever killed more mothers than all the other things put together. So the woman in this little drama should thank her lucky stars and Joseph Lister that she's living in an age of antisepsis. She may well be a bit bruised and stitched and shocked, but at least she's still here.

I can never get over what a short memory the human race has. It makes me impatient, it really does. Why, these days, you hardly know you're *born*.

From
Dear George

Dear George

She was trying to write an essay on the various sorts of humour in *As You Like It* at the same time, which didn't help. To her right was a pad of file paper on which she scrawled scathing comments about Shakespeare as they occurred. In front of her was her mother's block of Basildon Bond. She had used four sheets so far.

Dear George, she wrote for the fifth time, and added a curly little comma like a tadpole. She sat back and admired the comma. That was pure luck when it turned out like that. Sometimes if you concentrated on something too hard you ruined it.

She sauntered over to the mirror and stared at herself for a few minutes. 'You gorgeous creature you,' she murmured, sly but sincere, ogling herself from sideways on. A yawn overtook her and she watched her tongue arch like a leaf. Then she performed a floozie's bump and grind back to the *Complete Works*.

Jaq: What stature is she of?
Orl: Just as high as my heart.

George was tall, that was the best thing about him. She would be higher than his heart, of course, probably about level with his Adam's apple, but that was good enough for her. Already her feet were seven-and-a-halfs, and she was still not yet fifteen.

She turned back to her latest copy of the letter to George. She knew its phrases by heart now, and they were as spontaneous as two hours' effort could make them. 'Daniel Minter asked me to tell you that the Grindley match has been rearranged for the 16th because he thought you were coming back to the Bio Lab, but you didn't. So I thought I'd drop you a line to let you know. He asked me because I had to be there till five o'clock on the last day of term, collecting the results from our petri dishes.'

The handwriting was vital, that was what she was trying to perfect as she toiled over copy after copy. There must be nothing round or childish about it. She was dabbling now with italics like barbed wire. Sophistication was what she aimed for. A looped *f* would still creep in if she didn't watch it, or a silly swan-backed *s*.

There was her fat little sister, rattling the doorknob to be let in.

'I won't talk,' came the promises through the keyhole. 'I'll just sit on your bed and watch you.'

'Go away,' she drawled. 'You are banal.'

Silence. She thought of her sister's big baffled sheep's eyes and this made her giggle crossly and feel cruel.

'Banal!' she bellowed. 'Look it up in the dictionary.'

Her sister rushed heftily off downstairs towards the bookcase. From another part of the house drifted a weak howl from their mother, who was trying to get the new baby to sleep.

Disgust jerked her out of her seat. How *could* she, at *her* age, it was so *selfish* of her. It was just showing off. As everyone at school had pointed out, she'd probably been trying for a boy this time, so *served her right*.

She would never be able to bring George home. It would be too awful. Her mother would probably try to breastfeed it in front of him. She started to wriggle and giggle in horror.

Cel: I pray you, bear with me, I cannot go no further.
Tou: For my part, I had rather bear with you than bear you: yet I should bear no cross if I did bear you, for I think you have no money in your purse.

She picked up her pen and scribbled, 'This is obviously meant to be funny, but it is not. It is rubbish. People only say this is good because it is Shakespeare. It is really boring. It is not even grammar, e.g. I cannot go no further.' The hexagonal plastic shaft of the biro turned noisily in the grip of her front teeth as she paused to read through what she had written. Then she crossed out 'boring' and printed 'banal' in its place.

'Commonplace. Trite. Hackneyed,' came through the keyhole with a lot of heavy breathing; then a pause and, 'What do *they* mean?'

'Go away,' she said. 'Ask Mum.'

Served her mother right if she used up all the stamps and Basildon Bond. Spitefully she folded and inserted each of the four early drafts into separate envelopes, sealed them and wrote out George's address four times with self-consciously soppy relish. She had no intention of sending any of them, and stuck on the stamps in a spirit of wicked waste. Later today she would tear them up to show she had style, and send off this perfect fifth version.

She read it through again. It was making her cringe now, she couldn't see it fresh any more. She'd read those phrases so often, she couldn't tell whether they came across as casual or childish or too keen or what.

'I wish I was in 6B with you, all the GCSEs out of the way. Hope you have a good holiday. If you would possibly feel like meeting for any reason, I am fairly free this holiday. Maybe hear from you soon. Ciao.'

Was ciao too much? She hadn't thought it was till this moment. She couldn't put Yours sincerely, and shook at the thought of Love. Cheers was what the boys in 6B said to each other, but she wouldn't stoop that low.

'Dear George,' she scribbled again, this time on a naughty impulse and a sheet of scrap paper, 'I don't know I could stand to go out with you if Every Time We Said Goodbye you said Chiz instead. Why do you do it? It makes you sound really thick. Chiz chiz chiz chiz chiz. Try Ciao, it's more stylish — it's Italian in case you didn't know and it means the same as chiz — you look a bit Italian which is partly why I fancy you.'

The mournfulness of his image caught her, stopped her ticking for a second or two as a cameo of large meaty nobility filled her mind's eye.

She reread what she had written, then, sniggering, clattering her teeth together in enamelled applause, dipping her head down so that her hair piled up on one side of the paper in a foresty rustle, she scrawled, 'You can't be *that* thick. Anyone can have bad luck in GCSEs, ha ha, though two retakes in history is a bit much.'

Cupping her chin on the half shell of her hands, she made her mouth into a kissing shape. With the tip of her tongue she tenderly tapped inside each of the teeth in her upper jaw.

'I would like to feel your hands on the back of my waist (25"), with the thumbs round my sides,' she scrawled, chewing invisible gum, 'but only if they aren't sweaty. If you have wet hands it's all over before it's started, sorry Gorgeous George but that's the way I am.'

Holding her hands up in front of her, using them like boned fans to block the light, she spotted an incipient hangnail poking up from the cuticle of her left thumb and fell on it like a falcon, tearing at it with famished energy. When she had made it bleed she lost interest and stared out of the window.

There on the back lawn her galumphing little sister was helping their mother hang out baby vests and babygros and other baby rubbish in the sun. Her mother had it strapped to her front in a hideous pink nylon sling.

'No style,' she muttered, curling her lip. She pulled the curtains on them and made a warm gloom.

Once the candle was lit and positioned on her home-work table, she was able to ignore the worst aspects of her room, like the brainlessly 'cheerful' duvet cover with its sun, moon and poppy field. Her face's reflection was a blanched heart in the mirror on the back wall. When she came home on the last train she saw her reflection in the window like that, pale and pointed, looking sideways, fleering at the bugle eyes which were so very blot-like and black above cream-coloured cheeks. She had a vision of George coming up to her as she sat illegally alone in her accustomed first-class carriage, and saw his difficult smile.

Hugging herself as she rocked to and fro on the folding chair, adjusting her balance as it threatened to jack-knife her thighs to stomach in its fold-up maw, her hands became George's, firm and pressing around her waist. She stood up. Now one crept forward and undid the buttons of her shirt, stroked her neck down past the collar bone. Catching sight of herself in the mirror tweaking her own breast, the silly lost expression left her face instantly.

She reached across for Shakespeare and flicked through until she came to her latest discovery in *Antony and Cleopatra*. Holding her left hand palm out to her reflection, she touched wrist to wrist in the chill glass and murmured,

> There is gold and here
> My bluest veins to kiss, a hand that kings
> Have lipped, and trembled kissing.

This produced a reluctant simper and a slow shudder which wriggled through from head to foot finishing with a sigh. After a minute she tried it again but this time it did not work.

Lifting her knees and pointing her toes like a cartoon of stealth, she fell back onto her *As You Like It* essay with an angry groan.

It was a lover and his lass,
With a hey, and a ho, and a hey nonino
That o'er the green corn field did pass
In the spring time, the only pretty ring time
When birds do sing, hey ding a ding ding.

'Anybody could write this sort of stuff,' she wrote. 'If Madonna put it in one of her lyrics, English teachers everywhere would say, how moronic.' Then she dashed off an inspired demolition job on Touchstone before losing her drift.

Flicking through the rice-paper leaves, she came to another juicy bit.

Des: O, banish me, my lord, but kill me not!
Oth: Down, strumpet!
Des: Kill me tomorrow; let me live tonight!
Oth: Nay, if you strive —

There was George, big George, looming like a tower in the half-dark, and herself in a white nightdress with pintucks from shoulder seam to waist, quite plain, no lace, his hot hands round her neck . . . She inhaled slowly and closed her eyes; leaned forward and pressed a bit against her windpipe with her thumbs; blushingly smirked; then felt a chill tinge of shame, a prickling under her arms like cactus hairs, and busily started to biro a blue swallow on the inside of her elbow.

Tattoos only lasted when the ink got into your blood-stream.

Maybe she would get her ears pierced this afternoon at

Shangri La, she thought, though that was supposed to hurt a lot too, there was no anaesthetic, they just shot a spike through the lobe with a little gun like a paper punch.

She sniggered as she remembered something rude. According to Valerie Mitchell from 6B, who was a Saturday girl at Shangri La and who was doing Louis XIV for a special project, the Sun King's bed was heaped with pillows stuffed with his mistresses' hair. 'And not with the hair from their *heads*,' Valerie had leered.

Now she described this conversation to George in her make-believe letter, and even enclosed a clipping to launch his collection. When it came to signing off this time, she added fifty smacking Xs. She then spat on the paper before smearing it with her fist. Across the envelope's seal she wrote SWALK in lipstick and from the Queen's mouth on the stamp she drew a balloon saying, 'Who's a pretty boy then.'

'*Please* come and play,' whined her sister from the other side of the door. 'You've been up here for ages now and I don't believe you're just doing revision.'

'Go away,' she said.

'We could go roller skating,' said her sister.

'Mum won't let me go out till I've done the washing up,' she said, 'and I'm refusing on moral grounds since it's not my turn, so I *can't* go out.'

Once her sister had gone stump-stump-stumping off downstairs, she crept along the landing, pausing to stare and bite her thumb at the rumpled bedroom shared by her mother and stepfather. Then, when she was safely locked in the bathroom, she transferred the plastic ducklings, sailors, mechanically spouting whales and dinghies from the bath to the lavatory and closed the lid on them.

During the chin-high soak which followed, she lay poaching in water so hot that a clear Plimsoll line appeared on her skin, all fiery lobster-coloured flesh below the water's surface while above stayed white and sweat-pearled. The little bathroom was dense with steam, the wallpaper's paisley invisible and the gloss-painted ceiling lustrous with moisture. She closed her eyes and saw George opening her letter, his crooked smile, his reaching for the telephone. They talked with sophisticated ease, and soon they were sharing a fondue down at the Mousetrap.

There was silence except for the rustle from the boa of weightless scented bubbles sitting on her shoulders. It came into her mind that it would be much more natural to give him a ring straight off, and she decided not to send the letter after all.

When at last she tottered back, lurid and wrinkled and dizzy, her sister was sitting on the bed.

'You've *got* to play with me now,' said her sister. 'I've done all your washing up and Mum says you're horrible but you can go out on condition you take me roller skating.'

'Shift up,' she croaked, collapsing onto the bed, clutching at disappearing shreds of George as the towels came adrift all round her.

'So you *will* come when you're dry,' said her sister, gnatlike. 'I've got your skates out. I've tidied your room, see, so Mum won't go on about that either. There's no excuse. I even went down the road to post your letters.'

'Letters,' she said stupidly, still stunned by the equatorial bath, before it dawned on her.

Bed and Breakfast

They sat side by side not holding hands. Back on the platform and in the ticket office, people had turned to stare at them. It was visible, the intensity of their candle power, joined, no matter how they tried to bank it down and look everydayish.

Proud and shy out in the public air, they avoided the larky or lovey-dovey behaviour common to their age group. It was enough to allow themselves to glance at each other now and then, glances arrowing beams of sheepish delight.

With a swish of doors and a sigh the train slid away. Light poured in through the smeary windows. Nicola lowered her eyelids and broke into a half-smile, the edges of her teeth showing in the sunny flood like a fringe of daisy petals. She was very fair. Simon looked sideways at her face, the snowy printless forehead, and then she, turning, opened her eyes straight into his and he blushed, gasped, burrowed in his sports bag and brought out a mathematically arranged cheese sandwich. This he placed furtively in her lap.

'To keep your strength up,' he muttered, frowning at the couple opposite, fending off ridicule. The man was older than them, in his early twenties, stout, strong, sulky, his thumbs sunk angrily into the waistband of his jeans, muscular legs in a V-sign hogging more than their share of space. He was staring glumly out of the window as they sped past vegetable allotments and chimney stacks, his glare on autopilot. Beside him his girlfriend sat poring over a magazine article headed 'What Makes a Girl a Good Lay?'

These two ignored each other till the next station, when they slouched off the train like a couple of Alsatians. Nicola watched them snapping and snarling on the platform as the train pulled out.

'That's what we're *not* like,' she whispered, her lips like feathers against Paul's glowing ear-rim. 'We're not like that.'

'No!' he murmured, in frantic agreement.

All the talk of who fancied whom, who'd got off with whom, and words like shagging, she was above all that, he thought, it needed a quite different vocabulary to describe what was between them.

'Slag,' she'd said, for instance. 'If you ever use that word about anyone I'll never speak to you again. Or scrubber. Or dog.' He agreed with her, he was in no position not to. Half the time preoccupied, the *princesse lointaine*, miles away, and then the centre of attraction without even trying, you could feel the physical force of that phrase pulling power, she had it; though he should find a better way to put this, of course.

She had come into power certainly, but was, sweetly priggish, concerned not to abuse it. Daily she examined her emotions for signs of corruption.

Only last weekend she had told him about the two German students who had followed her round Boots, who'd kept asking her out, quite politely, and when finally she had said, no, really no, they had left meekly, one of them pausing first to say, 'Thank God indeed that he has made such beautiful faces for us to look at.'

'Bastard,' Simon had said before he could help it. Then, after a gratified smirk, she had looked embarrassed and even apologised.

The three other passengers in their carriage were all disembarking. Nicola and Simon looked at each other and waited, taut, until the doors sighed unevenly and they were quite out of the station, then collected themselves into each other's arms with a mutual groan. Their eyes flickered shut, their lips pressed open each to the other's, she curved her hand round his bare neck while he twisted his fingers in her hair during the unstoppered kisses. His hand moved to cover her breast, she smudged her heated face into his hot neck with a sigh, and his body pressed trembling, heavy and graceful against hers.

This was nothing to do with anybody else, and was certainly light years from those distant shameful sessions in the Bio Lab with the video and the Tupperware lunchbox full of contraceptives. There had been a pungent smell coming from the earthworms slit lengthwise in half and staked out with dressmaking pins half an hour earlier by the first year. *À propos* of nothing they had been plonked in front of the mooing woman, so hefty, so gross compared with the wildflower girls whom the documentary had devastated in front of the boys. Then the stirruped splay and bloody debouchment, to which the pious voiceover had instructed them to respond with wonder, with awe, had made even the snickering boys go green.

'They weren't being educational there, that was just

propaganda,' she'd fumed. 'That was meant as a deterrent. How dare they.' Therefore she had rejected the whole lot, the official sentimental education on offer, part and parcel, and was determined to reinvent the business of love for herself. Her attitude was the determined opposite of pragmatic. It took some nerve. She was the Lydia Languish of her set.

At the next station a flurry of new people piled in. This time the two of them sat opposite each other, looking out of the windows, turning occasionally for another secretive dazzled exchange of eyes. They rested their heads against carriage seats upholstered in shabby prickling green stuff which lit up under the sun like moss. They had never been properly alone together before, they were too young, they were both still living at home. They could not bear the thought of any of their various parents or step-parents or siblings knowing, so they had met in parks or walked by railway tracks, but it was the end of summer now and it was driving them mad.

They wanted something but weren't quite sure what they wanted. It was to do with something vital, though, it was there at the centre of their nascent sense of selfhood, and it was this which had caused to spring up the fierce protective hedge of silence and pride around the one area of their lives where they perceived their elders had no business, nor anybody else either.

'It's got to be *right*,' Nicola insisted.

'What will make it right?' asked Simon.

'We'll just know,' she said, confident, Rousseauesque.

It was difficult to convince her it was right when they could never be alone in a room together. Simon shared a room with two brothers, Nicola shared with her sister, their homes were packed to the gills and the fastidious simply did not thrive.

'I don't feel I belong to myself properly yet,' she had told him a while back. 'Dad's always on about how much I'm costing. I don't feel I'm my own property, not my body anyway. He does it sometimes to the plate of food in front of me, tots up how much the chips cost, the pie, the beans.'

That was why they were on this journey. Simon had found a guide in the library and chosen a place for the sake of its rural name, Meadowsweet, and, though he had not mentioned this, because it was the cheapest; although even so it was not cheap by the standards of what they could afford, in fact quite the opposite.

She leaned over and touched his arm. It was their station. All at once, there they were, deep in the country, standing on a tiny platform in the startlingly clean sweet air. Once the train had gone it was very quiet. They both jumped at a scuttering noise, but it was only a dry leaf bowling along the tarmac. Then they embraced, swaying, until they were light-headed, giddy, drawing away from each other with enormous smiles, almost shyly.

Simon got his map out.

'I think it might be quite a way,' he said, starting to look worried. 'There don't seem to be any buses either. Or taxis.'

'Oh, taxis,' said Nicola, as if she were sick to death of taxis. 'You don't go to the country for taxis. You *walk* in the country.'

They examined the map together, and it could have

meant anything since it was the first time either of them had tried to use one.

'Let's see where that leads,' he said, pointing to a green lane edged with hawthorn bushes, for no other reason than that he liked the look of it.

The first five miles or so were in daylight, or at least, dusk. They followed the single track road past flat tilting fields and hedgerows with little brown birds jumping in and out of them. A mistiness and moistness of rain in the air pressed coolness to their faces and blurred their hair with droplets. As they walked, they discussed life, death, and later on, when it became relevant, the weather.

Their voices piped away into the evening.

'Truth,' said Nicola.

'Not using other people,' they agreed solenmly.

'Love,' said Simon. 'Who you love.'

They stopped to hug each other. He squeezed her so hard that her breath came puffing out, her ribs creaked and her feet left the ground.

'I feel incredibly strong,' he marvelled. 'I feel I could lift you to the top of that tree with one hand.'

They compared notes on how, in each other's company, they felt full of power, flickering like flames, capable of tremendous effortless speed; and how this fading light was lovely and mysterious, seemingly criss-crossed with satiny threads of excitement. They made each other feel so alive, they agreed; all those other people on the train, they'd been dozy, half conscious in comparison.

She picked a blade of grass, stretched it between her thumbs and pursed her lips to blow. Kid's stuff, he pronounced this, copying her, and soon their piercing whistles split the air for half a mile around.

Time passed. It grew dark. The sky was a black meadow of silvered *petits moutons*; a gibbous moon backlit the scalloped border of each cloudlet. Some five or six fields away they could see a pub, a far-off gaudy box of rhythmic noise.

'We could ask there,' said Nicola.

'Too far,' said Simon. He peered at the map. 'Soon we hit a B-road, then we're laughing.'

'Can I have a look?' said Nicola. 'Ah. Mmm. I think we're here, look, that last church was marked. And, I see, that's where we're going. Yes. Quite a bit further.'

It started to rain.

By the time they reached the Meadowsweet Guest House it was nearly ten o'clock. They were drenched. Simon pressed the doorbell, and flashed her a desperate grin, like a plague victim. She returned a distant smile.

'We've got those chimes at home,' she said pensively. 'I didn't think they'd have them in the country.'

The door opened a crack and a suspicious bespectacled face peered at them over the guard-chain. Simon stepped forward.

'We booked,' he said. 'Simon Morrison.'

'It's ten o'clock,' said the face.

'It was a bit of a way from the station,' said Simon.

'You *walked*?' said the face disbelievingly. There was the scrabble and clink of various security measures being unfettered, then they were in, wiping their feet like a couple of children in the narrow hall.

'And you are Mr Morrison?' said their host, staring at Simon, who was looking his most half-baked.

'Thass right,' murmured Simon.

Their host's wife came to stare.

'I don't know,' she said at last. 'Come on, leave your wet shoes on the mat, then I'll bring you both a hot drink in the lounge.' She shook her head and bustled off, tutting, to the kitchen.

In the lounge, the leaping screen of the television was just one brightness among many. The room was small and savagely lit by a 150-watt bulb refracted through a complex chandelier which tinkled madly as Simon's head brushed it.

'Derek and Janet, I'd like you to meet our two strangers in the night,' said their host, who had decided to revert to jollity. 'Simon and, er.'

'Nicola,' said Nicola grimly. She and Simon stood awkwardly, sodden, in their socks. She glanced at him. He looked as though he wanted to hide behind the curtains. He looked, she thought, like a big child.

Derek and Janet gaped up at them from the settee.

'Raining, is it?' said Derek at last, gazing at Nicola's dripping elf-locks and rats-tails.

'Just a bit,' laughed their host, rubbing his hands. 'She looks like a little mermaid, doesn't she.' He put his arm matily round her shoulders. 'Sit ye down, Nicola, sit ye down.'

'Hot chocolate,' said his wife coldly from the door.

Up in their room at last, Nicola fell like a stone onto one of the twin beds.

'At least it's warm,' volunteered Simon. 'Clean. We can push the beds together.'

'No we can't,' snapped Nicola. 'I'd rather be under a haystack. This isn't the country. It's just like back at home.'

'It's the country outside, though,' said Simon, trying to draw her to him.

She shrugged him off.

'Nylon sheets,' she said bitterly. 'Horrible butterflies all over the duvet covers. Horrible little ornaments, rabbits in crinolines, mice on penny farthings.'

'But that sort of thing,' he said, amazed, 'it doesn't matter. I hadn't even noticed.'

'No, well,' she said. 'I thought, I thought at least there would be cotton sheets.'

'But that doesn't *matter*,' he persisted, earnest and gawky beneath another searchlight. 'Not at all. That's nothing.'

'Oh is it,' she sniffed.

'It sounded OK in the guide,' he said. '"Cosy and welcoming". We couldn't afford the ones with stars.'

'Don't,' she said, turning away from his boy's face. The caparisoned fairytale personage had reverted to plain lizard.

'You'd like me more if I was five years older. Ten. And my skin puts you off,' he said. 'Be honest.'

'Shut up,' she said, and started to cry. He sat down beside her and tried to draw her into his shoulder. She resisted. He swore. She cried harder.

'Please Nicola,' he said, pacing the room. 'It can't be just the duvet covers.'

'It's not!' she said wildly. 'It's life!'

'How do you mean?' he said. 'Life.'

'Look,' she snarled, 'can't you see it ahead? We're going to end up like them.'

'Never,' he soothed.

'Boring. Dead!'

She was restlessly beating her foot. A violent cyclonic mood would arrive like this sometimes, inexplicable, devastating, tearing through one or the other of them like a runaway freight train leaving maximum damage in its wake. She shuddered.

'Can't you see?' she said, trying to be calm. 'We'd struggle along for a bit but we'd never get beyond this. It's all mapped out.'

He held his arms out to her, trying to hug her, but she cackled like a witch and shrank away.

'All those feelings of flame,' she continued, 'speed, being strong, they're rubbish, you know. They're just like the adverts, rubbish to keep us quiet for a bit.'

'Not what I feel for you,' he said stubbornly. 'That's real.'

'No,' she said. She was hurtling downwards now, nothing could stop her. 'Like my dad says, it's shaft or be shafted.' She thumped the bouncy foam pillows. 'Like he says, what makes me think *I'm* so special?'

'You are,' he said.

'Not long before I'm screaming at some man in front of the children, just like Mum. *If* he's still there.'

'I'd never leave you,' he said sadly.

'You say that now,' she scoffed.

And so they continued under the comfortless white glare, for several hours, until they fell asleep at last athwart the winsome bed linen, fully dressed, clasped in each other's arms, as dawn broke over the fields outside their bedroom window.

Summoned to breakfast by a peremptory knock at the door and a brusque Wakeywakey! from their host, they shuffled downstairs white-faced and red-eyed. The morning sun winked on stainless steel toast racks and tea in tin pots, it put a shine on the varnished sausages, and cruelly exposed the pallor of bacon fat, the bluish jelly on fried eggs.

Nicola sat glowering at the pink-jacketed hunting melée on her table mat, ignoring everything and everybody around her. Even so, Simon was not cowed. An hour ago he had had an amazing dream, a tremendous panoply of sensualism, intensely gratifying, shudderingly happy, easy. It had unfurled a prospect of utmost melting pleasure, and she was in it all right, right at the heart of it. He felt full of optimism. He wanted to tell her, she looked so gloomy, but decided it could wait.

The room was cramped, and the two other couples at neighbouring tables were whispering like embarrassed children, although they were in late middle age. The clatter of cutlery was deafening in this tense demi-silence.

'Soft-boiled I think you said, Peter,' sang their host, re-entering the room with the air of a man under extreme pressure. 'And fried for you, Marjorie. Now have I got that right.'

'You're not from these parts originally?' chirruped Marjorie, cocking her head up at him, brave in the hushed room.

'No, no,' smiled their host. 'Does it show? We've only

recently moved from Berkshire. Hence the tablemats. And you?'

'We're from Norfolk,' said Marjorie. 'Originally.'

'Ah, from Norfolk are you. The land of the lazy wind – it doesn't go round you, it goes through you.'

'That's right!' said Marjorie gaily, as though this were a fresh thought to her, a surprise.

'Now, can I tempt you to another sausage, Marjorie?' said their host, courtly in his offer. 'There's one going begging here.'

'No really, I couldn't,' protested Marjorie. 'I've had sufficient.'

'Oh come now,' said their host roguishly. 'Haven't you got a little crack? A leetle leetle crack? I think you have!'

Simon was grabbed by a terrible rude desire to laugh. He frowned and coughed, but low down inside him it was taking over. He glanced at Nicola's stony face and away again quickly.

'Just one weeny sausage!' wheedled their host. 'Go on, Marjorie. I'm going to be very upset if you can't fit it in, very disappointed.'

With an imploring pout he waved his offering temptingly beneath her nose.

'Just for me!' he leered.

Simon's eyes started to stream. His face disintegrated and rapidly he took cover behind his napkin. He began to whimper softly, trying to disguise it with coughing. Now Nicola too unwillingly succumbed. Shoulders heaving, she looked at him, alarmed, her breath starting to come in uneven shudders. Hastily, they stumbled up from their table, appalled, jostling each other like cattle in their hurry to get through the doorway, then clattered up the stairs, almost out of control.

The door of their room closed safe behind them, they fell onto their beds, sobbed into the pillows, they hooted until their ribs hurt and they had to hold their sides. Whenever either of them showed signs of calming down, the other caught their eye and they were off again.

'Oh don't,' they groaned. 'No more.'

The gloomy shreds of the hateful night they had passed in that room flapped off into the hinterland on leathery broken wings. They paid and left as soon as they were able.

Outside it was a morning of hot sun with a cool surfy breeze, the air like clear liquid with bubbles rising, and they gulped great effervescent draughts as though newly escaped from prison.

Everything around them looked beautiful or interesting, freshly oxygenated as they were to the point of euphoria. Weeds, long and lush but on their last legs, fringed the lane, and they saw that the greenish-white flowers of the stinging nettles were giving way to tassels of seeds. Blackberries in the hedge were still pale pink or purplish, underjuiced, too sour to eat yet. They spat out sample mouthfuls.

Simon dethorned a branch of early rosehips, light orange, large and impeccably lacquered, broke off the top three inches, heavily fruited, and stuck it behind his ear. Considering what a disaster last night had been, he felt surprisingly jubilant, almost as though they had triumphed over circumstance after all. That was because he felt sure that nothing important was stopping them from doing so.

In fact, he realised, he was quite certain that it would be all right now. His dream warmed him, a smug heap of gold in some inward chamber of his mind. He smiled fatly, scooped Nicola up and swung her round in the air, ululating.

Having missed their breakfast earlier, they bought bread and cheese at the next village, silent while the elderly woman who was serving them chatted on to her crony about somebody else's unacceptable behaviour, cuddling the cordless phone between her chin and shoulder as she sliced the half-pound of cheddar.

Most of the cottages they passed had gardens visible from the road, all given over to vegetables. They paused to stare at a row of tall green teepees stuck with scarlet flowers.

'They're for cucumbers, aren't they?' said Simon uncertainly.

'I don't know,' said Nicola. 'But those over there are cabbages. Definitely. And that's rhubarb! I could grow rhubarb if I lived in the country.'

'Rhubarb?' said Simon, startled.

'Not *just* rhubarb,' she said, embarrassed. 'But, think, if you were vegetarian round here you'd need hardly any money.'

A few steps on by the side of the road was a carrier bag full of apples, in front of it a handwritten sign saying HELP YOURSELF.

'Look at that!' said Simon, amazed. He walked all round the bag as though some trick must be involved.

'You see?' said Nicola, choosing a couple of unbruised apples. 'You wouldn't need much money living out here. You could keep hens too. Bees, even.'

'I don't know about bees,' frowned Simon. 'You have to know about these things.'

As they walked on, they marvelled at how nobody in the country seemed much under sixty, and doubted they would ever be able to afford somewhere to live. They touched on the captiousness of their parents, the advantages of tents and caravans, and wondered whether or not common land really was common these days. They talked about who owned what, and how, and why, and contemplated the traveller's life, the blessed freedom, the openness to weather, even bad weather, and the fate of travellers who fell ill or grew old. Nicola put forward the view that it would have been preferable to live in the old days, at least you could put up a fight then, they'd got everybody taped now; Simon disagreed, pointing out that she would have been blackleading the grates up at the big house until carried off by TB or the umpteenth baby, they were better off now, more able to live free even if it seemed otherwise sometimes, and he had faith, things would change.

On they walked, past fields just harvested, the stubble in burnished zigzags against the earth, bales of straw stacked like great slabs of golden cake.

'This is what I wanted,' said Nicola, pausing at a gate and flinging out her arms towards the fields, the cool bright air, golds and ochres turning miles away to bluish greys and greens, and on, rising up to the sky, a fierce tender blue, and cohorts of cumulus clouds, banked and ranked as far as the eye could see, luminous, their top curves taking the sun.

They climbed over the gate and threw down their jackets under a tree in the corner of this field with a view. Here they spread their picnic and hungrily made up for their earlier frustrated breakfast.

'Last night,' she said as they finished eating, and she flushed a sudden miserable red. 'I didn't. I mean, I wasn't. I felt so, you know. I thought I could *kill* myself.'

'Don't,' he said. 'It's gone. But this morning . . . That business with the . . . "There's one going begging!"'

He started to gasp again, looking at her in momentary surprise.

'"Go on, Marjorie,"' she remembered, joining him. 'Oh her face!'

The irresistible joke had come to life again, helium-filled. They fell on their backs and abandoned themselves to it, it was like some drug, the laughing, leaving a wake of foamy euphoria.

When they calmed down at last they were lying side by side, quite private, looking at the leafy canopy above them from whose shelter issued the thoughtful soothings of wood-pigeons. They turned and lay in a sideways hug, staring into each other's eyes, smiling occasionally.

'Last night,' murmured Simon after a while. 'Last night wasn't so bad after all.'

He nuzzled up under her chin and blew softly into her hair, into her neck, to foment his nerve. Then, although no one else was anywhere in sight, let alone hearing distance, he began to whisper his dream into her ear.

When in Rome

They were standing in front of the bronze Etruscan she-wolf, staring at her eight pendant dugs and the two hearty Roman babies suckling there. It was quite early, but the July heat had collared them, limp as they already were after a broken night of what Geraldine was starting to call hate-making.

'Romulus and Remus,' read Paul from his guide book. 'Twin sons of Mars, set adrift in a basket on the Tiber, rescued and raised by a she-wolf. Later Romulus killed Remus and established the city of Rome on the Palatine Hill.'

'Let's move on,' said Geraldine. 'I want to see the Caravaggio.' She took her hair in one hand and gave it a sharp twist so that it stayed up for a few moments, a thick and fairish tangle, baring her neck. She had Germanic colouring but was now patchily brown-faced, with light eyes thrown into bizarre holiday relief like pieces of turquoise mosaic. Paul was as dark as a Roman to start with, and the sun had seeped into his skin like ink into blotting paper.

'Romulus' new city was exclusively male,' he continued. 'So to remedy this sorry state of affairs the first Romans kidnapped and raped the women of the neighbouring Sabine tribe.'

'Sorry state of affairs,' snorted Geraldine. 'Honestly.' Her hair tumbled down in slow motion like a pile of weeds.

They were stuck in an ageing deadlock, moody, critical, not sure how to leave each other or whether to carry on. Soon, they knew, the time would come to slough off lifelessness and stand apart in fully fledged separate fury. Meanwhile, since their arrival in Rome he had started flirting with a new idea in a dangerous last-ditch sort of way, and she had colluded to some extent. At any rate she had grown rather careless; not being happy made her childish. She buried the nagging thought alive.

'Strange to think *they* could do that,' said Paul, brushing his knuckles across her breasts.

'What?' she said, looking at the she-wolf. 'Oh. Ah.'

Outside in the Forum the heat was almost African. At first they tried to make sense of the bases of walls, the stumps of former colonnades.

'Remains of the Basilica Julia,' read Geraldine. 'A court of Civil Law. Forum of Augustus. The Mamertine Prison.'

Arches and columns and basilica fragments stood around them like meaningless mountains.

'Next on the list,' he said, taking the book from her. 'The Colosseum. Seated fifty-five thousand. Several hundredweight of sawdust was spread over the ring between each spectacle to absorb the blood.'

'Let's give it a miss,' she said.

'Don't move,' said Paul, pointing his camera at her. 'No, don't squint like that. Come on, Geraldine! You're on holiday, remember.'

She held still for some moments then lost patience and made an irritable movement just as he clicked the shutter. It was always like this when he was taking a photograph, she fumed to herself, the fatal lack of timing. Then the prints would come back with her face in a blur, or blinking, or glaring out with orange eyes like wasps.

'The sheer scale of it,' he said. He was polished with sweat, his skin like smooth dark marble.

'It's *too* big,' she sighed.

'It *was* the centre of the world,' he reproved.

Oh, we've got to talk on like this, ping, pong, for days and days yet, she thought. She turned her head restlessly, taking in the sepia-coloured landscape.

'The trouble was, of course, it went on too long,' he mused. 'The Roman empire. In the end it just crumbled.'

'Goths and Vandals,' she responded politely. 'Let's find an ice cream.'

By the time they reached the hotel for a siesta, the heat was stupendous. They had walked doggedly back in the sultry grey haze along packed roads buzzing with Vespas and helmetless boys and girls. Geraldine saw a man lean back at the traffic lights and kiss the girl sitting pillion, over his shoulder, almost upside down, top lip to bottom lip at any rate.

'All those obelisks and elephants,' she gasped, taking in their dim room, the *due letti* with narrow springless mattresses like squashed sandwiches, damp and white.

'You forget how close it is to Egypt,' Paul agreed. 'Carthage. The Phoenicians.' He stripped his clothes off and stood quietly in the shuttered gloom.

'You look like a statue,' she said.

She went and stood beside him, skated her fingertips idly over his damp torso. Their mouths smudged sideways into each other and she closed her eyes, started to lean into him and not think until, like a bee stinging, he bit the inside of her lip with a shade more spite than enthusiasm.

'Ouch,' she said, drawing back. 'I think I'll have a shower.'

'No,' he drawled, 'not yet,' and reeled her into him like a fisherman.

They cooled off each other for days at a time, then came together like this, almost in combat, gladiatorial. They turned cruel little blades on each other and wreaked havoc, and sulked; then made it up with a practised weariness – or in a fit of unpleasant excitement. This heat which so doped the mind did not similarly inhibit the body. They moved in on each other ferociously, both growing hotter by the second, so that it seemed for some blind free instants that it was not sweat in which their bodies were slithering and slapping, but blood.

Afterwards they slept, and woke, sad, self-contained, and solicitous towards each other. Either it was like that now, or it was pointless and petered out. He approached her body with boredom, really, if he was honest, pressing buttons as if he were entering his PIN number in the cash machine, the familiar formula. And she, she turned her head to one side, eyes scrolling back, and thought, 'If he does that once more . . .'

That evening they ate their meal under a wooden pergola twisted with vine leaves. The day's quilt of heat had not lifted and it was still suffocatingly hot and soupy. A storm was working itself up. They sat pushing scraps of squid round their plates, and their talk was quite dead.

'Oh,' said Geraldine. 'Oh . . . it's so . . .'

She was plagued by vanished words; what they used to affirm over meals on past holidays had sounded then in her ears with operatic courage and significance. The trouble was, she couldn't now remember what it was that had been said. She half rose from the table, sighing, staring at him.

'What is it?' he asked coldly.

She subsided. Her hands moved nervously, fingers raking her hair back, then arachnid, rolling bread pellets. He disliked intensely these fidgety hands, also the self-pitying twist of her mouth and the squawky shrillness that shredded her voice when she grew agitated. She glared at his shut face, and huffed and puffed, feeling his bulk across the table as if it were some piece of meaningless masonry she would have to drag along with her forever, uphill.

'It's this place,' she said wildly. 'Rome. It's so oppressive! All the hugeness and efficiency. Cruelty.'

'You mean ancient Rome,' he corrected her. 'There's nothing very efficient about it now. No hot water at our hotel for two days. Those Americans are going crazy.'

'You always,' said Geraldine, and stopped.

'I always what?'

'Nothing.'

'No, come on,' said Paul. 'What?'

'On and on,' moaned Geraldine. 'Relentless.'

'In what way precisely,' said Paul.

'Inexorable!'

'First Rome,' he said. 'Now me.'

'What I mean is,' she shrilled, and he wished he could

pick up that napkin and roll it into a ball and stuff it into her mouth. 'What I mean is, ancient Rome, it was all so bloody pragmatic. Baths and bridges and brothels and feasts and a special room to make yourself sick so you could go back and stuff more down your gullet. The vomitorium.'

'The vomitorium wasn't for vomiting in,' he said, scornful, pedantic. 'It was a particular sort of exit. From the Colosseum, actually, I think.'

'Shut up,' she shrilled. 'All I know is, there's more to life . . .'

'Oh yes, than the boring practical details,' he said nastily. 'Leave them to other people. Lesser mortals. Insurance and punctuality and all that. You're on the side of the Etruscans, aren't you, the shifty little singing dancing Etruscans with their sneaky little smiles.'

There was a silence, broken at last by a nervous bubbling giggle from Geraldine.

'You do hate me, don't you,' she smiled.

'Not at all, not at all,' he frowned – he was almost shouting now – 'But you're such a – such a dilettante, darling. Honestly.'

'How do you mean?' she asked, bridling, aware of the half-clothed affront waiting in the wings. He smiled.

'What I mean, Geraldine, what I mean is, all your talk of loving life, being happy just to be alive and so forth, as opposed to me, black and rigid and all that, well, it's just not on, is it. Life! You refuse to engage seriously with life at any level.'

They waited for the bill in silence, savouring the preceding exchange with a sort of scab-picking decadent relish; then walked slowly on to the Piazza Navona.

'I like the palm tree,' said Geraldine, as they walked around Bernini's Fontane dei Fumi. 'That must be the Nile. There's the Ganges, and see, on this corner is the Danube, and this last one's the Rio de la Plata. Look here, Paul, I don't want to settle down. Stay in.'

'That's just shallow talk,' said Paul. 'You can't know that.'

Lightning cracked the sky for an instant, a white flash, and then the rain came down in big warm splashy drops.

'Ah,' said Geraldine, 'I can't bear you,' and climbed into the floodlit fountain. The pale green water lapped round her legs, the rivergods lolled above in muscular abandon, and she stood in the drench, laughing, her streaming hair in long black rats-tails.

'For pity's sake,' said Paul in disgust. He turned on his heel and walked to the doorway of S. Agnese in Agone for shelter, and to disassociate himself from this display. A couple of Italian teenagers hooted and shouted before joining her in the water, and soon after that some American college girls jumped in and started singing 'I hear thunder'. This was what he couldn't stand about her, he muttered, as the rain drummed down so thickly that the fountain became a blur; this awful factitious edge. This hysteria.

The storm continued without any loss of energy, and a little while later the fountain dancers climbed out and shook themselves and embraced with laughter and yelling before running off for shelter. Geraldine started off in the direction of the hotel, and he had to run to catch her up.

'I thought you'd grown out of all that,' he shouted as they jogged on side by side.

'All what?' she said, not looking at him.

'That wild woman of the woods act,' he said grimly.

'You hate me,' she panted.

'I bought you those shoes,' he said, and his voice was peevish. 'They're ruined.'

'That does it,' she said. 'I must have been mad. For the rest of this holiday, I'm serious, I *won't*, unless you get some things.'

'What?'

'Look, Paul. You know exactly what I mean. You encouraged me to be careless. But I'm not risking it. It's not flirting any more. I can feel people want it, you do anyway, as a sort of revenge. You don't want me swanning around. So if you want to . . .'

He did, actually, want to, very much, annoyingly enough; he wanted her underneath him and crying. He felt furious. He stopped and yanked her head back, tugging on a handful of hair, pushing his mouth on hers so that their teeth clashed together. When she tried to wriggle off he stuck his thigh between her legs.

'All right,' she hissed when he let go at last. 'But I mean it.' She ran off in the rain towards the hotel, while he tracked down an all-night chemist.

Afterwards they lay exhausted, having battled their way to a weary state of truce, slogging it out like veterans.

'This is getting monotonous,' whispered Geraldine, stroking his arm. He teetered on the verge of sleep, then pushed himself to get up and go to the bathroom. Once there, he saw what had happened, and woke up.

'Bloody Catholic condoms,' he muttered. He washed and went back slowly to the bedroom. Crouching beside her on the bed, he put an ear down close to her belly.

'What are you doing?' she asked sleepily.

'Listening,' he said. 'I can hear a sort of ticking noise under the gurgles. But maybe it's just your watch.' He gave a guilty laugh. 'You'll never guess what just happened.'

'You wouldn't think of doing anything about it, would you,' he murmured, nuzzling her ear, turning his face into her hair.

They were lounging in the afternoon sun on the curving Spanish Steps, one among scores of couples, clasped in a baroque embrace.

'That would be my business,' she whispered, pulling his face down into her neck.

'Not really,' he said, smudging the words into her breast-bone. 'Not any more.'

'Listen, Paul,' she said, pulling away a little and kissing his eyelids. 'That's between me and my maker.'

Earlier that day they had visited the Vatican, and Geraldine had lain supine on a vacant stretch of marble in the Sistine Chapel in order to stare up for an unblinking minute at the creation of Adam, whose portrait was so astonishingly full of grace and power, half-rising to touch forefingers with God, so heart-stopping in its masculine beauty, that she had given an involuntary moan of pain when she saw, just beyond, the lumpish figure of Eve climbing from sleeping Adam's side as clumsily as if from a low slung sports car.

'It would be nothing but good for you,' he whispered, his arm over her shoulder and his lips brushing her earlobe, just like an Italian. 'You're not really rooted at the moment. You've said so yourself. Too light.' He punctuated these words with clever little kisses, beneath her eyebrow, by the corner of her eye, at the border of her upper lip. She gave a quivery laugh.

'It would be a sort of paperweight, you mean,' she suggested, butting her breasts against his ribs with a series of little sighs. He kissed her on the mouth, and they sat and rocked like this, locked, for a long time, as luxuriously tender as any couple there.

A little later, in Babington's Tea Rooms, they sat, hands linked across the tablecloth as though in farewell, and worked out that they were both almost ten years older than Keats had been when he died. At the table to their left were two palely glistening English couples of about their own age. These husbands and wives were giving each other long detailed descriptions of meals consumed, hoteliers' shortcomings, children's schools, own schools, and from there, amazing coincidences, greeted with faint screeches of delight.

'Johnny Pitlow? You know Johnny Pitlow? But that's incredible, he's godfather to my best friend's little girl, you know, the one who's at Lapwing House.'

'I simply could not, Paul,' whispered Geraldine in the silence which had thickened between them. 'I couldn't do it, you know.'

'It doesn't have to be like that,' he said testily.

'But don't you see?' she hissed. 'We've only got each other to take care of and we can't even manage that.'

'Rubbish,' he said.

'Look at Kate,' said Geraldine urgently. 'All that awful juggling and fretting she went through, about maternity leave and all the rest of it. Then Nick walked out, and you said, the last time we saw her, you weren't surprised, she'd grown so morose, what's the matter with her, it's healthy isn't it, she looks as old as the hills, she should pull herself together.'

'You'd manage it better,' said Paul, wincing as he chewed on cinnamon toast. 'I think I'm getting a mouth ulcer,' he added thoughtfully, probing the lining of his cheek with his tongue.

'Poor Kate,' sighed Geraldine. 'I must send her a postcard.'

Out in the heat, they smiled with relief to be among beautiful Romans again. The passeggiata had started in the via del Corso, and they strolled along in synch, thigh spliced to thigh, aware that they were considerably longer in the tooth than their Italian counterparts.

'You look so lovely,' said Paul, stopping in the middle of the street to frame her face with his hands. 'It's a pity you're so selfish.'

'Selfish?' said Geraldine, latching on to that word. 'I only want to stay as I am.'

'Exactly,' said Paul, and his mouth folded into a censorious line. He walked on alone.

'What's selfish about that?' said Geraldine, running after him.

'I don't know,' he snapped. 'Other women don't seem to make such a palaver about it. The most natural thing in the world.'

'What other women?' she said, incredulous, half laughing.

'Italian women.' He stopped in his tracks. 'For instance. They just get on with it. Look at them now. Che sera sera.'

'When did you get like this?' marvelled Geraldine.

'That's the trouble with you,' said Paul venomously. 'So keen on autonomy. So – so life-denying.'

'Now look here,' said Geraldine. 'You've gone wildly Lawrentian during this holiday and it's *ridiculous*.'

'It *is* part of life, though,' he snapped. 'You can't just say, no thank you.'

'I *am* on the side of life,' she protested. 'Far more than you are.'

'So you keep saying,' he sneered. 'Yours perhaps. Not anybody else's.'

Just then a crowd of babbling children surrounded them, shoving sheets of cardboard at them with knifing movements, jostling, chanting, feeling for their pockets, bright-eyed as birds.

'Ah, get away!' cried Paul, flailing helplessly. 'Vamoose! Leave us alone!'

The children surged against them, attacking and plucking and screeching, warm greedy fingers inside their pockets, dozens of fleshy little starfish hands reaching out. Then, pronto, the infant pack swarmed off, its retreat as instant as its attack, down an adjacent alleyway.

'They took my sunglasses,' said Geraldine. She was unreasonably upset, to the point of tears. A dull red line appeared round the edge of her mouth and she started to sniff. 'Did you see, some of them didn't have shoes on.'

'Like soldier ants,' said Paul, checking his pockets. 'Couldn't do a thing about it, either. They didn't get my wallet. Come on. I'll buy us a drink.'

'Wait a moment,' she said, dragging a knuckle across each of her eyes in turn. 'Do I look all right?'

'Yes,' he said, checking his watch.

In a dark bar lined with mirrors in a turning off the Piazza del Popolo, they stood at the counter and sipped cold beer alongside a handful of silent Italian men.

Paul said, 'I know I'm right.'

Geraldine caught sight of her reflection behind a row of brandy bottles. She looked swollen and green.

'You're such a consumer,' he continued. 'Such a wasteful throw-away artist. Fresh starts and blank screens – they're nonsensical concepts. The last five years, you can't just wipe them, you know.'

'Look, Paul,' she said carefully, after a long pause. 'It's all burnt out. You can see that. It's obvious. You're throwing *putti* onto the embers to try and revive them.'

'Don't,' he said, pulling her round against him, cradling her, his hands clasped over her stomach. 'Don't talk.'

'This holiday has been the decline and fall,' she said, styptic, relieved to be saying it but already full of dismay as the end of their five years together hurtled towards them like a juggernaut.

'No,' he sighed.

'Ciabatta and silly games,' she said. Her throat felt tight.

'We've still got passion,' he insisted, fingering a heather-coloured bruise on her forearm.

'That's not passion,' she said coldly. 'That's just nastiness.'

'What if you *are*, though?' Paul persisted. He smiled. 'Think of last night,' he said in a lower voice. 'How can you say it's over. In fact —' he patted her stomach — 'it might just be starting. Our *vita nuova*.'

She pulled away from him and hid her face behind her hand and the beer glass, letting her hair fall forward in two protective wings. Her knees and ankles were throbbing weakly, tingling, in fact so were all her joints. A gust of heat rushed through her, over her skin and away. Thoughts scrabbled like panicking rabbits, rising in a cyclonic swarm, until she thought the top of her head would take off like a helicopter.

'Don't cry,' he said as the tears fell in her beer.

'I'm not,' she said. 'I imagine it's just the hormones. You know. Women.'

She put on his sunglasses.

'Il gabinetto?' she asked the barman, and walked unsteadily off towards the back of the bar.

On her return she was radiant. Her face was alive and flickering with little smiles, like a fountain. He thought, so that's that, and felt surprisingly detached about it for a moment. She handed his sunglasses back to him, and said, 'It's all right.'

'What's all right?' he asked.

She leaned forward and dropped a syllable into his ear.

'Ah,' he said, and looked down at his hands lying in front of him on the marble counter like rubble.

'Blood,' she said again, softly, exultantly, woundingly.

'Thank God,' she said, more loudly.

And she drained her glass before unleashing a glad unexpected guffaw which had all the men turning to stare.

To Her Unready Boyfriend

If time sprawled ahead of us in a limitless and improving vista, your reluctance to consider the future wouldn't matter a scrap. We could lie in bed all afternoon browsing through the atlas to map out our itinerary for the next couple of decades or so.

We would discuss the politics of regions shaded in fondant pink and yellow and pistachio, skip to and fro across the equator, splash through the Tasman and Caspian seas, try our tongues round Kandy, Changchun, La Paz, Minsk. I would see you, racoon-furred and seal-booted in the winds of Nova Scotia, paddling our canoe from Natashquan to Sept-Iles, where we would disembark and joyfully climb up to and across the Otish mountains. At the ancient stadium of Olympia, to the susurrous applause of silver leaves we would take our marks on the line where Greek athletes crouched two thousand years ago, then race each other across a hundred yards, repeatedly. Our love would keep us young, along with the avoidance of strong sunlight. We would keep our options open.

Your fondness for dubiety, the way you prize the fluid and infinite possibilities which unfurl before an unattached person, these I sympathise with utterly. You cry freedom and I hear you. Harbouring the sense that there's an epiphany just around the corner, you wait, breath bated, creatively passive, for the chance phrase or glance that will crystallise it all, show you what your life is about and where it is leading. You lack the desire to commit yourself. You tell me you are not ready for the responsibility of a child, and why *should* you be, my darling? You're only thirty-six.

We have loved each other for over ten years now, but the night we met for the first time is like a photograph I carry in my wallet, clear as clear. I sat there in the White Hart, one of a group round a crowded table in a cloud of smoke. We hadn't spoken, you hadn't even seen me, but I was smitten by your heroic frowning profile, the stream of talk (of which I remember not one word, but it was in some way didactic, exhortatory), the glowing cigarette and your excitable hands transferring it to and from your mouth between castles of rhetoric. I wasn't particularly interested in what you were saying, but I wanted to be near you in the way I want to be near a successful log fire. I felt this so strongly I was afraid it would show, so I kept my eyes down, strictly away from your glamorous felty greatcoat, I adjusted my movement as my body swivelled towards you, heliotropic, like a plant towards the sun.

You got up and went to the bar for a round of drinks. Everyone else carried on talking, took no notice. To me it was as if a tooth had been pulled. By your place at the table was an overflowing ashtray and the box of matches you'd been using. I don't smoke. I leaned over, oh so casually, and hooked up that box of matches. I hid it in my hand, a gentle fist around it. Later I examined my trophy in private, sniffed the gunpowder smell and pushed out the miniature drawer with my thumb. Then I struck one of the precious batons and let the flame burn down until it reached my fingers. Ouch.

Since then you have rowed your boat less than merrily and with increasing lassitude down the stream of time. As long as outside events, not personal choice, make things happen, you can accept change with a good enough grace. Staying passive, you reason, is as though you haven't made a choice and your central purity is untouched.

Another woman might start to dream of accidents.

But imagine, just imagine if time were to dawdle and lose itself, as I wish it would; if the laws of mutability were to go a little bit haywire in our case; then perhaps one tender blue-grey evening in the third millennium we might find ourselves sitting by the fireside in our late fifties, our eyes would meet, and we would know we were ready at last. Our mortgage would be negligible by then, your thesis would at last be lapped in gold-tooled leather, and the worst of our wanderlust would have been slaked. Hand in hand we would climb the stairs that night to start a baby. And not before.

For, my dear love, you deserve acres of time, long red carpets of it; nor would I wish any less for you.

But, my sweet eternal boy, in recent months I've been dogged by a rhythmic noise, soft but distinct, tick-*tock*, tick-*tock* like the crocodile in Peter Pan. I've reached a certain age, you must remember, and this wretched clock noise, which increases in volume as the day progresses and is at its most distracting, menacing even, just when I'm undressing for bed, warns me, *Get*-a-move-on *hurry*-up, *Get*-a-move-on *not*-much-time.

It's all right for you, you're like the popes in the Renaissance, you can go on fathering children till you're eighty-three. But if you want us to stay together, and I say this as one who as you know has never used emotional blackmail in all our years together, if you want us to stay together, I say, then you must start telling the time by my clock. I can't ignore it.

You may prefer, of course, to wait another ten or fifteen years, as in my fireside fantasy. You may prefer to wait for the arrival of a paunch and root canal work before at last sowing the long-hoarded seed. If so, I won't be there. I'll be somewhere else, giggling with my adolescent daughter.

You say, our love for each other is enough, my talk is dangerously hubristic, let's take each day as it comes.

The trouble with that is, whether we like it or not we can't stay the same. It's not allowed. There's no procedure for freezing our present happiness, no insurance scheme against future grief or coldness and misunderstanding.

We can't mark time ad infinitum. Meanwhile, to our dismay, this baby denial will start to appear increasingly as a match that's not been struck. The irony is that you're the one who goes on about death all the time. What's it all about? Is there just nothing at the end? Can't you see this is your one sure way of cocking a snook at all that? All right, eventually, I admit, you will be forced by the laws of physics to unlink your molecules, to crumble into motes and spores and polycarbons, and your strongest comfort is that you might with luck become part of the atmosphere. But if your child is at the bedside when you draw your last breath, a child with your hunted look, your heroic profile, new-minted, then the baton will have been passed on.

A child would alter the balance between us, a child would turn the direction of our eyes away from the withering and fattening of our over-familiar selves towards the pleasure of a fresh new presence growing.

Forgive me for pointing this out, my love, but there is something lugubrious and loose-endish about you, a central glumness that my charming presence hasn't managed to melt entirely. You can warm your hands at the fire of other people's high jinks, but in your own kitchen there is a sadness, as of an uncooked cake. You're unfinished, some sort of refugee, abandoned early on and – despite my best efforts – not yet rescued.

You're wonderfully perspicacious, irresistibly beautiful, and you say I've pulled you out of the miseries that used to plague you. I can however only do so much for you; some mothering of course; but I am *not* your mother.

I would *like* to be a mother, not yours but still a mother. For this, though, I want your consent.

See me through nine months. I want to be a nice ripe pear on the sun-warmed bricks of a walled garden.

He'd look just like you. He could curl up in the crook of your arm at night. He'd stare at you in amazement at first, with a dazzled china-blue frown. When he meowed you could pass him over to me, I'd calm him down. I'd do it all, you wouldn't even notice.

Or perhaps we might have a girl, a baby girl, and after hacking through all those tiresome thorn-hedged years you would at last have found your own princess. You are capable of such generous secret tenderness that I think you couldn't fail to be a father both adoring and adored.

Let me see if I can draw a parallel to make you understand. I find it very peculiar that someone so clever can be so obtuse.

Do you remember the last time we saw Susan, just after she'd moved to the little house in Ansty with its south-facing garden, do you remember how she said she was home at last, this was the place she wanted to live in for the rest of her life? And as an acknowledgement of this fact she had planted a mulberry tree, knowing full well that she wouldn't be seeing any fruit on its branches for a good twenty-five years. I liked that. It was an act of faith. I'm fed up with us being so abjectly tentative.

If you carry on trying to rope us together with these massive cables of inertia, we'll fly apart at last. Time won't stand still just because we've been lucky in love, more's the pity.

Now, then: let's move on *now*. Let's abandon our fastidious comforts, wave goodbye to our turtledove snuggery while there's still time. Come on. You can't keep yourself to yourself forever. Be brave! Let's jump before we're pushed.

Come to bed. Unprotected. Now.

Heavy Weather

'You should never have married me.'

'I haven't regretted it for an instant.'

'Not *you*, you fool! *Me!* You shouldn't have got me to marry you if you loved me. Why *did* you, when you knew it would let me in for all *this*. It's not *fair!*'

'I didn't know. I know it's not. But what can I do about it?'

'I'm being mashed up and eaten alive.'

'I know. I'm sorry.'

'It's not your fault. But what can I do?'

'I don't know.'

So the conversation had gone last night in bed, followed by platonic embraces. They were on ice at the moment, so far as anything further was concerned. The smoothness and sweet smell of their children, the baby's densely packed pearly limbs, the freshness of the little girl's breath when she yawned, these combined to accentuate the grossness of their own bodies. They eyed each other's mooching adult bulk with mutual lack of enthusiasm, and fell asleep.

At four in the morning, the baby was punching and shouting in his Moses basket. Frances forced herself awake, lying for the first moments like a flattened boxer in the ring trying to rise while the count was made. She got up and fell over, got up again and scooped Matthew from the basket. He was huffing with eagerness, and scrabbled crazily at her breasts like a drowning man until she lay down with him. A few seconds more and he had abandoned himself to rhythmic gulping. She stroked his soft head and drifted off. When she woke again, it was six o'clock and he was sleeping between her and Jonathan.

For once, nobody was touching her. Like Holland she lay, aware of a heavy ocean at her seawall, its weight poised to race across the low country.

The baby was now three months old, and she had not had more than half an hour alone in the twenty-four since his birth in February. He was big and hungry and needed her there constantly on tap. Also, his two-year-old sister Lorna was, unwillingly, murderously jealous, which made everything much more difficult. This time round was harder, too, because when one was asleep the other would be awake and vice versa. If only she could get them to nap at the same time, Frances started fretting, then she might be able to sleep for some minutes during the day and that would get her through. But they wouldn't, and she couldn't. She had taken to muttering I can't bear it, I can't bear it, without realising she was doing so until she heard Lorna chanting I can't bear it! I can't bear it! as she skipped along beside the pram, and this made her blush with shame at her own weediness.

Now they were all four in Dorset for a week's holiday. The thought of having to organise all the food, sheets, milk, baths and nappies made her want to vomit.

In her next chunk of sleep came that recent nightmare,

where men with knives and scissors advanced on the felled trunk which was her body.

'How would you like it?' she said to Jonathan. 'It's like a doctor saying, now we're just going to snip your scrotum in half, but don't worry, it mends very well down there, we'll stitch you up and you'll be fine.'

It was gone seven by now, and Lorna was leaning on the bars of her cot like Farmer Giles, sucking her thumb in a ruminative pipe-smoking way. The room stank like a lion house. She beamed as her mother came in, and lifted her arms up. Frances hoisted her into the bath, stripped her down and detached the dense brown nappy from between her knees. Lorna carolled, 'I can sing a *rain*bow,' raising her faint fine eyebrows at the high note, graceful and perfect, as her mother sluiced her down with jugs of water.

'Why does everything take so *long*?' moaned Jonathan. 'It only takes *me* five minutes to get ready.'

Frances did not bother to answer. She was sagging with the effortful boredom of assembling the paraphernalia needed for a morning out in the car. Juice. Beaker with screw-on lid. Flannels. Towels. Changes of clothes in case of car sickness. Nappies. Rattle. Clean muslins to catch Matthew's curdy regurgitations. There was more. What was it?

'Oh, come on, Jonathan, think,' she said. 'I'm fed up with having to plan it all.'

'What do you think I've been doing for the last hour?' he shouted. 'Who was it that changed Matthew's nappy just now? Eh?'

'Congratulations,' she said. 'Don't shout or I'll cry.'

Lorna burst into tears.

'Why is everywhere always such a *mess*,' said Jonathan, picking up plastic spiders, dinosaurs, telephones, beads and bears, his grim scowl over the mound of primary colours like a traitor's head on a platter of fruit.

'I *want* dat spider, Daddy!' screamed Lorna. 'Give it to me!'

During the ensuing struggle, Frances pondered her tiredness. Her muscles twitched as though they had been tenderised with a steak bat. There was a bar of iron in the back of her neck, and she felt unpleasantly weightless in the cranium, a gin–drinking side effect without the previous fun. The year following the arrival of the first baby had gone in pure astonishment at the loss of freedom, but second time round it was spinning away in exhaustion. Matthew woke at one a.m. and four a.m., and Lorna at six-thirty a.m. During the days, fatigue came at her in concentrated doses, like a series of time bombs.

'Are we ready at last?' said Jonathan, breathing heavily. 'Are we ready to go?'

'Um, nearly,' said Frances. 'Matthew's making noises. I think I'd better feed him, or else I'll end up doing it in a lay-by.'

'Right,' said Jonathan. 'Right.'

Frances picked up the baby. 'What a nice fat parcel you are,' she murmured in his delighted ear. 'Come on, my love.'

'Matthew's not your love,' said Lorna. '*I'm* your love. You say, C'mon love, to *me*.'

'You're *both* my loves,' said Frances.

The baby was shaking with eagerness, and pouted his mouth as she pulled her shirt up. The little girl sat down beside her, pulled up her own teeshirt and applied a teddy bear to her nipple. She grinned at her mother.

Frances looked down at Matthew's head, which was shaped like a brick or a small wholemeal loaf, and remembered again how it had come down through the middle of her. She was trying very hard to lose her awareness of this fact, but it would keep re-presenting itself.

'D'you know,' said Lorna, free hand held palm upwards, hyphen eyebrows lifting, 'd'you know, I was sucking my thumb when I was coming downstairs, mum, mum, then my foot slipped and my thumb came out of my mouth.'

'Well, that's very interesting, Lorna,' said Frances.

Two minutes later, Lorna caught the baby's head a ringing smack and ran off. Jonathan watched as Frances lunged clumsily after her, the baby jouncing at her breast, her stained and crumpled shirt undone, her hair a bird's nest, her face craggy with fatigue, and found himself dubbing the tableau, Portrait of rural squalor in the manner of William Hogarth. He bent to put on his shoes, stuck his right foot in first then pulled it out as though bitten.

'What's *that*,' he said in tones of profound disgust. He held his shoe in front of Frances' face.

'It looks like baby sick,' she said. 'Don't look at me. It's not my fault.'

'It's all so bloody *basic*,' said Jonathan, breathing hard, hopping off towards the kitchen.

'If you think that's basic, try being me,' muttered Frances. 'You don't know what basic *means*.'

'Daddy put his foot in Matthew's sick,' commented Lorna, laughing heartily.

At Cerne Abbas they stood and stared across at the chalky white outline of the Iron-Age giant cut into the green hill.

'It's enormous, isn't it,' said Frances.

'Do you remember when we went to stand on it?' said Jonathan. 'On that holiday in Child Okeford five years ago?'

'Of course,' said Frances. She saw the ghosts of their frisky former selves running around the giant's limbs and up onto his phallus. Nostalgia filled her eyes and stabbed her smartly in the guts.

'The woman riding high above with bright hair flapping free,' quoted Jonathan. 'Will you be able to grow *your* hair again?'

'Yes, yes. Don't look at me like that, though. I know I look like hell.'

A month before this boy was born, Frances had had her hair cut short. Her head had looked like a pea on a drum. It still did. With each pregnancy, her looks had hurtled five years on. She had started using sentences beginning, 'When I was young.' Ah, youth! Idleness! Sleep! How pleasant it had been to play the centre of her own stage. And how disorientating was this overnight demotion from Brünnhilde to spear-carrier.

'What's that,' said Lorna. 'That *thing*.'

'It's a giant,' said Frances.

'Like in Jacknabeanstork?'

'Yes.'

'But what's that *thing*. That thing on the giant.'

'It's the giant's thing.'

'Is it his stick thing?'

'Yes.'

'My baby budder's got a stick thing.'

'Yes.'

'But I haven't got a stick thing.'

'No.'

'Daddy's got a stick thing.'

'Yes.'

'But *Mummy* hasn't got a stick thing. We're the same, Mummy.'

She beamed and put her warm paw in Frances's.

'You can't see round without an appointment,' said the keeper of Hardy's cottage. 'You should have telephoned.'

'We did,' bluffed Jonathan. 'There was no answer.'

'When was that?'

'Twenty to ten this morning.'

'Hmph. I was over sorting out some trouble at Clouds Hill. T. E. Lawrence's place. All right, you can go through. But keep them under control, won't you.'

They moved slowly through the low-ceilinged rooms, whispering to impress the importance of good behaviour on Lorna.

'This is the room where he was born,' said Jonathan, at the head of the stairs.

'Do you remember from when we visited last time?' said Frances slowly. 'It's coming back to me. He was his mother's first child, she nearly died in labour, then the doctor thought the baby was dead and threw him into a basket while he looked after the mother. But the midwife noticed he was breathing.'

'Then he carried on till he was eighty-seven,' said Jonathan.

They clattered across the old chestnut floorboards, on into another little bedroom with deep thick-walled windowseats.

'Which one's your favourite now?' asked Frances.

'Oh, still *Jude the Obscure*, I think,' said Jonathan. 'The tragedy of unfulfilled aims. Same for anyone first generation at university.'

'Poor Jude, laid low by pregnancy,' said Frances. 'Another victim of biology as destiny.'

'Don't *talk*, you two,' said Lorna.

'At least Sue and Jude aimed for friendship as well as all the other stuff,' said Jonathan.

'Unfortunately, all the other stuff made friendship impossible, didn't it,' said Frances.

'Don't *talk!*' shouted Lorna.

'Don't shout!' said Jonathan. Lorna fixed him with a calculating blue eye and produced an ear-splitting scream. The baby jerked in his arms and started to howl.

'Hardy didn't have children, did he,' said Jonathan above the din. 'I'll take them outside, I've seen enough. You stay up here a bit longer if you want to.'

Frances stood alone in the luxury of the empty room and shuddered. She moved around the furniture and thought fond savage thoughts of silence in the cloisters of a convent, a blessed place where all was monochrome and non-viscous. Sidling up unprepared to a mirror on the wall she gave a yelp at her reflection. The skin was the colour and texture of pumice stone, the grim jaw set like a lion's muzzle. And the eyes, the eyes far back in the skull were those of a herring three days dead.

Jonathan was sitting with the baby on his lap by a row of lupins and marigolds, reading to Lorna from a newly acquired guide book.

'When Thomas was a little boy he knelt down one day in a field and began eating grass to see what it was like to be a sheep.'

'What did the sheep say?' asked Lorna.

'The sheep said, er, so now you know.'

'And what else?'

'Nothing else.'

'Why?'

'What do you mean, why?'

'*Why?*'

'Look,' he said when he saw Frances. 'I've bought a copy of *Jude the Obscure* too, so we can read to each other when we've got a spare moment.'

'Spare moment!' said Frances. 'But how lovely you look with the children at your knees, the roses round the cottage door. How I would like to be the one coming back from work to find you all bathed and brushed, and a hot meal in the oven and me unwinding with a glass of beer in a hard-earned crusty glow of righteousness.'

'*I* don't get that,' Jonathan reminded her.

'That's because I can't do it properly yet,' said Frances. 'But, still, I wish it could be the other way round. Or at least, half and half. And I was thinking, what a cheesy business Eng. Lit. is, all those old men peddling us lies about life and love. They never get as far as this bit, do they.'

'Thomas 1840, Mary 1842, Henry 1851, Kate 1856,' read Jonathan. 'Perhaps we could have two more.'

'I'd kill myself,' said Frances.

'What's the matter with you?' said Jonathan to Matthew, who was grizzling and struggling in his arms.

'I think I'll have to feed him again,' said Frances.

'What, already?'

'It's nearly two hours.'

'Hey, you can't do that here,' said the custodian, appearing at their bench like a bad fairy. 'We have visitors from all over the world here. Particularly from Japan. The Japanese are a very modest people. And they don't come all this way to see THAT sort of thing.'

'It's a perfectly natural function,' said Jonathan.

'So's going to the lavatory!' said the custodian.

'Is it all right if I take him over behind those hollyhocks?' asked Frances. 'Nobody could possibly see me there. It's just, in this heat he won't feed if I try to do it in the car.'

The custodian snorted and stumped back to his lair.

Above the thatched roof the huge and gentle trees rustled hundreds of years' worth of leaves in the pre-storm stir. Frances shrugged, heaved Matthew up so that his socks dangled on her hastily covered breast, and retreated to the hollyhock screen. As he fed, she observed the green-tinged light in the garden, the crouching cat over in a bed of limp snapdragons, and registered the way things look before an onslaught, defenceless and excited, tense and passive. She thought of Bathsheba Everdene at bay, crouching in the bed of ferns.

When would she be able to read a book again? In life before the children, she had read books on the bus, in the bathroom, in bed, while eating, through television, under radio noise, in cafés. Now, if she picked one up, Lorna shouted, 'Stop reading, Mummy,' and pulled her by the nose until she was looking into her small cross face.

Jonathan meandered among the flowerbeds flicking through *Jude the Obscure*, Lorna snapping and shouting at his heels. He was ignoring her, and Frances could see he had already bought a tantrum since Lorna was now entered into one of the stretches of the day when her self-control flagged and fled. She sighed like Cassandra but didn't have the energy to nag as he came towards her.

'Listen to this,' Jonathan said, reading from *Jude the Obscure*. '"Time and circumstance, which enlarge the views of most men, narrow the views of women almost invariably."'

'Is it any bloody wonder,' said Frances.

'I want you to *play* with me, Daddy,' whined Lorna.

'Bit of a sexist remark, though, eh?' said Jonathan.

'Bit of a sexist process, you twit,' said Frances.

Lorna gave Matthew a tug which almost had him on the ground. Torn from his milky trance, he quavered, horror-struck, for a moment, then, as Frances braced herself, squared his mouth and started to bellow.

Jonathan seized Lorna, who became as rigid as a steel girder, and swung her high up above his head. The air was split with screams.

'Give her to me,' mouthed Frances across the awe-inspiring noise.

'She's a noise terrorist,' shouted Jonathan.

'Oh, please let me have her,' said Frances.

'You shouldn't give in to her,' said po-faced Jonathan, handing over the flailing parcel of limbs.

'Lorna, sweetheart, look at me,' said Frances.

'Naaoow!' screamed Lorna.

'Shshush,' said Frances. 'Tell me what's the matter.'

Lorna poured out a flood of incomprehensible complaint, raving like a chimpanzee. At one point, Frances deciphered, 'You always feed MATTHEW.'

'You should *love* your baby brother,' interposed Jonathan.

'You can't tell her she *ought* to love anybody,' snapped Frances. 'You can tell her she must behave properly, but you can't tell her what to feel. Look, Lorna,' she continued, exercising her favourite distraction technique. 'The old man is coming back. He's cross with us. Let's run away.'

Lorna turned her streaming eyes and nose in the direction of the custodian, who was indeed hotfooting it across the lawn towards them, and tugged her mother's hand. The two of them lurched off, Frances buttoning herself up as she went.

They found themselves corralled into a cement area at the back of the Smuggler's Arms, a separate space where young family pariahs like themselves could bicker over fish fingers. Waiting at the bar, Jonathan observed the comfortable tables inside, with their noisy laughing groups of the energetic elderly tucking into plates of gammon and plaice and profiteroles.

'Just look at them,' said the crumpled man beside him, who was paying for a trayload of Fanta and baked beans. 'Skipped the war. Nil unemployment, home in time for tea.' He took a great gulp of lager. 'Left us to scream in our prams, screwed us up good and proper. When our kids come along, what happens? You don't see the grandparents for dust, that's what happens. They're all off out enjoying themselves, kicking the prams out the way with their Hush Puppies, spending the money like there's no tomorrow.'

Jonathan grunted uneasily. He still could not get used to the way he found himself involved in intricate conversations with complete strangers, incisive, frank, frequently desperate, whenever he was out with Frances and the children. It used to be only women who talked like that, but now, among parents of young children, it seemed to have spread across the board.

Frances was trying to allow the baby to finish his recent interrupted feed as discreetly as she could, while watching Lorna move inquisitively among the various family groups. She saw her go up to a haggard woman changing a nappy beside a trough of geraniums.

'Your baby's got a stick thing like my baby budder.' Lorna's piercing voice soared above the babble. 'I haven't got a stick thing cos I'm a little gel. My mummy's got fur on her potim.'

Frances abandoned their table and made her way over to the geranium trough.

'Sorry if she's been getting in your way,' she said to the woman.

'Chatty, isn't she,' commented the woman unenthusiastically. 'How many have you got?'

'Two. I'm shattered.'

'The third's the killer.'

'That's my baby budder,' said Lorna, pointing at Matthew.

'He's a big boy,' said the woman. 'What did he weigh when he came out?'

'Ten pounds.'

'Just like a turkey,' she said, disgustingly, and added, 'Mine were whoppers too. They all had to be cut out of me, one way or the other.'

By the time they returned to the cottage, the air was weighing on them like blankets. Each little room was an envelope of pressure. Jonathan watched Frances collapse into a chair with children all over her. Before babies, they had been well matched. Then, with the arrival of their first child, it had been a case of Woman Overboard. He'd watched, ineffectual but sympathetic, trying to keep her cheerful as she clung on to the edge of the raft, holding out weevil-free biscuits for her to nibble, and all the time she gazed at him with appalled eyes. Just as they had grown used to this state, difficult but tenable, and were even managing to start hauling her on board again an inch at a time, just as she had her elbows up on the raft and they were congratulating themselves with a kiss, well, along came the second baby in a great slap of a wave that drove her off the raft altogether. Now she was out there in the sea while he bobbed up and down, forlorn but more or less dry, and watched her face between its two satellites dwindling to the size of a fist, then to a plum, and at last to a mere speck of plankton. He dismissed it from his mind.

'I'll see if I can get the shopping before the rain starts,' he said, dashing out to the car again, knee-deep in cow parsley.

'You really should keep an eye on how much bread we've got left,' he called earnestly as he unlocked the car. 'It won't be *my* fault if I'm struck by lightning.'

There was the crumpling noise of thunder, and silver cracked the sky. Frances stood in the doorway holding the baby, while Lorna clawed and clamoured at her to be held in her free arm.

'Oh, Lorna,' said Frances, hit by a wave of bone-aching fatigue. 'You're too heavy, my sweet.' She closed the cottage door as Lorna started to scream, and stood looking down at her with something like fear. She saw a miniature fee-fi-fo-fum creature working its way through a pack of adults, chewing them up and spitting their bones out.

'Come into the back room, Lorna, and I'll read you a book while I feed Matthew.'

'I don't want to.'

'Why don't you want to?'

'I just don't want to.'

'Can't you tell me why?'

'Do you know, I just don't WANT to!'

'All right, *dear*. I'll feed him on my own then.'

'NO!' screamed Lorna. 'PUT HIM IN DA BIN! HE'S RUBBISH!'

'Don't scream, you little beast,' said Frances hopelessly, while the baby squared his mouth and joined in the noise.

Lorna turned the volume up and waited for her to crack. Frances walked off to the kitchen with the baby and quickly closed the door. Lorna gave a howl of rage from the other side and started to smash at it with fists and toys. Children were petal-skinned ogres, Frances realised, callous and whimsical, holding autocratic sway over lower, larger vassals like herself.

There followed a punishing stint of ricochet work, where Frances let the baby cry while she comforted Lorna; let

Lorna shriek while she soothed the baby; put Lorna down for her nap and was called back three times before she gave up and let her follow her destructively around; bathed the baby after he had sprayed himself, Lorna and the bathroom with urine during the nappy changing process; sat on the closed lavatory seat and fed the baby while Lorna chattered in the bath which she had demanded in the wake of the baby's bath.

She stared at Lorna's slim silver body, exquisite in the water, graceful as a Renaissance statuette.

'Shall we see if you'd like a little nap after your bath?' she suggested hopelessly, for only if Lorna rested would she be able to rest, and then only if Matthew was asleep or at least not ready for a feed.

'No,' said Lorna, off-hand but firm.

'Oh thank God,' said Frances as she heard the car door slam outside. Jonathan was back. It was like the arrival of the cavalry. She wrapped Lorna in a towel and they scrambled downstairs. Jonathan stood puffing on the doormat. Outside was a mid-afternoon twilight, the rain as thick as turf and drenching so that it seemed to leave no room for air between its stalks.

'You're wet, Daddy,' said Lorna, fascinated.

'There were lumps of ice coming down like tennis balls,' he marvelled.

'Here, have this towel,' said Frances, and Lorna span off naked as a sprite from its folds to dance among the chairs and tables while thunder crashed in the sky with the cumbersomeness of heavy furniture falling down uncarpeted stairs.

'*S'il vous plaît,*' said Frances to Jonathan, '*Dansez, jouez avec le petit diable, cette fille. Il faut que je* get Matthew down for a nap, she just wouldn't let me. *Je suis tellement* shattered.'

'Mummymummymummy,' Lorna chanted as she caught some inkling of this, but Jonathan threw the towel over her and they started to play ghosts.

'My little fat boy,' she whispered at last, squeezing his strong thighs. '*Hey*, fatty boomboom, *sweet* sugar dumpling. It's not fair, is it? I'm never alone with you. You're getting the rough end of the stick just now, aren't you.'

She punctuated this speech with growling kisses, and his hands and feet waved like warm pink roses. She sat him up and stroked the fine duck tail of hair on his baby bull neck. Whenever she tried to fix his essence, he wriggled off into mixed metaphor. And so she clapped his cloud cheeks and revelled in his nest of smiles; she blew raspberries into the crease of his neck and onto his astounded hardening stomach, forcing lion-deep chuckles from him.

She was dismayed at how she had to treat him like some sort of fancy man to spare her daughter's feelings, affecting nonchalance when Lorna was around. She would fall on him for a quick mad embrace if the little girl left the room for a moment, only to spring apart guiltily at the sound of the returning Start-rites.

The serrated teeth of remorse bit into her. In late pregnancy she had been so sandbagged that she had had barely enough energy to crawl through the day, let alone reciprocate Lorna's incandescent two-year-old passion.

'She thought I'd come back to her as before once the baby arrived,' she said aloud. 'But I haven't.'

The baby was making the wrangling noise which led to unconsciousness. Then he fell asleep like a door closing. She carried him carefully to his basket, a limp solid parcel against her bosom, the lashes long and wet on his cheeks, lower lip out in a soft semicircle. She put him down and he lay, limbs thrown wide, spatchcocked.

After the holiday, Jonathan would be back at the office with his broad quiet desk and filter coffee while she, she would have to submit to a fate worse than death, drudging round the flat to Lorna's screams and the baby's regurgitations and her own sore eyes and body aching to the throb of next door's Heavy Metal.

The trouble with prolonged sleep deprivation was, that it produced the same coarsening side effects as alcoholism. She was rotten with self-pity, swarming with irritability and despair.

When she heard Jonathan's step on the stairs, she realised that he must have coaxed Lorna to sleep at last. She looked forward to his face, but when he came into the room and she opened her mouth to speak, all that came out were toads and vipers.

'I'm smashed up,' she said. 'I'm never alone. The baby guzzles me and Lorna eats me up. I can't ever go out because I've always got to be there for the children, but you flit in and out like a humming bird. You need me to be always there, to peck at and pull at and answer the door. I even have to feed the cat.'

'I take them out for a walk on Sunday afternoons,' he protested.

'But it's like a favour, and it's only a couple of hours,

and I can't use the time to read, I always have to change the sheets or make a meatloaf.'

'For pity's sake. I'm tired too.'

'Sorry,' she muttered. 'Sorry. Sorry. But I don't feel like me any more. I've turned into some sort of oven.'

They lay on the bed and held each other.

'Did you know what Hardy called *Jude the Obscure* to begin with?' he whispered in her ear. '*The Simpletons*. And the Bishop of Wakefield burnt it on a bonfire when it was published.'

'You've been reading!' said Frances accusingly. '*When* did you read!'

'I just pulled in by the side of the road for five minutes. Only for five minutes. It's such a good book. I'd completely forgotten that Jude had three children.'

'*Three?*' said Frances. 'Are you sure?'

'Don't you remember Jude's little boy who comes back from Australia?' said Jonathan. 'Don't you remember little Father Time?'

'Yes,' said Frances. 'Something very nasty happens to him, doesn't it?'

She took the book and flicked through until she reached the page where little Time and his siblings are discovered by their mother hanging from a hook inside a cupboard door, the note at their feet reading, 'Done because we are too menny.'

'What a wicked old man Hardy was!' she said, incredulous. 'How *dare* he!' She started to cry.

'You're too close to them,' murmured Jonathan. 'You should cut off from them a bit.'

'How *can* I?' sniffed Frances. '*Somebody's* got to be devoted to them. And it's not going to be you because you know I'll do it for you.'

'They're yours, though, aren't they, because of that,' said Jonathan. 'They'll love you best.'

'They're *not* mine. They belong to themselves. But I'm not allowed to belong to *my* self any more.'

'It's not easy for me either.'

'I know it isn't, sweetheart. But at least you're still allowed to be your own man.'

They fell on each other's necks and mingled maudlin tears.

'It's so awful,' sniffed Frances. 'We may never have another.'

They fell asleep.

When they woke, the landscape was quite different. Not only had the rain stopped, but it had rinsed the air free of oppression. Drops of water hung like lively glass on every leaf and blade. On their way down to the beach, the path was hedged with wet hawthorn, the fiercely spiked branches glittering with green-white flowers.

The late sun was surprisingly strong. It turned the distant moving strokes of the waves to gold bars, and dried salt patterns onto the semi-precious stones which littered the shore. As Frances unbuckled Lorna's sandals, she pointed out to her translucent pieces of chrysoprase and rose quartz in amongst the more ordinary egg-shaped pebbles. Then she kicked off her own shoes and walked wincingly to the water's edge. The sea was casting lacy white shawls onto the stones, and drawing them back with a sigh.

She looked behind her and saw Lorna building a pile

of pebbles while Jonathan made the baby more comfortable in his pushchair. A little way ahead was a dinghy, and she could see the flickering gold veins on its white shell thrown up by the sun through moving seawater, and the man standing in it stripped to the waist. She walked towards it, then past it, and as she walked on, she looked out to sea and was aware of her eyeballs making internal adjustments to the new distance which was being demanded of them, as though they had forgotten how to focus on a long view. She felt an excited bubble of pleasure expanding her ribcage, so that she had to take little sighs of breath, warm and fresh and salted, and prevent herself from laughing aloud.

After some while she reached the far end of the beach. Slowly she wheeled, like a hero on the cusp of anagnorisis, narrowing her eyes to make out the little group round the pushchair. Of course it was satisfying and delightful to see Jonathan − she supposed it *was* Jonathan? − lying with the fat mild baby on his stomach while their slender elf of a daughter skipped around him. It was part of it. But not the point of it. The concentrated delight was there to start with. She had not needed babies and their pleased-to-be-aliveness to tell her this.

She started to walk back, this time higher up the beach in the shade of cliffs which held prehistoric snails and traces of dinosaur. I've done it, she thought, and I'm still alive. She took her time, dawdling with deliberate pleasure, as though she were carrying a full glass of milk and might not spill a drop.

'I thought you'd done a Sergeant Troy,' said Jonathan. 'Disappeared out to sea and abandoned us.'

'Would I do a thing like that,' she said, and kissed him lightly beside his mouth.

Matthew reached up from his arms and tugged her hair.

'When I saw you over there by the rock pools you looked just as you used to,' said Jonathan. 'Just the same girl.'

'I am not just as I was, however,' said Frances. 'I am no longer the same girl.'

The sky, which had been growing more dramatic by the minute, was now a florid stagey empyrean, the sea a soundless blaze beneath it. Frances glanced at the baby, and saw how the sun made an electric fleece of the down on his head. She touched it lightly with the flat of her hand as though it might burn her.

'Isn't it mind-boggling,' said Jonathan. 'Isn't it impossible to take in that when we were last on this beach, these two were thin air. Or less. They're so solid now that I almost can't believe there was a time before them, and it's only been a couple of years.'

'What?' said Lorna. '*What* did you say?'

'Daddy was just commenting on the mystery of human existence,' said Frances, scooping her up and letting her perch on her hip. She felt the internal chassis, her skeleton and musculature, adjust to the extra weight with practised efficiency. To think, she marvelled routinely, to think that this great heavy child grew in the centre of my body. But the surprise of the idea had started to grow blunt, worn down by its own regular self-contemplation.

'Look, Lorna,' she said. 'Do you see how the sun is making our faces orange?'

In the flood of flame-coloured light their flesh turned to coral.

From
Hey Yeah Right Get a Life

Lentils and Lilies

Jade Beaumont was technically up in her bedroom revising for the A levels which were now only weeks away. Her school gave them study days at home, after lectures on trust and idleness. She was supposed to be sorting out the differences between Wordsworth and Coleridge at the moment.

Down along the suburban pleasantness of Miniver Road the pavements were shaded by fruit trees, and the front gardens of the little Edwardian villas smiled back at her with early lilac, bushes of crimson flowering currant and the myopic blue dazzle of forget-me-nots. She felt light on her feet and clever, like a cat, snuffing the air, pinching a pungent currant leaf.

There was a belief held by Jade's set that the earlier you hardened yourself off and bared your skin, the more lasting the eventual tan; and so she had that morning pulled on a brief white skirt and T-shirt. She was on her way to an interview for a holiday job at the garden centre. Summer! She couldn't wait. The morning was fair but chilly and the white-gold hairs on her arms and legs stood up and curved to form an invisible reticulation, trapping a layer of warm air a good centimetre deep.

I may not hope from outward forms to win
The passion and the life, whose fountains are within.

That was cool, but Coleridge was a minefield. Just when you thought he'd said something really brilliant, he went raving off full steam ahead into nothingness. He was a nightmare to write about. Anyway, she herself found outward forms utterly absorbing, the colour of clothes, the texture of skin, the smell of food and flowers. She couldn't see the point of extrapolation. Keats was obviously so much better than the others, but you didn't get the choice of questions with him.

She paused to inhale the sweet air around a philadelphus Belle Etoile, then noticed the host of tired daffodils at its feet.

Shades of the prison-house begin to close
Upon the growing boy,
But he beholds the light, and whence it flows,
He sees it in his joy.

She looked back down her years at school, the reined-in feeling, the stupors of boredom, the teachers in the classrooms like tired lion-tamers, and felt quite the opposite. She was about to be let out. And every day when she left the house, there was the excitement of being noticed, the warmth of eye-beams, the unfolding consciousness of her own attractive powers. She was the focus of every film she saw, every novel she read. She was about to start careering round like a lustrous loose cannon.

Full soon thy soul shall have her earthly freight,
And custom lie upon thee with a weight,
Heavy as frost, and deep almost as life!

She was never going to go dead inside or live somewhere boring like this, and she would make sure she
was in charge at any work she did and not let it run
her. She would never be like her mother, making
rotas and lists and endless arrangements, lost forever in
a forest of twitching detail with her tense talk of juggling
and her self-importance about her precious job and
her joyless 'running the family'. No, life was not some
sort of military campaign; or, at least, *hers* would not
be.

When she thought of her mother, she saw tendons and
hawsers, a taut figure at the front door screaming at them
all to do their music practice. She was always off out; she
made them do what she said by remote control. Her trouble
was, she'd forgotten how to relax. It was no wonder Dad
was like he was.

And everybody said she was so amazing, what she
managed to pack into twenty-four hours. Dad worked
hard, they said, but she worked hard too *and* did the home
shift, whatever that was. Not really so very amazing though;
she'd forgotten to get petrol a couple of weeks ago, and
the school run had ground to a halt. In fact some people
might say downright inefficient.

On the opposite side of the road, a tall girl trailed past
with a double buggy of grizzling babies, a Walkman's
shrunken tinkling at her ears. Au pair, remarked Jade
expertly to herself, scrutinising the girl's shoes, cerise plastic

jellies set with glitter. She wanted some just like that, but without the purple edging.

She herself had been dragged up by a string of au pairs. Her mother hated it when she said that. After all, she *was* supposed to take delight in us! thought Jade viciously, standing stock-still, outraged; like, *be* there with us. For us. Fair seed-time had my soul I *don't* think.

Above her the cherry trees were fleecy and packed with a foam of white petals. Light warm rays of the sun reached her upturned face like kisses, refracted as a fizzy dazzle through the fringing of her eyelashes. She turned to the garden beside her and stared straight into a magnolia tree, the skin of its flowers' stiff curves streaked with a sexual crimson. She was transported by the light and the trees, and just as her child self had once played the miniature warrior heroine down green alleys, so she saw her self now floating in this soft sunshine, moving like a panther into the long jewelled narrative which was her future.

Choice landscapes and triumphs and adventures quivered, quaintly framed there in the zigzag light like pendant crystals on a chandelier. There was the asterisk trail of a shooting star, on and on for years until it petered out at about thirty-three or thirty-four, leaving her at some point of self-apotheosis, high and nobly invulnerable, one of Tiepolo's ceiling princesses looking down in beautiful amusement from a movie-star cloud. This was about as far as any of the novels and films took her too.

A pleasurable sigh escaped her as the vision faded, and she started walking again, on past the tranquil houses, the coloured glass in a hall window staining the domestic light, a child's bicycle propped against the trunk of a standard rose. She sensed babies breathing in cots in upstairs rooms, and solitary women becalmed somewhere downstairs, chopping fruit or on the telephone organising some toddler tea. It really was suburban purdah round here. They were like battery hens, weren't they, rows of identical hutches, so neat and tidy and narrow-minded. Imagine staying in all day, stewing in your own juices. Weren't they bored out of their skulls? It was beyond her comprehension.

And so materialistic, she scoffed, observing the pelmetted strawberry-thief curtains framing a front room window; so bourgeois. Whereas her gap-year cousin had just been all over India for under £200.

> The world is too much with us; late and soon,
> Getting and spending, we lay waste our powers.
> Little we see in Nature that is ours;
> We have given our hearts away, a sordid boon!

Although after a good patch of freedom she fully intended to pursue a successful career, the way ahead paved by her future degree in Business Studies. But she would never end up anywhere like here. No! It would be a converted warehouse with semi-astral views and no furniture. Except perhaps for the ultimate sofa.

Jade rounded the corner into the next road, and suddenly there on the pavement ahead of her was trouble. A child was lying flat down on its back screaming while a man in a boilersuit crouched over it, his anti-dust mask lifted to his forehead like a frogman. Above them both stood a broad fair woman, urgently advising the child to calm down.

'You'll be better with a child than I am,' said the work-man gratefully as Jade approached, and before she could agree – or disagree – he had shot off back to his sand-blasting.

'She's stuck a lentil up her nose,' said the woman crossly, worriedly. 'She's done it before. More than once. I've got to get it out.'

She waved a pair of eyebrow tweezers in the air. Jade glanced down at the chubby blubbering child, her small squat nose and mess of tears and mucus, and moved away uneasily.

'We're always down at Casualty,' said the mother, as rapidly desperate as a talentless stand-up comedian. 'Last week she swallowed a penny. Casualty said, a penny's OK, wait for it to come out the other end. Which it did. But they'd have had to open her up if it had been a five-pence piece, something to do with the serration or the size. Then she pushed a drawing pin up her nose. They were worried it might get into her brain. But she sneezed it out. One time she even pushed a chip up her nostril, really far, and it needed extracting from the sinus tubes.'

Jade gasped fastidiously and stepped back.

'Maybe we should get her indoors,' suggested the woman, her hand on Jade's arm. 'It's that house there across the road.'

'I don't think . . .' started Jade.

'The baby, oh the baby!' yelped the woman. 'He's in the car. I forgot. I'll have to . . .'

Before Jade could escape, the woman was running like an ostrich across the road towards a blue Volvo, its passenger door open onto the pavement, where from inside came the sobbing of the strapped-in baby. Jade tutted, glancing down at her immaculate clothes, but she had no option really but to pick up the wailing child and follow the mother. She did not want to be implicated in the flabby womany-ness of the proceedings, and stared crossly at this overweight figure ahead of her, ludicrously top-heavy in its bulky stained sweatshirt and sagging leggings.

Closer up, in the hallway, her hyperaesthetic teenage eyes observed the mother's ragged cuticles, the graceless way her heels stuck out from the backs of her sandals like hunks of Parmesan, and the eyes which had dwindled to dull pinheads. The baby in her arms was dark red as a crab apple from bellowing, but calmed down when a bottle was plugged into its mouth.

It was worse in the front room. Jade lowered her snuffling burden to the carpet and looked around her with undisguised disdain. The furniture was all boring and ugly while the pictures, well the pictures were like a propaganda campaign for family values – endless groupings on walls and ledges and shelves of wedding pictures and baby photos, a fluttery white suffocation of clichés.

The coffee table held a flashing ansaphone and a hideous orange Amaryllis lily on its last legs, red-gold anthers shedding pollen. Jade sat down beside it and traced her initials in this yolk-yellow dust with her fingertip.

'I used to love gardening,' said the woman, seeing this. 'But there's no time now. I've got an Apple up in the spare room, I try to keep a bit of part-time going during their naps. Freelance PR. Typing CVs.'

She waved the tweezers again and knelt above her daughter on the carpet.

I wouldn't let you loose on my CV, thought Jade, recoiling. Not in a million years. It'd come back with jam all over it.

The little girl was quite a solid child and tried to control her crying, allowing herself to be comforted in between the probings inside her face. But she was growing hotter, and when, at the woman's request, Jade unwillingly held her, she was like a small combustion engine, full of distress.

'See, if I hold her down, you have a try,' said the woman, handing her the tweezers.

Jade was appalled and fascinated. She peered up the child's nose and could see a grey-green disc at the top of one fleshy nostril. Tentatively she waved the silver tongs. Sensibly the child began to howl. The mother clamped her head and shoulders down with tired violence.

'I don't think I'd better do this,' said Jade. She was frightened that metal inside the warm young face combined with sudden fierce movement could be a disastrous combination.

The woman tried again and the walls rang with her daughter's screams.

'Oh God,' she said. 'What can I do?'

'Ring your husband?' suggested Jade.

'He's in Leeds,' said the woman. 'Or is it Manchester. Oh dear.'

'Ha,' said Jade. You'd think it was the fifties, men roaming the world while the women stayed indoors. The personal was the political, hadn't she heard?

'I've got to make a phone call to say I'll be late,' said the woman, distracted yet listless. She seemed unable to think beyond the next few minutes or to formulate a plan of action, as though in a state of terminal exhaustion. Jade felt obscurely resentful. If she ever found herself in this sort of situation, a man, babies, etcetera; when the time came; IF. Well, he would be responsible for half the child-care and half the housework. At least. She believed in justice, unlike this useless great lump.

'Why don't you ring Casualty?' she suggested. 'See what the queues are like?'

'I did that before,' said the woman dully. 'They said, try to get it out yourself.'

'I'm sorry,' said Jade, standing up. 'I'm on my way to an interview. I'll be late if I stay.' People should deal with their own problems, she wanted to say; you shouldn't get yourself into situations you can't handle then slop all over everybody else.

'Yes,' said the woman. 'Thank you anyway.'

'You could ring the doctor,' said Jade on the way to the front door. 'Ask for an emergency appointment.'

'I'll do that next,' said the woman, brightening a little; then added suddenly, 'This year has been the hardest of my life. The two of them.'

'My mother's got four,' said Jade censoriously. '*And* a job. Goodbye.'

She turned with relief back into the shining spring morning and started to sprint, fast and light, as quick off the blocks as Atalanta.

Hey Yeah Right Get a Life

Dorrie stood at the edge of the early morning garden and inhaled a column of chilly air. After the mulch of soft sheets and stumbling down through the domestic rubble and crumbs and sleeping bodies, it made her gasp with delight, outside, the rough half-light of March and its menthol coldness.

The only other creature apart from herself was next door's cat which sauntered the length of the fence's top edge stately as a *fin de siècle* roué returning from a night of pleasure. That was what she was after, the old feline assurance that she had a place here. Of course you couldn't expect to remain inviolate; but surely there had to be some part of yourself you could call your own without causing trouble. It couldn't *all* be spoken for. She watched the cat hunch its shoulders and soundlessly pour itself from the fence onto the path.

Nowadays those few who continued to see Dorrie at all registered her as a gloomy, timid woman who had grown rather fat and over-protective of her three infants. They sighed with impatient pity to observe how easily small anxieties took possession of her, how her sense of proportion appeared to have receded along with her horizons.

She was never still, she was always available, a conciliatory twittering fusspot. Since the arrival of the children, one, two and then three, in the space of four years, she had broken herself into little pieces like a biscuit and was now scattered all over the place. The urge – indeed, the necessity – to give everything, to throw herself on the bonfire, had been shocking; but now it was starting to wear off.

Back in the warmth of her side of the bed she lay listening to Max's breathing, and the clink and wheezing protest of a milk float, then the first front doors slamming as the trainee accountants and solicitors set off for the station. There was a light pattering across the carpet and a small round figure stood by the bed. She could see the gleam of his eyes and teeth smiling conspiratorially in the blanching dark.

'Come on then,' she whispered. 'Don't wake Daddy.'

He climbed into bed and curled into her, his head on her shoulder, his face a few inches from hers, gazed into her eyes and heaved a happy sigh. They lay looking at each other, breathing in each other's sleepy scent; his eyes were guileless, unguarded and intent, and he gave a little occasional beatific smile.

'Where's your pyjama top?' she whispered.

'Took it *off*,' he whispered back. 'Too itchy.'

'It's *not* itchy,' she tutted. 'I'll put some special oil in your bath tonight.'

His chest was like a huge warm baroque pearl. She satined the side of her face against it for a moment.

'When are you going to stop wearing nappies at night?' she scolded in a whisper.

'When I'm four,' he chuckled, and shifted his pumpkin padding squarely onto her lap.

Max stirred and muttered something.

'Ssssh,' said Robin, placing a forefinger against his mother's lips and widening his eyes for emphasis.

They watched Max's dark bearded face break into a yawn, a seadog or a seagod about to rally his crew. He was waking up. Robin wriggled under the bedclothes to hide. Last night it had been her under the bedclothes and Max's hands on her head while she brought him off with her mouth. Then she had curled into him, her head on his shoulder, until he fell into a dense sleep, and she basked like a lioness in the sun. Next, gently unwinding herself from his knotty embrace she had glided along to the next room and plucked this heavy boy from his bed, standing him, sleep-dazed, in front of the lavatory, pointing the shrimp of his penis for him, whispering encouragement as the water hissed, before closing in on him with the midnight nappy.

Max's eyes flickered awake and he smiled at Dorrie.

'Mmmm,' he said. 'Come here.' He reached over and grabbed her, buried his face in her neck, and then as he reached downwards his hands encountered his son.

'No! No!' screeched Robin, laughing hectically. 'Get *away*, Daddy!'

This brought his siblings, Martin and Maxine, running from their bedroom and they hurled themselves into the heap of bodies. Max struggled out of it growling, and was gone.

The three children shoved and biffed their way into shares of her supine body. Robin clung to his central stake, arms round her neck, head between her breasts, kicking out at attempts to supplant him. Martin hooked his legs round her waist and lay under her left arm gnawing his nails and complaining it wasn't fair. Maxine burrowed at her right side, all elbows and knees, until she settled in the crook of her other arm, her head beside Dorrie's on the pillow.

'Mummy. A good heart is never proud. Is that true?' said Maxine.

'What?'

'It was on my *Little Mermaid* tape. I can make my eyes squelch, listen.'

'Oof, careful, Robin,' said Dorrie, as Robin brought his head up under her chin and crashed her teeth together.

'Goodbye,' said Max from the doorway.

'Don't forget we're going out tonight,' said Dorrie from the pillows.

'Oh yes,' said Max. He looked at the heap of bodies on the bed. 'Your mother and I were married eight years ago today,' he said into the air, piously.

'Where was *I*?' said Maxine.

'*Not* going out,' hissed Robin, gripping Dorrie more tightly. 'Stay inner house, Mummy.'

'And I'm not going to stand for any nonsense like that,' growled Max. He glared at his youngest son. 'Get off your mother, she can't move. It's ridiculous.'

'It's all right, Max,' said Dorrie. 'Don't make yourself late.'

'Go away, Daddy,' shouted Robin.

'Yeah,' joined in Martin and Maxine. 'Go away, Daddy.'

Max glared at them impotently, then turned on his heel like a pantomime villain. A moment later they heard the front door slam.

'Yesss!' said Robin, punching the air with his dimpled fist. The bed heaved with cheers and chuckles.

'You shouldn't talk to Daddy like that,' said Dorrie.

'Horble Daddy,' said Robin dismissively.

'He's not horble,' huffed Dorrie. 'Horrible. Time to get up.'

They all squealed and clutched her harder, staking her down with sharp elbows and knees wherever they could.

'You're hurting me,' complained Dorrie. 'Come on, it really is time to get up.' And at last she extracted herself like a slow giantess from the cluster of children, gently detaching their fingers from her limbs and nightdress.

When she turned back from drawing the curtains, Martin was painting his shins with a stick of deodorant while Maxine sat on the floor, galloping her round bare heels in the cups of a discarded bra, pulling on the straps like a jockey, with shouts of 'Ya! Ya! Giddy up boy!' Robin ran round and round his mother's legs, wrapping and rewrapping her nightdress. Then he rolled on the carpet with both hands round her ankle, a lively leg-iron, singing alleluia, alleluia, alleluia.

'Don't do that, Martin,' said Dorrie as she climbed into yesterday's jeans and sweatshirt. But he was already on to something else, crossing the floor with a bow-legged rocking gait, a pillow across his shoulders, groaning under its imaginary weight and bulk.

'I'm Robin Hood carrying a deer,' he grinned back over his shoulder. Maxine roared with laughter, hearty as a Tudor despot.

'Come on, darlings,' Dorrie expostulated feebly. 'Help me get you dressed.'

They ran around her and across the landing, ignoring her, screeching, singing, bellowing insults and roaring into the stairwell. She pulled vests and socks and jumpers from various drawers, stepping around them like a slave during a palace orgy. Their separate energies whizzed through the air, colliding constantly, as random as the weather. She grabbed Martin as he shot past and started to strip off his nightclothes.

'No!' he yelled and tore himself free, running off trouser-less. He was as quick as she was slow. It was like wading through mud after dragonflies.

'I hate you!' he was screaming at Maxine now for some reason. 'I wish you were dead!'

'Now now,' said Dorrie. 'That's not very nice, is it.'

Then there were pinches and thumps and full-chested bellows of rage. By the time she had herded them down for the cornflakes stage, they had lived through as many variants of passion as occur in the average Shakespeare play. She looked at their momentarily woebegone faces streaked with tears of fury over whichever was the most recent hair-pulling or jealousy or bruising, she had lost track, and said with deliberate cheer, 'Goodness, if we could save all the tears from getting ready in the mornings, if we could collect them in a bucket, I could use them to do the washing up.'

All three faces broke into wreathed smiles and apprecia-tive laughter at this sally, and then the row started up again. They did not take turns to talk, but cut across each other's words with reckless thoughtlessness. She was trying to think through the hairbrushing, shoe-hunting, tooth-cleaning, packed lunch for Martin, empty toilet roll cylinder for

Maxine's Miss Atkinson, with an eye on the clock, but it was a non-starter.

'SHUSH,' she shouted. 'I can't hear myself THINK.'

'Are you thinking?' asked Maxine curiously.

'No,' she said. 'Hurry UP.'

It was not in fact possible to think under these conditions; no train of thought could ever quite leave the platform, let alone arrive at any sort of destination. This was what the mothers at the school gates meant when they said they were brain-dead, when they told the joke about the secret of childcare being a frontal lobotomy or a bottle in front of me. This was why she had started waking in the small hours, she realised, even though heaven knew she was tired enough without that, even though she was still being woken once or twice a night by one or the other of them; not Max because he had to be fresh for work and anyway they wouldn't want him. They wanted *her*. But when they were all safe, breathing regularly, asleep, quiet, she was able at last to wait for herself to grow still, to grow still and alive so that the sediment settled and things grew clearer. So that she could *think*.

'Mrs Piper said Jonathan had nits and she sent him home,' said Martin, lifting his face up. She was brushing his hair, and pushed his brow back down against her breastbone. Then, more muffled, came, '*Don't* make me look like Elvis de Presto.'

'What I want to know, Mum,' he said as she pushed him back and knelt at Maxine's feet to struggle with her shoe buckles. 'What I *need* to know, nobody will tell me,' he continued crossly, 'is, is God there, *can* he hold the whole world in his hand – or is he like the Borrowers? I mean, what is he? Is he a man? Is he a cow?'

She was working grimly against the clock now. Her hands shook. She was shot to hell. Maxine was complaining of a blister on her little toe. Dorrie ran off upstairs like a heifer for the plaster roll and cut a strip and carefully fitted it round the pea-sized top joint of the toe. Maxine moaned and screamed, tears squirted from her eyes, her face became a mask of grief as she felt the plaster arrangement inside her sock even more uncomfortable once strapped into her shoe. It all had to be removed again and a square quarter inch of plaster carefully applied like a miniature postage stamp to the reddened area.

'We're late,' hissed Dorrie, but even in the middle of this felt a great sick thud of relief that it was not two years ago when she had been racing against the clock to get to work pretending to them there that all this had not just happened. When at last she had caved in, when she had given in her notice, it felt like giving up the world, the flesh and the devil. It had been terrible at first, the loss of breadth, the loss of adult company. There were the minutes at various school gates with the other mothers, but you couldn't really call that proper talk, not with all the babies and toddlers on at them. After all she had not managed to keep both worlds up in the air. She knew she had failed.

She picked Robin up and jammed him into the buggy.

'Teeth!' said Martin, baring his own at her. 'You've forgotten about teeth!'

'Never mind,' she said through hers, gritted, manoeuvring the buggy across the front doorstep. 'Come on.'

'Why?' asked Martin, pulling his school jumper up to

his eyes and goggling at himself in front of the hall mirror. 'Burglars don't show their noses, Mum. Look. Mum.'

These days Martin flew off towards the playground as soon as they reached the school gate, for which she was profoundly grateful. For his first five years he had been full of complaints, fault-finding and irritability. He still flew into towering rages and hit her and screamed until he was pink or blue in the face, often several times a day. As he was her first child this had come as a shock. She even asked the doctor about it, and the doctor had smiled and said his sounded a fiery little nature but he would no doubt learn to control himself in time. 'Also, all behaviour is *learned* behaviour,' said the doctor reprovingly. 'Never shout back or you'll just encourage him.' Plenty of the other mothers had children who behaved similarly, she noticed after a while. You just had to take it, and wait for time to pass. It could take years. It did. He was loud, waspish, frequently agitated and a constant prey to boredom. When she saw him nibbling his nails, tired and white as a cross elf, she would draw him onto her lap and make a basket of her arms around him. She saw his lack of ease in the world, and grieved for him, and knew it was her fault because she was his mother.

Maxine was less irritable but more manipulative. Her memory was terrifyingly precise and long – yesterday, for example, she had raged at Dorrie for stealing a fruit pastille, having remembered the colour of the top one from several hours before. She relished experiments and emotional mayhem. Her new trick this week was to fix you with her pale pretty eye, and say, quite coolly, 'I hate you.' This poleaxed Dorrie. And yet this little girl was also utterly unglazed against experience, as fresh and easily hurt as one of those new daffodil shoots.

Only when Robin was born had she realised what it was to have what is commonly known as an easy child. No rhyme nor reason to it. Same treatment, completely different. They were as they were as soon as they were born, utterly different from each other. That was something at least. It couldn't *all* be her fault.

Now it was halfway through Martin's first school year and he had settled in well. It was wonderful. She glanced in passing at other less fortunate mothers talking low and urgent with their infants, entwined and unlinking, like lovers, bargaining with furtive tears, sobs, clinging arms, angry rejections, pettishness and red eyes.

It was the same when she dropped Maxine off at nursery school half an hour later. On the way out she and Robin passed a little girl of three or so saying to her mother, 'But Mummy I *miss* you'; and the mother, smartly dressed, a briefcase by her, rather tightly reasoning with her, murmuring, glancing at her watch. Dorrie felt herself break into a light sympathetic sweat.

The little scene brought back Robin's trial morning there last week. He had refused to walk through the nursery school's entrance and was shouting and struggling as she carried him in. She had set him down by a low table of jigsaw puzzles and told him sternly that she would sit over there in that corner for five minutes, that his sister was just over there in the Wendy house, and that he must let her go quietly. From the toy kitchen he had brought her a plastic cupcake with a fat ingratiating smile.

'Here y'are,' he'd said.

'Save it for when I come to pick you up,' Dorrie had said, handing it back to him, pity and coldness battling through her like warring blood corpuscles. At last he had given her a resigned kiss on the cheek and gone off to the painting table without another look. (Two hours alone, for the first time in months. Wait till he's at school, said the mothers; you won't know yourself.) She dashed a tear away, sneering at her own babyishness.

Now, today, there was this precious time with Robin. He liked to be around her, within a few yards of her, to keep her in his sight, but he did not pull the stuffing out of her as the other two did. He did not demand her thoughts and full attention like Maxine; nor that she should identify and change colour like litmus paper with his every modulation of emotion as it occurred, which was what Martin seemed to need. Sometimes those two were so extravagantly exacting, they levied such a fantastic rate of slavish fealty that they left her gasping for air.

No, Robin talked to his allies and foes, *sotto voce*, in the subterranean fields which ran alongside the privet-hedged landscape in which they moved together. He sent out smiles or little waves while Dorrie was working, and took breaks for a hug or to pause and drink squash, him on her lap like a stalwart beanbag.

She sorted the dirty whites from the coloured wash up on the landing, and he put them into the washing basket for her. Up and down the stairs she went with round baskets of washing, the smell of feet and bottoms, five sets, fresh and smelly, all different. Robin stuffed the garments into the washing machine one by one, shutting the door smartly and saying 'There!' and smiling with satisfaction. She did some handwashing at the sink, and he pushed a chair over across the floor to stand on, and squeezed the garments, then took handfuls of the soap bubbles that wouldn't drain away and trotted to and from the bucket on the mat with them.

'What a helpful boy you are!' she said. He beamed.

'Now I'm going to iron some things including Daddy's shirt for tonight,' she said. 'So you must sit over there because the iron is dangerous.'

'Hot,' he agreed, with a sharp camp intake of breath.

He sat down on the floor with some toys in a corner of the kitchen and as she ironed she looked over now and then at his soft thoughtfully frowning face as he tried to put a brick into a toy car, the curve of his big soft cheek like a mushroom somehow, and his lovely close-to-the-head small ears. He gave an unconscious sigh of concentration; his frequent sighs came right from deep in the diaphragm. Squab or chub or dab had been the words which best expressed him until recently, but now he was growing taller and fining down, his limbs had lost their chubbiness and his body had become his own.

No longer could she kiss his eyelids whenever she wished, nor pretend to bite his fingers, nor even stroke his hair with impunity. He was a child now, not a baby, and must be accorded his own dignity. The baby was gone, almost.

Abruptly she put the iron on its heel and swooped down on him, scooped him up and buried her nose in his neck with throaty growling noises. He huffed and shouted and laughed as they swayed struggling by the vegetable rack.

She tickled him and they sank down to the lino laughing and shouting, then he rubbed his barely-there velvet nose against hers like an Eskimo, his eyes close and dark and merry, inches from hers, gazing in without shame or constraint.

It was going to be a long series of leave-takings from now on, she thought; goodbye and goodbye and goodbye; that had been the case with the others, and now this boy was three and a half. Unless she had another. But then Max would leave. Or so he said. This treacherous brainless greed for more of the same, it would finish her off if she wasn't careful. If she wasn't already.

She took Max's shirt upstairs on a hanger and put the rest of the ironing away. What would she wear tonight? She looked at her side of the wardrobe. Everything that wasn't made of T-shirt or sweatshirt fabric was too tight for her now. Unenthusiastically she took down an old red shirt-dress, looser than the rest, and held it up against her reflection in the full-length mirror. She used to know what she looked like, she used to be interested. Now she barely recognised herself. She peeled off her sweatshirt and jeans and pulled the dress on. She looked enormous. The dress was straining at the seams. She looked away fast, round the bedroom, the unmade bed like a dog basket, the mess everywhere, the shelves of books on the wall loaded with forbidden fruit, impossible to broach, sealed off by the laws of necessity from her maternal eyes. During the past five years, reading a book had become for her an activity engaged in at somebody else's expense.

The doorbell rang and she answered it dressed as she was. Robin hid behind her.

'Gemma's got to be a crocodile tomorrow,' said Sally, who lived two roads away. 'We're desperate for green tights, I've tried Mothercare and Boots and then I thought of Maxine. I don't suppose?'

'Sorry,' said Dorrie, 'Only red or blue.'

'Worth a try,' said Sally, hopeless. 'You look dressed up.'

'I look fat,' said Dorrie. 'Wedding anniversary,' she added tersely.

'Ah,' said Sally. 'How many years?'

'Eight,' said Dorrie. 'Bronze. Sally, can you remember that feeling before all the family stuff kicked in, I know it's marvellous but. You know, that spark, that feeling of fun and – and lightness, somehow.'

Immediately Sally replied, 'It's still there in me but I don't know for how much longer.'

'You could try Verity,' said Dorrie. 'I seem to remember she put Hannah in green tights last winter to go with that holly berry outfit.'

'So she did!' said Sally. 'I'll give her a ring.'

'Kill,' whispered Robin, edging past the women into the tiny front garden; 'Die, megazord,' and he crushed a snail shell beneath his shoe. Half hidden beneath the windowsill he crouched in a hero's cave. Across the dangerous river of the front path he had to save his mother, who was chatting to a wicked witch. He started round the grape hyacinths as though they were on fire and squeezed his way along behind the lilac bush, past cobwebs and worms, until he burst out fiercely into the space behind the hedge. She was being forced to walk the plank. He leaped into the ocean and cantered sternly across the waves.

★   ★   ★

They were late coming out of nursery school, and Dorrie stood with the other mothers and au pairs in the queue. Some were chatting, some were sagging and gazing into the middle distance.

In front of her, two women were discussing a third just out of earshot.

'Look at her nails,' said the one directly in front of Dorrie. 'You can always tell. Painted fingernails mean a rubbish mother.'

'I sometimes put nail polish on if I'm going out in the evening,' said the other.

'*If,*' scoffed the first. 'Once in a blue moon. And then you make a mess of it, I bet. You lose your touch. Anyway, you've got better things to do with your time, you give your time to your children, not to primping yourself up.'

Robin pushed his head between Dorrie's knees and clutched her thighs, a mini Atlas supporting the world.

Dorrie saw it was Patricia from Hawthornden Avenue.

'*I* was thinking of doing my nails today,' said Dorrie.

'What on earth *for?*' laughed Patricia. She was broad in the beam, clever but narrow-minded.

'Wedding anniversary,' said Dorrie. 'Out for a meal.'

'There you are then,' said Patricia triumphantly, as though she had proved some point.

'I had a blazing row with *my* husband last night,' said Patricia's friend. 'And I was just saying to myself, Right that's it, I was dusting myself down ready for the off, when I thought, No, hang on a minute, I *can't* go. I've got three little children, I've *got* to stay.'

Patricia's eyebrows were out of sight, she reeled from

side to side laughing. They all laughed, looking sideways at each other, uneasy.

'Have you noticed what happens now that everyone's splitting up,' snorted Patricia's friend. 'I've got friends, their divorce comes through and do you know they say it's amazing! They lose weight and take up smoking and have all the weekends to themselves to do *whatever they want* in because the men take the children off out then.'

'Divorce,' said Dorrie ruminatively. 'Yes. You get to thirty-seven, married, three kids, and you look in the mirror, at least I did this morning, and you realise – it's a shock – you realise nothing else is supposed to happen until you die. Or you spoil the pattern.'

The nursery school doors opened at last. Dorrie held her arms out and Maxine ran into them. Maxine had woken screaming at five that morning, clutching her ear, but then the pain had stopped and she had gone back to sleep again. Dorrie had not. That was when she had gone downstairs and into the garden.

'The doctor's going to fit us in after her morning surgery, so I must run,' said Dorrie, scooping Maxine up to kiss her, strapping Robin into the buggy.

'Mum,' called Maxine, as they galloped slowly along the pavement, 'Mum, Gemma says I must only play with her or she won't be my friend. But I told her Suzanne was my best friend. Gemma's only second best.'

'Yes,' said Dorrie. 'Mind that old lady coming towards us.'

'Suzanne and me really wanted Gemma to play Sour Lemons but Shoshaya wanted her to play rabbits,' panted Maxine. 'Then Shoshaya cried and she told Miss Atkinson.

And Miss Atkinson told us to let her play. But Gemma wanted to play Sour Lemons with me and Suzanne and she did.'

'Yes,' said Dorrie. She must get some milk, and extra cheese for lunch. She ought to pick up Max's jacket from the cleaners. Had she got the ticket? Had she got enough cash? Then there was Max's mother's birthday present to be bought and packed up and posted off to Salcombe, and a card. She had to be thinking of other people all the time or the whole thing fell apart. It was like being bitten all over by soldier ants without being able to work up enough interest to deal with them. Sometimes she found herself holding her breath for no reason at all.

'Why do you always say yes?' said Maxine.

'What?' said Dorrie. They stood at the kerb waiting to cross. She looked up at the top deck of the bus passing on the other side and saw a young man sitting alone up there. He happened to meet her eye for a moment as she stood with the children, and the way he looked at her, through her, as though she were a greengrocer's display or a parked car, made her feel less than useless. She was a rock or stone or tree. She was nothing.

'Why do you always say yes?' said Maxine.

'What?' said Dorrie.

'Why do you always say YES!' screamed Maxine in a rage.

'Cross *now*,' said Dorrie, grabbing her arm and hauling her howling across the road as she pushed the buggy.

They turned the corner into the road where the surgery was and saw a small boy running towards them trip and go flying, smack down onto the pavement.

'Oof,' said Maxine and Robin simultaneously.

The child held up his grazed hands in grief and started to split the air with his screams. His mother came lumbering up with an angry face.

'I told you, didn't I? I told you! You see? God was looking down and he saw you were getting out of control. You wouldn't do what I said, would you. And God said, *right*, and He made you fall down like that and that's what happens when you're like that. So now maybe you'll listen the next time!'

Dorrie looked away, blinking. That was another thing, it had turned her completely soft. The boy's mother yanked him up by the arm, and dragged him past, moralising greedily over his sobs.

'She should have hugged him, Mummy, shouldn't she,' said Maxine astutely.

'Yes,' said Dorrie, stopping to blow her nose.

The tattered covers of the waiting room magazines smiled over at them in a congregation of female brightness and intimacy. The women I see in the course of a day, thought Dorrie, and it's women only (except Max at the end of the day), we can't really exchange more than a sentence or two of any interest because of our children. At this age they need us all the time; and anyway we often have little in common except femaleness and being in the same boat. Why should we? She scanned the lead lines while Robin and Maxine chose a book from the scruffy pile – 'How to dump him: twenty ways that work', 'Your hair: what does it say about you?' 'Countdown to your best orgasm'. Those were the magazines for the under-thirties, the free-standing feisty girls who had not yet crossed the ego line. And of course some girls never did cross the ego line. Like men, they stayed the stars of their own lives. Then there was this lot, this lot here with words like juggle and struggle across their covers, these were for her and her like – 'Modern motherhood: how do you measure up?'; 'Is your husband getting enough: time management and you'; 'Doormat etiquette: are you too nice?'

Am I too *nice*? thought Dorrie. They even took *that* away. Nice here meant weak and feeble, *she* knew what it meant. Nice was now an insult, whereas self had been the dirty word when she was growing up. For girls, anyway. She had been trained to think of her mother and not be a nuisance. She couldn't remember ever saying (let alone being asked) what she wanted. To the point of thinking she didn't really mind what she wanted as long as other people were happy. It wasn't long ago.

The doctor inspected Maxine's eardrum with her pointed torch, and offered a choice.

'You can leave it and hope it goes away. That's what they'd do on the Continent.'

'But then it might flare up in the night and burst the eardrum. That happened to Martin. Blood on the pillow. Two sets of grommets since then.'

'Well, *tant pis*, they'd say. They're tough on the Continent. Or it's the usual Amoxcyllin.'

'I don't like to keep giving them that. But perhaps I could have some in case it gets very painful later. And not give it otherwise.'

'That's what I'd do,' said the doctor, scribbling out a prescription.

'How are you finding it, being back at work?' asked Dorrie timidly but with great interest. The doctor had just returned after her second baby and second five-month maternity leave.

'Fine, fine,' smiled the doctor, rubbing her eyes briefly, tired blue eyes kind in her worn face. 'In fact of course it's easier. I mean, it's hard in terms of organisation, hours, being at full stretch. But it's still easier than being at home. With tiny children you really have to be so . . . selfless.'

'Yes,' said Dorrie, encouraged. 'It gets to be a habit. In the end you really do lose yourself. Lost. But then they start to be not tiny.'

'Lost!' said Maxine. 'Who's lost? What you talking about, Mum? *Who's* lost?'

The doctor glanced involuntarily at her watch.

'I'm sorry,' said Dorrie, bustling the children over to the door.

'Not at all,' said the doctor. She did look tired. 'Look after yourself.'

Look after yourself, thought Dorrie as she walked the children home, holding her daughter's hand as she skipped and pulled at her. She glanced down at her hand holding Maxine's, plastic shopping bags of vegetables over her wrist, and her nails looked uneven, not very clean. According to the nursery school queue, that meant she was a good mother. She did nothing for herself. She was a vanity-free zone. Broken nails against that tight red dress wouldn't be very alluring, but all that was quite beyond her now. By schooling herself to harmlessness, constant usefulness to others, she had become a big fat zero.

By the time they got home Dorrie was carrying Robin

straddled African-style across her front, and he was alternately sagging down protesting, then straightening his back and climbing her like a tree. He had rebelled against the buggy, so she had folded it and trailed it behind her, but when he walked one of his shoes hurt him; she knew the big toenail needed cutting but whenever his feet were approached he set up a herd-of-elephants roar. She made a mental note to creep up with the scissors while he slept. I can't see how the family would work if I let myself start wanting things again, thought Dorrie; give me an inch and I'd run a mile, that's what I'm afraid of.

Indoors, she peeled vegetables while they squabbled and played around her legs. She wiped the surfaces while answering long strings of zany questions which led up a spiral staircase into the wild blue nowhere.

'I know when you're having a thought, Mummy,' said Maxine. 'Because when I start to say something then you close your eyes.'

'Can I have my Superman suit?' said Robin.

'In a minute,' said Dorrie, who was tying up a plastic sack of rubbish.

'Not in a minute,' said Robin. '*Now*.'

The thing about small children was that they needed things all day long. They wanted games set up and tears wiped away and a thousand small attentions. This was all fine until you started to do something else round them, or something that wasn't just a basic menial chore, she thought, dragging the hoover out after burrowing in the stacking boxes for the Superman suit. You had to be infinitely elastic and adaptable; all very laudable but this had the concomitant effect of slowly but surely strangling your powers of concentration.

Then Superman needed help in blowing his nose, and next he wanted his cowboys and Indians reached down from the top of the cupboard. She forgot what she was thinking about.

Now she was chopping onions finely as thread so that Martin would not be able to distinguish their texture in the meatballs and so spit them out. (Onions were good for their immune systems, for their blood.) She added these to the minced lamb and mixed in eggs and breadcrumbs then shaped the mixture into forty tiny globes, these to bubble away in a tomato sauce, one of her half-dozen flesh-concealing ruses against Maxine's incipient vegetarianism. (She knew it was technically possible to provide enough protein for young children from beans as long as these were eaten in various careful conjunctions with other beans – all to do with amino acids – but she was not wanting to plan and prepare even more separate meals – Max had his dinner later in the evening – not just yet anyway – or she'd be simmering and peeling till midnight.)

The whole pattern of family life hung for a vivid moment above the chopping board as a seamless cycle of nourishment and devoural. And after all, children were not teeth extracted from you. Perhaps it was necessary to be devoured.

Dorrie felt sick and faint as she often did at this point in the day, so she ate a pile of tepid left-over mashed potato and some biscuits while she finished clearing up and peace-keeping. The minutes crawled by. She wanted to lie down on the lino and pass out.

Maxine's nursery school crony, Suzanne, came to play after lunch. Dorrie helped them make a shop and set up tins of food and jars of dried fruit, but they lost interest after five minutes and wanted to do colouring in with felt tips. Then they had a fight over the yellow. Then they played with the Polly Pockets, and screamed, and hit each other. Now, now, said Dorrie, patient but intensely bored, as she pulled them apart and calmed them down and cheered them up.

At last it was time to drop Suzanne off and collect Martin. Inside the school gates they joined the other mothers, many of whom Dorrie now knew by name or by their child's name, and waited at the edge of the playground for the release of their offspring.

'I can't tell you anything about Wednesday until Monday,' said Thomas' mother to a woman named Marion. A note had been sent back in each child's reading folder the previous day, announcing that the last day before half term would finish at twelve. The women who had part-time jobs now started grumbling about this, and making convoluted webs of arrangements. 'If you drop Neil off at two then my neighbour will be there, you remember, he got on with her last time all right, that business with the spacehopper; then Verity can drop Kirsty by after Tumbletots and I'll be back with Michael and Susan just after three-thirty. Hell! It's ballet. Half an hour later. Are you *sure* that's all right with you?'

'They're late,' said Thomas' mother, glancing at her watch.

'So your youngest will be starting nursery after Easter,' said Marion to Dorrie. 'You won't know yourself.'

'No,' said Dorrie. She reached down to ruffle Robin's feathery hair; he was playing around her legs.

'Will you get a job then?' asked Marion.

'Um, I thought just for those weeks before summer I'd get the house straight, it's only two hours in the morning. And a half,' said Dorrie in a defensive rush. 'Collect my thoughts. If there are any.'

'Anyway, you do your husband's paperwork in the evenings, don't you?' said Thomas' mother. 'The accounts and that. VAT.'

'You get so you can't see the wood for the trees, don't you,' said Dorrie. 'You get so good at fitting things round everything else. Everybody else.'

'I used to be in accounts,' said Marion. 'B.C. But I couldn't go back now. I've lost touch. I couldn't get into my suits any more, I tried the other day. I couldn't do it! I'd hardly cover the cost of the childcare. I've lost my nerve.'

'My husband says he'll back me up one hundred per cent when the youngest starts school,' said Thomas' mother pensively. 'Whatever job I want to do. But no way would he be able to support change which would end by making his working life more difficult, he said.'

'That's not really on, then, is it?' said Marion. 'Unless you get some nursery school work to fit round school hours. Or turn into a freelance something.'

'Some people seem to manage it,' said Thomas' mother. 'Susan Gloverall.'

'I didn't know she was back at work.'

'Sort of. She's hot-desking somewhere off the A3, leaves the kids with a childminder over Tooting way. Shocking journey, but the devil drives.'

'Keith still not found anything, then? That's almost a year now.'

'I know. Dreadful really. I don't think it makes things any, you know, easier between them. And of course she can't leave the kids with him while he's looking. Though she said he's watching a lot of TV.'

'What about Nicola Beaumont, then?' said Dorrie.

'Oh her,' said Marion. 'Wall-to-wall nannies. No thank you.'

'I could never make enough to pay a nanny,' said Thomas' mother. 'I never earned that much to start with. And then you have to pay their tax on top, out of your own taxed income. You'd have to earn eighteen thousand at least before you broke even if you weren't on the fiddle. I've worked it out.'

'Nearer twenty-two these days,' said Marion, 'In London. Surely.'

'Nicola's nice though,' said Dorrie. 'Her daughter Jade, the teenage one, she's babysitting for us tonight.'

'Well she never seems to have much time for me,' said Marion.

'I think she just doesn't have much time full stop,' said Dorrie.

'Nor do any of us, dear,' said Thomas' mother. 'Not *proper* time.'

'Not time to yourself,' said Marion.

'I bet she gets more of that than I do. She commutes, doesn't she? There you are then!'

They were all laughing again when the bell went.

'Harry swallowed his tooth today,' said Martin. 'Mrs Tyrone said it didn't matter, it would melt inside him.' He wiggled his own front tooth, an enamel tag, tipping it forward with his fingernail. Soon there would be the growing looseness, the gradual twisting of it into a spiral, hanging on by a thread, and the final silent snap.

'He won't get any money from the Tooth Fairy, will he, Mum,' said Martin. 'Will he, Mum? Will he, Mum? Mum. Mum!'

'Yes,' said Dorrie. 'What? I expect so dear.' She was peeling carrots and cutting them into sticks.

'And Kosenia scratched her bandage off today, and she's got eczema, and she scratched off, you know, that stuff on top, like the cheese on Shepherd's Pie, she just lifted it off,' Martin went on.

'Crust,' said Dorrie.

'Yes, crust,' said Martin. 'I'm not eating those carrots. No way.'

'Carrots are very good for you,' said Dorrie. 'And tomorrow I'm going to pack some carrot sticks in your lunch box and I want you to eat them.'

'Hey yeah right,' gabbled Martin. 'Hey yeah right get a life!'

And he marched off to where the other two were watching a story about a mouse who ate magic berries and grew as big as a lion. Television was nothing but good and hopeful and stimulating compared with the rest of life so far as she could see. Certainly it had been the high point of her own childhood. Her mother thought she spoiled her children, but then most of her friends said their mothers thought the same about them. She was trying to be more tender with them – she and her contemporaries – to offer them choices rather than just tell them what to do; to be more patient and to hug them when they cried rather than briskly talk of being brave; never to hit them. They felt, they all felt they were trying harder than their parents had ever done, to love well. And one of the side effects of this was that their children were incredibly quick to castigate any shortfall in the quality of attention paid to them.

Now they were fighting again. Martin was screaming and chattering of injustice like an angry ape. Maxine shrilled back at him with her ear-splitting screech. Robin sat on the ground, hands to his ears, sobbing deep-chested sobs of dismay.

She groaned with boredom and frustration. Really she could not afford to let them out of her sight yet; not for another six months, anyway; not in another room, even with television.

'Let's all look at pictures of Mummy and Daddy getting married,' she shouted above the din, skilfully deflecting the furies. Sniffing and shuddering they eventually allowed themselves to be gathered round the album she had dug out, while she wiped their eyes and noses and clucked mild reproaches. The thing was, it did not do simply to turn off. She was not a part of the action but her involved presence was required as it was necessary for her to be ready at any point to step in as adjudicator. What did not work was when she carried on round them, uninvolved, doing the chores, thinking her own thoughts and making placatory noises when the din grew earsplitting. Then the jaws of anarchy opened wide.

Soon they were laughing at the unfamiliar images of their parents in the trappings of romance, the bright spirited faces and trim figures.

'Was it the best day in your life?' asked Maxine.

There was me, she thought, looking at the photographs; there used to be me. She was the one who'd put on two stone; he still looked pretty fit. The whole process would have been easier, she might have been able to retain some self-respect, if at some point there had been a formal handing over like Hong Kong.

At the end of some days, by the time each child was breathing regularly, asleep, she would stand and wait for herself to grow still, and the image was of an ancient vase, crackle-glazed, still in one piece but finely crazed all over its surface. I'm shattered, she would groan to Max on his return, hale and whole, from the outside world.

Now, at the end of just such a day, Dorrie was putting the children down while Max had a bath after his day at work. It was getting late. She had booked a table at L'Horizon and arranged for Jade to come round and babysit at eight. They had not been out together for several months, but Dorrie had not forgotten how awful it always was.

It was twenty to eight, and Robin clung to her.

'Don't go, Mummy, don't go,' he sobbed, jets of water spouting from his eyes, his mouth a square buckle of anguish.

'Don't be silly,' said Dorrie, with her arms round him. 'I've got to go and change, darling. I'll come straight back.'

'No you won't,' he bellowed. Martin watched with interest, nibbling his nails.

'He's making me feel sad, Mum,' commented Maxine. 'I feel like crying now too.'

'So do I,' said Dorrie grimly.

'What's all the noise?' demanded Max, striding into the room drubbing his hair with a towel. 'Why aren't you children asleep yet?'

Robin took a wild look at his father and, howling with fresh strength, tightened his grip on Dorrie with arms, legs and fingers.

'Let go of your mother this minute,' snarled Max in a rage, starting to prise away the desperate fingers one by one. Robin's sobs became screams, and Maxine started to cry.

'Please, Max,' said Dorrie. 'Please don't.'

'This is ridiculous,' hissed Max, wrenching him from her body. Dorrie watched the child move across the line into hysteria, and groaned.

'Stop it, Daddy!' screamed Martin, joining in, and downstairs the doorbell rang.

'Go and answer it then!' said Max, pinning his frantic three-year-old son to the bed.

'Oh God,' said Dorrie as she stumbled downstairs to open the door to the babysitter.

'Hello, Jade!' she said with a wild fake smile. 'Come in!'

'Sounds like I'm a bit early,' said Jade, stepping into the hall, tall and slender and dressed in snowy-white shirt and jeans.

'No, no, let me show you how to work the video, that's just the noise they make on their way to sleep,' said Dorrie, feeling herself bustle around like a fat dwarf. It seemed pathetic that she should be going out and this lovely girl staying in. The same thought had crossed Jade's mind, but she had her whole life ahead of her, as everyone kept saying.

'Any problems, anything at all, if one of them wakes and asks for me, please ring and I'll come back, it's only a few minutes away.'

'Everything'll be *fine*,' said Jade, as if to a fussy infant. 'You shouldn't worry so much.'

'I'll swing for that child,' they heard Max growl from the landing, then a thundering patter of feet, and febrile shrieks.

'Eight years, eh,' said Max across the candlelit damask. 'My Old Dutch. No need to look so tragic.'

Dorrie was still trying to quiet her body's alarm system, the waves of miserable heat, the klaxons of distress blaring in her bloodstream from Robin's screams.

'You've got to go out sometimes,' said Max. 'It's getting ridiculous.'

'I'm sorry I didn't manage to make myself look nice,' said Dorrie. '*You* look nice. Anyway, it's four pounds an hour. It's like sitting in a taxi.'

Max was big and warm, sitting relaxed like a sportsman after the game, but his eyes were flinty.

'It's just arrogant, thinking that nobody else can look after them as well as you,' he said.

'They can't,' mumbled Dorrie, under her breath.

'You're a dreadful worrier,' said Max. 'You're always worrying.'

'Well,' said Dorrie. 'Somebody's got to.'

'Everything would carry on all right, you know, if you stopped worrying.'

'No it wouldn't. I wish it would. But it wouldn't.'

Lean and sexually luminous young waiting staff glided gracefully around them.

'Have you chosen,' he said, and while she studied the menu he appraised her worn face, free of make-up except for an unaccustomed and unflattering application of lipstick, and the flat frizz of her untended hair. She was starting to get a double chin, he reflected wrathfully; she had allowed herself to put on more weight. Here he was on his wedding anniversary sitting opposite a fat woman. And if he ever said anything, *she* said, the children. It showed a total lack of respect; for herself; for him.

'I just never seem to get any time to myself,' muttered Dorrie. She felt uneasy complaining. Once she'd stopped bringing in money she knew she'd lost the right to object. So did he.

'It's a matter of discipline,' said Max, sternly.

He felt a terrible restlessness at this time of year, particularly since his fortieth. The birthday cards had all been about being past it. Mine's a pint of Horlicks, jokes about bad backs, expanding waistlines, better in candlelight. There it stretched, all mapped out for him; a long or not-so-long march to the grave; and he was forbidden from looking to left or right. He had to hold himself woodenly impervious, it would seem, since every waking moment was supposed to be a married one. All right for her, she could stun herself with children. But he needed a romantic motive or life wasn't worth living.

He could see the food and drink and television waiting for him at each day's end, and the thickening of middle age, but he was buggered if he was going to let himself go down that route. He watched Dorrie unwisely helping herself to sautéed potatoes. Her body had become like a car to her, he thought, it got her around, it accommodated people at various intervals, but she herself seemed to have nothing to do with it any more. She just couldn't be bothered.

What had originally drawn him to her was the balance between them, a certain tranquil buoyancy she had which had gone well with his own more explosive style. These days she was not so much tranquil as stagnant, while all the buoyancy had been bounced off. He wished he could put a bomb under her. She seemed so apathetic except when she was loving the children. It made him want to boot her broad bottom whenever she meandered past him in the house, just to speed her up.

The children had taken it out of her, he had to admit. She'd had pneumonia after Maxine, her hair had fallen out in handfuls after Robin, there had been two caesareans, plus that operation to remove an ovarian cyst. The saga of her health since babies was like a seaside postcard joke, along with the mothers-in-law and the fat-wife harridans. After that childminder incident involving Martin breaking his leg at the age of two, she'd done bits of part-time but even that had fizzled out soon after Robin, so now she wasn't bringing in any money at all. When he married her, she'd had an interesting job, she'd earned a bit, she was lively and sparky; back in the mists of time. Now he had the whole pack of them on his back and he was supposed to be as philosophical about this as some old leech-gatherer.

He didn't want to hurt her, that was the trouble. He did not want the house to fly apart in weeping and wailing and children who would plead with him not to go, Daddy. He did not want to seem disloyal, either. But, he thought wildly, neither could he bear being sentenced to living death. Things were going to have to be different. She couldn't carry on malingering round the house like this. It wasn't fair. She shouldn't expect. He felt a shocking contraction of pity twist his guts. Why couldn't she bloody well look after herself better? He took a deep breath.

'Did I mention about Naomi,' he said casually, spearing a floret of broccoli.

Naomi was Max's right-hand woman at the builder's yard. She oversaw the stock, manned the till when necessary, sorted the receipts and paperwork for Dorrie to deal with at home and doled out advice about undercoats to the customers. She had been working for them for almost two years.

'Is she well?' asked Dorrie. 'I thought she was looking very white when I saw her last Wednesday.'

'Not only is she not well, she's throwing up all over the place,' said Max heavily. 'She's pregnant,' he added in a muffled voice, stuffing more vegetables into his mouth.

'Pregnant?' said Dorrie. 'Oh!' Tears came to her eyes and she turned to scrabble under the table as if for a dropped napkin. So far she had managed to hide from him her insane lusting after yet another.

'That's what I thought,' sighed Max, misinterpreting her reaction.

'I'm so pleased for her, they've been wanting a baby for ages,' said Dorrie, and this time it was her voice that was muffled.

'So of course I've had to let her go,' said Max, looking at his watch.

'You've *what*?' said Dorrie.

'It's a great shame, of course. I'll have to go through all that with someone else now, showing them the ropes and so on.'

'How *could* you, Max?'

'Look, I knew you'd be like this. I *know*. It's a shame isn't it, yes; but there it is. That's life. It's lucky it happened when it did. Another few weeks and she'd have been able to nail me to the wall, unfair dismissal, the works.'

'But they need the money,' said Dorrie, horrified. 'How are they going to manage the mortgage now?'

'He should pull his finger out then, shouldn't he,' shrugged Max. 'He's public sector anyway, they'll be all right. Look, Dorrie, I've got a wife and children to support.'

'Get her back,' said Dorrie. 'Naomi will be fine. She's not like me, she'll have the baby easily, she won't get ill afterwards, nor will the baby. We were unlucky. She's very capable, she's not soft about things like childminders. You'd be mad to lose her.'

'Actually,' said Max, 'I've offered her a part-time job when she is ready to come back, and I rather think that might suit us better too. If I keep her below a certain number of hours.'

'What did Naomi say to *that*?'

'She was still a bit peeved about being let go,' said Max. 'But she said she'd think about it. If she could combine it with another part-time job. Beggars can't be choosers. I mean, if she chooses to have a baby, that's her choice.'

'I see,' said Dorrie carefully. 'So who will take over her work at the yard meanwhile?'

'Well, you, of course,' said Max, swallowing a big forkful of chop, his eyes bulging. He hurried on. 'Robin starts at nursery after Easter, Maxine's nearly finished there, and Martin's doing fine at school full-time now. So you can work the mornings, then you can collect Robin and Maxine and bring them along for a sandwich and work round them from then till it's time to pick up Martin. We can leave the paperwork till the evening. We'll save all ways like that. He's a big boy now, he can potter around.'

'He's only three and a half,' she said breathlessly. 'And when would I do the meals and the ironing and the cleaning and the shopping in all this?'

'Fit it in round the edges,' said Max. 'Other women do. It'll be good for you, get you out of the house. Come on, Dorrie, I can't carry passengers forever. You'll have to start pulling your weight again.'

It was towards the end of the main course and they had both drunk enough house white to be up near the surface.

'They're hard work, young children, you know,' she said.

'You said yourself they're getting easier every day. You said so yourself. It's not like when they were all at home all day screaming their heads off.'

'It is when they're on holiday,' she said. 'That's nearly twenty weeks a year, you know. What happens *then*?'

'You're off at a tangent again,' he said, sighing, then demanded, 'What *do* you want out of life?'

'It's not some sort of anaconda you've got to wrestle with,' said Dorrie. She realised that this latest sequestration of her hours would send her beside herself. Loss of inner life, that's what it was; lack of any purchase in the outside world, and loss of all respect; continuous unavoidable

Lilliputian demands; numbness, apathy and biscuits. She was at the end of her rope.

'We can't just wait for things to fall into our laps though,' said Max, thinking about his own life.

'We're doing all right,' said Dorrie.

'That doesn't mean to say we couldn't do better. We need to expand.'

'We're managing the mortgage,' said Dorrie. 'I think we should be grateful.'

'That's the spirit,' said Max. 'That's the spirit that made this island great. Stand and stare, eh. Stand and stare.'

'What would you prefer?' said Dorrie. 'Life's a route march, then you die?'

'But then *you've* got what you wanted, haven't you – the children.'

'You are horrible,' said Dorrie. She took a great gulp of wine and drained her glass. 'It's about how well you've loved and how well you've been loved.' She didn't sound very convincing, she realised, in fact she sounded like Thought for the Day. She sounded like some big sheep bleating.

'I don't know what it is, Dorrie,' he said sadly, 'But you're all damped down. You've lost your spirit. You're not there any more.'

'I know. I know. But that's what I'm trying to say. You think I've just turned into a boring saint. But I'm still there. If you could just take them for a few hours now and then and be *nice* to them, if I just had a bit of quiet time . . .'

'I'm not exactly flourishing either, you know. You're getting to me.'

'Sorry. Sorry. I seem to be so dreary these days. But . . .'

'That's what I mean. Such a victim. Makes me want to kick you.'

'Don't Max. Please don't. We've got to go back to that girl and pay her first.'

'Just being miserable and long-suffering, you think that'll make me sorry for you.'

'Max . . .'

'But it makes me hate you, if you must know.'

Back at the house, Max handed Dorrie his wallet and went off upstairs. He was tired as he brushed his teeth, and angry at the way the evening had gone; nor did he like his bad-tempered reflection in the bathroom mirror. Soon he was asleep, frowning in release like a captive hero.

Dorrie meanwhile was fumbling with five-pound notes, enquiring brightly as to whether Jade had had a quiet evening.

'Oh yes, there wasn't a sound out of them once you'd gone,' said Jade, not strictly truthfully, still mesmerised by the beautiful eyes of the sex murderer with the razor on the screen. There had actually been a noise from the boys' bedroom and when she had put her head around the door sure enough the younger one was lying in a pool of sick. But he was breathing fine so she left him to it, it wasn't bothering him and no way was she going to volunteer for that sort of thing. She was getting paid to babysit, not to do stuff like that. That would have been right out of order.

'Would you like to stay and finish your video?' asked Dorrie politely, flinching as she watched the razor slit through filmstar flesh.

'No, that's all right,' said Jade reluctantly. She flicked the remote control and the bloody image disappeared. She sighed.

'Well, thank you again,' said Dorrie. 'It's lovely to know I can leave them with someone I can trust.'

'That's OK' said Jade. 'No problem.' And with a royal yawn she made her exit.

It took Dorrie half an hour or so to bathe the dazed Robin, to wash the acrid curds holding kernels of sweet-corn and discs of peas from his feathery hair and wrap him in clean pyjamas and lay him down in the big bed beside his noble-looking father, where he fell instantly asleep, slumbering on a cloud of beauty.

She kissed his warm face and turned back, her body creaking in protest, to the job in hand. Downstairs in the midnight kitchen she scraped the duvet cover and pillow case with the knife kept specifically for this purpose, dumping the half-digested chyme into the sink, running water to clear it away, then scraping again, gazing out of the window into the blackness of the wild garden, yearning at the spatter of rain on the glass and the big free trees out there with their branches in the sky.

Their needs were what was set. Surely that was the logic of it. It was for *her* to adapt, accommodate, modify in order to allow the familial organism to flourish. Here she was weeping over her own egotism like a novice nun, for goodness sake, except it was the family instead of God. But still it was necessary, selflessness, for a while, even if it made you spat on by the world. By your husband. By your children. By yourself.

She wanted to smash the kitchen window. She wanted to hurt herself. Her ghost was out there in the garden, the ghost from her freestanding past. If she kept up this business of reunion, it would catch hold of her hands and saw her wrists to and fro across the jagged glass. It would tear her from the bosom of this family she had breastfed. No. She must stay this side of the glass from now on, thickening and cooling like some old planet until at last she killed the demands of that self-regarding girl out there.

She twisted and squeezed water from the bedlinen she had just rinsed. If she were to let herself be angry about this obliteration, of her particular mind, of her own relish for things, then it would devour the family. Instead she must let it gnaw at her entrails like some resident tiger. This was not sanctimony speaking but necessity. All this she knew but could not explain. She was wringing the sheet with such force that it creaked.

'Fresh air,' she said aloud, and tried to open the window in front of her. It was locked, clamped tight with one of the antiburglar fastenings which they had fitted on all the windows last summer. She felt around in the cupboard above the refrigerator for the key, but it wasn't in its usual place. She hunted through the rows of mugs, the tins of tuna and tomatoes, the bags of rice and flour and pasta, and found it at last inside the glass measuring jug.

Leaning across the sink she unlocked the window and opened it onto the night. A spray of rain fell across her face and she gasped. There was the cold fresh smell of wet earth. It occurred to her that this might not necessarily be killer pain she was feeling, not terrible goodbyeforever pain as she had assumed; and she felt light-headed with the shock of relief.

Perhaps this was not the pain of wrist-cutting after all. Instead, the thought came to her, it might be the start of that intense outlandish sensation that comes after protracted sleep; the feeling in a limb that has gone numb, when blood starts to flow again, sluggishly at first, reviving; until after a long dormant while that limb is teeming again, tingling into life.

Out in the garden, out in the cold black air, she could see the big trees waving their wild bud-bearing branches at her.

Burns and the Bankers

They were sitting down at last. There were over a thousand of them. All that breath and flesh meant the air beneath the chandeliers had very soon climbed to blood heat despite the dark sparkle of frost outside on Park Lane. An immense prosperous hum filled the hotel ballroom, as if all the worker bees of the British Isles were met to celebrate industriousness.

Nicola Beaumont used her tartan-ribboned menu to fan herself. The invitation had said six-thirty, so she had dashed straight from Ludgate Hill, having changed in literally two minutes in the Ladies, after a meeting with Counsel which had stretched out far too long; at the end of a day which had started with an eight o'clock meeting; with heels, earrings and lipstick going on in the back of the cab here; only to find that they were expected to stand around drinking alcohol for over an hour. And she'd somehow forgotten to prepare herself for the inevitable Caledonian overkill, all these sporrans and dirks and coy talk of the lassies.

Big Dougal was down from Edinburgh for the occasion, she'd noted, encircled by a servile coterie of younger men. She had been standing near enough to hear fragments of the incredibly circumlocutory anecdote with which he was, as he would no doubt have put it, regaling them. '. . . And that young gentleman, desirous of purchasing a property not a million miles away from the aforementioned office in Dumfries, then found himself embroiled in negotiations of a not entirely shall we say *salubrious* nature . . .'

Oh what windbags the Scots are, thought Nicola, she always forgot in between, but what blowhard old windbags they are really. Look at these young men smiling like stiff-necked nutcrackers, the ricti of slavish mirth baring their teeth. It was a terrible thing, ambition; or, as Dougie would doubtless have put it, the desire for advancement. She herself had climbed the greasy pole a while back, she had been a full partner for six years now, so that slavish part of it was behind her, thank heavens; although of course the business of winning and pleasing clients was ongoing. That was why she was here now holding a tumbler of whisky – how she hated whisky, the stink of it, the rubbish they talked about it. But this was an important anniversary year for the Federation of Caledonian Bankers and they had decided to mark it by bringing together senior staff, clients and professional advisers for a mega-Burns Night.

She turned towards another group. Here, a lawyer she knew who had recently been made a partner at Clarence Sweets was talking to the head leasing partner at Iddon Featherstone, each with a black-tied husband at her elbow.

'But is he good with them at weekends?' the Clarence Sweets woman was eagerly demanding. 'Hands on, I mean.'

'Oh yes, he takes them swimming,' said the head leasing partner. 'Out on their bikes.' She shrugged. 'Though of course he's usually working at weekends.'

The husbands under discussion gazed into their tumblers of whisky like wordless children. Each of the four standing there had that day crammed twelve hours' worth of work into ten in order to attend this banquet, and the whisky was hitting stomachs which had long since forgotten the snatched midday sandwich.

No, I do not want to compare nightmare journey times to the Suzuki session, thought Nicola, whose four-year-old twins went to the same violin teacher as the Clarence Sweets woman's daughter, somewhere out in Surrey, every Saturday. She scanned the packed room and caught sight of her husband Charlie on the other side, arriving late. He was looking stockier than ever. All that flying he'd had to do in the last year hadn't helped, she thought; six or seven times a month recently, including Japan and Australia. Not good for the waistline. Not good for the heart.

By the time she'd threaded her way across through the crowd, Torquil Cameron had got his mitts on Charlie. That was sharp of him, to remember him from Goodwood.

'A-*ha*,' smiled Torquil above his frilly jabot, then he bowed from the hips in that way men do in kilts, the better to show off his pleats, the swing of them. 'Delighted you could be here, Nicola. As you can see I've located your other half for you. Now I don't think you've met my own good lady wife, Jean.' Jean stood by him, the colour of a brick, free of make-up, in her fifties and a girlish white ballgown with a plaid sash athwart her bosom.

She smiled at Nicola, who was wearing a black crêpe trousersuit, and her eyes showed disapproval mixed with shyness and fear.

'So, Nicola!' boomed Torquil. 'When was it exactly, the last time we had the pleasure of seeing you up in Auld Reekie?'

'Oh, not long ago, I think,' smiled Nicola, wondering why he had to be so ponderous. 'It was October, wasn't it? There was that day of meetings about the Yellow Target business. You took us all out for a good lunch at the Witchery, I seem to remember.'

'That's right, that's right!' crowed Torquil as though delighted and relieved. He turned to Charlie. 'You'll be looking forward to your haggis then?' he enquired. Charlie smiled wanly.

Following this welcome there had been an interminable stretch of time during which the thousand guests drifted slow as plankton past the seating plan and from there down the huge staircase into the ballroom.

'The things I do for you,' Charlie had muttered as they shuffled down the stairs.

'I sat through *Die* mostincrediblyboringold *Meistersinger* only last week for your lot,' she had reminded him. 'Four hours.'

'This'll be longer.'

'And *Orpheus and Eurydice* the week before.'

'That was *short*.'

'You'll be all right,' she had said crossly. 'Lots of whisky.'

'Did Harry make it into the team, d'you know?'

'As a reserve.'

Charlie had given a vexed snort.

'That boy. He's perfectly capable of it. He just doesn't try.'

'He said he missed the shot which would have got him a place. Just bad luck. He's very disappointed.'

'So he should be.'

Their lives were both so busy that times of idleness alone together like this, on the staircase in a queue, were few and far between. They had over the years developed a breezy shorthand for talking about their four children, for exchanging vital information and intimate views as economically as possible, rather like a couple of fighter pilots crewing the same Mosquito.

Nicola had an extraordinarily retentive memory, which was invaluable not only in the practice of law but also at this sort of event, as she could memorise the seating plan and prime herself to ask the right questions about the various sporting activities and children of the clients involved. She was excellent on names and faces. So, as she and Charlie had made their slow way down, her mental picture had been as follows:

Susan Buchanan
Stay-at-home. Winsome.
Vegetarian. Three boys
under six.

Brian Mahon
Fifty-something. In Structured
Finance at Bank of Hibernia.
Tennis, squash.
Originally Belfast.
Heavy drinker.
Nice eyes.

Charlie Beaumont
Senior executive at
Schnell-Darwittersbank.
Mustn't get too drunk,
please.

Lily Forfar
Unknown quantity.

Deborah Mahon
Three girls, all grown up.
Hospital visiting. Bridge.
Ealing. Portugal.

Iain Buchanan
Glaswegian *émigré*.
London branch of Bank of
Alba. Lanky, hyper. Golf,
football, supports Partick
Thistle (cue football banter).
Heavy drinker.

Donald Forfar
Unknown quantity.
Doing well in the
heavy-hitting Edinburgh
branch of Bank of Alba.
Possible future work here;
currently with Clarence
Sweets but they
messed up a big case
for him last year.
Golf?

Nicola Beaumont
Partner at Littleboy & Pringle.

The table was bristling with slim silver vases of orchids
and bottles of wine standing ready uncorked before forests
of glasses and napkins pleated into white cockades and
even little silver-plated quaichs, one each engraved with a
guest's name, the date and the crest of the Caledonian
Banking Federation.

'Well, Iain,' said Nicola to the man seated on her left.
'This is all very impressive.'

'And it hasn't even started yet,' said Iain. 'Here, let me pour you a glass. White or red? Have you been to a Burns Night before? No, well, there are a lot of speeches I can warn you, so you'll be glad of a glass in front of you.'

'Cheers,' said Nicola, who knew this man slightly and liked him, his sharpness and frankness.

'*Slanjiva*,' he replied, or something like it.

She was aware of Donald Forfar on her right, a strong thick-set presence, the sort of build that looked good in a kilt. Whereas tall lean men like Iain Buchanan were far better off in jeans. She was about to turn and introduce herself but then Iain was tapping her arm.

'Here's Torquil Cameron now,' he said, directing her gaze towards the top table on its platform hundreds of metres away from them. 'He'll be giving the welcome and he'll take his time because he's a big balloon, but then he'll say grace and we can all get started.'

'Oh good,' said Nicola.

It was very hot. She picked up the menu to fan herself, and her mind stretched back through the packed day. Every minute had been spoken for. Her chargeable hours were on target so far this year but it was a constant battle. She hadn't managed a full half-hour with the children this morning; it couldn't be helped but it made her feel a bit sick considering she was out tonight again for the second time this week and it was only Wednesday. Jade was so sarcastic these days but she liked the benefits, the good school, the nice holidays. She, Nicola, would make up that twenty-minute shortfall, she would squeeze it in somehow tomorrow.

She took a sip of wine and immediately the alcohol rose up behind her face to somewhere at eyebrow level and she thought, that's hit the spot. The one thing all us hard-working and often successful people can't have, she realised as she gazed around her at the sea of heated faces, is TIME. She took another sip and felt a number of tiny muscles in her shoulders relax like a sigh. That's it, she decided. Water from now on or I'll never last.

It made her crisp with irritation, that she could have arrived half an hour later and no harm done. But that's the deal, she reminded herself. She had always to be thinking ahead. That was what she had to do. She was unable to sit inside the minute; it was a joke in their family that she couldn't sit still. She had a beautiful house and she was never in it. She knew what the children were doing at every hour of the day, and she wasn't there. She kept it all up in the air, she never lost her grip. So much so that it would be positively dangerous for her to relax. If she were to let go it didn't bear thinking about, the fall-out.

The waiters were moving in massed ranks across the floor, bearing soup to the tables while Torquil Cameron carried on. He was paying lip service to Burns now.

'And where, ladies and gentlemen,' boomed Torquil Cameron, 'Where would we be without poetry?'

Nicola caught Charlie's eye across the table and smothered a giggle. She glanced at other faces and saw the pained expressions of piety, as though God had been mentioned, or cancer.

The moment passed. Poetry! thought Nicola. That's all we need. Doubtless some Scot would start spouting Burns later and it was in dialect if she remembered rightly. Wee sleekit cowrin timrous beastie. As the man boomed on, she became aware of an unfamiliar feeling: boredom. Of course one ought to be able to make these dead patches of time work for one. She had friends who recommended meditation techniques for just such occasions. Om, wasn't it. Or was it visualise a beach. Which reminded her, she *must* get that cheque off to Better Villas asap.

At last the big balloon had finished. Now he was announcing grace, and they all had to bow their heads over their soup bowls.

> Some hae meat that canna eat,
> And some wad eat that want it;
> But we hae meat, and we can eat,
> And sae the Lord be thankit.

Then the hubbub started up again and there was the chinking of a thousand spoons as they tackled their Cullen Skink.

Nicola glanced around their table. She realised with relief that, so great was the noise, she would not be obliged to talk to anyone beyond Iain Buchanan on her left and this other man on her right. Iain's wife Susan, directly opposite, was giving Charlie the sparrow's bright look askance, while he smiled falsely back. Susan was smart and chirpy, as Nicola remembered, but not very deep. Also she was a full-time mother of the sort who drew their skirts away when Nicola approached, while exuding a neediness to freeze the cockles of your heart. This man Iain on her left was working all the hours of the day and night, Nicola happened to know, as he badly wanted to be made deputy head of the branch, and that move was still a good year off.

On the other side of Charlie was Deborah Mahon, a vaguely smiling woman of fifty-five or fifty-six, who had not earned any money for over thirty years. She had had a front-of-house job in the bank for a little while before she got married, back in the mists of time, when she was still in her decorative early twenties, and since then had stayed indoors to look after her husband and three demanding, confident and ambitious daughters, the youngest of whom had just started university.

Nicola knew how the talk went at this kind of mixed do with spouses. The men would address the women beside them with bored chivalry, feeding them brief obvious questions about their children or their house or their little part-time jobs and then the women would chat on, working away at keeping the conversational bonfire alight, pulling more than their weight in an exchange which really was nineteen to the dozen. But she herself was not one of these women. She had a foot in both camps. Not only had she borne four children but she also earned as much as her husband and more than Iain Buchanan. So she would be able to talk with the men about money and the new Japanese restaurant near Gracechurch Street and – barring sport, of course – things that really interested them. Still she wore high heels and earrings and noticed that this man on her right, Donald Forfar, was quite appealing in a solid saturnine sort of way.

'"The Selkirk Grace",' he said, waving his soup spoon at her. 'So called because Robert Burns repeated those lines when he dined with the Earl of Selkirk. Although the fact of the matter is, he didn't write them, they were around well before he was born and were known as "The Covenanter's Grace".'

'How interesting,' said Nicola; and then, in case that sounded satirical, 'I love Scotland but I've never been to Selkirk,' which was inane but somehow less hostile.

'Unfortunately my wife has just gone down with the flu,' said Donald Forfar, when Nicola enquired about her absence. She herself never got ill. Apart from three months' maternity leave around each of her labours, she had never taken a day off sick. Touch wood.

It turned out that Donald was a fan of Robert Burns. He was reading a new biography of Burns at the moment.

'Oh dear,' said Nicola, whose busy life did not allow for this although she always read at least two books when they went away on holiday and one of her New Year's resolutions had been to join a Book Club. 'I really must read more.'

'But as a pleasure,' smiled Donald. 'You make it sound like a duty.'

Yes well, thought Nicola. The packed quality of her life meant that it was physically, mentally, impossible for her to sit inside the minute like a thin-skinned raindrop proud on a nasturtium leaf, impossible for her to sit still and read a book. Her nights were necessarily short and her sleep was a dreamless passing out. No drowsing in the morning was possible, ever.

Iain Buchanan was leaning forwards now to talk to Donald Forfar.

'That's right, we moved six months ago,' he was saying.

'It's a mansion, so I've heard,' said Donald Forfar. 'Acres of green sward.'

'Och, it's nice for Susan and the boys to have a bit of a garden to run around in,' said Iain. 'They love the tennis court. Talking of which. You know Roderick MacKenzie? Excuse me, Nicola. Perhaps you know him too? Investments at the Lombard Street branch of the Bank of Auld Scotia?'

'Married to Lucy MacKenzie over at Leviathan?'

'That's the one. Dropped down dead during a game of tennis, the day after Boxing Day. Heart attack.'

'Yes. Four children. Shocking.'

'He was from Aberdeen originally, wasn't he?'

'I thought she was Irish.'

'No, no, she's English. Very English.'

'And what is this?' said Brian Mahon, leaning across the space left by Donald Forfar's absent wife, peering across Iain Buchanan and joining in. 'Are we now reduced to comparing the English, the Irish and the Scots? Is that the game?' He looked fairly drunk already, his colour high and his eyes blue as the sea.

'Donald was just saying how industrious us Scots are compared to the feckless feckin Irish,' said Iain. 'And how we carry our drink better too.'

'Don't listen to them, now, Nicola,' said Brian, turning his dark-fringed blue gaze on her. 'We have the better poetry and music. What's Burns to Yeats?'

'We've got Shakespeare,' said Nicola, but they ignored her.

'The Irish,' said Iain. 'Not to put too fine a point on it, are no so gifted in the intellectual department.'

'The Scots are always thinking of number one, Nicola,' said Brian. 'It's impossible for a Scotsman to fall in love.'

'Och aye, that describes Robert Burns perfectly,' hooted Iain.

'Nature over nurture,' mused Donald Forfar. It was rather sweet, thought Nicola, the way he spoke like a schoolmaster. 'He was steeped in the disciplines of survival and repression,' he continued, 'but still the poetry in him triumphed.'

'Education,' declared Iain, swirling his whisky glass then sniffing it. 'Application. They're the reason why Scotland's best.'

At the mention of education, Nicola began to salivate like Pavlov's dog, and was just preparing to quiz these men about the schools their children attended when she was deflected by Brian Mahon.

'Scots on the make,' he scoffed. 'That's what they do, Nicola, they emigrate as soon as they can in order to better themselves, even if it's only down south to Guildford like Iain here, then they lecture anyone who'll bear it on the virtues of the auld country.'

'Of course Scotland stayed with the traditional teaching methods at the time England abandoned them,' mused Donald Forfar. 'And the presence of an educated working class has meant we have a more genuinely democratic society than the English in consequence.'

'Donald went to Fettes,' said Iain Buchanan drily.

'Oh, *Fettes!*' said Nicola, riveted.

Before she could cross-question him about old school-mates, however, she was interrupted by someone in a kilt shouting for them all to stand for the arrival of the haggis. She glanced at her watch during the general upheaval this involved. Gone nine. The twins would have been asleep for over an hour. Then there was an awful whining noise as a piper threaded his way through the tables, followed by a chef carrying something beige on a silver plate, then a third play actor holding a bottle of whisky aloft in each hand. These three certainly took their time, apparently pacing themselves by the slow handclap that accompanied them to the top table.

'Will you look there, Donald,' said Iain Buchanan, craning to see the hefty old Scot rising to his feet on the top table's dais as the rest of the room sat down again. 'It's old Shoogie Henderson who'll be giving the address to the haggis. He was in with the bricks right enough. When's he due to retire, d'you think?'

'He's past sixty,' said Donald, pouring whisky into the little silver quaichs and passing them round the table.

'That's the trouble with this organisation,' fumed Iain, tipping the contents of his quaich into his mouth. 'Nae movement. Blocked at the top.'

'I prefer the Tamdhu,' said Donald. 'The Speyside malt is softer.'

Iain's face was redder than it had been an hour ago. He held his quaich out for a refill. He was at that crucial age, somewhere around thirty-seven or thirty-eight, when his work life must either take off very soon with the rocket fuel of promotion and increased power, or stick for good in a rut until retirement age.

Up at the crackling microphone Shoogie Henderson cleared his resented old throat, and some sort of hush crept by degrees across the huge room. Then, in the manner of Father Christmas, he read:

Fair fa' your honest, sonsie face,
Great Chieftain o'the Puddin-race!
Aboon them a' ye tak your place,
Painch, tripe, or thairm:
Weel are ye worthy of a grace
As lang's my airm.

And it was as lang as his airm, too. On and on it went, incomprehensible to Nicola, and smug and ridiculous.

'His knife see Rustic-labour dight,' continued old Shoogie with relish, 'An' cut you up wi' ready sleight . . .'

He paused and smiled at the kilted loon beside him, who seized a knife and plunged it histrionically into the haggis. A cheer went up.

'What exactly is in it?' asked Nicola, as a plate of tweedy brownish morsels was placed in front of her.

'Och, it's just a sausage,' said Donald, brushing her arm as he reached for the whisky. 'But they use the stomach bag as casing rather than the more usual intestinal tubing.'

'But what's *in* it?' said Nicola, meeting his eyes, which were like black glass and slightly hooded. 'I want to know what it's made of.'

'The liver, lights and windpipe of a sheep,' said Donald, glittering at her.

'Right,' said Nicola. 'Thank you.'

'Over here with the tatties and neeps,' Iain Buchanan sang out to a waiter.

On every table Nicola could see men in kilts smacking their lips and going for seconds. She tasted a scrap of haggis and found it both mealy and salty. An ocean of alcohol was being drained in nips and sips and gulps, in a steamingly hot room on a thousand empty stomachs. Faces were red and damp, and drastically split with laughter. The noise was tremendous. It was almost ten o'clock, Nicola saw with another covert glance at her watch, and they weren't even on the main course, the haggis being in the nature of an entrée as far she could tell.

'Here we are, Nicola,' said Iain Buchanan as a bevy of Scottish country dancers trooped onto the raised square platform in the middle of the room. 'Here comes the heedrum hodrum. Listen out for the noise they make. One or the other of them will give a wee hooch now and then to show their particular enjoyment.'

'I've not seen dancing at a Burns Supper before,' mused Donald. 'It's obviously no expense spared tonight.'

The young dancers were a sad, odd-looking crew, and the platform shook as they leaped and jumped. Hi-yeuch! they went in a scrubbed desperate way, baring their teeth brightly and panting. It was almost as sexless as Irish dancing, thought Nicola, with the upper body having nothing to do with the rest, as if some radical divorce went on at hip level. She looked around her. All this archness and stiffness and verbosity! You shuddered to think of bedtime.

She eyed her table, which had temporarily given up on conversation because of the heedrum hodrum, and considered the men. Charlie was still a main contender, though he must have put on twenty pounds since the summer. Iain wasn't bad-looking but for some reason he came nowhere. Tolerable, she smiled to herself, but not handsome enough to tempt *me*. Brian Mahon now, although well into his fifties, was obviously still interested, whereas his wife, just as obviously, had the dusty look of one who has no desires of her own. No, it would have to be this man Donald Forfar, he was definitely the favourite, although his thick black hair looked worryingly turfy. She was fascinated by the way the shadow on his jaw was growing darker as the evening progressed. At this rate he'd have a beard by midnight. He had drawn his chair out a little in order to watch the dancing and Nicola was able to steal a look at his stout calves in their woolly knee socks, and at his big bare knees.

The meal dragged on, through warm sliced meat then some sort of muesli concoction until at last they reached the coffee stage. Not long now, thought Nicola, unwrapping a mint. It was a nasty shock, then, when Donald, turning a genial eye upon her, declared, 'Now at last the evening proper can begin!'

'But that business before the haggis,' faltered Nicola, 'that poem, wasn't that *it?*'

'No, no,' laughed Donald. 'The heart of a Burns Night is the Immortal Memory. Someone has to make a speech in praise of Burns, and that's what it's called – the Immortal Memory.'

'Look who's giving it tonight,' crowed Brian Mahon from further up the table. 'It's Rory McCrindle. Have you seen his place in Farnham? Tartan sofas, tartan carpets, views of the heather-covered highlands. It's like Rob Roy's Cave.'

'Nothing to Iain's mansion in Guildford, so I've been told,' said Donald. 'I hear it has a swimming pool, Iain; am I right?'

I'm not sure I'll be able to last through this, thought Nicola. I've had enough. Across the table, Charlie winked at her. He looked red and pie-eyed. A few minutes earlier she had heard him ask their waiter for more walt misky. No help from that quarter, she thought, wondering how she would get him home.

'And this Immortal Memory event,' said Nicola. 'Roughly how, er, *long* does it tend to go on?'

'Och, the Immortal Memory is only the start of it,' said Iain. 'Don't worry. You'll love it.'

'The Immortal Memory is a moral dose of salts,' said Donald. 'Once a year you listen to the story of Burns' life and poetry, then you examine your own life in the light of his. It's an improving speech, Nicola.'

'So he's like a saint?' said Nicola.

'Not exactly a saint,' said Donald.

'A man's a man for a' that,' burst in Iain.

'The social, friendly, honest man,' rolled out Donald, 'Whate'er he be.'

'For a' that,' said Iain again.

'Yes, the English all know bits of Shakespeare,' said Nicola. 'To be or not to be, is this a dagger which I see before me. But we don't try to copy his life, leaving Anne Hathaway in the lurch. With twins, too.'

'Oor Rab had mair twins than Shakespeare,' said Iain aggressively. 'He had them coming oot his ears.'

'No, Nicola, it's the litany of his life which has taken hold,' said Donald. 'Barefoot, boxbed, homespun, peat fires by which he listened to Old Betty's ghost stories, hard labour on father's failing farm from age of seven. They were poor but they were happy. See "The Cotter's Saturday Night" which is the great Scottish Family Values poem.'

'Aye one for the lassies, but,' said Iain.

'Oh, aye one for the lassies,' agreed Donald with a nasal

whine of mock–disapprobation. 'Enough babies fathered to get him denounced from the kirk pulpit and make him consider sailing for Jamaica . . . But in the nick of time a publisher takes up his collection of dialect poems and they are a huge hit with everyone buying them from the crème de la crème of Edinburgh society . . .'

'Like your good self, Donald,' remarked Iain.

'. . . From the literati in Edinburgh to the farm labourers and maidservants for miles around,' continued Donald mildly. 'Highland Mary dies in childbirth, his wean of course . . .'

'But he married Bonny Jean thingwy, right enough,' said Iain.

'Yes, he marries faithful Jean Armour, mother of nine of his children . . .'

'Oh, that's why the pudding was called Jean's Brose,' interrupted Nicola. 'That muesli thing.'

'. . . Fails at farming, gets a job as an exciseman, gets ill,' continued Donald. 'Dies aged thirty-seven.'

'Thirty-seven!' exclaimed Nicola. 'Shakespeare was over fifty.'

'Burns had more *twins*, though,' insisted Iain.

'Not only that, Nicola,' Donald continued, 'But the Immortal Memory will be built round one of several well-worn themes.'

'Burns Mark One,' cut in Iain. 'The Ploughman Poet.'

'"To a mountain daisy, on turning one down with a plough",' said Donald. 'Burns Mark Two, the Lover. Aye one for the lassies, heh heh. O my luve's like a red red rose. Burns Mark Three, the convivial man . . .'

'. . . Burns was nae an alkie,' glossed Iain. 'Enjoyed a wee dram with his friends but did not get regularly paralettic.'

'We are na fou, we're nae that fou,' quoted Donald.

'And so on,' said Iain with an air of resignation, pouring more whisky. 'But look, McCrindle's on his way up to the microphone.'

It was not really possible to see the man, so far away was the top table. He was a tartan ant in a tartan formicary.

'Of course, Burns was — not to put too fine a point on it — a *peasant*,' came his amplified voice.

'Burns Mark One,' hissed Donald and Iain each side of her, one in each ear.

She turned off, as she did when she had to sit through an opera. She decided to regard this as relaxation time. Looking across the table at Charlie she felt relief again at not having to talk to the wives. She knew their type, particularly Brian Mahon's wife, the older one, whose eye she caught for a moment before looking away. Oh yes, that one had a look that said, 'You, with your four-wheel drive and your greedy ways. I don't know why you bother to have children if you don't look after them.'

She tuned into Rory McCrindle to see how it was going.

'As teenagers Burns and his young friends formed a club, the Tarbolton Bachelors,' he announced with laborious pleasure. 'The rules laying down no admittance to snobs — here I quote — "*and especially no mean-spirited, worldly mortal, whose only will is to heap up money*".'

A ripple of laughter swept through the room like a gust of wind in a barleyfield.

'"*Why is the bard unfitted for the world*",' he continued, '"*yet has so keen a relish of its pleasures?*"'

Well, quite, thought Nicola. Absolutely. There was her daughter Jade insisting that she didn't want a life like hers, but where did she think it all came from? Her latest talk was of being an events organiser, of how she was going to have a portfolio career and lots of fun. Just to irritate Nicola (Nicola felt sure) she wore a T-shirt with a slogan across her breasts – 'ALL OF THIS and my dad's loaded too'. Would she really rather be like that woman, Brian Mahon's wife, whose high point of the year was probably masterminding her fifties-style turkey-and-sprouts family Christmas? Whereas she, Nicola, had been able to deal with the festive season by sweeping the whole lot off to Lapland. Granted it had been a nightmare to pack for with the nanny back up to Sheffield on Christmas Eve, then Chloe had broken the little finger on her left hand slipping on a patch of ice at Rovaniemi airport, but still it had been *amazing*. All that snow, and the children had adored the sleigh ride with Santa's elves.

Now he was quoting from one of the ploughman poet's letters. "*If miry ridges and dirty dunghills are to engross the best part of my soul immortal, I had better been a rook or a magpie and then I should not have been plagued with any ideas superior to the breaking of clods and picking up of grubs.*"

Home was a wasteland during the week anyway as she'd discovered during her maternity leaves, just nannies or women like Deborah Mahon for company. Your eyes went dull inside three days, your thighs turned to Turkish Delight, you put on half a stone a week. She loved her children more than life itself (forced as one was into Goneril-and-Regan hyperbole), and so did Charlie in his way; but, like him, she preferred to subcontract out much of the work of parenthood. She had a wonderful nanny, worth her weight in gold, she'd had her for four years now and dreaded to think what would happen when she left.

Burns was exchanging the dirty dunghills of Mossgiel for lionisation in the drawing rooms of Edinburgh, where his delight in educated talk sat painfully alongside his contempt for hereditary privilege. She could feel it all around her, history, these chaps, their wives, waiting to drive her back indoors. But, like Burns in the Edinburgh drawing rooms, she would not be intimidated; she had considered her position and thought out where she stood on this one.

When Nicola was a child, her mother had existed in a maroon cloud of rage and frustration. If ever the guiltwagon comes within five miles of me now, she thought, I remember that cloud and shout with relief. She hadn't exactly been born with a silver spoon in her mouth but the eleven plus had allowed her into the game. She had stretched and competed and done well. Minutes became meaningful units, hours added up to something. Then came the children and working for a partnership, and all her time management skills had come into their own.

Sometimes the stay-at-home mothers tried to pick her brains about the best schools for their daughters. Why bother? she wanted to say, Why bother flogging them over exam hurdles if your girls are going to end up like you, sipping coffee in between school runs? And of course there were no men at home during the days – they sped off early to be where the action was. To work. To make money.

Rory McCrindle was winding up his Immortal Memory with a few lofty homiletic insights. 'That human decency and human worth have for the most part their dwelling among the poor he had a perception more constant, more pressing and more experienced than any other man of his epoch,' he intoned.

I don't buy that old idea of poverty being a virtue, thought Nicola. What's *wrong* with money? Money's good for people. That she should earn her living had been an article of faith. She hadn't slaved at her exams and said no to fun for all those years of torts and statutes, just for something to pass the time until she started a family. What a waste of government money, for a start. And she couldn't take a couple of years off. *No.* She'd be dead in the water. She wouldn't be allowed back in.

Also, they *needed* her money. It would be too dangerous to rely on Charlie's income alone with job security as it was. It took an incredible amount to keep the show on the road, what with the mortgage and childcare, not to mention Charlie's alimony payments to the dreaded Joanne. She felt many years old for an instant, a hard-worked horse. 'Driven' was the adjective that had always been applied to her, usually as a compliment, but –

Her thoughts were interrupted by a sudden pandemonium of scraping chairs and shouts of 'Rabbie!' and 'Rabbie Burns!' as all around her people rose to their feet, tossing back the contents of their quaichs with stagey bravado. An emotional wave of applause followed. These hard-working cautious bankers and their like had been moved to the edge of tears by this account, familiar to them all, of the poet's reckless, penurious life and of his death made fearful by the terror of debt.

★   ★   ★

'I hear there was a fair bit of trouble over planning the speeches,' said Donald, sipping his way towards incaution. 'Apparently Alistair Wallace, he's the head of the Aberdeen branch, well he was the obvious choice to give the Toast to the Lassies.'

'Toast to the *Lassies*?' said Nicola disdainfully.

'Yes, the Toast to the Lassies usually comes directly after the Immortal Memory, but because of the numbers involved tonight they have to take things a wee bit slower to allow for the food to be served and taken away and so on.'

'Why Alistair Wallace?' asked Iain. 'Why not a younger man? Though *most* of us are younger than Alistair Wallace. It wouldnae be difficult to be younger than Alistair Wallace.'

'His Toast to the Lassies has been in demand with Burns Societies all along the East Coast for the past thirty years,' said Donald. 'He's a local hero. But when it finally came to the run-through down in London, much to everybody's dismay his famous speech was obviously impossible. Offensive. Sexist.'

'Oh, not that P.C. stuff again,' said Iain in disgust.

'You could see where the problem lay,' brooded Donald. 'Your average traditional Burns Supper, it's nearly all men that go along. The wives stay at home. It's a wee bit Masonic, if you like. And of course the organiser of this big Caledonian Federation anniversary event realised in the nick of time that mibbe half the guests here tonight were likely to be female. Things would have to be updated.'

'So what did they do?' asked Nicola, intrigued despite herself. She loved management issues.

'Well, they couldn't drop Alistair altogether, that would have been offensive too. He'd never have understood, and neither would his fans. So they decided to shunt him into a less controversial slot, the Reply to the Immortal Memory. That's usually just a brief vote of thanks if it's included at all. And he was requested to keep the obscenities to a minimum.'

'Oh great,' said Iain angrily. 'The classic sense-of-humour failure. That's great.'

'Not when you think about it,' Donald demurred. 'You can see their point. It would have been like asking an audience where half the guests were black to sit and laugh at racist jokes. You wouldn't call that a sense-of-humour failure.'

'That's different,' growled Iain. 'Anyway, who *will* be giving the Toast to the Lassies now?'

'They found an academic with an interest in Scottish Literature,' shrugged Donald. 'Birkbeck College, I think it was.'

'Oh how super, an *academic*,' said Iain. 'Are they bringing back that Talisker then?'

'Is this the man who's been causing all the trouble?' asked Nicola.

'The very one,' said Donald, craning his neck towards the top table.

This controversial old speaker Alistair Wallace rattled out anecdotes in thick hawking gutturals. Nicola's ears took in about half of what he said, while for the rest of it she sat with the strained expression of one who is hard of hearing. I can't believe the time, she thought; we're never going to be allowed home. His voice was like artillery, and his tone was brutal, laconic, almost East European she decided; although there was also something purely Scottish in its blend of romantic stoicism. As far as she could tell, his speech had had nothing at all to do with Burns. At least it didn't go on as long as the one before. Now it was drawing to a close with a joke for the bankers.

"'Och, this way of life is all fine and dandy," says Angus to his friend Gavin. "The money's fine, the job's great, but I find the stress is getting to me. I get that hyped up sometimes I don't know what to do with myself."

"'You know fine well that's an occupational hazard in jobs like ours, big hitters in the City," says Gavin. "Big swinging dicks as we are. I'll tell you what I do when I get that way myself, when I get stressed out. When I get like that, first opportunity occurs, I drive back to my house, kiss the wife at the front door, take her upstairs to the bedroom. And half an hour later I'm right as rain. Feeling like a million dollars. Ready to get back into the fray. You should try it."

"'Well," says Angus. "Thanks for the tip. It certainly seems to work for you."'

The men were sniggering quietly over their whisky. Susan Buchanan had her head cocked on one side to listen, like a bright-eyed sparrow, while Deborah Mahon had assumed her vague all-purpose smile. Nicola regarded the grin on her husband's tired grey face. Charlie was still her darling, but he wasn't exactly Young Lochinvar any more.

'A week later,' the speaker continued, 'Angus and Gavin meet again. "You're looking much better, Angus," cries Gavin. "You're looking years younger, relaxed, not a care in the world." "Thanks to you," smiles Angus. "I took your advice. Next time I felt stressed out I drove back to the house. Knocked at the door. Kissed the wife. Took her upstairs to the bedroom. Half an hour later, right as rain. Just as you said. She was a bit surprised at first, your good lady, but after I explained it was you that had sent me round she was fine about it.'"

The enormous room erupted. All around, hot red faces were disintegrating into guffaws and whinnying. Nicola smiled politely and felt a shudder run through her.

Stress! She could handle it. She positively enjoyed jumping in its salty waves. The danger was, you got *too* good at it. You started to see time that was not paid time – chargeable hours – as dead time; unprofitable; unless it was directly recuperative – the gym, for example, twice a week to keep up this level of energy – servicing the machine. There was of course another rhythm, the rhythm of children and old people, being patient, watching the grass grow; but she couldn't see herself doing that for another thirty years at least. She didn't *want* to take it easy. She was young, or at least in the prime of life; she loved stirring productive movement. Stillness just didn't do it for her.

And why is it always down to me, thought Nicola, this talk of having it all and so on? I took the top first in my year. I'm cleverer than him though I don't rub it in. We have four children. But there's no question of him adapting his hours to the family or helping manage the nanny and the house and all that *that* involves. There is never for one moment a suggestion that Charlie should budge.

To be fair, he never suggested she stop working either.

*   *   *

'Iain, it's gone eleven,' said Nicola. 'I don't want to sound rude but I'm wondering about the babysitter.'

'There's a way to go yet. You can't hurry a Burns Night. You shouldnae worry, your sitter will be fine, she'll be asleep in front of the telly.'

'It's true,' said Donald. 'There is no getting round it. You might as well enjoy it. Would you like another glass?'

'No thank you,' said Nicola, not smiling.

She must be the only person in the room who wasn't drunk. How much more of this Burns stuff could there possibly be?

'Here we are, Nicola,' said Iain. 'Here's the Toast to the Lassies about to start. Here's the *academic*. Now we're in for a treat.'

As it happened, this next speech was so direct and affecting that Nicola found herself listening with all her attention for the first time.

The poet's mother Agnes had been the eldest of six, and when she was ten her mother had died, first telling Agnes that she must look after her little brothers and sisters. Not much later Agnes was courted by a ploughman, the two of them working daily together in the fields; but then, after seven years of this, she found him with another woman and finished with him. On the rebound she married William Burns, a tenant-farmer years older than herself. Their eldest son Robert did not inherit his mother's strict ideal of fidelity. He described himself as having a tinder heart always alight for some girl or other.

Famously there was Highland Mary, Mary Campbell, with whom he joined hands under the current of the brook where they met in a private marriage pledge, and who died in childbirth with his baby about the time Jean Armour was having his twins. Then there was May Cameron, a servant girl, and Jenny Clow, and Agnes McLehose (his Clarinda) in Edinburgh, and Anna Park, barmaid at the Dumfries Globe, who bore his daughter Betty nine days before Jean presented him with his third son.

Thank God I live in an age of contraception, thought Nicola. Of all the blessings of the modern world, that must be the greatest.

It was Jean Armour he eventually married, banishing thoughts of the intellectual disparity between them in a stoutly worded letter – '*A wife's head is immaterial compared with her heart. My Jean has the kindest heart in the county, gratefully devoted with all its powers to love me. Indeed the poor girl has the most sacred enthusiasm for me and has not a wish but to gratify my every idea of her deportment.*' She bore nine of his children, four of whom died. '*Of the four children she bore me in seventeen months, two sets of twins, my eldest boy only is living,*' he wrote to a friend in 1788. '*But I reckon a twelve brace of children against I celebrate my twelfth wedding day – twenty-four christenings, twenty-four useful members of society! I am so enamoured of her prolific twin-bearing merit that I have given her the legal title which I now avow to the world.*'

There was something rather fab about having had the twins at forty, thought Nicola; bringing in new life when others that age were starting to worry about death. And she still wasn't too old, there was still just about time to squeeze in one last baby if she really felt like it.

Once Burns had married Jean Armour, he arranged for

the babies he continued to father by other women to go to her rather than to his mother as before. 'Oor Rab could hae done wi' twa' wives,' Jean commented. On the day of his funeral, she gave birth to their ninth baby, a boy. She was left with five sons and little Betty Park. She was to live on for another thirty-eight years, two more of her sons dying early during that time.

'In his own time Burns was criticised for immorality,' concluded the speaker. 'He wrote,

> O ye douce folk that live by rule
> Grave, tideless-blooded, calm an' cool
> Your hearts are like a standing pool
> Ye *never* stray . . .

That sort of love, the sort that moved Burns to poetry, it's like the sea. It ebbs and flows. It doesn't last. What remains when it's over? Why, the poetry of course. And the babies.'

'Oh dear,' said Nicola to Iain, wiping her eyes, while the applause died down around them. 'That was sad. That poor woman Jean.'

'Och aye, bonnie Jean,' said Iain. 'These days she'd have been a teleworker for the bank, right enough.'

'More security in that than in farming,' said Nicola.

'Security. Babies. I don't know.' Iain shook his head and poured more whisky. 'I'm no being rude, Nicola, but can I ask you something? Why do you have *four*? We've got the three and that's as much as Susan can cope with, and she doesn't work.'

Nicola was used to men asking this question. Usually it

came with the unspoken accusation that she was just being greedy, which was a bit rich coming from a banker as it so often did. Because I *want* them and I can *afford* them, she felt like saying; because I'm thinking of the future, when I retire at fifty; because, *more life*; because – why *not*?

But this man was not attacking her, he was in his befuddled way genuinely curious.

'I would never have had so many if I'd had to stay at home and look after them myself,' she said, as she always said, to take the heat off. Then she continued, less guarded because she liked this man – 'I mean, I was tempted during my third pregnancy to take some time off. Charlie was seriously worried about the mortgage, I can tell you. I'd had a bad run of nannies. I'd missed all Jade's sports days and prize-givings that year because of work. But as soon as the scan showed it was twins, that did it. I knew I'd be back at work as soon as I could crawl out of the house. Twins!'

'Susan says a nanny wouldn't be the same,' Iain persisted. He was pushing it now. 'She says they want *her* there.'

'Yes they'd prefer a mother at home,' said Nicola crisply. 'But I couldn't do that. I'm their mother, that's what they've got.'

Iain sat, shaking his head dolefully, and staring into his glass. Irritated, Nicola shifted in her seat and turned towards Donald.

'You'll be looking forward to the Reply from the Lassies,' he said.

'More?' said Nicola in horror, without thinking. He laughed.

'This should be the last. Truly.'

In the distance a young woman could be seen standing at the microphone consulting her notes.

'Isn't that Fiona MacPherson's new assistant?' asked Donald, leaning over her towards Iain. She felt his weight against her arm. 'Fiona MacPherson that's head of H.R. at the Auld Scotia?'

'Don't mess with that MacPherson woman, I'm telling you,' said Iain, mournfully shaking his head. Drink turned him into a clown, noticed Nicola.

'Behind every successful man there's a woman,' began the young woman at the microphone, and her voice was surprisingly loud and clear. 'Behind every successful woman is . . . what? That is the question I'd like to consider this Burns Night.'

Here we go, thought Nicola. What every woman needs is a wife. She saw Donald raise an eyebrow at Brian Mahon, and Brian Mahon reply with a comical turning down of the corners of his mouth. Did this girl realise how little people liked to be lectured, wondered Nicola, wincing for her, and at the same time admiring her; more particularly how men hate to be lectured by women?

'Men ask, what is it women want?' the girl continued.

'A thundering scalade right enough!' shouted a frisky Scot on his eleventh whisky.

The most hurtful thing always was the assumption that because she was successful at work she must have sacrificed her children; that her children must have suffered. But if anybody had suffered, she now saw, it was her.

'Women want love and they want work, just the same as men,' declared the girl. 'And they want children to be seen as a fact of life not as a personal weakness. So if you love your women, all you men out there, take your share of what's called women's work so that us women can take some of the bread-winning burden off *your* shoulders. Get a life. Outside the office. It'll be better for your health. Better for your love life. And, if you're interested, since Burns mentions it, better for your immortal soul. *Aux armes, citoyens!* In the name of the love you claim to feel for us lassies.'

She left the dais to ragged applause and uncertain wolf whistles. She did not smile or look back.

'Well, for the majority of us, of course, that's luckily the case, the bit about having the wife at home taking care of all that side of things,' chuckled Iain Buchanan. 'And don't think it's not appreciated, Susan, because it is! Sorry, Nicola. But it's true. I can't see any reason why I should change a state of affairs that works, that allows me to work. Let's face it, this sort of job needs total support and backup. We all need a bonny Jean to keep the home fires burning.'

'I suppose that was what you might call a professional suicide note,' said Donald. 'I wonder if Fiona MacPherson vetted that little diatribe. I rather think not.'

'And I'm not having some fat hen from H.R. telling me how to run my life. Or how to have weans, for Chrissake,' continued Iain. 'Pass that bottle of Deanston's, Brian.' He waved his quaich in the air. 'Freedom and whisky gang thegither.'

'I must say I've never heard that lesson drawn from Burns' life before,' mused Donald. 'Burns the family man. By all accounts he was the ultimate bastard when it came to loving them and leaving them.'

'He looked after his bairns, though,' said Iain hotly.

'Excuse me,' said Nicola. 'I was under the impression that it was his mother and his wife who looked after them. If I understood rightly.'

'Haw hey,' said Iain, fuddled. 'Right enough. But he didnae leave them to die in a ditch.'

'The trouble is, these days at work you have to put in the hours and be *sheen* to be putting in the hours,' said Brian Mahon, very slurred. 'I mean in a proper job. Not just teaching or journalism.'

'No, you couldn't call being a poet a proper job,' agreed Nicola, following her own line of thought. 'What did they used to say about Friday being Poet's Day? Piss Off Early Tomorrow's Saturday, that's right. Whereas Friday in this day and age is Dress Down day.'

'He did have a proper job, he was a farmer,' said Iain. 'He just didnae do very well at it. Then he was an exciseman. He was no idler.'

Hours are not a measure of love, Nicola assured her children; the number of hours I spend with you has nothing to do with how much I love you; you can ring me at work any time you want. Which was probably just what these three men, Iain and Donald and Brian, said to their wives. This man Donald had a lovely mouth, she noticed. She lifted her eyes and saw he was glowering at her.

'Family man,' he said, and his voice was hard and flat. 'That's the euphemism for a lazy bastard not pulling his weight.'

They lapsed into silence, broodingly, as more music started up. The piano was some way across on the other side of the hall, and Nicola could not see who was playing. If you got them up to Grade IV by the age of ten, you could enter them for a music scholarship. They hadn't twigged, first time round with Jade and Harry, but by the time the twins were born they'd got wise to it. Hence the Suzuki lessons.

Allowing herself at last to listen to the music, its solitary thoughtful quality affecting her like alcohol, she relaxed for the first time that evening. She let go, and of course that was a mistake.

Usually she bowed to the tyranny of postive thinking as anything else was not exactly very helpful. Now fissures of doubt and ambivalence raced along the walls of the fortress. Charlie was off to Australia next week and she would be in Frankfurt. She wasn't easy when they were both out of the country at the same time. Harry had recently been diagnosed as dyspraxic, but she simply hadn't had time to follow it up. The nanny had been with them so long that she regarded herself as part of the family. And she wasn't. So *that* would end badly. Roderick MacKenzie was buried and dead, a man of forty-three, and Charlie's PA had just been diagnosed as having breast cancer, and she was only thirty-eight. Burns had been thirty-seven, but that was then. She was older than that, they were all getting older all the time. As for sex, it was efficient these days but not exactly exciting. The pilot light was still there and the usual procedure led to a reliable enough firing up. But it had become something that was good for them, like going to the gym. Where was the wild restlessness she could hear in this music? She was aware of Donald Forfar's solid unfamiliar body beside hers, and wondered whether he was very hairy. She wouldn't mind. What a coward she was to have slept with only one man since marriage. You have one life, and the way to keep your life alive was through the sexual flame, she had seen that tonight, falling in love with new others, the tinder heart catching fire again and again. Yet *she* had chosen monogamy.

The piano playing drew to a close. Never had an evening gone on quite like this before. Those on her table had been bearing each other company for many hours like a little band of passengers in a lifeboat, and were now sagging with fatigue and alcohol. When yet another tartan-clad lassie walked up to the microphone clasping her hands soulfully before her, several of them clearly wished to lay their heads on the tablecloth in front of them and give up. Brian Mahon looked less than half-conscious. Charlie was rolling his eyes. This is ridiculous, thought Nicola; how are we supposed to get up in the morning after this? It's not like we've got the weekend to recover. It's a Wednesday. It's probably Thursday by now actually. She felt angry and sad. A bread roll flew through the air past the next table leaving a wake of tutting.

The girl's voice made a rich pompous warbling noise above them, but at least you could hear all the words.

> John Anderson my jo, John,
> When we were first acquent;
> Your locks were like the raven,
> Your bonny brow was brent;
> But now your brow is beld, John,
> Your locks are like the snow.
> But blessings on your frosty pow
> John Anderson my Jo.

'Jo means sweetheart,' whispered Donald. 'It's a song from an old wife to her wrinkled old baldy husband.'

She felt his whispering breath in her hair, and glowed. His arm was touching hers and it seemed to give off heat.

> John Anderson my jo, John,
> We clamb the hill the gither;
> And mony a canty day, John,
> We've had wi' ane anither:
> Now we maun totter down, John,
> And hand in hand we'll go;
> And sleep the gither at the foot,
> John Anderson my Jo.

'And are you looking forward to tottering down towards old age with your wife eventually?' she asked Donald politely, daringly, once it was finished.

He scowled at her as if through a cloud.

'My wife's just left me.'

'Oh, ah. *Ah*,' said Nicola. 'I'm sorry.'

Charlie's voice, slurred and fruity, drifted across the table.

'It's a braw bricht moonlicht nicht the nicht. You see, I have a very *good* Scotch accent,' he was boasting to Susan Buchanan's glassy smile. He turned his head and gradually focused an eye on Nicola and her demon lover.

'Donald whar's yur troosers?' he demanded, dissolving into foolish sleepy laughter.

Then they were dazedly hauling themselves to their feet. The end had heaved into sight. Big Dougal was thanking them for coming and hoping they would all join in singing

Burns' most famous song of all; but first he would like to thank . . .

Nicola turned to Iain Buchanan, who stared at her angrily.

'That poor bastert Burns,' he growled. 'Always on the edge of bankruptcy, the farm failing. All those mouths to feed, those women and children. Never any fucking security.'

'I suppose not,' said Nicola, thinking, I'm glad I'm not the one who's responsible for getting you home. All the way to Guildford, too.

'He worked hard to keep his family,' said Iain fiercely, as though she were denying it. 'When he didnae make it as a farmer he changed his career, he became an exciseman. Did you know that? He wasnae a drinker. The occasional bender like us all, *then* he might end up having one too many, but right enough he wasnae a drinker.'

'No, no,' said Nicola.

'It was the rheumatoid endocarditis, actually,' said Donald. 'That killed him.'

'Naw, he didnae die of drink, you know,' said Iain Buchanan, his face up close to hers, belligerent, and she realised he was very drunk. 'It wasnae the drink.'

'So you said,' said Nicola.

She could see Susan Buchanan staring across at her husband with a look of hopeless hungry grief.

'Burns was dying,' Donald Forfar announced in his stately fashion. 'The doctor sent him off alone to the Solway Firth. The doctor's orders were, to wade out to sea daily until he was up to his armpits, then to stand there in the freezing cold grey Atlantic for as long as he could. For some reason this did not improve his health. Then a bill for seven pounds and four shillings arrived from his tailor, and it struck deathly fear in his heart. He was hard pressed for money and he could not pay it. It became a gigantic sum in his mind, a horrifying debt. It tormented him. A few days later he was dead.'

Iain Buchanan gave a groan and tossed another few gills of whisky down his throat.

'That's very sad,' said Nicola, recognising for a fact that Iain had, in banking parlance, over-extended himself.

The pipers started up their wailing. It was nearly one o'clock. Side by side around the tables the guests stood up and swayed with varying degrees of self-consciousness and tiredness to the dismal strains of Auld Lang Syne.

> Should auld acquaintance be forgot
> And never brought to mind?
> Should auld acquaintance be forgot,
> And auld lang syne!

She wouldn't care if she never saw any of them again. Her right hand was in Iain's, who was on her left, and her left hand was in Donald's, who was on her right. She felt uneasy, as though she had become a conduit for their misery, which was, in each case, both inflammable and sodden, dangerously so, and not to be trusted.

'I'm in the middle of my life,' thought Nicola. 'I'm rooted in. I have four healthy children.' She felt a wave of gratitude break over her head.

Donald and Iain were gripping her hands too hard, Iain was droning away about cups o' kindness.

'I work hard, I earn good money, I'm able to take care

of my family,' she added to herself. 'My precious children. *And* I'm not a drunk.'

Verse followed verse of Auld Lang Syne to general incomprehension, even among the Scots. Then it did end. It was over, and people were sheepishly seizing their neighbours for hugs and kisses, unable to meet each other's eyes. It was like the cringe-making conclusion to a happy clappy evangelical service, she thought; forced contact. Although the emotion here was more what you might call fearful tearful. Or just plain maudlin.

Donald Forfar grabbed her to him and kissed her on the mouth. Oh good, was her first thought, before common sense kicked in, and she closed her eyes and leaned into his hot body, into the heat and darkness of the kiss. She even liked the smell and the taste of the whisky. Again, like everything else that night, it seemed to last forever, though it couldn't have been more than a few seconds.

Then Charlie was beside them saying, 'Hey, excuse me,' very unsteady on his feet. He started to prod Donald on the shoulder when Iain stepped in and growled, 'Whit ye think ye're doing to ma friend?'

'Your friend?' said Charlie, looking baffled.

'Are you deaf, pal?' snarled Iain, 'Or just plain stupid?'

'Are you talking to me, Jocko?' said Charlie, turning away from Donald and squaring up to Iain.

'Een! Een!' squeaked Susan Buchanan, hopping around them and plucking at his sleeve. 'Come away from him! Come away now!'

Nicola went to join in, but found she was about to start laughing uncontrollably and so held back. It wasn't funny, it wasn't in the least bit funny. Donald touched her arm but she shrugged it off. No, I don't want you, she thought. I really don't. Rabbie Burns notwithstanding, that would be a very bad idea indeed.

Bystanders from the neighbouring tables stood gawping in a circle as though they could not believe their eyes. Iain got hold of Charlie's lapels and Charlie got hold of Iain's lapels. This wouldn't do her relationship with the Bank much good, realised Nicola, and her mind leaped ahead inventing damage limitation strategies. The men were both so stupefied with whisky that they could barely stand.

'*Naw*, Ee-yen,' screeched Susan Buchanan, 'Heh *naw!*'

Wrestling like two sleepy bears in a snowdrift, they fell, growling, slowly and heavily, the Scotsman and the auld enemy, down onto the white tablecloth at which they had sat politely facing each other for so many hours that night, crashing into the china and cutlery with a noise that was enough to bring a moment's silence to the rest of the vast room.

I even love my husband, thought Nicola in that moment, continuing to count her blessings. Even now. She watched him as he sprawled and brawled in the churning tartan-flashing stramash of bottles and leftovers. You are the father of my children, she said silently. But don't push it too far. Pal.

Café Society

Two shattered women and a bright-eyed child have just sat down at the window table in the café. Both women hope to talk, for their minds to meet; at the same time they are aware that the odds against this happening are about fifty to one. Still they have decided to back that dark horse Intimacy, somewhere out there muffledly galloping. They order coffee, and toast for the boy, who seizes a teaspoon and starts to bash away at the cracked ice marbling of the formica table.

'No, Ben,' says his mother, prising the spoon from his fingers and diverting his attention to the basket of sugar sachets. She flings discreet glances at the surrounding tables, gauging the degrees of irritability of those nearest. There are several other places they could have chosen, but this sandwich bar is where they came.

They might have gone to McDonald's, so cheap and tolerant, packed with flat light and fat smells and unofficial crêche clamour. There they could have slumped like the old punchbags they are while Ben screeched and flew around with the other children. McDonald's is essentially a wordless experience, though, and they both want to see if they can for a wonder exchange some words. Then there is Pete's Café on the main road, a lovely steamy unbuttoned room where men sit in their work clothes in a friendly fug of bonhomie and banter, smoking, stirring silver streams of sugar into mugs of bright brown tea. But it would not be fair to take this child in there and spoil that Edenic all-day-breakfast fun. It would take the insensitivity of an ox. Unthinkable.

Here is all right. They get all sorts here. Here is used to women walking in with that look on their faces – 'What hit me?' Even now there is a confused-looking specimen up there ordering a decaffitated coffee, takeaway, at the counter.

'Every now and then I think *I* might give it up, see if that helps,' says Frances. 'Caffeine. But then I reckon it's just a drop in the ocean.'

Ben rocks backwards in his chair a few times, seeing how far he can go. He is making a resonant zooming noise behind his teeth, but not very loudly yet. Sally keeps her baggy eye on him and says, 'Sometimes I think I'm just pathetic but then other times I think, I'm not a tank.'

'Cannonfodder,' observes Frances.

'It's all right if you're the sort who can manage on four hours,' says Sally. 'Churchill. Thatcher. Bugger.'

Ben, having tipped his chair to the point of no return, carries on down towards the floor in slow motion. Frances dives in and with quiet skill prevents infant skull from hitting lino-clad concrete.

'Reflexes,' says Sally gratefully. 'Shot to pieces.'

She clasps the shaken child to her coat with absent fervour. He is drawing breath for a blare of delayed shock when the arrival of the toast deflects him.

'The camel's back,' says Sally obscurely.

'Not funny,' comments Frances, who understands that she is referring to sleep, or its absence.

Ben takes the buttery knife from the side of his plate and waves it in the air, then drops it onto his mother's coat sleeve. From there it falls to her lap and then, noisily, to the floor. She dabs at the butter stains with a tissue and bangs her forehead as she reaches beneath the table for the knife. Ben laughs and sandpapers his chin with a square of toast.

This woman Sally has a drinker's face, but her lustreless grey skin and saurian eye come not from alcohol but from prolonged lack of sleep.

As a former research student it has often occurred to her that a medical or sociology post-graduate might profitably study the phenomenon in society of a large number of professional women in their thirties suffering from exhaustion. Her third child, this bouncing boy, has woken at least four times a night since he was born. Most mornings he won't go back to sleep after five, so she has him in with her jumping and playing and singing. She hasn't shared a bedroom with her husband for eighteen months now. She'd carried on full-time through the first and second. They slept. Luck of the draw. Yes of course she has talked to her health visitor about this, she has taken the boy to a sleep clinic, she has rung Cry-sis and listened to unseen mothers in the same foundering boat. The health visitor booked her into a sleep counselling course which involved her taking an afternoon every week off work, driving an hour's round trip on the North Circular, only to listen to some well-meaning woman tell her what damage this sleep pattern was causing to the family unit, to her health, to her marriage, to the boy's less demanding siblings. Well she knew all that anyway, didn't she? After the third session she said, what's the point? Not every problem has a solution, she decided, and here it is obviously a brutally simple question of survival, of whether she cracks before he starts sleeping through. It's years now.

These thoughts flash through her mind, vivid and open, but must remain unspoken as Ben's presence precludes anything much in the way of communication beyond blinking in Morse. The few words she has exchanged with this woman Frances, known only by sight after all from the nursery school queue, are the merest tips of icebergs. Such thoughts are dangerous to articulate anyway, bringing up into the air what has been submerged. Nearly all faces close in censorship at the merest hint of such talk. Put up and shut up is the rule, except with fellow mothers. Even then it can be taken as letting the side down. She yawns uncontrollably so that her eyes water, leaving her with the face of a bloodhound.

From her handbag this tired woman Sally takes a pad and felt tips and places them in front of her son Ben, who is rolling his eyes and braying like a donkey.

'Shush Ben,' she says. 'You're not a donkey.'

He looks at her with beautiful affectless eyes. He sucks in air and starts up a series of guttural snorts.

'You're not a piggy, Ben, stop it,' says Sally.

'Piggy,' says Ben, laughing with lunatic fervour.

'They were brilliant at work, they bent over backwards,' says Sally, rapidly, anyway. 'It was me that resigned, I thought it wasn't fair on them. I was going into work for a rest. Ben!'

'That's hard,' says Frances, watching as Sally straightens

the boy in his chair and tries to engage him in colouring a picture of a rabbit in police uniform.

'Do you work then?' asks Sally, filling in one long furry ear with pink.

'Yes. No,' says Frances. 'I shouldn't be here! You know, round the edges at the moment. I mean, I must. I have. Always. Unthinkable! But, erm. You know. Freelance at the moment.'

Ben pushes the paper away from him and grasps at a handful of felt tips. He throws them against the window and cheers at the clatter they make on impact.

'No, Ben!' growls Sally through clenched teeth. 'Naughty.'

The two women grovel under the table picking up pens. Ben throws a few more after them.

What Frances would have said had there been a quiet patch of more than five seconds, was, that she had worked full-time all through the babyhood of her first child, Emma, and also until her second, Rose, was three, as well as running the domestic circus, functioning as the beating heart of the family while deferring to the demands of her partner's job in that it was always her rather than him who took a day off sick when one of the girls sprained a wrist or starred in a concert, and her too of course who was responsible for finding, organising and paying for childcare and for the necessary expenditure of countless megavolts of the vicarious emotional and practical energy involved in having someone else look after your babies while you are outside the house all day, all the deeply unrestful habits of vigilance masquerading as 'every confidence' in the girl who would, perfectly reasonably, really rather be an aerobics instructor working on Legs Tums 'n Bums.

Then there was one childcare-based strappado too many; and she cracked. After all those years. She had come home unexpectedly in the afternoon to find the girl fast asleep on the sofa, clubbed out as she later put it, while Emma and Rose played on the stairs with needles and matches or some such. Could be worse, her sensible woman-in-the-workplace voice said; she's young, she likes a good time and why shouldn't she; nothing happened, did it? To hell with that, her mother-in-the-house voice said; I could be the one on the sofa rather than out there busting a gut and barely breaking even.

She needed work, she loved work, she was educated for it. Didn't she, Sally, feel the same way? She'd never asked her partner for money; no, they were equals, pulling together. Well, work was fabulous while you were there, it was what you had to do before and after work that was the killer. It was good for the girls to see their mother out working in the real world, he said when she talked of feeling torn apart; a role model. There's no need to feel guilty, he would begin, with God-like compassion. It's not guilt, you fool. It's the unwelcome awareness that being daily ripped in half is not good, not even ultimately. I agree with all the reasons. 'I'm sorry, they've got to realise that you are a person in your own right and have work to do.' I couldn't agree more. 'Women have always worked, except for that brief sinister time in the fifties.' Yes. But had they always had to work a ten-hour day at a full hour's commuting distance from their babies while not showing by a murmur or a flicker what this was doing to them?

So here she was after all these years 'gone freelance', that coy phrase, cramming a full-time job into their school hours and also the evenings once they'd gone to bed. She had a large envelope of sweets pinned to the wall by the telephone so that she could receive work calls to the noise of lollipop-sucking rather than shrilling and howls. And now, of course, she had no sick pay, paid holiday, pension or maternity leave should she be so foolish as to find herself pregnant again. Just as the Welfare State she'd been raised to lean on was packing up.

Unfortunately not one word of this makes it into the light of day, as Ben is creating.

'It was more fun at work,' Frances bursts out, watching Sally wipe the child's buttery jawline with another of the inexhaustible supply of tissues from her bag. 'You get some *respect* at work.'

'My last childminder,' says Sally. She flinches.

'Snap,' says Frances.

The two women sip their powerless cappuccinos.

'In a couple of years' time, when this one starts school,' says Sally, 'I could probably get back, get by with an au pair in term-time. Someone to collect them from school, get their tea. But then there's the holidays.'

'Very long, the holidays,' agrees Frances.

'Not fair on the poor girl,' says Sally. 'Not when she doesn't speak English. Now if it was just Leo he'd be fine,' she continues, off on another tack, thinking aloud about her two eldest children. 'But Gemma is different.'

The child Ben slides off his chair and runs over to the glass-fronted display of sandwich fillings, the metal trays of damp cheese, dead ham and tired old tuna mixed with sweetcorn kernels. He starts to hit the glass with the flat of his hand. There is a collective intake of breath and everyone turns to stare. As she lurches over to apologise and expostulate, Sally's mind continues to follow her train of thought, silently addressing Frances even if all that Frances can see of her is a bumbling, clucking blur.

Children are all different, Sally thinks on, and they are different from birth. Her own son Leo has a robust nature, a level temperament and the valuable ability to amuse himself, which is what makes him so easy to care for. He has smilingly greeted more than half a dozen childminders in his time, and waved them goodbye with equal cheeriness. Gemma, however, was born more anxious, less spirited. She cries easily and when her mother used to leave for work would abandon herself to despair. She is crushingly jealous of this youngest child Ben. She wants to sit on Sally's lap all the time when she is there, and nags and whines like a neglected wife, and clings so hard that all around are uncomfortably filled with irritation. She has formed fervid attachments to the aforementioned childminders, and has wept bitterly at their various departures. Well, Gemma may thrive better now her mother is at home, or she may not; the same could be said of her mother. Time will tell, but by then of course it will be then and not now, and Sally will be unemployable whichever way it has turned out.

'Oof,' grunts Sally, returning with her son, who leaps within her arms like a young dolphin. She sits him firmly on his chair again.

'My neighbour's au pair wrote their car off last week,' says Frances. 'Nobody hurt, luckily.'

They both shudder.

'We're so lucky,' they agree, po-faced, glum, gazing at zany Ben as he stabs holes into the police rabbit with a sharp red pen. Sally yawns uncontrollably, then Frances starts up where she leaves off.

After all, they're getting nowhere fast.

An elderly woman pauses as she edges past their table on the way to the till. She cocks her head on one side and smiles brightly at Ben, whose mouth drops open. He stares at her, transfixed, with the expression of a seraph who has understood the mystery of the sixth pair of wings. His mother Sally knows that he is in fact temporarily dumb-struck by the woman's tremendous wart, which sits at the corner of her mouth with several black hairs sprouting from it.

'What a handsome little fellow,' says the woman fondly. 'Make the most of it, dear,' she continues, smiling at Sally. 'It goes so fast.' Sally tenses as she smiles brightly back, willing her son not to produce one of his devastating monosyllables. Surely he does not know the word for wart yet.

'Such a short time,' repeats the woman, damp-eyed.

Well, not really, thinks Frances. Sometimes it takes an hour to go a hundred yards. Now she knows what she knows she puts it at three and a half years per child, the time spent exhausted, absorbed, used up; and, what's more, if not, then something's wrong. That's a whole decade if you have three! This is accurate, wouldn't you agree, she wants to ask Sally; this is surely true for all but those women with Olympic physical stamina, cast-iron immune systems, steel-clad nerves and sensitivities. Extraordinary women; heroines, in fact. But what about the strugglers? The ordinary mother strugglers? Why do they educate us, Sally, only to make it so hard for us to work afterwards? Why don't they insist on hysterectomies

for girls who want further education and have done with it? Of
course none of this will get said. There is simply no airspace.

Ben's eyes have sharpened and focused on his admirer's
huge side-of-the-mouth wart.

'Witch,' he says, loud and distinct.

'Ben,' says Sally. She looks ready to cry, and so does the
older woman, who smiles with a hurt face and says, 'Don't
worry, dear, he didn't mean anything', and moves off.

'WITCH,' shouts Ben, following her with his eyes.

At this point, Sally and Frances give up. With a scraping
of chairs and a flailing of coats, they wordlessly heave
themselves and Ben and his paraphernalia up to the counter,
and pay, and go. They won't try that again in a hurry.
They smile briefly at each other as they say goodbye, wry
and guarded. They have exchanged little more than two
hundred words inside this hour, and how much friendship
can you base on that?

After all, it's important to put up a decent apologia for
your life; well, it is to other people, mostly; to come up
with a convincing defence, to argue your corner. It's
nothing but healthy, the way the sanguine mind does leap
around looking for the advantages of any new shift in
situation. And if you can't, or won't, you will be shunned.
You will appear to be a whiner, or a malcontent. Frances
knows this, and so does Sally.

Even so they pause and turn and give each other a
brief, gruff, foolish hug, with the child safely sandwiched
between them.

Hurrah for the Hols

These were the dogdays all right, these last flyblown days of August. Her maternal goodwill was worn threadbare. This was the nadir of Dorrie's year, all this holiday flesh needing to be tended and shameless bad temper on display.

She was sitting at a table in the unshaded barbecue area by the pool over a cup of terrible coffee. And yet it was supposed to be the annual high-water mark, their summer fortnight, particularly this year when they had rejected camping or self-catering in favour of splashing out on a room in this value-for-money family hotel.

'You really are a stupid little boy. You're really pushing your luck,' said the man at the next table to one of the three children sitting with him. 'I want to see that burger finished *now*. Can't you for once in your whole life . . .'

His voice was quiet and venomous. What was he doing here alone with his children? It must be the same as Max was doing with their three now, playing crazy golf to give her some time to herself. This man's wife was probably just round the corner over just such another cup of coffee. Was she too feeling panic at not making good use of that dear-bought commodity, solitude?

'If you don't do what I say right now there'll be no ice cream. No swimming. No puppet show. I mean it.'

The small boy beside him started to cry into his burger, wailing and complaining that his teeth hurt.

'And don't think you're going to get round me like that,' snarled the man. 'I'm not your *mother*, remember!'

All over the place, if you listened, you could hear the steady exasperated undertone of the unglamorously leisure-clad parents teasing their tempestuous egomaniacal little people into, for example, eating that sandwich up 'or I tell you what, and you're being very silly, but you won't be going to the Treasure Island club tonight and *I mean it.*' It stuck in her throat, the bread of the weeping child. The parents said nothing to each other, except the names of sandwich fillings. She and Max were the same, they couldn't talk over, under or round the children and so it turned them sour and obdurate in each other's company. They held each other at night in bed but again could say or do nothing for fear of their children beside them, sleeping like larks, like clean-limbed breathing fruit.

She sipped and grimaced and watched the snail's progress of the combine harvester on the adjacent cliff. There was a splash as someone jumped into the pool, and a flapping over wasps and a dragging round of high chairs to plastic tables, and howls, hoots, groaning and broken-hearted sobbing, the steady cacophony which underscores family life en masse. At least sitting here alone she had been noticing the individual elements of the composition, she realised with surprise and some pleasure. When she was with her brood she noticed nothing of the outside world, they drank up all her powers of observation.

Here they came now, off the crazy golf course, tear-stained, drooping, scowling. Here comes the big bore, and here come the three little bores. Stifle your yawns. Smile. On holiday Max became a confederate, saying things like 'They never stop' and 'That child is a cannibal.' Their constant crystalline quacking, demanding a response, returning indefatigable and gnat-like, drove him mad. There must be something better than this squabbly nuclear family unit, she thought, these awful hobbling five- and six-legged races all around her.

She could see they were fighting. She saw Martin hit Robin, and Robin clout him back. It was like being on holiday with Punch and Judy – lots of biffing and shrieking and fights over sausages. What a lumpen, moping, tearful, spiritless mummy she had become, packing and unpacking for everybody endlessly, sighing. Better sigh, though, than do as she'd done earlier that day, on the beach when, exasperated by their demands, on and on, all afternoon, she'd stood up and held out her hands to them.

'Here, have some fingers,' she'd snarled, pretending to snap them off one by one. 'Have a leg. Have an ear. Nice?' And they had laughed uproariously, jumping on her and pinning her to the rug, sawing at her limbs, tugging her ears, uprooting her fingers and toes. Such a figure she cut on the beach these days, slumped round-shouldered in the middle of the family encampment of towels, impatience on a monument growling at the sea. Or was it Mother Courage of the sand dunes, the slack-muscled white body hidden under various cover-ups, headgear, dark glasses, crouched amidst the contents of her cart, the buckets, wasp spray, suncream, foreign legion hats with neck-protective flaps, plastic football, beach cricket kit, gaggle of plastic jelly sandals, spare dry swimsuits, emergency pants. If she lumbered off for a paddle all hell broke loose.

'Did you have a nice time?' she said weakly as they reached her table.

Martin was shrieking about some injustice, his father's face was black as thunder. Robin sprinted to her lap, then Maxine and Martin jumped on her jealously, staking their claim like settlers in some virgin colony.

'She's not your long-lost uncle, your mother,' said Max, unable to get near her. 'You only saw her half an hour ago.'

Things got worse before they got better. There was a terrible scene later on. It was in the large room by the bar, the Family Room, where at six o'clock a holiday student surf fanatic led all the young children in a song and dance session while their parents sagged against the walls and watched.

> And a little bit of this
> And a little bit of that
> And shake your bum
> Just like your mum

sang the children, roaring with laughter as they mimed the actions. After this, glassy lollipops were handed out, and then the surfer started to organise a conga. The children lined up, each holding the waist of the one in front, many of them with the lollipops still in their mouths, sticks stuck outwards.

'That's dangerous,' mumured Dorrie. 'If they fell,' and

she and other mothers discreetly coaxed the sweets from the mouths of their nearest offspring with earnest promises that these would be returned immediately the dance had finished. Then she glanced across the room and saw Martin in the line, lollipop stick clamped between his teeth. Max just beyond him, sipping from his first bottle of beer, caught her eye; she, without thinking as hard as she might have done, indicated to him the lollipop peril, miming and pointing.

The conga had started, the music was blasting out, and yet when Max wrenched the stick from between Martin's clenched teeth the boy's screams were louder even than the very loudly amplified Birdy song. Martin broke out of the line and fought his father for the lollipop. Max, looking furious, teeth bared inside his dark beard, was a figure both ridiculous and distressing, like a giant Captain Haddock wrestling with an hysterical diminutive Tintin. Their battle carried on out in the hall, where Max dragged Martin just as the conga was weaving past, with screaming and shouting and terrible fury between them. They were hating each other.

Dorrie edged up to them, horror-struck, and the next thing was that Max was shouting at *her*. All right, it was their first day, they were all tired from the journey, but this was dreadful. The other parents, following the conga, filtered past interestedly watching this scene.

'Don't, don't, don't,' said Dorrie several times, but softly. The other two children joined them, sobbing.

At last she got them all past reception and up the stairs.

'I don't like you, Daddy,' wailed Martin through tears.

'I know you don't, Martin,' huffed Max, storming off ahead.

Really, he was very like Martin, or Martin was very like him – both prone to explosions of aggressive self-defensiveness – although of course Martin was six, whereas Max was forty. Because Max did this, she had to do the opposite in order to redress the balance, even though doing so made her look weak and ineffective. He sometimes pointed this out, her apparent ineffectiveness. But what would he rather? That she scream at them like a fishwife? Hit them? Vent her temper or ignore them, like a man? Let them get hurt? Let them eat rubbish? Let them watch junk? Just try doing it all the time before you criticise, not only for a few hours or days, she reflected, as she reined herself in and wiped tears from blubbing faces and assisted with the comprehensive nose-blowing that was needed in the wake of such a storm.

At least he didn't hit them when he lost his temper. She had a friend whose husband did, and then justified it with talk of them having to learn, which she, Dorrie, could not have borne. She really would much rather be on her own with them, it was much easier like that. Like a skilful stage manager she had learned how to create times of sweetness and light with the three of them; she could now coax and balance the various jostling elements into some sort of precarious harmony. It was an art, like feeding and building a good log fire, an achievement. Then in Max would clump, straightways seizing the bellows or the poker, and the whole lot would collapse in ruins.

'I'll get them to bed, Max,' she said. 'Why don't you go for a swim or something.'

'I'll wait for you in the bar,' he said frostily. 'Remember they stop serving dinner at eight.'

'Yes.'

'Don't forget to turn the listening service on.'

'No.'

'I know when I'm not wanted.'

She choked down her reply, and gently closed the door behind him.

'Now then,' she said, smiling at their doleful tear-smeared faces. 'What's up? You look as though you've swallowed a jellyfish!'

They looked at her, goggling with relief, and laughed uncertainly.

'*Two* jellyfish!' she said, with vaudeville mirth.

They laughed harder.

'And an *octopus*!' she added.

They fell on the floor, they were laughing so hard.

The second day was an improvement on the first, although, as Dorrie said to herself, that would not have been difficult. They turned away from the glare of the packed beach towards leafy broken shade, walking inland along a lane whose hedges were candy-striped with pink and white bindweed. A large dragonfly with marcasite body and pearl-ised wings appeared in the air before them and stopped them in their tracks. Then they struck off across a path through fields where sudden clouds of midges swept by without touching them. When they reached a stream over-arched by hawthorn trees the children clamoured to take off their sandals and dip their feet in the water.

'This is the place for our picnic,' said Dorrie, who had brought supplies along in a rucksack, and now set about distributing sandwiches and fruit and bottles of water.

'We can't walk across the strand today,' said Max,

consulting his copy of the Tide Tables as he munched away at a ham roll. 'Low tide was earlier this morning, then not again till nine tonight. Fat lot of good that is. But tomorrow looks possible.'

He had heard about an island not far from here which, once a day, for a short time only, became part of the mainland. When the tide was out you could walk across the strand to the island and visit the ancient cell of the hermit who had lived centuries before in the heart of its little woods.

'There doesn't seem to be any logic to it,' said Dorrie, looking over his shoulder at the week's chart. 'No pattern to the tides, no gradual waxing and waning as with the moon. I thought the tides were supposed to be governed by the moon, but they're all over the place.'

The children sat by them, each with a bag of crisps, nibbling away busily like rodents.

'There *is* a pattern, though,' said Max. 'When there's a new moon or an old moon, the tides are at their highest and also at their lowest. It's all very extreme at those times of the month, when the earth, moon and sun are directly in line.'

Martin, having finished his own bag of crisps, was now busily capturing ants from the grass and dropping them into his sister's bag.

'Don't do that,' said Dorrie.

'And when the moon's at right angles to the sun, that's when you get neap tides,' continued Max. 'Less extreme, less dramatic. What the hell's the matter *now*.'

Maxine had been trying to pull her bag of crisps away from Martin, who had suddenly let go, with the result that Maxine's crisps had flown into the air and over the grass, where Martin was now rolling on them and crushing them into salty fragments.

'Stop it!' called Dorrie.

'Get up this minute!' shouted Max.

'Why should I, it's a free country,' gabbled Martin, rolling back and forth, enjoying the noise and drama.

'My crisps!' sobbed Maxine. 'They're all squashed!'

'What's your problem,' said Martin with spiteful pleasure, getting up as his father approached, and brushing yellow crumbs from his shorts. 'You threw them away, so that means you didn't want them.'

'I *didn't* throw them away!' screamed Maxine.

'Liar, I saw you,' goaded Martin. 'I saw you throw them in the air. Little liar.'

Maxine howled, scarlet in the face, struggling with her mother, who was trying to hold her, while Martin ran off out of range, dancing on the spot and fleering and taunting.

'Why is he such a poisonous little tick?' said Max, though without his usual fury.

On their way back to the hotel they passed a camp-site, and stopped by the gate to read its painted sign.

'Families and mixed couples only,' Maxine read aloud. 'What does that mean, Mum? What are mixed couples? Mum? Mum?'

'I'm not sure,' said Dorrie. She was reminded of her parents' description of looking for somewhere to rent when they first came to London, with the signs up in the windows reading 'No Blacks, No Irish' and her father with his Dublin accent having to keep quiet for a change and let her mother do the talking.

'Why do you suppose they want mixed couples only?' she murmured to Max. 'Why would they worry about gayness?'

'I don't think it's that,' said Max. 'I think it's more to put off the eighteen-thirty element; you know, bikers and boozers and gangs getting into fights.'

'You twenty years ago,' said Dorrie.

'Martin in ten years' time,' said Max.

'What's a couple?' persisted Maxine. 'What's a couple, Dad?'

'A couple here means a man and a woman,' said Max.

'Oo–a–ooh!' exclaimed Martin, giving Maxine a lewd nudge in the ribs and rolling his eyes.

'A husband and wife,' said Dorrie deflatingly.

'So a couple's like a family?' said Maxine.

'Yes,' said Dorrie.

'No,' said Max. 'A couple is *not* like a family. That's far too easy, just two people. It doesn't qualify.'

Dorrie was laughing now, and put her arms round his waist, her head in his shoulder. He kissed the top of her head and stroked her hair. The three children stood round looking at them with big smug smiles, beaming with satisfaction.

'Come in for a hug,' said Dorrie, holding out her arm to them, and they all five stood rocking by the side of the road locked into an untidy, squawking clump.

'You're looking well,' said Max, gazing at her that evening across the mackerel pâté and the bud vase holding the miniature yellow carnations. 'You've caught the sun. It suits you.'

'It was a good walk today,' said Dorrie, suddenly shy.

'They're lovely but they're very tiring,' said Max, draining his glass of beer. 'Exhausting. You should be more selfish.'

How can I, thought Dorrie, until you are less so? It's a seesaw. But she kept quiet. He went on to talk about the garden centre, how it was doing all right but they couldn't afford to rest on their laurels with all these small businesses going down all round them.

'We're a team,' declared Max, grandiose, pouring another glass for them both.

'Ye-es,' said Dorrie. 'But it's a bit unbalanced, don't you think, the teamwork, at the moment?'

'Are you saying I don't work hard enough?' demanded Max.

'Of course not,' said Dorrie. 'You work too hard. Don't be silly. No, I meant, you do all the work that gets somewhere and gives you something to show for the effort and pulls in money, but the work I do doesn't seem to get anywhere, it doesn't show, it somehow doesn't count even though it needs doing of course.'

'I don't see what you're driving at,' said Max, starting to look less cheerful.

'I don't know,' said Dorrie. 'At the moment I feel sub. Sub something.'

'Suburban?' suggested Max.

'Subordinate?' said Dorrie. 'No.'

'Submerged, then. How about submerged.'

'That's nearer. Still not quite . . . I know! Subdued. Though submerged is growing on me. Submerged is accurate too. That time at Marks, all my twenties, half my thirties, it's like a dream. I've almost forgotten what it used to be like.'

And she tried to explain to Max her feeling about this encroaching blandness, adaptability, passivity, the need for one of them at least to embrace these qualities, even if this made them shudder, if the family was going to work.

'We all have to knuckle down,' he said. 'Sooner or later.'

'It's just it seems, some of us more than others.'

'If we want to join in at all,' opined Max. 'Life. It's called growing up.'

'It doesn't feel like growing up,' she muttered from her side of the fence. Rather it felt like being freeze-dried and vacuum-packed. Knuckled down was putting it mildly.

'Well, as I said, whatever you're feeling like, you're looking well,' said Max; and that made them both feel better.

'Lovely, in fact,' he added, leaning across to touch her face meaningly.

After dinner, sitting in the Family Room drinking coffee, they found themselves drawn into a quiz game provided by the hotel as the adult equivalent of the children's conga. The quizmaster was a sparky woman in an emerald green jacket and pleats. She split them into groups and bossed them through an unnecessary microphone.

'What's the other name for kiwifruit?' she demanded, and echoes bounced off the ceiling. The groups whispered and giggled and scribbled on their scoresheets.

'What flag is all one colour?' she asked. 'Here's a clue, somewhere not very nice. Ooh, I hope no one from there is in this room!'

'Birmingham?' suggested Max.

'Very funny, the bearded gentleman,' said the woman.

'Now we're out of Miscellaneous and onto the Human Body. Let's see how much you all know about the body, you jolly well should considering your age. And the one who's paying for the holiday will certainly be hoping to know a bit more about the human body of the opposite sex or else they'll have wasted their money, won't they?'

Dorrie's mouth fell open, she nearly dropped her drink, but nobody else batted an eyelid.

'And we've quite enough children here thank you very much while we're on the subject so let's hope you all know what you're up to,' continued the woman, arching a roguish eyebrow. 'Right. Now. Where are the cervical nerves?'

'And where's your sense of humour?' Max whispered into Dorrie's ear, observing her gape rudely at the woman.

In bed that night surrounded by their sleeping children, they held each other and started to kiss with increasing warmth. He grabbed shamelessly between her legs, her body answered with an enthusiastic twist, a backward arch, and soon he was inside her. There must be no noise, and she had pulled the sheet up to their necks. Within a couple of minutes they were both almost there, together, when there came a noise from Martin's bed.

'Mum,' he said sleepily, and flicked his lamp on. 'Mum, I'm thirsty.'

Max froze where he was and dropped his head and swore beneath his breath. Martin got out of bed and padded over towards them.

'Did you *hear* me, Mum?' he asked crossly. 'I want some water. *Now.*'

Dorrie was aware of her hot red face looking up from under Max's, and heard herself say, 'In a minute, dear. Go back to bed now, there's a good boy.' Martin paused to stare at them, then stumbled over back towards his bed.

'Do you think he's been traumatised?' she whispered to Max, mortified, cheated of the concentrated pleasure which had been seconds away, the achievement of it, the being made whole.

'Do I think *he's* been traumatised?' growled Max incredulously, rolling off her.

'Where's your sense of humour, then?' she murmured in his ear, but he pulled away and turned his back on her. She didn't blame him.

Their third day's adventure was planned by Max. They were going to cross the strand and explore the hermit's island. Today the tide was out at a reasonable time of the morning and the sun was up too. They stood and gazed across the shining sands at the exposed island, which was now, for an hour or so only, part of the mainland.

'It's further than I thought,' said Dorrie. 'It looks well over a mile. Maybe two.'

'Half a mile at most,' said Max heartily. 'Let's get going, remember we're racing the tide. Come on you lot, shoes and socks in the boot.'

'I think they should wear their plastic sandals,' said Dorrie. 'I can see stones. Weed.'

'Nonsense,' said Max. 'Lovely sand, skipping across the golden sand. Don't fuss, don't spoil it all with fussing.'

'Skippety skip,' sang Robin.

'I still think,' said Dorrie.

'Give us a break,' said Max.

'I'm not wearing my jellies,' said Martin. 'No way.'

'No way,' echoed Maxine.

When they started walking they were less downright, but by then it was too late. The gleaming silver-pink sand was knotted with wormcasts which made the children shudder, and studded with pebbles, and sharp-edged broken shells, which made them wince and squawk.

'Come on,' called Max, striding ahead on his prime-of-life leathery soles. 'We've got to keep moving if we're going to be there and back in time. Or we'll be cut off.'

Dorrie helped the children round the weeds, through ankle-deep seawater rivulets blue as the sky above, clucking, and lifting, and choking down irritation at the thought of the plastic sandals back in the boot.

'You were right, Mum,' groaned Martin mournfully. 'I wish I'd worn them.'

'So do I,' said Maxine, picking her way like a cross hen.

'So do I,' wept Robin, who was walking on tiptoe, as though that might spare his soft pink feet the wormcasts, and slowing them all down considerably.

'Come on,' yelled Max, a couple of hundred yards ahead.

'We can't,' yelled Dorrie, who was by now carrying Robin across her front.

It felt desperate, like the retreat from Moscow or something. Trust Max to engineer a stressful seaside event, trust Max to inject a penitential flavour into the day. They were by now half a mile out; it would be mad to go on and dismal to turn back. The sun was strong but muffled by haze, and the sky glared with the blanched fluorescence of a shaving light.

'What's all the fuss about?' said Max, having unwillingly rejoined them.

'I think we'll have to turn back,' said Dorrie. 'Look at the time. Even if we make it to the island we won't be able to explore, we'll have to turn round and come straight back and even then we'd be cutting it fine. Why don't you go alone, darling, you're quicker on your own.'

'You always have to spoil it, don't you?' said Max, furious as a child. 'You never want anything I plan to work.'

'Their feet hurt,' pleaded Dorrie. 'Don't let's quarrel in front of them.'

'Robin, you'll come with me, won't you?' said Max, squatting down beside his son. 'I'll give you a piggyback.'

'Max,' said Dorrie. 'It's nearly midday, it's not safe, why don't you go ahead with the camera and take photos so we'll all be able to see the hermit's house when the film's developed.'

'Robin?' said Max.

'I don't know what to choose,' said Robin, looking from his father to his mother and back again. He was out of his depth.

Dorrie felt anger bulge up as big as a whale surfacing, but breathed it down and said again, 'Take the camera, darling, that way we'll all see the secret island,' and hung the camera round his neck. She made herself kiss him on the cheek. He looked at her suspiciously. The children brightened. She forced herself to hug him. The children cheered.

'All right,' he said at last, and set off across the wet sand, running simple and free as a Red Indian.

'I didn't know what to say, Mum,' said Robin, spreading

his hands helplessly. 'Daddy said go on go with me not Mummy. You said no. I felt splitted in half.'

'It's all right,' said Dorrie. 'Now everybody's happy. Look at that seagull.'

Above them, floating on a thermal, was a big, white, cruel-beaked bird. Seagulls were always larger than you expected, and had a chilly fierce look to them, without gaiety. She could barely speak for rage, but did not assign it much importance, so used was she by now to this business of ebb and flow. Who else, she wondered, could be living at such a pitch of passion as she in the midst of this crew; so uncontrolled, so undefended?

Having poked around the hermit's mossy cell and raced the tide back, white-toothed wavelets snapping at his heels, Max was in a good mood for the rest of the day, and they all benefited. He felt he had achieved something. He *had* achieved something. He had conquered the island, he had patterned it with his footprints, he had written his name on the sandy floor of the hermit's very cell with his big toe. Next week he would show them the photographs to prove it.

When the sun was low in the sky and the children were asleep, Max suggested to Dorrie that she should go for a walk on her own, just down to the beach below the hotel.

'It'll do you good,' he said.

He was going to sit by the bedroom's picture window in the half-dark with a beer, and would probably be able to make out her figure if the light didn't go too fast.

'Are you sure you'll be all right?' she said.

'Go on,' he snorted. 'Before I change my mind.'

She walked down barefoot through the hotel gardens, across trim tough seaside turf bordered by white-painted palisades and recently-watered fuchsia bushes. Then she turned on to the low cliff path which zigzagged down to the beach and felt the longer grass brush against her legs, spiky marram grass softly spangled in the dusk with pale flowers, sea pinks and thrift and white sea campion.

Robin had had trouble getting to sleep that evening. Stay here, he had demanded tearfully, his hand on her arm; don't go. I won't go, she had said; close your eyes. She had stroked his temple with the side of her little finger. Gradually he had allowed himself to be lowered down, a rung at a time, towards the dark surface of sleep. He had given a tiny groan as she moved to get up, but he was too far gone to climb back. She had sat by him for a little longer, creaking with fatigue, looking at his quiet face, his still hand on her arm, savouring the deep romance and boredom of it.

There were no buildings now between her and the beach except for this last snug cottage to her left shedding light from its windows. She paused to look up at it. It must surely house an ideal family, sheltered and enclosed but with a view of the bay too. The father was reading his children a story, perhaps, while the mother brushed their hair. Where did this cosy picture come from? Certainly not from her own childhood. She turned away and carried on down to the beach.

It was lovely to stand barefoot, bare-legged indeed, invisible in the deep dusk, a great generous moon in the sky and her feet at the edge of the Atlantic. She looked out over the broad bosom of the sea and it was like an old engraving, beautiful and melancholy, and the noise it made was a sighing, a rhythmic sighing.

As sailors' ghosts looked back on their drowned selves, dismantled, broken up, sighing like the sea for the collar-bone lost somewhere around the equator, the metatarsals scattered across the Indian Ocean, so she wondered whether there could ever be a reassembly of such scattered drowned bodies, a watery *danse macabre* on the wreckers' rocks beneath a full moon. Was it possible to reclaim the scattered-to-the-winds self? She was less afraid of death, or under-stood it a shade more, purely through coming near it each time she had had a baby; but apart from that, this puzzle was to do with the loss of self that went with the process, or rather the awareness of her individuality as a trouble-some excrescence, an obsoletism. What she wanted to know was, was this temporary, like National Service used to be, or was it for good?

She was filled with excitement at standing by the edge of the sea alone under the sky, so that she took great clear breaths of air and looked at the dimming horizon, opening her eyes wider as if that might help her to see more. It filled her with courage and made her want to sing, some-thing Irish or Scottish, sad and wild and expressive of this, this wild salt air, out here, and of how it was thrilling, being alive and not dead.

When she turned back across the beach, away from the water, it was dark. The orange lights of the hotel up on the hill lengthened on the wet black sand like pillars of flame. She reached the edge of the beach, where it met the rocks and turf above, and started to climb back. A bat bounced silently past her ear as she crossed the little bridge over the stream, and then she felt the dust of the earth path beneath her feet again. As she walked on, hugging herself against the fresh chill of the dark, she looked at the cottages built on the hills around the bay, their windows yellow lozenges of enclosed warmth in the night.

Now she was walking back past the house she had envied on the way down, the house which was so secure and self-sufficient with its warm lit windows and snug family within. And from this house came the wailing of a child, a desolate hopeless noise. It was coming from this very house. On and on it went, the wailing, steady and miserable, following her up the path. Her throat tightened and her eyes prickled, she called herself every sort of fool as she trudged on; and she physically ached to pick up and hold the weeping child, and tell it there there, there there, then smooth it down and stroke its hand until it slept. The comfortless noise continued, not a baby's crying but the sobbing of a child. No child should be left to cry like that, she thought, ambushed by pity, by memory; and − in a rage − people aren't bloody well nice enough to their children!

Don't be so soft, came the advice; crying never did any harm, you can't allow them to run the show or where will that land you? Let them take themselves to hell, those hard hearts who leave their children to cry themselves to sleep alone, and in hell they will have to listen to the sound of a child crying and know that they can never comfort it. That was what Dorrie was thinking as she climbed back up the hill.

From
Constitutional

Early One Morning

Sometimes they were quiet in the car and sometimes they talked.

'Mum.'

'Yes?'

'Can I swear one time in the day? If I don't swear in the others?'

'Why?'

'In the morning. When you come and wake me. Can I say, "Bollocks"?'

'No.'

He's the only person in the world who listens to me and does what I tell him, thought Zoe. That morning when she had gone to wake him he had groaned, unconscious, spontaneous – 'Already?' Then he had reached up from his pillow to put strong sleepy arms round her neck.

For these years of her life she was spending more time alone with her boy, side by side in the car, than with anybody else, certainly far more than with her husband, thirty times more, unless you counted the hours asleep. There was the daily business of showing herself to him and to no one else; thinking aloud, urging each other on in the hunt for swimming things, car keys, maths books; yawning like cats, as they had to leave soon after seven if they were going to get to school on time. Then they might tell each other the remains of a dream during the first twenty-five minutes on the way to Freda's house, or they might sit in comfortable silence, or sometimes they would talk.

This morning when she had pointed out the sun rising in the east to hit the windscreen and blind them with its flood of flashy light, her nine-year-old boy had scoffed at her and said the earth twizzled on its axis and went round the sun, and how she, his mother, was as bad as the ancient Egyptians, how they sacrificed someone to Ra if the sun went in and finished off everybody when there was an eclipse. It's running out, this hidden time (thought Zoe). You're on your own at eleven, goes the current unwritten transport protocol, but until then you need a minder. Less than two years to go.

'I remember when I was at school,' she'd said that morning while they waited for the Caedmon Hill lights. 'It seemed to go on forever. Time goes by slowly at school. Slowly. Slowly. Then, after you're about thirty, it goes faster and faster.'

'Why?' asked George.

'I don't know,' she said. 'Maybe it's because after that you somehow know that there'll be a moment for you when there isn't any more.'

'Ooh-ah!'

Then he looked at a passing cyclist and commented, 'Big arse.'

'George!' she said, shocked.

'It just slipped out,' he said, apologetic, adult. 'You know, like when that man in the white van wouldn't let you in and you said, "Bastard."'

Sometimes this daily struggle and inching along through filthy air thick with the thwarted rage of ten thousand drivers gave her, Zoe, pause. It took forty-five minutes to travel the two and three-quarter miles to George's school (Sacred Heart thanks to his father's faith springing anew, rather than Hereward the Wake half a mile along), and forty-five minutes for her to come back alone in the empty car. In the afternoons it was the same, but the other way round of course, setting off a little after two thirty and arriving back well after four. There was no train. To do the journey by bus, they would have had to catch a 63A then change and wait for a 119 at Sollers Junction. They had tried this, and it had doubled the journey time. Why couldn't there be school buses for everyone as there were in America, the mothers asked each other. Nobody knew why not, but apparently there couldn't. They were just about able to walk it in the same time as it took in the car, and they had tried this too, carrying rucksacks of homework and packed lunch and sports equipment through the soup of fumes pumped out by crawling cars. Add wind and rain, and the whole idea of pavement travel looked positively quixotic.

'I'll get it, Mum,' said George, as her mobile beeped its receipt of a text.

It was from her friend Amy, whose husband had recently left her for one of his students.

– If I say anything, he gets very angry (Amy had told her on their last phone call); he doesn't allow me to be angry.

– But he was the one to leave you.

– Yes. But now he's furious with me, he hates me.

– Do you still love him?

– I don't recognise him. I can't believe this man I ate with and slept beside for fifteen years is capable of being so cold and so, yes, cruel.

Is it true, then, that women can take grief as grief (thought Zoe), but men refuse to do that, they have to convert it into diesel in order to deal with it, all the loss and pain converted into rage?

Her husband had looked around and said, Why don't you do like Sally and Chitra and Mo, organise an au pair, pay for a few driving lessons if necessary, hand it over to someone who'll be glad of the job. She, Zoe, had thought about this, but she'd already been through it all once before, with Joe and Theresa, who were both now at secondary school. She'd done the sums, gone through the interviews in her imagination, considered the no-claims bonus; she'd counted the years for which her work time would be cut in half, she'd set off the loss of potential income against the cost of childcare, and she'd bitten the bullet. 'It's your choice,' said Patrick. And it was.

'You're a loser, Mum,' her daughter Theresa had told her on her return from a recent careers convention. But she wasn't. She'd done it all now – she'd been through the whole process of hanging on to her old self, carving out patches of time, not relinquishing her work, then partly letting go in order to be more with the children, his work taking precedence over hers as generally seemed to be the case when the parents were still together. Unless the woman earned more, which opened up a whole new can of modern worms. Those long forgotten hours and days were now like nourishing leaf mould round their roots. Let the past go (sang Zoe beneath her breath), time to move on; her own built-in obsolescence could make her feel lively rather than sad. And perhaps the shape of life would be like an hour-glass, clear and wide to begin with, narrowing down to the tunnel of the middle years, then flaring wide again before the sands ran out.

'Mum, can you test me on my words?' asked George. He was doing a French taster term, taking it seriously because he wanted to outstrip his friend Mick who was better than him at maths.

'Well I'm not supposed to,' said Zoe. 'But we're not moving. Here, put it on my lap and keep your eye open for when the car in front starts to move.'

When I was starting out, leaving babies till after thirty was seen as leaving it late (thought Zoe). Over thirty was the time of fade for women, loss of bloom and all that. Now you're expected to be still a girl at forty-two – slim, active, up for it. But if I hadn't done it, had Joe at twenty-six and Theresa at twenty-eight, hammered away at work and sweated blood in pursuit of good childminders, nurseries, au pairs, you name it, and finally, five years later when George came along, slowed down for a while at least; then I wouldn't know why so many women are the way they are. Stymied at some point; silenced somewhere. Stalled. Or, merely delayed?

'It's who, when, where, how and all that sort of thing,' said George. 'I'll tell you how I remember *quand*. I think of the Sorcerer's Apprentice, because you know he had a WAND, rhymes with *quand*, and then he goes away with all those buckets of water and then WHEN he comes back

. . . Get it? WHEN he comes back! That's how it stays in my mind. And *qui* is the KEY in a door and you answer it and who is there? WHO! I thought of all that myself, yeah. Course. And *où* is monkeys in the rainforest. Oo oo oo. Hey look, it's moving.'

They crawled forward, even getting into second gear for a few seconds, then settled again into stasis.

'Why the rainforest?' asked Zoe. 'Monkeys in the rainforest?'

'Because, WHERE are they?' he asked. 'Where *are* they, the trees in the rainforest. That's what the monkeys want to know, oo oo oo. Cos they aren't there any more, the trees in the rainforest.'

'You remember everything they teach you at school, don't you,' said Zoe admiringly.

'Just about,' said George with a pleased smile. 'Mum, I don't want you to die until I'm grown up.'

There was a pause.

'But I don't want to die *before* you,' he added.

'No, I don't want that either,' said Zoe.

This boy remembers every detail of every unremarkable day (thought Zoe); he's not been alive that long and he's got acres of lovely empty space in his memory bank. Whereas I've been alive for ages and it's got to the point where my mind is saying it already has enough on its shelves, it just can't be bothered to store something new unless it's *really* worth remembering.

I climb the stairs and forget what I'm looking for. I forgot to pick up Natasha last week when I'd promised her mother, and I had to do a three-point turn in the middle of Ivanhoe Avenue and go back for her and just hope that none of the children already in the car would snitch on me. But that's nothing new. I can't remember a thing about the last decade or so, she told other mothers, and they agreed, it was a blur, a blank; they had photographs to prove it had happened, but they couldn't remember it themselves. She, Zoe, saw her memory banks as having shrivelled for lack of sleep's welcome rain; she brooded over the return of those refreshing showers and the rehydration of her pot-noodle bundles of memories, and how (one day) the past would plump into action, swelling with import, newly alive. When she was old and free and in her second adolescence, she would sleep in royally, till midday or one. Yet old people cannot revisit that country, they report; they wake and listen to the dawn chorus after four or five threadbare hours, and long for the old three-ply youth-giving slumber.

They had reached Freda's house, and Zoe stopped the car to let George out. He went off to ring the bell and wait while Freda and also Harry, who was in on this lift, gathered their bags and shoes and coats. It was too narrow a road to hover in, or rather Zoe did not have the nerve to make other people queue behind her while she waited for her passengers to arrive. This morning she shoehorned the car into a minute space three hundred yards away, proudly parking on a sixpence.

What's truly radical now though (thought Zoe, rereading the text from Amy as she waited) is to imagine a man and woman having children and living happily together, justice and love prevailing, self-respect on both sides, each making sure the other flourishes as well as the children. The windscreen blurred as it started to rain. If not constantly, she modified, then taking turns. Where *are* they?

But this wave of divorces (she thought), the couples who'd had ten or fifteen years or more of being together, her feeling was that often it wasn't as corny as it seemed to be in Amy's case – being left for youth. When she, Zoe, looked closely, it was more to do with the mercurial resentment quotient present in every marriage having risen to the top of the thermometer. It was more to do with how the marriage had turned out, now it was this far down the line. Was one of the couple thriving and satisfied, with the other restless or foundering? Or perhaps the years had spawned a marital Black Dog, where one of them dragged the other down with endless gloom or bad temper or censoriousness and refused to be comforted, ever, and also held the other responsible for their misery.

There had been a scattering of bust-ups during the first two or three years of having babies, and then things seemed to settle down. This was the second wave, a decade or so on, a wild tsunami of divorce as children reached adolescence and parents left youth behind. The third big wave was set to come when the children left home. She, Zoe, had grown familiar with the process simply by listening. First came the shock, the vulnerability and hurt; then the nastiness (particularly about money) with accompanying baffled incredulity; down on to indignation at the exposure of unsuspected talents for treachery, secretiveness, two-faced liardom; falling last of all into scalding grief or adamantine hatred. Only last week her next door neighbour, forced to put the house on the market, had hissed at her over the fence, 'I hope he gets cancer and dies.' Though when it came to showing round prospective purchasers, the estate agents always murmured the word 'amicable' as reassurance; purchasers wanted to hear it was amicable rather than that other divorce word, acrimonious.

She peered into the driver's mirror and saw them trudging towards her with their usual heaps of school luggage. It was still well before eight and, judging herself more bleached and craggy than usual, she added some colour just as they got to the car.

'Lipstick, hey,' said George, taking the front seat. The other two shuffled themselves and their bags into the back.

'I used to wear make-up,' said Zoe. 'Well, a bit. When I was younger. I really enjoyed it.'

'Why don't you now?' asked Freda. Freda's mother did, of course. Her mother was thirty-eight rather than forty-two. It made a difference, this slide over to the other side, reflected Zoe, and also one was tireder.

'Well, I still do if I feel like it,' she said, starting the car and indicating. She waited for a removal van to lumber along and shave past. 'But I don't do it every day like brushing my teeth. It's just another thing.' Also, nobody but you lot is going to see me so why would I, she added silently, churlishly.

She was aware of the children thinking, what? *Why* not? Women *should* wear make-up. Freda in particular would be on the side of glamour and looking one's best at all times.

'We had a Mexican student staying with us once,' she told them, edging on to the main road. 'And at first she would spend ages looking after her long glossy hair, and more ages brushing make-up onto her eyelids and applying that gorgeous glossy lipgloss. But after a while she stopped, and she looked just like the rest of us – she said to me that it was a lovely holiday after Mexico City, where she really couldn't go outside without the full works or everybody would stare at her. So she kept it for parties or times when she felt like putting it on, after that.'

'Women look better with make-up,' commented Harry from the back. Harry's mother dropped him off at Freda's on Tuesday and Thursday mornings, and, in the spirit of hawk-eyed reciprocity on which the whole fragile schoolrun ecosystem was founded, Zoe collected George from Harry's house on Monday and Wednesday afternoons, which cut *that* journey in half.

'Well I'm always going to wear make-up when I'm older,' said Freda.

'Women used to set their alarm clocks an hour early so they could put on their false eyelashes and lid liner and all that,' said Zoe. 'Imagine being frightened of your husband seeing your bare face!'

There was silence as they considered this, grudging assent, even. But the old advice was still doing the rounds, Zoe had noticed, for women to listen admiringly to men and not to laugh at them if they wanted to snare one of their very own. Give a man respect for being higher caste than you, freer, more powerful. And men, what was it men wanted? Was it true they only wanted a cipher? That a woman should not expect admiration from a man for any other qualities than physical beauty or selflessness? Surely not. If this were the case, why live with such a poor sap if you could scrape your own living?

'Do you like Alex?' asked Harry. 'I don't. I hate Alex, he whines and he's mean and he cries and he whinges all the time. But I pretend I like him, because I want him to like me.'

There was no comment from the other three. They were sunk in early-morning torpor, staring at the static traffic around them.

'I despite him,' said Harry.

'You can't say that,' said Freda. 'It's despise.'

'That's what I said,' said Harry.

George snorted.

It was nothing short of dangerous and misguided (thought Zoe) not to keep earning, even if it wasn't very much and you were doing all the domestic and emotional work as well, for the sake of keeping the marital Black Dog at bay. Otherwise if you spoke up it would be like biting the hand that fed you. Yes you wanted to be around (thought Zoe), to be an armoire, to make them safe as houses. But surrendering your autonomy for too long, subsumption without promise of future release, those weren't good for the health.

'I hate that feeling in the playground when I've bullied someone and then they start crying,' said Harry with candour.

'I don't like it if someone cries because of something I've said,' said Freda.

'I don't like it when there's a group of people and they're making someone cry,' said George over his shoulder. 'That makes me feel bad.'

'Oh I don't mind that,' said Harry. 'If it wasn't me that made them cry. If it was other people, that's nothing to do with me.'

'No, but don't you feel bad when you see one person like that,' replied George, 'and everyone picking on them, if you don't, like, say something?'

'No,' said Harry. 'I don't care. As long as *I'm* not being nasty to them I don't feel bad at what's happening.'

'Oh,' said George, considering. 'I do.'

'Look at that car's number plate,' said Freda. 'The letters say XAN. XAN! XAN!'

'FWMM!' joined in Harry. 'FWMMFWMM! FWMMFWMMFWMM!'

'BGA,' growled George. 'BGA. Can you touch your nose with your tongue?'

Zoe stared out from the static car at the line of people waiting in the rain at a bus stop, and studied their faces. Time sinks into flesh (she mused), gradually sinks it. A look of distant bruising arrives, and also for some reason asymmetry. One eye sits higher than the other and the mouth looks crooked. We start to resemble cartoons or caricatures of ourselves. On cold days like today the effect can be quite trollish.

'Who would you choose to push off a cliff or send to prison or give a big hug?' George threw over his shoulder. 'Out of three – Peter Vallings–'

'Ugh, not Peter Vallings!' shrieked Freda in an ecstasy of disgust.

'Mrs Campbell. And – Mr Starling!'

'Mr Starling! Oh my God, Mr Starling,' said Harry, caught between spasms of distaste and delight. 'Yesterday he was wearing this top, yeah, he lets you see how many ripples he's got.'

Your skin won't stay with your flesh as it used to (thought Zoe); it won't move and follow muscle the way it did before. You turn, and there is a fan of creases however trim you are; yet once you were one of these young things at the bus stop, these over-eleven secondary school pupils. Why do we smile at adolescent boys, so unfinished, so lumpy (she wondered) but feel disturbed by this early beauty of the girls, who gleam with benefit, their hair smooth as glass or in rich ringlets, smiling big smiles and speaking up and nobody these days saying, 'Who do you think you are?' or 'You look like a prostitute.' It's not as if the boys won't catch up with a vengeance.

'I love my dog,' said Harry fiercely.

'Yes, he's a nice dog,' agreed Freda.

'I love my dog so much,' continued Harry, 'I would rather die than see my dog die.'

'*You* would rather die than your *dog*?' said George in disbelief.

'Yes! I love my dog! Don't you love *your* dog?'

'Yes. But . . .'

'You don't really love your dog. If you wouldn't die instead of him.'

Zoe bit her tongue. Her rule was, never join in. That way they could pretend she wasn't there. The sort of internal monologue she enjoyed these days came from being round older children, at their disposal but silent. She was able to dip in and out of her thoughts now with the freedom of a bird. Whereas it was true enough that no thought could take wing round the under-fives; what they needed was too constant and minute and demanding, you had to be out of the room in order to think and they needed you *in* the room.

When George walked beside her he liked to hold on to what he called her elbow flab. He pinched it till it held a separate shape. He was going to be tall. As high as my heart, she used to say last year, but he had grown since then; he came up to her shoulder now, this nine-year-old.

'Teenagers!' he'd said to her not long ago. 'When I turn thirteen I'll be horrible in one night. Covered in spots and rude to you and not talking. Jus' grunting.'

Where did he get all that from? The most difficult age for girls was fourteen, they now claimed, the parenting experts, while for boys it was nineteen. Ten more years then. Good.

'Would you like to be tall?' she'd asked him that time.

'Not very,' he'd said decisively. 'But I wouldn't like just to be five eight or something. I'd want to be taller than my wife.'

His *wife*! Some way down the corridor of the years, she saw his wife against the fading sun, her face in shade. Would his wife mind if she, Zoe, hugged him when they met? She might, she might well. More than the father giving away his daughter, the mother must hand over her son. Perhaps his *wife* would only allow them to shake hands. When he was little his hands had been like velvet, without knuckles or veins; he used to put his small warm hands up her cardigan sleeves when he was wheedling for something.

They were inching their way down Mordred Hill, some sort of delay having been caused by a juggernaut trying to back into an eighteenth-century alley centimetres too narrow for it. Zoe sighed with disbelief, then practised her deep breathing. Nothing you could do about it, no point in road rage, the country was stuffed to the gills with cars and that was all there was to it. She had taken the Civil Service exams after college and one of the questions had been, 'How would you arrange the transport system of this country?' At the time, being utterly wrapped up in cliometrics and dendrochronology, she had been quite unable to answer; but now, a couple of decades down the line, she felt fully qualified to write several thousand impassioned words, if not a thesis, on the subject.

But then if you believe in wives and steadfastness and heroic monogamy (thought Zoe, as the lorry cleared the space and the traffic began to flow again), how can you admit change? Her sister Valerie had described how she was making her husband read aloud each night in bed from *How to Rescue a Relationship*. When he protested, she pointed out that it was instead of going to a marriage guidance counsellor. Whoever wants to live must forget, Valerie had told her drily; that was the gist of it. She, Zoe, wasn't sure that she would be able to take marriage guidance counselling seriously either, as she suspected it was probably done mainly by women who were no longer needed on the school run. It all seemed to be about women needed and wanted, then not needed and not wanted. She moved off in second gear.

No wonder there were gaggles of mothers sitting over milky lattes all over the place from 8.40 a.m. They were recovering from driving exclusively in the first two gears for the last hour; they had met the school deadline and now wanted some pleasure on the return run. Zoe preferred her own company at this time of the morning, and also did not relish the conversation of such groups, which tended to be fault-finding sessions on how Miss Scantlebury taught long division or post-mortems on reported classroom injustices, bubblings-up of indignation and the urge to interfere, still to be the main moving force in their child's day. She needed a coffee though – a double macchiato, to be precise – and she liked the café sensation of being alone but in company, surrounded by tables of huddled intimacies each hived off from the other, scraps of conversation drifting in the air. Yesterday, she remembered, there had been those two women in baggy velour tracksuits at the table nearest to her, very solemn.

'I feel rather protective towards him. The girls are very provocative the way they dress now. He's thirteen.'

'Especially when you're surrounded by all these images. Everywhere you go.'

'It's not a very nice culture.'

'No, it's not.'

And all around there had been that steady self-justificatory hum of women telling each other the latest version of themselves, their lives, punctuated with the occasional righteous cry as yet another patch of moral high ground was claimed. That's a real weakness (she thought, shaking her head), and an enemy of, of – whatever it is we're after. Amity, would you call it?

'Last year when we were in Cornwall we went out in a boat and we saw sharks,' said Harry.

'Sharks!' scoffed George. 'Ho yes. In *Cornwall*.'

'No, really,' insisted Harry.

'It's eels as well,' said Freda. 'I don't like them either.'

'Ooh no,' Harry agreed, shuddering.

'What about sea-snakes,' said George. 'They can swim into any hole in your body.'

The car fell silent as they absorbed this information.

'Where did you hear this?' asked Zoe suspiciously; she had her own reservations about Mr Starling.

'Mr Starling told us,' smirked George. 'If it goes in at your ear, you're dead because it sneaks into your brain. But if it goes up your . . .'

'What happens if it gets in up there?' asked Harry.

'If it gets in there, up inside you,' said George, 'you don't die but they have to take you to hospital and cut you open and pull it out.'

The talk progressed naturally from here to tapeworms.

'They hang on to you by hooks all the way down,' said Harry. 'You have to poison them, by giving the person enough to kill the worm but not them. Then the worm dies and the hooks get loose and the worm comes out. Either of your bottom or somehow they pull it through your mouth.'

'That's enough of that,' said Zoe at last. 'It's too early in the morning.'

They reached the road where the school was with five minutes to spare, and Zoe drew in to the kerb some way off while they decanted their bags and shoes and morning selves. Would George kiss her? She only got a kiss when they arrived if none of the boys in his class was around. He knew she wanted a kiss, and gave her a warning look. No, there was Sean McIlroy – no chance today.

They were gone. The car was suddenly empty, she sat unkissed, redundant, cast off like an old boot. 'Boohoo,' she murmured, her eyes blurring for a moment, and carefully adjusted her wing mirror for something to do.

Then George reappeared, tapping at the window, looking stern and furtive.

'I said I'd forgotten my maths book,' he muttered when she opened the car door, and, leaning across as though to pick up something from the seat beside her, smudged her cheek with a hurried – but (thought Zoe) unsurpassable – kiss.

The Door

Organising a new back door after the break-in was more complicated than you might imagine. Even sourcing a ready-made door to fit the existing frame took some doing. After following a couple of false trails I drove to a little DIY shop five miles away, in a draughty row of shops just off the A3 after the Tolworth Tower turning.

Bleak from outside, this charmless parade supplied all sorts of seductive and useful items when you looked more closely. Under the dustbin lid of a sky were: a travel agent offering cut-price controlled escapes; a newsagent with a bank of magazine smiles on entry and a surprisingly choice collection of sweets (real Turkish Delight, macadamia praline, Alpine milk chocolate); an art shop with dusty sleeping cat at the foot of a good wooden easel; a café with Formica tables, a constant frying pan and a big steel teapot. If you looked closely and in the right way, all the pleasures and comforts were accessible here in this dog-leg just off the Tolworth turning, as well as all the nuts and bolts. It was the first time for months that I'd been able to entertain such a thought. In the iron light of February I entered the hardware shop and inside was a little community of goodwill and respect.

The woman on the other side of the counter listened
to me attentively, looked at me with kind eyes from behind
her glasses, and explained the sizes, finishes, charges and
extras for the various models of ready-made doors they
could supply. While she did this she also dealt with a couple
of phone calls, politely and efficiently, and paused for a
few seconds to admire the baby asleep in the arms of the
café owner from next door who had come round with
some query about his ceiling, promising herself aloud a
cuddle once my order had been taken. Since the seven-
teenth of August I had grown unimaginative about others,
selfishly incurious and sometimes downright hostile. Now,
here, some sort of thaw was taking place. A tall man in
overalls was talking to the shop's manager, telling him about
the progress of a job out in West Molesey, and it seemed
it was going well.

There was an atmosphere of good temper which was
rare and warming, none of the usual sighs or in-staff carping
or reined-in impatience when you wanted to know how
much it would be with extra safety bolts or with three
coats of paint rather than two. I was charmed. I wanted
to stay in this dim toasty light amid the general friendliness
and walls festooned with hosepipes, tubes of grouting and
sealant, boxes of thumbtacks, lightbulbs, my mind soothed
by the industrious but not frantic atmosphere.

Everything here had to do with maintenance and sound-
ness. Grief kept indoors grows noxious, I thought, like a
room that can't be aired; mould grows, plants die. I wanted
to open the windows but it wasn't allowed.

The order was complicated — did I want full or partial
beading; what about a weatherboard; the door furniture,

would I prefer a silver or gold finish, or perhaps this brushed aluminium – and it took quite a while. Even so, I was sorry when it was finished and Sally – the young woman's name – had handed me my carbon copy and swiped a hundred pounds from my Barclaycard as the deposit. Because even a very ordinary ready-made back door was going to cost £400 in total to supply, fit, hang and paint.

'They're not cheap, are they, doors,' I said, as I signed the slip.

'They're not,' she sighed in agreement, not taking my comment in any way personally. 'But they're well-made, these doors. Nice and strong.'

'Good,' I said, tucking the Visa slip into my wallet. For a moment I toyed with the idea of telling her how they'd kicked the last one in, but I couldn't face the effort. Even so I felt she was like a sister to me.

'So Matthew will be along on the twenty-second to hang the door and paint it,' she said.

'You've got my number in case he needs to change the date.'

'Yes, that's right, but expect him on the twenty-second at about nine thirty,' she said. 'Matthew is very dependable.'

At nine thirty-five on the twenty-second I had a phone call, and I relaxed at the sound of Sally's calm voice, even though I was expecting her to cancel the door-fitting appointment with all the irritation that would involve. I had with difficulty arranged a day at home to deal with a couple of files from the office, without having to take it off my annual holiday allowance. But she was not ringing to cancel, no, she was only ringing to let me know that the traffic was terrible that morning and Matthew had rung her to say he was stuck out in a jam near Esher but should be with me before ten.

He arrived at two minutes to, the tall man in overalls I had seen earlier in the shop; he had a frank open face and unforced smile. As he walked into the kitchen at the back my shoulders dropped and I gave a sigh as thorough as a baby's yawn. It was going to be all right.

'Would you like tea or coffee?' I asked, raising the kettle to show this was no idle offer.

'Not just now, thank you,' he said. 'Later would be good, but I'd better get cracking on straight away.'

Again he smiled that nice natural smile. He was not going to be chatty, how wonderful; I would be able to trust him and leave him to it and get on with my work. He did not need respectful hovering attendance, as the man who had recently mended the boiler had done; nor me running around for stepladders and spare bits and pieces that he might have forgotten, like the electrician before Christmas just after I'd moved in. That had been three months after the funeral I wasn't at. First I'd chucked things out in a sort of frenzy, bin bags to Oxfam, but then I'd realised that wouldn't be enough, I'd have to move. Which I'd done, somehow.

I waited around a bit while he brought in his toolboxes. Then, staggering only slightly and with a shallow stertorousness of breathing and blossom of sweat on his forehead, he carried in the door itself, a raw glazed slab of timber that looked too narrow for the destined frame.

'I didn't quite realise . . .' I said. 'I thought it was going to be ready-painted, ready to hang today.'

'It is ready to hang,' he said. 'But first I must see how it fits; I must shave anywhere it's a bit tight. I must see wherever it needs adjusting to the frame.'

'Oh, so it's not just standard; I see,' I said.

'The frame is a standard size from the measurements you took, but they're always a few millimetres out here and there,' he explained. He wasn't irritated or bored by my questions, but at the same time he continued to prepare for work, spreading a groundsheet, setting out his tools.

'We want a perfect fit,' he said, looking up, looking me in the eye. 'But don't worry, it'll all be done by the end of today.'

I hardly ever believe a man when he says that sort of thing, but this one I did. I went into the front room and sat down to work. The disabling sluggishness which had dogged me ever since I'd moved here, stagnant as my reflection in the mirror, seemed to have beaten a temporary retreat. It was over two hours before I looked up again, though I had been distantly aware of the sounds of drilling and tapping, finding them reassuring rather than distracting. There was satisfaction in two people working separately but companionably in the flat. It was dignified.

I went through to the kitchen.

'Are you ready for a coffee now?' I asked. 'It's nearly twelve thirty. I'll be making myself a sandwich, shall I do one for you too? Just cheese and tomato.'

I hadn't cooked anything in this kitchen. Nuts and raisins, toast, that was about it. I really couldn't be bothered.

'I'll say yes to the coffee and no to the sandwich,' he said, looking briefly in my direction, his concentration needed for the door, which he appeared to have in a wrestling hold halfway into the frame. 'Thank you.'

'Can I help?' I said feebly, despising myself immediately for putting him under the necessity of making a polite refusal while struggling with a seven-foot door. The wood was still in its patchy undercoat. Outside, the air was the opposite of crisp, and chill with it.

'Not brilliant painting weather,' I commented as I sawed away at the loaf.

'I don't think it'll rain quite yet,' he said. 'Not till the evening. And the paint should have gone off by then. You'll know when it's gone off, when you're safe, by licking your finger and then just touching the surface of the gloss. If it's smooth, you're safe. If it's still tacky you'll have to wait a bit longer.'

Safe — that word — I thought I'd never hear it again. And of course there *is* no safety but it's nice to hear it spoken of.

'Will you really have time to give it two coats?' I said. 'What happens after you've applied the first one?'

'Then I have to be a bit patient but it doesn't take as long as you'd think,' he said, at work now on lining up the hinges with the places marked for them on the frame.

'Watching paint dry,' I suggested, and smiled. I felt better than I had for weeks; I'd worked hard and happily this morning and would continue to do so after my sandwich, with him round the corner. I saw what a ghost I'd become in these rooms, invisible, restless, talking to myself and leaving half-finished sentences in the air.

He had a row of little brass screws held by the line of his lips, like a seamstress with her mouthful of pins, and frowned as he prepared the path for the first of them with the tip of a bradawl. I put his coffee on the draining board beside him, then perched on a kitchen stool over by the breadbin while I ate my sandwich. The hinges went on well and without trouble. He stood up at last and straightened his back.

'That's more like it,' he said, and picked up the mug of coffee.

'It looks lovely,' I said truthfully. 'The last one was too old, I think, the wood was rotten in the corner and really it wouldn't have kept a squirrel out if it was determined. Let alone a burglar.'

'You had a break-in then,' he said, shaking his head.

'"Opportunistic" the police said when they came round,' I replied, remembering the two young boys with their notebooks and curt chivalry. One of them had had a large fading bruise on his cheekbone.

'I've got a couple of good sliding bolts to fit on this door,' he said. 'That and the Chubb lock mean that things should be as secure as they can be.'

'Excellent,' I said. I wanted to tell him, that meant nothing. Out of the blue your heart can stop beating and you're dead. All finished in twenty minutes. No warning. I'd finished my sandwich. I should have gone back to the front-room table then and made a start on the next file, but somehow I felt like loitering in the kitchen.

'Funny how things come all at the same time,' I continued. The business of trying to utter natural words from the heart, frank and clear, struck me with dismal force, the inevitable difficulty involved in discovering ourselves to others; the clichés and blindness and inadvertent misrepresentations; but I thought I would have a go anyway.

'Yes, all sorts of things,' I said, but I suddenly couldn't be bothered to mention personal details. One step at a time. One day at a time. Yeah, yeah. 'You just have to put your head down and keep walking, sometimes,' I blurted. 'Keep on keeping on. Never mind the weather.'

He nodded and sipped his coffee. He didn't think I was mad. I *wasn't* mad, but I was very shaken, very shuddery inside when I remembered things. My mind had been behaving like a bonfire, feed it a dry and crackling little worry and it would leap into flame.

'I know what you mean,' he said. 'When something happens. Takes over. I've had a few weeks when it's been hard to think of anything else. Well, me and my wife both, really.'

He paused, took another sip of coffee.

'These friends of ours,' he continued, 'A month ago, their flat caught fire, they lived above a garage, it was the wiring, and they lost their two youngest. In the fire. It was in the papers.'

'Oh God,' I groaned. 'How terrible.'

My eyes were filling up, my throat had a rock halfway down.

'We've been trying to help see them through it,' he said. 'But there's not much you can say.'

'No,' I said.

'You can be there, though,' he added, turning back to the door.

'You have to watch it, pity,' I said in a rush. 'Pity could finish you off.'

'That's right,' he said. 'In the end you have to say to yourself, "No I'm not going to think about that for now." We had to do that, me and my wife, we weren't getting to sleep at night.'

'Because it doesn't help anyone in the end,' I snorted. 'If you go under yourself then you certainly won't be able to hold out a strong hand to help.'

'That's right,' he said again, and his smile was full of honesty and warmth. I wondered what his wife was like, whether she was equally generous-natured. My dead love had been married, married with a vengeance though he'd never shown me her photo.

'I must get back to my files,' I said.

'And I can start on the painting now,' he replied, glancing anxiously at the sky.

I had another restorative work session, concentrating well and thoroughly absorbed. Thank God for work. Save us from the obsessive mental mill which constantly grinds but never digests. Secrecy doesn't come naturally to me, and this enforced silence was a punishment for which even his wronged wife might have pitied me, had she known about me. For the first time I wondered what *she* was going through, wherever she was.

Later in the afternoon, Matthew called to me from the kitchen that I should come and have a look.

The door was glossy with its second white coat, immaculate. It had two silver bolts, which he demon-strated would slide easily and slickly into the plates he'd fitted in the frame, and along with the Chubb lock these two would make the door trebly secure. He handed me the small silver key which would fasten them in place, and the larger one for the Chubb, which was gold in colour.

'Better not shut it for another couple of hours,' he suggested. 'With luck the rain'll hold off that long; I think it will, but if you shut it before then the paint won't have hardened enough, it'll stick to the frame when you shut it then rip away and leave raw wood when you open it again. So leave it to harden for as long as you can before you shut the door.'

I can recognise good advice when I hear it. This was what I'd needed to know.

'Thank you,' I said. 'Thank you.'

If I'm Spared

'What are you wearing,' he muttered into his mobile, non-committal.

She told him, in detail, and while he listened he drew down deep draughts of nicotine and narrowed his eyes. She had a small hard waist, Fiona, and was proud of what in Pilates-speak was described as her inner corset.

'Are you coming in?' called Barbara, plaintive, from the back door. 'It's gone ten.'

'In a minute,' he replied.

'Tom . . .'

'I said, in a minute.'

The row of tall terraced houses in which he lived backed on to the little gardens of another row of tall terraced houses. Many of the windows within his view were lit, displaying rectangular yellow interiors, noiseless genre scenes of pasta pots, embracing or retreating couples, cats, squabbles, and, three houses down, a solitary smoker sitting in the dark by an open window, cigarette end glowing scarlet.

He wrapped up the stirring conversation with Fiona then took a drag on his own cigarette and tipped his head back to exhale, looking up at a jewelled aeroplane in the sky, following its trajectory hungrily with his eyes even though he had only two days ago returned from Belarus and would be off again in two days if not sooner to Haiti.

Adrenalin junkies was what they called themselves, he and his fellow foreign correspondents. It was undeniably addictive, the lure of being away, of being witness to the unfolding of important events, and also of being in some heady way exempt. At the end of the day, with any luck at all they went back to their foreign correspondents' hotel and had a drink together.

He was exempt at home too. He could not be expected to latch straight back into the mundane daily round after what he had seen. So when Barbara in a crass moment asked him to do something like take out the rubbish, as she had tonight, it jarred.

'Sorry, I was miles away,' he'd said. 'Can't get that child out of my mind, the one I was telling you about who lost both her legs in the bombing. What did you say?'

'Nothing,' Barbara had mumbled, tying up the black plastic sack.

Anyway, she'd left him alone to take care of Daisy for fifty minutes this afternoon while she went off to do some shopping or whatever. 'Bond with your daughter!' she'd ordered, heavily waggish, before disappearing off to do whatever it was she wanted to do. She was crap at jokes.

There was no guilt. Feelings are after all involuntary. The holiness of the heart's affections, and so on. As Fiona said, it was ridiculous to talk about someone else breaking up a marriage; a marriage would have to be in trouble already for the husband to want to sleep with someone else. Or the wife, she'd added, scrupulously fair.

Not that any boats had yet been burned. Or launched,

for that matter; Fiona was a tad too cut and dried to get romantic about. Thing was, he wanted his cake and eat it. Barbara could be a wet blanket all right, nothing to talk about except the child and the dripping tap. On the other hand he wouldn't actually like to live with one of the Fionas. As that guy from Reuters had said one night when they were getting out of it on the local champagne, what you wanted when you were fresh back from a war zone was a vase of flowers and your dinner on the table, not some ambitious female cutting you up at the lights – 'Oh yeah, I'm off to Tashkent tomorrow', that sort of thing.

Even so, it was only his second night back and already they were reduced to penne with pesto and frozen peas. 'I could have stayed in Belarus for that,' he'd joked. She blamed it on the traffic and Daisy teething; and then she sat gnawing her cuticles while he drank his coffee. When he asked her not to, she proceeded to play with her hair instead, using a strand to floss her teeth when she thought he wasn't looking. She couldn't keep her hands still, it was probably her most infuriating habit, they were always up near her face, her mouth, her hair; if he snapped at her to keep them below shoulder level she would sit with them in her lap and twist her wedding ring round and round.

That really got to him. She'd been doing it tonight.

He decided on one last cigarette before going in. It was the sovereign cure. Not only did it make his irritation melt away, but it dropped his shoulders and sharpened his mind so that he started to concentrate on the Belarus piece, even scribbled a few words onto the back of his Marlboro packet.

That done, he inhaled luxuriously and toyed with certain

useful clichés. 'I need some space' was so obviously code for something else, like 'I need some time alone', that its use these days was the lazy man's insult. 'Life is not a dress rehearsal' was more interesting because, while widely used as a get-out clause, what it really meant was, 'I'm about to do something incredibly rash and ill-advised.' No, the loftiest current euphemism had to be, 'Time to move on.' That would do if it came to it. Dignified, non-specific, fabulously exculpatory. Time to move on. There was no answer to that.

He shivered. It had been a moody day, typical April in England, half-hours of hot sun then quick banks of cool storm cloud draining the light. It was cold now. Grinding his cigarette stub into the grass, he groaned inwardly and went indoors.

'The only appointment they have is at eight twenty,' said Barbara, appearing beside him with a cup of tea.

'What time is it?' he murmured, keeping his eyes shut against her.

'Seven thirty-five. I've been up since five with Daisy, it's her teeth again. But I really think you should go, Tom, he said you should go back within two weeks if it didn't clear up but you've been away so much it's more like two months . . .'

'Yeah yeah yeah,' said Tom, hauling himself up against the pillows.

The trouble with Barbara was that she made such a production out of being a misery. She huffed, she sighed, her face drooped with reproach whenever she saw him. Or, mute appeal was how she would probably put it. It was a habit she couldn't kick and, as he told her, every bit as bad as his smoking, which she went on about incessantly.

Right on cue he broke into a brief harsh fit of coughing.

'You see? I worry about you, flying all the time and the superbugs in the air conditioning.'

'But eight twenty. Christ.'

'I'm sorry, darling, it's the only one they had, I had to make it a same-day appointment, they keep a few open every morning and you have to wait in the phone queue at seven thirty to get one,' she intoned, drawing the curtains.

'OK, OK,' he said.

She had a bloody nice life, part-time and all the rest of it, yet she was ravenous for pity, addicted to it. He even had to commiserate with her, for fuck's sake, he actually had to join in with her moaning on about what a hard row she had to hoe before she'd let him get his leg over.

'And I couldn't make you an ordinary appointment because they're booking three weeks ahead, and we never know what you'll be doing in three weeks' time. Couldn't you have a word at work about that? Little Daisy never knows when she'll be seeing you . . .'

'Shut UP,' said Tom softly, eyes closed, sucking in his first draught of tea.

'It's only you I'm thinking of.'

She was hurt now; but then, when wasn't she.

'Reach me my fags,' he demanded, silently daring her to deliver them with a health lecture. He kept his eyes shut. There was a long pause.

'Fuck's sake, I'll go to the quack at eight twenty. Now give me my cigarettes,' he said, opening one eye to menace her with.

With a gusty sigh she brought them to him.

'You promise?' she said.

'Yes,' he said, lighting up.

There came a yell from Daisy in her cot.

'Smoking can cause a slow and painful death,' she quoted, scurrying from the bedroom.

'Careful, darling, don't go giving me ideas,' he muttered.

I arrive on time, they're late, he thought, tapping his foot, looking round with distaste at the waiting room full of sore-eyed sneezers and losers. He was down to see a Dr Cooling and didn't know whether this would be a man or a woman. It had been a man when he came six weeks ago. A viral infection of the respiratory tract, he'd announced. Brilliant.

'It still hasn't cleared up,' he said to Dr Cooling, who turned out to be an uncharming young female with little glasses like arrow-slits.

'Smoker?'

'Yes, but I think it's a bug I've picked up abroad.'

'How long?'

'How long what?'

'How long have you been a smoker?'

'What's that got to do with it? Since I was fifteen. Fourteen.'

She tapped something into the computer, then gave him a cursory examination with a stethoscope.

'Any blood in the sputum?'

'There has been a bit, probably just broken capillaries because it's a really hacking cough, this one.'

'Night sweats?'

'Look, I've been in a war zone for the last week. I simply wouldn't notice something like that,' he said. You tended to be more concerned about landmines and snipers than your nicotine intake, was what he wanted to convey. She was remarkably unresponsive. He had, actually, been waking drenched in sweat in the small hours for a while now.

'Weight loss?'

'Some,' he said grudgingly, 'But that goes with the job. Pot Noodles and cold baked beans can take the edge off your appetite.'

She glanced at her watch.

'I'd like you to go along for an X-ray,' she said, scribbling something on a pad. 'You don't need to book, just turn up at the hospital and wave this form. We'll let you know when we get the results if you need to see us again.'

She wouldn't give him any drugs, told him to take paracetamol if his chest hurt. Great. 'Waste of time,' he told Barbara when he got home.

A week later, when he got back from Haiti, there was a letter asking him to come in and discuss the X-ray results. Barbara once again arranged a same-day appointment for him.

'So what does a shadow on the lung actually mean?' he asked Dr Minton, a middle-aged man this time, breezy and positive. 'It sounds like something out of a Victorian novel.'

'It may mean nothing very much,' twinkled Dr Minton, indicating the darker claw-shaped area spread over the upper lobes of the lung X-ray. 'But just to be on the safe side I'd like you to go for a few more tests.'

'I'm off to Malawi on Wednesday,' said Tom. 'Can't it wait?'

'I really do think it would be a good idea to get the tests done as soon as possible,' Dr Minton said, looking hard at the backs of his hands. 'By all means let's see if we can't fast-track it. Does your work provide health insurance?'

And so, within forty-eight hours, Tom was sitting opposite Mr Orlando Horton, one of London's leading respiratory physicians. Between them was Mr Horton's immense desk. Mr Horton was himself immense, a great gloomy tree of a man. When Tom had first entered the room, the tree had advanced towards him with outstretched hand, and Tom, who was over six feet tall, had found himself looking up at him like a child. He must be six six, thought Tom now, stupidly; six seven.

'So what do you think this shadow thing is?' he had asked him, cheerfully enough.

'I think it is lung cancer,' Mr Horton had said in a grave voice, lacing his long white surgeon's fingers together on his blotter.

'Cancer?' Tom had yelped.

'Of course I cannot give a cast-iron diagnosis until the results of your bronchoscopy and sputum tests are on my desk. But that is what it looks like to me.'

'Cancer?' Tom had repeated, in more of a bleat this time.

'I'm sorry if this has come as a shock to you,' said Mr Horton. 'But I believe in telling the truth.'

'Oh so do I,' Tom had agreed, nodding his head vigorously. 'The truth is very, yes, absolutely.'

Mr Horton had gone on talking but Tom somehow hadn't heard what he was saying. The man was huge. There was something of Belgium about him, the lack of life in the streets, the uncurtained windows. He saw him lurking in some airless Victorian interior crammed with greedy aspidistra plants, more outside in the garden, gluttonous evergreens, fat rank graveyard swathes of ivy and laurel and yew. An arboretum, murmured Tom, a pinetum.

'Sorry?'

'No, no,' said Tom. 'Carry on.'

He was interested to see how Mr Horton was pushing himself further and further back from his desk during this consultation. He was almost backing out of the window by the end. You could imagine him as a child waiting for punishment, enormous in shorts, lugubrious, at Eton or one of those places where they made you line up outside the door then show your bottom. But he was up again with his hand stuck out to be shaken, and it seemed it was time to be off.

'Very often people do not take in everything I have told them,' the talking tree said mournfully. 'Should you find this to be your own case, my secretary will give you written details of where to go and so on for the further tests I have advised.'

'Thank you,' said Tom, pumping his hand witlessly and grinning like a zany.

He found himself gasping for a cigarette, trembling all over with desire and need, but smoking was banned on the underground. There was this unattractive female waiting beside him on the bench, and she was eating a bean salad with brown rice and smelly vinaigrette. She was oblivious to the fact that the smell of her food was turning people away from her, that she was hogging the bench. She ate carefully and greedily, chasing the last recalcitrant beans round the plastic box with her metal fork. (More than twenty-five years of heavy smoking, Mr Treetrunk had said, shaking his head.) She must have cooked it and packed it the night before. No make-up, a bogbrush hairdo, but she knew what was good for her and she was looking after her health. Tom hated her with all his heart. He had to move away in case he took her fork off her and stabbed her with it.

He walked back home from the station, through the park, looking around him with peeled eyes. All about him were the cherry cheeks and Lycra of people out doing themselves good. He stopped to examine the criss-crossed cable-like flexibility of some late catkins. Plants! They were incredible. Look at the shape of that leaf! The wasteful little knots and garlands of buds gave him pause, some like fat beads and others full but pointed, little pleated leaves still fresh, not quite unpacked. All winter these trees had stood bare-boned, and now this. It wasn't fair.

Barbara was wonderful. When he got back to the house and told her, she went white then held him hard in her arms. It was gratifying, frankly.

He lay winded on the sofa while she sat on the floor beside him and clasped his hands, kissing them, her face concealed by the pale curtain of her hair.

'I just didn't take any of it in after he'd told me it was lung cancer,' he said. 'I don't honestly remember anything. I think the secretary gave me some bits of paper about tests. Christ, I'd better look up my pension details. Work. What do I do about work? I'm supposed to be in Malawi in two days. How long have I got? I mean, here on the planet, as opposed to London or wherever.'

'We should find out what we can,' said Barbara. 'Some facts. Statistics. Then maybe we can work out what it is we have to face.'

He loved her sanity, her gravity, her sweet round face and long fair hair like an early Flemish Madonna. There was something a little disquieting about the way she was rising to the occasion, as though it was what she'd been waiting for all these years, but he brushed that thought aside and concentrated on the way she'd said we and not you.

Gingerly they surfed the net together. Carcinogens in cigarette smoke cause nearly nine in ten deaths from lung cancer. Abnormal cells dividing uncontrollably. Travelling in the blood and lymph. Secondary tumours. Metastasis. Chemotherapy. Palliative care. The five-year survival rate, so hopeful in testicular cancer at nine in ten, was here more like one in twenty.

'Let's turn off the computer,' said Barbara.

'Too much information,' quipped Tom. Everything felt speeded up, as though he was in a cartoon.

'Let's wait until your next appointment with the consultant,' said Barbara. 'It's not long, we can get our questions ready for him then.'

The cartoon quality stayed with him while she went to collect Daisy from the nursery. He was fascinated by this stroke of ill fortune, how to take it, how to absorb it, in what posture to meet it. He was used to catastrophes, but only to the catastrophes of others. Now he had one of his own. What was it you said in this situation, wasn't there some phrase? I've had a good innings, that was it, to show you were a good sport. No, he couldn't say that.

My number's up. That was better. He saw himself in a paddle boat on a pond, as a megaphoned voice ordered, 'Come in number seven, your time is up.' Then he saw himself frantically paddling the boat away to the far shore, trying to escape the black-cowled park keeper.

They were back. Daisy ran to him and he stooped to pick her up and swing her in the air. The child, the poor child, he thought; they're so defenceless, children. She laughed with surprise as he whirled her round the room, and he wondered why he hadn't noticed before that emergent blue-white frill of tooth. She would soon be fatherless.

'How will she remember me?' he asked Barbara, and answered before she could – 'With a cigarette hanging out of my mouth.' He swore then and there that he would never smoke again. He shuddered at his selfish self of yesterday, this morning; found it inconceivable that he should have puffed away so blithely, poisoning the air where his own baby daughter was growing.

'How do I tell people?' he asked.

'Let's not tell anyone yet,' said Barbara.

How wise she was, and how patient and kind! It was a bloody good job one of them was patient and kind – where would their poor child be otherwise? He saw now that these were the qualities he needed in a woman, the timeless womanly qualities of fidelity and selflessness and compassion. Plus, he couldn't help but add, full-time nursing skills. How could he have berated her for being boring? Stimulation he could do without, he got enough of that at work surely. There were always books for fuck's sake. It was the balance of the yin and the yang, they'd had their own dynamic all along; he saw that now.

There was one other person he felt he had to tell.

'It's not something for over the phone,' he muttered into his mobile from inside the garden shed. He had offered to unearth Daisy's tricycle and have another go at teaching her how to use it. Well, a first go, if he was honest.

'That sounds intriguing,' came Fiona's laid-back drawl.

She was less amused when he told her his news over a glass of wine at her flat. She stopped looking sleek and smiling and pleased with herself. Her face went blank as though a cloud had gone over the sun.

'The thing about lung cancer is that the, ah, prognosis is not good. The outlook.'

'I know what prognosis means,' she said, lowering her beautiful eyelids.

'And yet the extraordinary thing is, I keep forgetting for a moment and imagining everything's all right again. You know, like when there's five minutes of blue sky after a month of rain and immediately you assume it's going to stay like that for good.'

'Mm,' said Fiona, sipping her wine.

'There's this deep brainless underlying optimism,' said Tom with a shaky laugh.

'You're in denial,' said Fiona in a flat voice. 'There are four stages, you know. Denial, anger, depression, acceptance. You're still in the first.'

'Not really. God, I wake in the night and it's real enough then. Why me and all that. Why me.'

'You should stop being such a victim and take control of your treatment,' Fiona opined, and this time there was no mistaking the tone of her voice.

'Victim?' spluttered Tom.

Her revulsion was palpable. When he reached across and touched her neck, she got up and crossed the room to get away from him.

'It's not catching, you know,' he said.

'Why don't you try that juice cure,' she said, lighting a cigarette. 'Flush all the toxins out.'

'Forgive me.' he murmured into Barbara's hair that night.

'What for?'

'I haven't been very . . . I've taken you for granted.'

She had had a lot to put up with over the years, he saw that now. He felt remorse for the times when he had been unkind and, yes actually, even cruel. Now that he was about to be plucked away from it, his life with her seemed foolishly underappreciated. The boats were burnt at last, if not in the way he had envisaged.

Gone were thoughts of sexual boredom. Gratefully he dived into Barbara. Vanished was his chilliness towards the under-threes. Ardently he courted Daisy, dazzling her with his funny faces and noises and tricks. Held in the unaccustomed beam of his goodwill, their smiles were pleased but cautious.

Four in the morning became the new time of waking. It was obviously an unconscious urge to be sentient for as much of his remaining non-ash time as possible. He wavered on the threshold of how to face the future. Would he brave it out with stoicism? Or not? The ideal held up for a dying man was of a good-humoured lack of self-mourning. Yet, was it really such a virtue not to mind? Or to lie and claim you didn't mind? It would be a gallant pulling of the wool over the eyes to let the living off the hook by not showing pain or fear; but on the other hand, they weren't the ones on the way out.

I'm crocked, he thought, hands behind head staring up at the ceiling; I'm finished. From some bleak dawn corner of his brain came the new voice.

– Go to sleep quietly; you knew all along it ended like this. For everybody. Who cares? In the end, so what. Who do you think you are? Why should you matter?

He listened to Barbara's breathing and felt her warm thigh against his.

– Who cares? Friends? Family? Your other half?

– Yes no yes.

– Harm and grief. You don't want to rip them out of their own lives.

– I do.

– Is life so fabulous after all?

– Yes.

– All the same, you'll be dead soon, whether you like it or not. You know that, don't you.

He lay there and waited, and gradually grey light crept above the curtains across the ceiling.

If, he vowed in his mind, IF I am spared, never again will I complain about anything. I will accept life as it comes and I will not waste any more of it in pandering to the greedy restless self. I see it all now, how it is and how life should be lived.

★   ★   ★

Barbara came with him to the next appointment. She paused at the majestic front door to breathe on the brass plaque where clusters of letters swarmed after Mr Orlando Horton's name.

'Impressive, eh?' said Tom. 'They're only called mister when they're really top of the pile. He's obviously one of the best men for what I've got, at least there is that.'

He broke off into a fit of coughing, and spat the frightening blood-flecked results into a tissue. Barbara turned her head away and reached for more tissues. She handed him one and dabbed at her tears with another.

'Do I look as though I've been crying?' she asked.

'Not at all,' he lied, moved by the scarlet and turquoise of her eyes, and drew her into him, tucking her bowed head beneath his chin.

Fifteen minutes later they were standing out on the steps again in a very different state.

'You haven't got cancer,' said Barbara, clutching his hand, his loose fist, and moving it with little rocking movements along her cheek, under her jaw. She hung on to his hand and kissed it.

'I'm not going to die,' marvelled Tom. He had his arm round her shoulders, sagged onto her.

'You'll get better,' sniffed Barbara, holding his hand to her wet face. She wouldn't let go.

'It'll take five sets of drugs,' said Tom. 'A cocktail of drugs as he put it. But there's no question. They'll work.'

'Tuberculosis!' marvelled Barbara. 'I thought it had disappeared.'

'I can't believe it,' he said, propelling her down to the pavement. 'Let's find somewhere for coffee.'

'Did he actually say he'd made a mistake at any point?' asked Barbara, her face in ruins after the last half-hour, ruins through which the sun now shone.

'No he didn't, did he,' said Tom, halting again.

'It was when he said, "In retrospect",' said Barbara. 'Then I knew there was a chance.'

'In retrospect,' said Tom. 'You're right. It's one of those phrases. Same as, "With the benefit of hindsight". Bastard. Why didn't I say anything? I just felt so stunned. I'm going back in right now.'

'Oh Tom please,' said Barbara. 'You're alive. I need a coffee.'

'In retrospect,' snarled Tom, leading her off to the nearest Starbucks.

That afternoon they had a celebration with Daisy; they collected her from the nursery and sat out on the pocket-handkerchief of lawn in the back garden with a cake and candles. 'Happy birthday', sang Daisy, and Barbara couldn't stop smiling. I've been allowed back on, thought Tom. When Daisy blew out the candles, he lit them again. I didn't want to have to get off the train yet, he thought, and in the end I didn't have to. Barbara cut the cake into slices, and he ate more than his fair share, though neither she nor Daisy seemed to mind.

Some weeks later, one fine warm evening late in May, Tom was standing out in the garden. It was almost dark, and Barbara was at the back door. She'd been nagging him about taking more time off, but nothing was going to stop him leaving tomorrow early. He was off to Islamabad and had just been informed that the lovely Sophie would be coming along as research assistant.

'Tom,' called Barbara softly from the back door.

'In a minute,' he replied.

She had been doing that thing she did. After they'd eaten their pasta, in the space where normally he'd be enjoying a cigarette with his coffee, she'd been fiddling with her wedding ring, twisting it round and round. It drove him mad. Why did she carry on doing it when she knew how much it irritated him? Then, when she thought he wasn't looking, he saw her floss the gap between her front teeth with a strand of her long hair.

From his jeans pocket now he extracted the contraband pack of Marlboro. There was the brief flare of a match in the dark, then the end of his cigarette glowed scarlet. He pulled out his mobile and tapped in a number. As he waited for the connection he took a draught of nicotine, bathing himself like a Roman emperor in its fabulous drench.

'Is that Sophie?' he murmured. 'Ah, just the goddess I wanted to talk to. Now, tell me . . .'

He was standing in the lush dusk of early summer, his shoes white with petals in grass still wet from the afternoon rain. The yellow-lit windows of the terraced houses opposite were silent pictures of talk and appetite and solitude. All round the back gardens the candles of horse chestnut trees glowed creamy in the gloom and a soft marzipan scent blew from their clusters over and around him. He didn't really notice any of that; he was too busy talking, soft and urgent, into his mobile.

The Phlebotomist's Love Life

Sun slid early over the curtains and woke her still smiling from their victorious photo finish of the night before. They had been together for a year and together was the word. She saw now that without this private truthful allying in powerful pairs all over the globe, without this nothing would work and the world would come to an end.

Then came the tide of unease like a body blush, the flush of dismay. What had they done in the night? She flicked on the radio and he moaned in his sleep beside her.

'Sorry,' she whispered, remembering he was on a late, and slipped off to the kitchen with her work clothes. She put some toast on and filled the kettle. 'Has he killed as many people as Stalin?' came the voice from the radio, keen as mustard, 'Proportionately, that is?'

How eager they had all been to step out of the blood-boltered twentieth century, she thought as she pulled on her tights; how sick to the back teeth of the fangs of history and misery they all were. Now look. Some belle époque. Not even one prelapsarian decade this time; not even one paltry year of peace.

Stopping at the corner shop to buy a paper, she scanned the photos beneath the headlines on display, palm trees and oily black cumulus clouds and silent howling faces.

'Lovely morning,' said Ahmed as she paid him.

'Beautiful,' she agreed. 'Terrible,' she added, indicating the front page of her paper.

'Terrible, terrible,' muttered Ahmed. 'The poor people. What have they done? They have done nothing.'

She stifled the impulse to apologise. He too, presumably, had helped to vote in this government.

On the bus it was standing room only. It had always caused her trouble with men – war. She dreaded its approach, from the moment when they first mentioned its possibility on the news to the pretend discussion about rights and wrongs in the run-up. She remembered her first proper boyfriend, Ewan, and his rage at her objections to the Gulf War. True, her talk had sounded childish even to her, even then when she was only twenty – wishing that women could go off and live on another continent, man-free, war-free. Or at least, go to that neutral continent taking the children with them for the duration of any war the men had created. Without testosterone and the desire for phallic toys, she'd argued, the world would be a better place.

Bollocks, he'd said.

Who had she been with during the Kosovo conflict? With Dan, of course. War is the worst, she'd told him; living in a state of murder and the reversal of all things good.

What about the Second World War? he demanded. Eh? Wasn't that a just war? You'd have been wringing your hands along with Neville Chamberlain, wouldn't you, all out for appeasement.

At times like this, she cried, women get put in their place. They go horribly quiet. It comes down to rape and babies. Ah, ah, you don't like me going on at you like this. You'd prefer me in a chador! A burqa!

You're like a fox terrier, aren't you, he'd said when she'd continued to disagree with him; you get hold of an idea and then nothing'll stop the yapping.

Up on the fifth floor in Haematology, they were slopping around with their early-morning caffè lattes and setting up for the day ahead. Ambulance sirens hooted like owls, the noise drifting up from the roads round the hospital. She took her own coffee to a grime-streaked window and looked down over the waking city, its tower blocks and churches and grids of terraced houses spread out to the sun, some hundreds of thousands of lives within her purlieu, and as she looked her eye's imagination pumped clouds of poison in an unnerving pall across the landscape.

Soon there were twenty or so patients clutching numbered paper tickets in the waiting room where she was. Her job was to take blood, but not till nine o'clock and it was still only five to. A mournful-faced elderly man appeared at the door, clutching a big pink plastic-covered number eight.

'Is this where I should be?' he asked.

'No, you're a Warfarin if you've been given that plastic number,' she told him. 'You want the anti-coagulant clinic down on the third floor.'

'Are you sure?' he said. 'This is the blood department,

isn't it? Some other young woman assured me it was up here.'

'Well yes, this is one part of it, but you need the other part, and that's on the third floor.'

'Just my luck. The lift's broken.'

'There's one that works on the other side of the building,' she told him. 'If you walk along that corridor, follow it along to the swing doors, then keep left.'

I'll never believe the government again when it says there's no money for public services, she thought; not after this, not after it's written a blank cheque to the army without a murmur.

In her side room of sharps and vacutainers she passed her working days in a sequence of three-minute cycles. 'Hello!' she said with a reassuring smile, 'Yes one arm out of a sleeve please', some random chat if they wanted that while she hunted for the vein; then they looked away often talking rapidly while she slowly drew off a dark crimson tubeful. Occasionally someone would express surprise at the blood being purple-crimson, and she would take another half-minute to explain that this was venous blood as opposed to the oxygenated arterial scarlet sort that flows from cuts and wounds.

These days, rather than quiz them about holiday plans before she inserted the needle, she simply said in a neutral voice: 'So what do you think of the war, then?' She found the daily montage of opinion this tactic produced addictively compelling.

It's all wrong that they're e-mailing home, said one; soldiers should cut off from the soft domestic side of things, they shouldn't be thinking about whether their boy was

Man of the Match; you know he sends his football team to be tortured if they lose? I'm fifty, said another, and this is the first time in my life I've felt ashamed of my country; I wake up and I feel ashamed. War is inevitable, shrugged the third in line, it's part of human nature; they haven't had one for a while. *Why* is war inevitable? fumed the next one on; who *says*? People no longer fight duels to settle arguments, so why continue to do so at a national level? There are other ways to get what you want.

'Here we all are,' declared a stout well-dressed old man. 'We've been managing to live alongside Muslims for the last thousand years – and now this! Don't they know anything? Haven't they read *any* history? Ouch.' He rolled his eyes up to the sky with dismal sarcasm. 'Maybe *Jesus* will save us.'

'Everybody's got used to it now, because it's not affecting our lives here,' claimed a large woman with a toddler in tow. 'We're all still doing what we normally do. It's awful really, the way the children sit in front of the television and say "Oh not the war again", and zap it with the remote. Ben, put that down. *Now.*'

He's a vile dictator and he cannot be allowed to go on torturing and murdering his own people and manufacturing chemical weapons, she was told; he's in breach of UN resolutions; he's a menace to everyone and it's high time he was taken out.

Surely there are other ways of saving a country than by making it uninhabitable, she heard; what they've spent on bombs in the last fortnight would have covered the cost of providing clean water for the entire world.

Her last of the morning was American, heavily pregnant

and incandescent with indignation. 'It's like a bad dream,' she cried, not waiting to be prompted. 'But the trouble is when I wake up each morning I realise it's not a dream. You know he's from Texas? Did you know it's legal there to carry a gun but against the law to own a vibrator? Make war not love, hey! I'm glad I'm not in the war zone right now, I'd be in the queue of pregnant women at the hospital begging for a Caesar. Cluster bombs, shrapnel, did you see that bus they bombed last night, killed eight children, the baby in a shroud . . .'

'Shhh, shhh,' she said to her once she'd sealed up her blood and put it safely to one side. She handed her a tissue. 'You mustn't think about it for the next few days, you must avoid the papers and the news generally or your blood pressure will go sky high and they'll haul you in for observation and you don't want *that*.'

'Right,' agreed the woman, blowing her nose. 'But it's hard not to think about it all the time, you know?'

Down in the staff canteen, she took her tray of lasagne over to a table of her friends.

'Very anti this morning,' she said as she sat down. 'Five for, sixteen against, three undecided.'

'You could be on to a nice little earner there,' said Agnes. 'You should get on to Gallup Poll or whoever it is that comes up with these statistics.'

'Pre-emptive strike,' said Femi as she reached across and grabbed the last bread roll.

'Widespread confusion and dismay,' she added. 'Nobody's very happy about it. It's as though the national auto-immune system was starting to pack up. I still haven't met anyone who knows what it's *for*.'

'Can we not talk about the war for a change?' asked Femi plaintively. 'Look, I've got pictures of my new niece to show you.'

'She's gorgeous,' said Agnes, studying the proffered photographs. 'She's scrumptious. She's got a face like a flower.' Agnes was gentle and indecisive generally, a dove if ever there was, but had flown out hawkishly over the war. Her brother-in-law had been in his prisons, and, though she would not say what had happened to him there, Agnes thought even war was better than letting such things exist.

But if we remove one tyrant, then why not another, she'd said to Agnes; most of the staff at this hospital could give ample reason for us to go to war with their country of origin – every single one of them, if you were to ask the cleaners.

True, said Agnes; and maybe that's the way ahead.

'She's her third,' said Femi. 'My sister says that's it, three girls are as much as she can cope with. But I tell her not to be so sure, her husband's always on about wanting a boy to play football with.'

Three girls, she thought. Three girls in pinafores and four boys with side-partings her great-grandmother had raised – the hundred-year-old photograph was in a shoebox at home somewhere. One son had been killed in each year of the First World War. Apparently their mother had not done much after 1918; there was nothing physically wrong with her but after the last boy was killed she hadn't really got out of bed, though she'd lived another thirty years, tended by her daughters.

'Room for a little one?' said fifteen-stone Patricia, fellow phlebotomist, breezing up with a plate of fish and chips. 'I've been taking blood all morning in a draughty old church hall and I'm starving.'

'Aren't they letting us have the school gym any more?' she asked.

'No, they decided the little bleeders were missing too much PE so that was that,' said Patricia, shaking on the vinegar. 'Joke, ladies, joke. We're allowed to say bloody and bleeder, perks of the job.'

'Is it because stocks are low?' asked Agnes. 'Is it because of the war?'

'They're always a bit low,' said Patricia, tucking in. 'People are squeamish, Tony Hancock's got a lot to answer for. As well as the other one. So yes, supplies can always do with being beefed up, and of course blood doesn't store terribly well, it's only got a shelf life of a week or two.'

'I would like to give blood,' said Femi.

'Good for you,' said Patricia. 'Though honestly, they've turned it into such a palaver that if you're not careful it'll take you half a day rather than half an hour, you have to fill in questionnaires about drugs and travel and whether you've had a new sexual partner in the last three months, and you can't be on any sort of medication.'

'Hmm,' said Femi. 'I wouldn't have to take the time as holiday, would I?'

'I'll do you upstairs after lunch, love, if they can spare you over in Casualty,' said Patricia. 'You'll have to wait till I've had my pudding, though.'

'So what do *you* think of the war, then, Patricia?' she asked, despite herself.

'She can't leave it alone, that one,' tutted Femi.

'It feels wrong because we started it and it wasn't in self-defence,' said Patricia, 'and it feels perverse because we're not going to get anything out of it, least of all safety or honour. Not bleeding likely. *That's* what I think.'

'Nobody will join the army after this,' she said, staring at images of dust and tanks and gunfire.

'Oh but they will,' he said. 'Of course they will. They'll sign up in their thousands. This is what you want if you're attracted to the army. What's the point if you don't get to fight? Especially if you're on the side with the best guns and you know you've got a hundred times the firepower of the enemy.'

'But how can they want this?' she asked.

'What,' he said, half listening.

'How can they want *this*.'

'Men like fighting,' he said simply, staring at the screen. 'They always have. Action. Competition, aggression, call it what you like.'

'What?' she said.

'The challenge. Adrenalin. Fitness, strength. Pitting yourself against the enemy. Targets. Explosions.'

He picked up the remote control and pointed it at the television.

Mothers repeating their grief, she thought. If she had a son, where would she hide him? She imagined a future call-up, the open-faced conscripts; a quick horrid fantasy of fear and protections; taking milk to the cellar.

'You'd want a boy,' she said. 'Wouldn't you. You would.'

'What?' he said, absently, staring at the little brightly coloured manikins that had appeared on the screen. 'Oh! Nice one!'

He had been flipping between channels for a while now, the flares and flashes and explosions changing place with roaring and balls and goals. Men are for Mars, she thought; is *that* it?

'Can't you stay with one channel?' she asked.

'I just wanted to see how Arsenal were doing.'

'Come on the Gunners!' she sneered.

'What?' he said, startled.

'I don't know what you think about the war,' she said. 'You never talk to me.'

'Yes I do!' he said, rising to the attack.

'We only ever watch television and go to bed.'

'No we don't!'

'Yes we do,' she said. Oh yes we do. Were they clowns arguing in a pantomime?

'Look, I'm tired. I've had a long day. But if you want to "talk" – FINE,' he said. He pressed the mute button on the remote control; not the off button, she noticed; the football was in its eighty-third minute. 'What about?'

'The war,' she said.

He made a noise somewhere between fury and disgust.

'I just can't believe you get so angry when I try to talk to you about the war,' she said.

'I'm not angry,' he said. 'You just go on and on.'

'Don't hate me,' she said. 'I put up with sitting in front of hours of football because I love sitting with your arm round me and my head on your shoulder.'

'I don't hate you,' he said. 'I love you.'

'I know. But I need to know what you think about the war because we're part of each other.'

'Right. Yes. This is what I think. If it's over fast, with few civilian casualties, there will be a feeling of, it's all been worth it. It was justified. Whereas if it goes on for months and eats up the national budget and there are more casualties on both sides than expected, then it will *not* be seen as good.'

'But what do *you* feel?'

'I've just told you!'

'What, so how it turns out will justify it or not?'

'Yes.'

'But surely there are first principles? The end doesn't justify the means?'

'I've said what I think,' he shrugged, his eyes back on the screen. He pressed a button and the crowd started roaring again.

Even she could see that she wasn't going to get any more out of him in the eighty-sixth minute of the game; and it wouldn't be just four minutes to wait, it always went into extra time. She decided to get ready for bed. In the shower she soaped and scrubbed and loudly sang until the tiles echoed – 'And another one gone and another one gone, another one bites the dust . . .'

In bed, he turned to her and held her. Don't mention the war must be her motto now, on the home front at least. He buried his face in her neck. She stiffened and willed herself not to shrug him off. If she stayed with him, she'd have to button her lip. He put his hands in her hair and his mouth on hers, and moved to lie on top of her. At this point usually her arms would clasp him and her legs twine round his as she returned his kisses; but now she found herself heaving his weight off with unexpected violence.

'What's the matter?' he asked, baffled.

'I don't know,' she said, sitting up.

'Nothing's the matter,' he murmured. 'Come here,' and pulled her back down to him.

'Don't,' she said loudly, surprising them both.

'What?' he said.

'My body can't pretend,' she found herself saying. 'You always said you liked that about me. My body can't tell lies.'

'What?' he said again, trying to draw her to him.

'Unless you're happy with forcing legs open and spit in your face,' she hissed. 'Yes you *would* like that, I bet.'

'No,' he said, aghast.

'Then you can just fuck off,' she said.

'What?' he said.

But she had already left the bedroom, slamming the door behind her. She stormed off to the sofa and to late-night television. There, she lay down and watched the war and wept.

Constitutional

'I just think she's a bit passive-aggressive,' said the woman to her friend. 'In a very sweet way. D'you know what I mean?'

This is so much the sort of thing you hear on the Heath that I couldn't help smiling, straight from Stella's funeral though I was, standing aside to let them past me on to the pavement. Even five minutes later, almost at the ponds, I'm smiling, but that could be simple relief at being outside in some November sun.

The thing about a circular walk is that you end up where you started – except, of course, that you don't. My usual round trip removes me neatly from the fetid staffroom lunch-hour, conveniently located as the school is on the very edge of the Heath. And as Head of Science I'm usually able to keep at least two lunch-hours a week free by arranging as many of the departmental meetings and astronomy clubs and so on as I possibly can to take place after school.

Because I know exactly how long I have – quick glance at my watch, fifty-three minutes left – and exactly how long it takes, I can afford to let my mind off the lead. Look at the sparkle of that dog's urine against the dark green of the laurel, and its wolfish cocked leg. In the space of an hour I know I can walk my way back to some sort of balance after my morning-off's farewell distress before launching into sexual reproduction with Year Ten at five past two.

When the sun flares out like this, heatless and long-shadowed, the tree trunks go floodlit and even the puddles in the mud hold flashing blue snapshots of the sky. You walk past people who are so full of their lives and thoughts and talk about others, so absorbed in exchanging human information, that often their gaze stays abstractedly on the path and their legs are moving mechanically. But their dogs frisk around, curvetting and cantering, arabesques of pink tongues airing in their broadly smiling jaws. They bound off after squirrels or seagulls, they bark, rowrowrow, into the sunshine, and there is no idea anywhere of what comes next.

This walk is always the same but different, thanks to the light, the time of year, the temperature and so on. Its sameness allows me to sink back into my thoughts as I swing along, while on the other hand I know and observe at some level that nothing is ever exactly the same as it was before.

It's reminding me of that card game my grandfather taught me, Clock Patience, this circuit, today. I'm treading the round face of a twelve-hour clock. Time is getting to be a bit of an obsession but then I suppose that's only natural in my condition. So, it's a waiting game, Clock Patience. You deal the fifty-two cards in the pack, one for each week of the year, face down into a circle of twelve, January to December, and there is your old-fashioned clock face. I didn't find out till last week so that's something else to get used to. Stella would have been interested. Fascinated.

The queen is at the top, at twelve o'clock, while ace is low at one.

Forty-nine minutes. From that hill up there to my left it's possible to see for miles, all over London, and on a clear day I'm pretty sure I can pinpoint my road in Dalston. A skipper on the Thames looked up here at the northern heights three centuries ago and exclaimed at how even though it was midsummer the hills were capped with snow. All the Heath's low trees and bushes were festooned with clean shirts and smocks hung out to dry, white on green, this being where London's laundry was done.

So you deal the first twelve cards face down in the shape of a clock face, then the thirteenth goes, also face down, into the middle. Do this three times more and you end up with four cards on every numeral and four in a line across the clock.

As I overtake an elderly couple dawdling towards the ponds, these words drift into my ears – '. . . terrible pain. Appalling. They've tried this and that but nothing seems to help. Disgusting . . .' The words float after me even though I speed up and leave the two of them like tortoises on the path behind me.

Start by lifting one of the four central cards. Is it a three of hearts? Slide it face up under the little pile at three o'clock, and help yourself to the top card there. Ten of spades? Go to ten o'clock and repeat the procedure. Ah, but when you turn up a king, the game gains pace. The king flies to the centre of the clock and lies face upwards. You lift his down-turned neighbour and continue. Nearly always the kings beat the clock – they glare up at you from their completed gang before you have run your course, four scowling tyrants. But occasionally you get the full clock out before that happens, every hour completed; and that's very satisfying.

'Patience is more of a woman's card game,' said Aidan, who prefers poker. 'The secretaries at work got hooked on computer Solitaire. We had to get the IT department to wipe it from the memories.'

We were lying in bed at the time.

'Have you noticed how on rush-hour trains,' I countered, 'a seated man will open up his laptop in the middle of the general crush and you'll think, *he* must have important work to do. Then you peep round the edge of the screen and he's playing a game of exploding spaceships.'

I don't know when I should tell him about this latest development. Pregnancy. Or even, whether.

One thing the doctor asked my grandfather to do early on, before his diagnosis, was to draw a simple clock face on a piece of paper and then sketch in the hands at five past ten. He couldn't do it. I was there. His pencil seemed to run away with him. His clock had wavy edges, it had gone into meltdown, the numerals were dropping off all over the place and the whole thing was a portrait of disintegration.

Forty-five minutes left. I can't believe my body has lasted this long, said Stella the last time I visited her in her flat. When you think (she said), more than ninety years, it seems quite incredible. She had few teeth, three or four perhaps, and didn't seem to mind this, although one of them came out in her sandwich that day while we were having lunch, which gave us both a shudder of horror. When she had the first of her funny turns and I visited her in hospital, she said, 'I don't care what's wrong with me. Either they put it right or not. But what's the point? Just to go on and on?'

For some reason the fact that she was ninety-three when she died and that her body was worn out did not make her death any more acceptable to this morning's congregation. The church was rocking with indignant stifled sobs at the sight of the coffin in front of the altar, and her old body in it. She had no children but hundreds of friends. Her declared line had always been that since death is unknowable it's simply not worth thinking about. She didn't seem to derive much comfort from this at the end, though.

Prolongation of morbidity is what they're calling this new lease of life after seventy. I turned to the sharp-looking woman brushing away tears beside me in the pew this morning, and said, 'You'd think it would be easier on both sides to say goodbye; but ninety-three or not, it isn't.'

'That's why I won't allow myself to befriend old people any more,' said my sharp neighbour. 'I can't afford to invest my time and emotion in them when the outcome's inevitable.'

'That's hard!' I exclaimed.

'So's grief,' she growled. 'Don't give me grief. I'm not volunteering for it any more.'

Look at these benches, inscribed with the dates of the various dear departed, positioned at the side of the path so the living can rest on the dead and enjoy the view. There seems to be a new one every time I go for a walk. They're the modern version of a headstone or a sarcophagus. 'David Ford – A Kindly Man and a Good Citizen.' How distant he must have been from the rest, to have this as his epitaph. Or here, equally depressing,

'Marjorie Smith – Her Life Was Devotion to Others.' We all know what *that* means.

The sharp woman this morning, she had a whiff of therapy-speak about her. What she said, the way she said it, reminded me of my father in some way. Let the past go, he declares; what's the point in raking over the past, chewing over old news. As my mother would say, how *convenient*. And when, precisely, does the past begin, according to him? Last year? Yesterday? A minute ago?

My father, living in Toronto at the moment, has a deliberately poor memory and refuses nostalgia point blank. There has been a refreshing lack of clutter in the various places he's lived since leaving home when I was five. He treats his life as a picaresque adventure, sloughing off old skin and moving on, reinventing himself on a regular basis. He lives with the freshness and brutality of an infant. He can't see the point of continuity, he feels no loyalty to the past. What he values is how he feels now. That phrase, 'Where are we going?', he's allergic to it, and from the moment a woman delivers herself of those words to him she's on the way out as far as he is concerned. Goodbye Sarah, Lauren, Anna, Phoebe and countless others, the women whom he refers to as romantic episodes.

I don't see my life in quite the same way, though I have a certain sympathy for that nonchalant approach. Aidan, for example, likes to identify his objectives and be proactive at taking life by the scruff of the neck; whereas I prefer to nose forward instinctively, towards some dim but deeply apprehended object of desire which I can't even put into words. He says that's our age difference showing: I've inherited a touch of the old hippy whereas he's free of those sentimental tendencies. Anyway, I used to say to him, what if nothing much happens to you, or lots of different disjointed things? Does that make you any less of a person? I suppose I was being aggressive-passive.

At least I was being open, unlike Aidan, who has a selective memory and failed to mention he was married. When I found out, then it was time for *me* to let the past go, to move on, despite his talk of leaving. I wasn't born yesterday.

My mother could not be more different from my father. Why they married is a mystery. She is perpetually at work on weaving the story of her life; she sees herself as the central figure in her own grand tapestry. She carries her past with her like a great snail shell, burnished with high-density embellishments. She remembers every conceivable anniversary – birthdays, deaths, first kisses, operations, house moves – and most of her talk starts 'Do you remember?' There is quite a lot I don't remember, since I left home and Scotland as soon as I could, not popular with my stepfather, the Hero in her quest, her voyage-and-return after the false start that was my father. I was heavily abridged in the process. I'd be willing to bet a thousand pounds that her main concern once I tell her about the baby will be how to incorporate the role of grandmother into her carefully woven narrative. Still, Aberdeen is a long way off.

I'm finding more and more when I meet new people that, within minutes of saying hello, they're laying themselves out in front of me like scientific diagrams which they then explain, complex specimens, analysed and summed up in their own words. They talk about their past in great detail, they tell me their story, and then – this is what passes for intimacy now – they ask me to tell them mine. I have tried. But I can't. It seems cooked up, that sort of story. And how could it ever be more than the current version? It makes me feel, no *that's* not it and *that's* not it, as soon as I've said something. Perhaps I'm my father's daughter after all. It's not that I'm particularly secretive – it's more to do with whatever it is in us that objects to being photographed.

And here's the oldest jogger I've seen for a while, barely moving, white-bearded – look, I'm going faster than him even at walking pace. It's hard not to see a bony figure at his shoulder, a figure with a scythe.

I was on the tube this morning minding my own business when I realised that the old fellow standing beside me – not quite Zimmer frame, but bald, paunchy, in his early seventies – was giving me the eye. I looked back over my shoulder instinctively. Then I realised that it was *me* he was eyeing and couldn't restrain a shocked snort of laughter. The parameters shift once you're past forty, it seems, when it comes to the dance of wanting and being wanted. Though that was always very good with Aidan, whatever else was wrong between us, and he's seven years younger than me.

You would think that a science teacher and tutor of PHSE would know how not to get pregnant. You would think so. Once again it was to do with my age. My GP noticed that I'd just had another birthday and advised me to stop taking the Pill. It was time to give my system a rest, she suggested, time to get back in touch with my natural cycle again now that I was so much less fertile because of the years. There are other methods of contraception far more natural, she continued, and far less invasive than stroke-inducing daily doses of oestrogen and progestogen. She sent me off to a natural family-planning guru.

I learned to chart the months, colouring my safe days in blue and my fertile days in red, in advance, thanks to the clockwork regularity of my cycle. It was pretty much half and half, with the most dangerous time from day thirteen to day seventeen, day one being the first day of my period. I took my temperature with a digital thermometer every morning and believed that I was safe once it had risen by 0.2 degrees from a previous low temperature for three days in a row. The onset of a glossy albuminous secretion, though, meant I had to be on red alert.

Emboldened by contact with my own inner calendar, its individual ebb and flow, I took a pair of compasses and made a circular chart for each monthly revolution onto tracing paper, with several inner circles all marked with the days of my private month, recording dates of orgasm, vivid dreams, time of ovulation, phases of the moon and so on. I was steadier and more pedestrian during the first half of my inner month, I noticed – and more thin-skinned, clever and volatile in the fortnight before my period.

When after several months I placed the translucent sheets of tracing paper on top of each other, I was able to see both the regularly repeated events and also the slight variations over time as a wheeling overlap, so that looking back down the past year was like gazing into a helix with seashell striations.

'My cycle seems rather disturbed,' I said to the Wise Woman at one of our consultations.

'Two teaspoons of honey daily should regularise that,' she said. And I nodded and smiled. No kidding. Me, with a Biology degree from a good university and a keen interest in neuroscience. Then, of course, three weeks after saying goodbye forever to Aidan, I found I was pregnant. Talk about the biological clock.

Thirty-six minutes left. See the sun on the bark of this sweet chestnut tree, and how it lights up the edges of these spiralling wrinkled grooves. Our brain cortex looks like wet tree bark, as I was telling Year Eleven only yesterday. This expansive outer layer with its hundred billion nerve cells has to contract itself into tightly concertinaed ripples and ridges; it has to pleat and fold back on itself in order to pack down far enough to fit inside the skull.

It's hard to think of Stella this morning in her coffin, her bones, her skull with the brain annihilated. She could remember ninety years ago, as many nonagenarians can, as though it were yesterday; but − unusual, this − she could also remember yesterday. That is a great thing in extreme old age, to be both near- and far-sighted. Once I asked her what was her earliest memory, and she thought it might have been when she was one or possibly two, sitting outside the post office in her pram on a snowy day. She was watching the boy in the pram on the other side of the doorway as he howled and howled − 'And I thought, "Oh do be quiet! They're coming back, you know. It's really ridiculous to make a noise like that. They haven't left us here forever." He was wearing a white fur bonnet which I wanted for myself.'

This memory of hers sent some messenger running in my brain, zigzagging along corridors and byways of the mind, and triggered the retrieval of my own earliest memory, which she heard with a hoot of incredulity. I was standing outside my parents' bedroom door and for the first time felt flood over me the realisation that they were not part of me. They were separate. And I thought of my own selfish demands, and wanted to go into them and say how sorry I was for being a burden to them and how considerate they would find me now that I had realised I was not part of them. The bedroom door was tall as a tree in front of me.

'Very guilty,' I told Stella. 'I feel guilty generally. Don't you?'

She paused and we both waited to see what she would come up with. Talking to her was like mackerel fishing, the short wait and then the flash of silver.

'I don't feel guilty *enough*,' she said, with emphasis, at last.

When her doorbell rang, she would open the front room window of her first-floor flat and let down a fishing line with a key attached to the end of it where the hook would otherwise have been. That way her visitors could unlock the front door and let themselves in, saving her the stairs.

She listened with interest while I tried to describe the latest theories about memory, how they now think that when you try to remember something you are not going to your mental library to take a memory-book off the shelf or to play back a memory-video. No, you are remembering the original memory; you are reconstructing that memory. The more frequently you chase a particular memory and reconstruct it, the more firmly established in the brain that memory track becomes.

This short cut I've just taken – thirty-one minutes, I'm watching the time – at first it was nothing but that the grass had been walked on once or twice; but it's obviously been trodden over again and again, hundreds of times, and has become an established path. Repetition – repeated reconstruction of the memory – strengthens it.

'So, Stella,' I said, 'you remember that fur bonnet from ninety years ago because you've remembered it so often that by now it's an established right of way, it's on all your maps.'

'I am not aware of having called up that memory more than once or twice,' said Stella. 'In fact I could have sworn it appeared for the first time last week. But you may be right.'

Occasional Bentleys used to glide down our mean street and disgorge a superannuated star or two – a fabled ex-Orsino, a yesteryear Hamlet. Stella had been a well-known actress, she had travelled the world with various theatre companies; she had never married, nor apparently had she ever made much money, for here she was in extreme old age living in a rented room on next to nothing. She was still working, for heaven's sake. Three times a week she would creep painfully down the stairs a step at a time, allowing a good twenty minutes for the descent, then wait for the bus to take her into Gower Street, where she introduced her students to Beatrice and Imogen and Portia and the traditional heartbeat of the iambic pentameter. She remained undimmed, without any of the usual inward-turning self-protective solipsism, open like a Shakespearean heroine to grief and chance and friendship even in her tenth decade.

If it is true that each established memory makes a track, a starry synaptic trail in the brain, and that every time we return to (or as they insist, *reconstruct*) that particular constellation of memory, we strengthen it, then so is the following. Stella's billion lucent constellations may have been extinguished at her death, but she herself has become part of my own brain galaxy, and part of the nebulous clusters of all her myriad friends. Every time I remember Stella, I'll be etching her deeper into myself, my cells, my memory.

Twenty-nine minutes until I'm due back at school. That staffroom yesterday was like a rest home for the elderly. The young ones had all gone off to leap around at some staff-pupil netball match, leaving the over-thirties to spread out with their sandwiches. I sat marking at a table near to where Max, Head of Maths, was chatting with Lower School History Peter and the new Geography woman.

'It's on the tip of my tongue,' said Max, his eyes locking hungrily onto Peter's. 'You know, the one that looks like . . .'

'In Year Eight?' said Peter.

'Bloody hell, I've got that thing,' groaned Max. 'You know, that disease, what the hell's it called, where you can't remember anything . . .'

'No you haven't!' snapped Peter. He fancies him.

'I went to get some money out on Sunday,' he fretted. 'I stood in the queue for the cash machine for ten minutes then when it was my turn I couldn't remember my PIN number. I'm Head of Maths, for pity's sake. So I tapped in 1989 – in case I'd used my memorable date, because that's it – but apparently I hadn't because the machine then swallowed my card.'

'You read about people being tortured for their PIN number,' said the new Geography woman – what *is* her name? – 'Well, they could torture me to within an inch of my life and I still wouldn't know it. I'd be dead and they still wouldn't have the money.'

'What happened in 1989?' asked Peter keenly.

'Arsenal beat Liverpool 2–0 at Anfield,' said Max.

'Did they?' said Peter.

'You're not into football, then,' said Max as he turned to the crossword, shaking out his newspaper, and Peter's face fell.

It reminded me of that scene in the restaurant last time I was out for a meal with Aidan. The couple at the neighbouring table were gaping at each other wordlessly, silent with frustration. Then he electrified everyone within earshot by softly howling, 'It's gone, it's gone.' I thought he'd swallowed a tooth, an expensive crown. His expression seemed to bear this out – anguish and a mute plea for silence. But no – it was merely that he had forgotten what he was halfway through saying. He was having a senior moment.

I've always had a very good memory. It used to be that any word I wanted would fly to me like a bird, I'd put my hand up and pluck it out of the air. Effortless. Gratifying. Facts, too, came when called, and when someone gave me their phone number I would be able to hold it in my head till later when I had a pen – even several hours later.

Thanks to this, I never had any trouble with exams, unlike my GP cousin who spent her years at medical school paddling round frantically in a sea of mnemonics. 'Two Zulus Buggered My Cat,' she'd say. 'Test me, I've got to learn the branches of the facial nerve.' And what was the one she found so hideously embarrassing? See if I can remember. It was the one for the cranial nerves.

Oh	Optic
Oh	Olfactory
Oh	Oculomotor
To	Trochlear
Touch	Trigeminal
And	Abducent
Feel	Facial
Veronica's	Vestibulocochlear
Glorious	Glossopharyngeal
Vagina	Vagus
And	Accessory
Hymen	Hypoglossal

Not that she's prudish, but she was in a predominantly male class of twenty-two-year-olds at the time, and that's her name – Veronica.

The minute I hit forty, I lost that instant recall. I had to wait for the right cue, listen to the cogs grinding, before the word or fact would come to me. Your brain cells are dying off, Aidan would taunt.

Even so, I sometimes think my memory is too good. I don't forget *enough*. I wish I could forget *him*. It's all a question of emotional metabolism, whether you're happy or not. You devour new experience, you digest and absorb what will be nourishing, you let the rest go. And if you can't shed waste matter, you'll grow costive and gloomy and dyspeptic. My mother always says she can forgive (with a virtuous sigh); but she can never forget (with a beady look). She is mistaken in her pride over this. Not to be able to forget is a curse. I read somewhere a story that haunted me, about a young man, not particularly clever or remarkable in any way except that he remembered everything that he had ever seen or heard. The government of whatever country it was he lived in grew interested, thinking this might be useful to them, but nothing came of it. The man grew desperate, writing out sheets of total recall and then setting fire to them in the hope that seeing them go up in flames would raze them from his mind. Nothing worked. He was a sea of unfiltered memories. He went mad.

Max is worried that forgetting his PIN number is the first step to losing his mind, but really his only problem is that he knows too much. How old is he? Near retirement, anyway. Twenty years older than me. After a certain age your hard disk is much fuller than it's ever been, thanks to the build-up of the years. Mine has certainly started refusing to register anything it doesn't regard as essential – I frequently find myself walking back down the road now to check I've locked the front door behind me. Your internal organs stop self-renewing at a certain point, and at the same time your mind begins to change its old promiscuous habits in the interests of managing what it's already got.

I sometimes taunt Max with the crossword if I'm sitting near him in the staffroom in the lunch-hour. 'It's on the tip of my tongue,' he moans. Last week there was a brilliant clue, tailor-made for a mathematician too – 'Caring, calm, direct – New Man's sixty-third year (5, 11).' He rolled his eyes and scowled and moaned, followed various trails up blind alleys, barked with exasperation, and his mind ran around all over the place following various scents. It was interesting to observe him in the act.

Twenty-five minutes, and I've reached the tangled old

oak near the top fence with its scores of crooked branches and thousands of sharp-angled twigs. I use trees to help when I'm explaining to my sixth-form biologists how the brain works. 'Neurons are the brain's thinking cells,' I say, and they nod. 'There are billions of neurons in everyone's brain,' I say, and they nod and smile. 'And each one of these billions of neurons is fringed with thousands of fine whiskers called dendrites,' I continue, while they start to look mildly incredulous – and who can blame them? The word dendrite comes from the Greek for tree, I tell them, and our neuron-fringing dendrites help create the brain's forest of connectivity. Dendrites are vital messengers between neuron and neuron, they cross the little gappy synapses in between, they link our thoughts together. It's as though several hundred thousand trees have been uprooted and had their heads pushed together from every direction – there is an enormous interlocking tangle of branches and touching twigs.

While I waited for Max as he wrestled with that clue, I could almost hear the rustle and creak of trees conferring. 'I'll give you another clue,' I said. 'You're in it.' But even that didn't help him.

It's not that my mind is going, it's more like my long-term memory is refusing to accept any more material unless it's really unmissable. When I was young I remembered everything because it was all new. I could remember whether I'd locked the door because I'd only locked it a few hundred times before. Now I can't ever remember whether I've locked it as I've done it thousands of times and my memory will no longer deign to notice what is so old and stale.

My short-term memory is in fact wiping the slate clean

disconcertingly often these days. Like an autocratic secretary, it decides whether to let immediate thoughts and impressions cross over into the long-term memory's library – or whether to press the delete button on them. 'I've got an enormous backlog of filing and I simply can't allow yet more unsifted material to accumulate,' it snaps, peering over its bifocals. 'It's not that there isn't enough space – there is – but it's got to the point where I need to sort and label carefully before shelving, or it'll be lost forever – it'll be in there somewhere, but irretrievable.'

The thing about my sixth-formers – about all my pupils, in fact – is that it is not necessary for them to commit anything to memory. Why should they store information in their skulls when they've got it at their fingertips? Yet Stella's decades of learning speeches by heart meant that when age began its long war of attrition her mind was shored up with great heaps of blank verse. I have noticed myself that if I don't continue to learn by repetition, even just the odd phone number, then my ability to do so starts to slide away. I will not, however, be trying to learn Russian in my old age as I once promised myself. No, I'll follow the progress of neuroscientific research, wherever it's got to. I've learned from Jane Blizzard's example that you have to find a way to graft new stuff onto old in order to make it stick.

My ex-colleague Jane had been teaching French and Latin for as long as anyone could remember. She decided when she took early retirement at fifty-five last year that she wanted to study for the three sciences at A-level, and came to me for help in organising this. Forty years ago she had not been allowed to take science at her all-girls school, even at a lower level, and felt this was a block of ignorance she wanted to melt. She's clever, and passed the three A-levels with flying colours, but to her horror discovered a few months later that all her newly acquired knowledge had trickled away. She had not been able to attach it to anything she already knew, and her long-term memory had refused to retain it.

As I overtake a couple of pram-pushing mothers in their early thirties, I hear 'Her feet were facing the wrong way'. Would this mean anything to a girl of seventeen? Or to a man of sixty-three? My pupils will balk at my pregnancy. The younger ones will find it positively disgusting. I speed up and pass two older women, late fifties perhaps, free of make-up, wrapped in a jumble of coloured scarves and glasses on beaded chains, escorting a couple of barrel-shaped Labradors as big as buses. 'She was just lying on the pavement panting, refusing to move,' one of them announces as I pass. They have moved on from the dramas of children to the life-and-death stuff of dogs. And I, I who am supposed to be somewhere between these two stages, where am *I* in this grand pageant? My colleagues will say to each other, so why didn't she get rid of it?

Eighteen minutes left, and I'm making good time. If I'm lucky I might even catch Max groaning over his unsolved clues and help put him out of his misery.

It was my grandfather again who introduced me to crosswords – first the general knowledge ones, then, as I left childhood, the cryptics. He had an acrobatic mind and a generous nature. I used to stay with him and my grand-mother for long stretches of the school holidays, as we liked each other's company and my parents were otherwise involved.

When my grandfather started to forget at the age of eighty-one – by which time I had long since finished at university and was on to my second teaching job – it was not the more usual benign memory loss. It was because his short-term memory, his mind's secretary, was being smothered and throttled by a tangle of rogue nerve fibres.

Since different sorts of memory are held in different parts of the brain, the rest stayed fine for a while. He could tell me in detail about his schooldays, but not remember that his beloved dog had died the day before. It reminded me of the unsinkable *Titanic* with its separate compartments. In time his long-term memory failed as well. The change was insidious and incremental, but I noticed it sharply as there would usually be several months between my visits.

Talking to someone whose short-term memory has gone is like pouring liquid into a baseless vessel. Your words go in then straight through without being held at all. That really is memory like a sieve. While I was digging the hole in his back garden in which to bury the dog, he stood beside me and asked what I was doing.

'Poor Captain was run over,' I replied, 'so I'm digging his grave.'

'Oh that's terrible,' he exclaimed, tears reddening his rheumy old eyes. 'How terrible! How did it happen?'

I described how Captain's body had been found at the kerbside on the corner of Blythedale Avenue, but he was examining the unravelled cuff of his cardigan by the time I'd finished.

'What's this hole you're digging, then?' he asked, a moment or two after I'd told him; and I told him again, marvelling to see new grief appear in his eyes. As often as he asked I answered, and each time his shocked sorrow about the dog was raw and fresh. How exhausting not to be able to digest your experience, to be stalled on the threshold of your own inner life. For a while he said that he was losing himself, and then he lost that.

Finding his way back into a time warp some fifty years before, he one night kicked my terrified old grandmother out of bed because, he said, his parents would be furious at finding him in bed with a stranger.

'I'm not a stranger,' she wept. 'I'm your wife.'

'You say so,' he hissed at her, widening his eyes then narrowing them to slits. 'But I know better.'

From then on, he was convinced that she was an impostor, a crafty con-artist who fooled everybody except himself into thinking that she was his eighty-year-old wife.

In the evenings he would start to pace up and down the length of their short hallway, muttering troubled words to himself, and after an hour or so of this he would take the kettle from the kitchen and put it in the airing cupboard on the landing, or grab a favourite needlepoint cushion from the sofa and craftily smuggle it into the microwave. He wrote impassioned incomprehensible letters in their address book, and forgot the names of the most ordinary things. I mean, *really* forgot them. 'I want the thing there is to drink out of,' he shouted when the word 'cup' left him. He talked intimately about his childhood to the people on the television screen. He got up to fry eggs in the middle of the night. He accused me of stealing all their tea towels.

'I want to go home,' he wept.

'But you *are* home,' howled my grandmother.

'And who the hell are *you*?' he demanded, glaring at her in unfeigned dismay.

But, because muscle memories are stored in quite another part of the brain, the cerebellum at the back, he was still able to sit at the piano and play Debussy's *L'isle joyeuse* with unnerving beauty.

Thirteen minutes. It always surprises me how late in the year the leaves stay worth looking at. November gives the silver birches real glamour, a shower of gold pieces at their feet and still they keep enough to clothe them, thousands of tiny lozenge-shaped leaves quaking on their separate stems. That constant tremor made them unpopular in the village where I grew up – palsied, they called them.

Trees live for a long time, much longer than we do. Look at this oak, so enormous and ancient standing in the centre of the leaf-carpeted clearing, it must be over five hundred years old. It's an extremely slow developer, the oak, and doesn't produce its first acorn until it's over sixty. Which makes me feel better about the elderly prima gravida label.

They have been known to live for a thousand years, oak trees, and there are more really old ones growing on the Heath than in the whole of France. Look at it standing stoutly here, all elbows and knees. When the weather is stormy, they put up signs round here – 'Beware of falling limbs'. It was these immensely strong and naturally angled branches, of course, which gave the Elizabethans the crucks they needed for their timber-framed houses and ships.

Stella was like seasoned timber, she stayed strong and flexible almost until the end. When she had her second stroke, three weeks after the first, she was taken to a nursing home for veterans of the stage and screen, somewhere out in Middlesex. In the residents' lounge sat the old people who were well enough to be up. They looked oddly familiar. I glanced round and realised that I was recognising the blurred outlines of faces I had last seen ten times the size and seventy years younger. Here were the quondam matinee idols and femmes fatales of my grandparents' youth.

Then I went to Stella's room. I held her strong long hand and it was a bundle of twigs in mine. There was an inky bruise to the side of her forehead. Her snowy hair had been tied in a little topknot with narrow white satin ribbon.

I talked, and talked on; I said I'd assume she understood everything – 'Squeeze my hand if you can to agree' – and felt a small pressure. I talked about Shakespeare and the weather and food and any other silly thing that came into my head. Her blue eyes gazed at me with such frustration – she couldn't move or speak, she was locked in – that I said, 'Patience, dear Stella. It's the only way.'

Her face caved in on itself, a theatrical mask of grief. Her mouth turned into a dark hole round her toothless gums, a tear squeezing from her old agonised eyes, and she made a sad keening hooting noise.

Afterwards, in the corridor, I stood and cried for a moment, and the matron gave me automatic soothing words.

'Not to worry,' I said. 'I'm not even a relative. It's just the pity of it.'

'Yes, yes,' she said. 'The pity of it, to be sure. Ah but during the week I nurse on a cancer ward, and some of those patients having to leave their young families . . .'

I really did not want to have to think about untimely

death on top of everything else, and certainly not in my condition; so I returned to the subject of Stella.

'Walled up in a failed body,' I said. 'Though perhaps it would be worse to be sound in body but lost in your mind, dipping in and out of awareness of your own lost self. Which is worse?'

'Ah well, we are not to have the choice anyway,' she said, glancing at her watch. 'We cannot choose when the time comes.'

The trouble is, old age has moved on. Three score years and ten suddenly looks a bit paltry, and even having to leave at eighty would make us quite indignant these days. Sixty is now the crown of middle age. And have you noticed how ancient the parents of young children are looking? Portly, grizzled, groaning audibly as their backs creak while they lean over to guide tiny scooters and bicycles, it's not just angst at the work-life balance that bows them down. Last time I stopped for a cup of tea at the café over by the bandstand, I saw a lovely new baby in the arms of a white-haired matriarch. Idly I anticipated the return of its mother from the Ladies' and looked forward to admiring a genera-tional triptych. Then the baby started to grizzle, and the woman I'd taken for its grandmother unbuttoned her shirt and gave it her breast. No, it's not disgust or ridicule I felt, nothing remotely like – only, adjustment. And of course that will probably be me next year.

My baby is due early in summer, according to their dates and charts. If it arrives before July, I'll still be forty-three. Who knows, I might be only halfway through; it's entirely possible that I'll live to be eighty-six. How times change. My mother had me at thirty-two, and she will become a grandmother at seventy-five. Her mother had her at twenty-one, and became a grandmother at fifty-three. At this rate my daughter will have her own first baby at fifty-four and won't attain grandmotherhood until she's a hundred and nineteen.

I'd better take out some life insurance. I hadn't bothered until now because if I died, well, I'd be dead so I wouldn't be able to spend it. But it has suddenly become very necessary. I can see that. Maternity leave and when to take it; childminders, nurseries, commuting against the clock; falling asleep over marking; not enough money, no trees in Dalston; the lure of Cornwall or Wales. I've seen it all before. But it's possible with just the one, I've seen that too.

I'm not quite into the climacteric yet, that stretch from forty-five to sixty when the vital force begins to decline; or so they used to say. And a climacteric year was one that fell on an odd multiple of seven (so seven, twenty-one, thirty-five and so on), which brings me back to my glee at that crossword clue last week, and the way I taunted old Max with it – 'Caring, calm, direct – New Man's sixty-third year (5,11).' Grand climacteric, of course. The grand climacteric, the sixty-third year, a critical time for men in particular.

To think that my grandfather had three more decades after *that*. Towards the end of his very long life – like Stella, he lived to ninety-three – it was as though he was being rewound or spooled in. He became increasingly childish, stamping his feet in tantrums, gobbling packets of jelly babies and fairy cakes, demanding to be read aloud to from *The Tale of Two Bad Mice*. He needed help with dressing and undressing, and with everything else. Then he became a baby again, losing his words, babbling, forgetting how to walk, lying in his cot crying. Just as he had once grown towards independence, so, with equal gradualness, he now reverted to the state of a newborn. Slowly he drifted back down that long corridor with fluttering curtains. At the very end, if you put your finger in the palm of his hand, he would grasp it, as a baby does, grab it, clutch at it. When at last he died, his memory was as spotless as it had been on the day he first came into the world.

Seven minutes left, and I'll pause here at the home-run ash tree to pull off a bunch of keys, as children do, for old times' sake. So ingenious, these winged seeds drying into twists which allow them to spin far from the tree in the wind; nothing if not keen to propagate. I have a particular liking for this ash tree; it's one of my few regular photographic subjects.

I'm careful how I take photographs. I've noticed how you can snap away and fail to register what you're snapping; you can take a photograph of a scene instead of looking at it and making it part of you. If you weren't careful, you could have whole albums of the years and hardly any memories of them.

I take my camera onto the Heath, but only on the first of the month, and then I only take the same twelve photographs. That is, I stand in exactly the same twelve places each time – starting with the first bench at the ponds and ending with this ash tree – and photograph the precise same views. At the end of the year I line up the twelves in order, the February dozen beneath the January dozen and so on, and in the large resultant square the year waxes and wanes. You don't often catch time at work like this. Aidan was quite intrigued, and soon after we met he was inspired to add a new Monday-morning habit on his way to work. He left five minutes early, then paused to sit in the kiosk near the exit at Baker Street to have four of those little passport photos taken. He stuck these weekly records into a scrapbook, and after eighteen months it was nearly full. It was what I asked for in September when I found out that he already had a wife and child. He refused. So, in a rage, I took it. I was going to give it back, it belonged to him; but now clearly it doesn't belong to him in the same way any more. It's his baby's patrimony.

I have a feeling that this baby will be a girl. In which case, of course, I'll call her Stella. If the dates are accurate, then she'll be born in early summer. I might well be pushing her along this very path in a pram by then, everything green and white around us, with all the leaves out and the nettles and cow parsley six feet high.

Four minutes to go, and I'm nearly there. Walking round the Heath on days like this when there is some colour and sun, I can feel it rise in me like mercury in a thermometer, enormous deep delight in seeing these old trees with their last two dozen leaves worn like earrings, amber and yellow and crimson, and in being led off by generously lit paths powdered silver with frost. It must be some form of benign forgetfulness, this rising bubble of pleasure in my chest, at being here, now, part of the landscape and not required to do anything but exist. I feel as though I've won some mysterious game.

Two minutes to spare, and I'm back where I started, off the path and on to the pavement. That got the blood circulation moving. It's not often that I beat the four scowling kings. There's the bell. Just in time.

From

In-Flight Entertainment

Diary of an Interesting Year

12th February 2040
My thirtieth birthday. G gave me this little spiral-backed notebook and a biro. It's a good present, hardly any rust on the spiral and no water damage to the paper. I'm going to start a diary. I'll keep my handwriting tiny to make the paper go further.

15th February 2040
G is really getting me down. He's in his element. They should carve it on his tombstone – 'I Was Right.'

23rd February 2040
Glad we don't live in London. The Hatchwells have got cousins staying with them, they trekked up from Peckham (three days). Went round this afternoon and they were saying the thing that finally drove them out was the sewage system – when the drains packed up it overflowed every-where. They said the smell was unbelievable, the pavements were swimming in it, and of course the hospitals are down so there's nothing to be done about the cholera. Didn't get too close to them in case they were carrying it. They lost their two sons like that last year.

'You see,' G said to me on the way home, 'capitalism cared more about its children as accessories and demonstrations of earning power than for their future.'

'Oh shut up,' I said.

2nd March 2040

Can't sleep. I'm writing this instead of staring at the ceiling. There's a mosquito in the room, I can hear it whining close to my ear. Very humid, air like filthy soup, plus we're supposed to wear our face-masks in bed too but I was running with sweat so I ripped mine off just now. Got up and looked at myself in the mirror on the landing – ribs like a fence, hair in greasy rat's tails. Yesterday the rats in the kitchen were busy gnawing away at the breadbin, they didn't even look up when I came in.

6th March 2040

Another quarrel with G. OK, yes, he was right, but why crow about it? That's what you get when you marry your tutor from Uni – wall-to-wall pontificating from an older man. 'I saw it coming, any fool could see it coming especially after the Big Melt,' he brags. 'Thresholds crossed, cascade effect, hopelessly optimistic to assume we had till 2060, blahdy blahdy blah, the plutonomy as lemming, democracy's massive own goal.' No wonder we haven't got any friends.

He cheered when rationing came in. He's the one that volunteered first as car-share warden for our road; one piddling little Peugeot for the entire road. He gets a real kick out of the camaraderie round the stand-pipe.

– I'll swop my big tin of chickpeas for your little tin of sardines.

– No, no, my sardines are protein.

– Chickpeas are protein too, plus they fill you up more. Anyway, I thought you still had some tuna.

– No, I swopped that with Astrid Huggins for a tin of tomato soup.

Really sick of bartering, but hard to know how to earn money since the Internet went down. 'Also, money's no use unless you've got shedloads of it,' as I said to him in bed last night, 'the top layer hanging on inside their plastic bubbles of filtered air while the rest of us shuffle about with goitres and tumours and bits of old sheet tied over our mouths. Plus, we're soaking wet the whole time. We've given up on umbrellas, we just go round permanently drenched.' I only stopped ranting when I heard a snore and clocked he was asleep.

8th April 2040

Boring morning washing out rags. No wood for hot water, so had to use ashes and lye again. Hands very sore even though I put plastic bags over them. Did the face masks first, then the rags from my period. Took forever. At least I haven't got to do nappies like Lexi or Esme, that would send me right over the edge.

27th April 2040

Just back from Maia's. Seven months. She's very frightened. I don't blame her. She tried to make me promise I'd take care of the baby if anything happens to her. I havered (mostly at the thought of coming between her and that throwback Martin – she'd got a new black eye, I didn't ask). I suppose there's no harm in promising if it makes her feel better. After all, it wouldn't exactly be taking on a responsibility – I give a new baby three months max in these conditions. Diarrhoea, basically.

14th May 2040
Can't sleep. Bites itching, trying not to scratch. Heavy thumps and squeaks just above, in the ceiling. Think of something nice. Soap and hot water. Fresh air. Condoms! Sick of being permanently on knife edge re pregnancy.

Start again. Wandering round a supermarket – warm, gorgeously lit – corridors of open fridges full of tiger prawns and fillet steak. Gliding off down the fast lane in a sports car, stopping to fill up with thirty litres of petrol. Online, booking tickets for *The Mousetrap*, click, ordering a crate of wine, click, a holiday home, click, a pair of patent leather boots, click, a gap year, click. I go to iTunes and download *The Marriage of Figaro*, then I chat face to face in real time with G's parents in Sydney. No, don't think about what happened to them. Horrible. Go to sleep.

21st May 2040
Another row with G. He blew my second candle out, he said one was enough. It wasn't though, I couldn't see to read any more. He drives me mad, it's like living with a policeman. It always was, even before the Collapse. 'The Earth has enough for everyone's need, but not for everyone's greed' was his favourite. Nobody likes being labelled greedy. I called him Killjoy and he didn't like that. 'Every one of us takes about twenty-five thousand breaths a day,' he told me. 'Each breath removes oxygen from the

atmosphere and replaces it with carbon dioxide.' Well, pardon me for breathing! What was I supposed to do – turn into a tree?

6th June 2040

Went round to the Lumleys for the news last night. Whole road there squashed into front room, straining to listen to radio – batteries very low (no new ones in the last govt delivery). Big news though – compulsory billeting imminent. The Shorthouses were up in arms, Kai shouting and red in the face, Lexi in tears. 'You work all your life', etc, etc. What planet is he on. None of us too keen, but nothing to be done about it. When we got back, G checked our stash of tins under the bedroom floorboards. A big rat shot out and I screamed my head off. G held me till I stopped crying then we had sex. Woke in the night and prayed not to be pregnant, though God knows who I was praying to.

12th June 2040

Visited Maia this afternoon. She was in bed, her legs have swollen up like balloons. On at me again to promise about the baby and this time I said yes. She said Astrid Huggins was going to help her when it started – Astrid was a nurse once, apparently, not really the hands-on sort but better than nothing. Nobody else in the road will have a clue what to do now we can't google it. 'All I remember from old films is that you're supposed to boil a kettle,' I said. We started to laugh, we got a bit hysterical. Knuckledragger Martin put his head round the door and growled at us to shut it.

1st July 2040
First billet arrived today by army truck. We've got a Spanish group of eight including one old lady, her daughter and twin toddler grandsons (all pretty feral), plus four unsmiling men of fighting age. A bit much since we only have two bedrooms. G and I tried to show them round but they ignored us, the grandmother bagged our bedroom straight off. We're under the kitchen table tonight. I might try to sleep on top of it because of the rats. We couldn't think of anything to say – the only Spanish we could remember was *Muchas gracias*, and as G said, we're certainly not saying *that*.

2nd July 2040
Fell off the table in my sleep. Bashed my elbow. Covered in bruises.

3rd July 2040
G depressed. The four Spaniards are bigger than him, and he's worried that the biggest one, Miguel, has his eye on me (with reason, I have to say).

4th July 2040
G depressed. The grandmother found our tins under the floorboards and all but danced a flamenco. Miguel punched G when he tried to reclaim a tin of sardines and since then his nose won't stop bleeding.

6th July 2040
Last night under the table G came up with a plan. He thinks we should head north. Now this lot are in the flat

and a new group from Tehran promised next week, we might as well cut and run. Scotland's heaving, everyone else has already had the same idea, so he thinks we should get on one of the ferries to Stavanger then aim for Russia.

'I don't know,' I said. 'Where would we stay?'

'I've got the pop-up tent packed in a rucksack behind the shed,' he said, 'plus our sleeping bags and my wind-up radio.'

'Camping in the mud,' I said.

'Look on the bright side,' he said. 'We have a huge mortgage and we're just going to walk away from it.'

'Oh shut up,' I said.

17th July 2040

Maia died yesterday. It was horrible. The baby got stuck two weeks ago, it died inside her. Astrid Huggins was useless, she didn't have a clue. Martin started waving his Swiss Army knife around on the second day and yelling about a Caesarean, he had to be dragged off her. He's round at ours now drinking the last of our precious brandy with the Spaniards. That's it. We've got to go. Now, says G. Yes.

1st August 2040

Somewhere in Shropshire, or possibly Cheshire. We're staying off the beaten track. Heavy rain. This notebook's pages have gone all wavy. At least biro doesn't run. I'm lying inside the tent now, G is out foraging. We got away in the middle of the night. G slung our two rucksacks across the bike. We took turns to wheel it, then on the fourth morning we woke up and looked outside the tent flap and it was gone even though we'd covered it with leaves the night before.

'Could be worse,' said G, 'we could have had our throats cut while we slept.'

'Oh shut up,' I said.

3rd August 2040

Rivers and streams all toxic – fertilisers, typhoid etc. So, we're following G's DIY system. Dip billycan into stream or river. Add three drops of bleach. Boil up on camping stove with T-shirt stretched over billycan. Only moisture squeezed from the T-shirt is safe to drink; nothing else. 'You're joking,' I said, when G first showed me how to do this. But no.

9th August 2040

Radio news in muddy sleeping bags – skeleton govt obviously struggling, they keep playing the *Enigma Variations*. Last night they announced the end of fuel for civilian use and the compulsory disabling of all remaining civilian cars. As from now we must all stay at home, they said, and not travel without permission. There's talk of martial law. We're going cross-country as much as possible – less chance of being arrested or mugged – trying to cover ten miles a day but the weather slows us down. Torrential rain, often horizontal in gusting winds.

16th August 2040

Rare dry afternoon. Black lace clouds over yellow sky. Brown grass, frowsty grey mould, fungal frills. Dead trees come crashing down without warning – one nearly got us today, it made us jump. G was hoping we'd find stuff growing in the fields, but all the farmland round here is surrounded by razor wire and armed guards. He says he knows how to grow vegetables from his allotment days, but so what. They take too long. We're hungry *now*, we can't wait till March for some old carrots to get ripe.

22nd August 2040

G broke a front crown cracking a beechnut, there's a black hole and he whistles when he talks. 'Damsons, black-berries, young green nettles for soup,' he said at the start of all this, smacking his lips. He's not so keen now. No damsons or blackberries, of course – only chickweed and ivy.

He's just caught a lame squirrel, so I suppose I'll have to do something with it. No creatures left except squirrels, rats and pigeons, unless you count the insects. The news says they're full of protein, you're meant to grind them into a paste, but so far we haven't been able to face that.

24th August 2040

We met a pig this morning. It was a bit thin for a pig, and it didn't look well. G said, 'Quick! We've got to kill it.'

'Why?' I said. 'How?'

'With a knife,' he said. 'Bacon. Sausages.'

I pointed out that even if we managed to stab it to death with our old kitchen knife, which looked unlikely, we wouldn't be able just to open it up and find bacon and sausages inside.

'Milk, then!' said G wildly. 'It's a mammal, isn't it?'

Meanwhile the pig walked off.

25th August 2040
Ravenous. We've both got streaming colds. Jumping with fleas, itching like crazy. Weeping sores on hands and faces – unfortunate side-effects from cloud-seeding, the news says. What with all this and his toothache (back molar, swollen jaw) and the malaria, G is in a bad way.

27th August 2040
Found a dead hedgehog. Tried to peel off its spines and barbecue it over the last briquette. Disgusting. Both sick as dogs. Why did I use to moan about the barter system? Foraging is MUCH MUCH worse.

29th August 2040
Dreamt of Maia and the Swiss Army knife and woke up crying. G held me in his shaky arms and talked about Russia, how it's the new land of milk and honey since the Big Melt. 'Some really good farming opportunities opening up in Siberia,' he said through chattering teeth.

'We're like in the *Three Sisters*,' I said, '"If only we could get to Moscow." Do you remember that production at the National? We walked by the river afterwards, we stood and listened to Big Ben chime midnight.'

Hugged each other and carried on like this until sleep came.

31st August 2040
G woke up crying. I held him and hushed him and asked what was the matter. 'I wish I had a gun,' he said.

15th September 2040
Can't believe this notebook was still at the bottom of the
rucksack. And the biro. Murderer wasn't interested in them.
He's turned everything else inside out (including me). G
didn't have a gun. This one has a gun.

19th September 2040
M speaks another language. Norwegian? Dutch? Croatian?
We can't talk, so he hits me instead. He smells like an
abandoned fridge, his breath stinks of rot. What he does
to me is horrible. I don't want to think about it, I won't
think about it. There's a tent and cooking stuff on the
ground, but half the time we're up a tree with the gun.
There's a big plank platform and a tarpaulin roped to the
branches above. At night he pulls the rope ladder up after
us. It's quite high, you can see for miles. He uses the platform for storing stuff he brings back from his mugging
expeditions. I'm surrounded by tins of baked beans.

3rd October 2040
M can't seem to get through the day without at least two
blowjobs. I'm always sick afterwards (sometimes during).

8th October 2040
M beat me up yesterday. I'd tried to escape. I shan't do
that again, he's too fast.

14th October 2040
If we run out of beans I think he might kill me for food.
There were warnings about it on the news a while back.
This one wouldn't think twice. I'm just meat on legs to

him. He bit me all over last night, hard. I'm covered in bite marks. I was literally licking my wounds afterwards when I remembered how nice the taste of blood is, how I miss it. Strength. Calves' liver for iron. How I haven't had a period for ages. When that thought popped out I missed a beat. Then my blood ran cold.

15th October 2040
Wasn't it juniper berries they used to use? As in gin? Even if it was I wouldn't know what they looked like, I only remember mint and basil. I can't be pregnant. I won't be pregnant.

17th October 2040
Very sick after drinking rank juice off random stewed herbs. Nothing else, though, worse luck.

20th October 2040
Can't sleep. Dreamed of G, I was moving against him, it started to go up a little way so I thought he wasn't really dead. Dreadful waking to find M there instead.

23rd October 2040
Can't sleep. Very bruised and scratched after today. They used to throw themselves downstairs to get rid of it. The trouble is, the gravel pit just wasn't deep enough, plus the bramble bushes kept breaking my fall. There was some sort of body down there too, seething with white vermin. Maybe it was a goat or a pig or something, but I don't think it was. I keep thinking it might have been G.

31st October 2040
This baby will be the death of me. Would. Let's make that
a conditional. 'Would', not 'will'.

7th November 2040
It's all over. I'm still here. Too tired to

8th November 2040
Slept for hours. Stronger. I've got all the food and drink,
and the gun. There's still some shouting from down there
but it's weaker now. I think he's almost finished.

9th November 2040
Slept for hours. Fever gone. Baked beans for breakfast.
More groans started up just now. Never mind. I can wait.

10th November 2040
It's over. I got stuck into his bottle of vodka, it was the
demon drink that saved me. He was out mugging – left
me up the tree as usual – I drank just enough to raise my
courage. Nothing else had worked so I thought I'd get
him to beat me up. When he came back and saw me
waving the bottle he was beside himself. I pretended to
be drunker than I was and I lay down on the wooden
platform with my arms round my head while he got the
boot in. It worked. Not right away, but that night.

Meanwhile M decided he fancied a drink himself, and
very soon he'd polished off the rest of it – more than
three-quarters of a bottle. He was singing and sobbing and
carrying on, out of his tree with alcohol, and then, when
he was standing pissing off the side of the platform, I crept

along and gave him a gigantic shove and he really was out of his tree. Crash.

13th November 2040
I've wrapped your remains in my good blue shirt; sorry I couldn't let you stay on board, but there's no future now for any baby above ground. I'm the end of the line!

This is the last page of my thirtieth birthday present. When I've finished it I'll wrap the notebook up in six plastic bags, sealing each one with duct tape against the rain, then I'll bury it in a hole on top of the blue shirt. I don't know why as I'm not mad enough to think anybody will ever read it. After that I'm going to buckle on this rucksack of provisions and head north with my gun. Wish me luck. Last line: good luck, good luck, good luck, good luck, good luck.

The Tipping Point

Look at that sky. it's almost sitting on the windscreen. Whose idea was it to hold the Summer School up in the wilds this year? I know my sweet Americans would follow me to the ends of the Earth for my thoughts on the Bard; and I know Stratford venues are stratospheric these days. But all this way to study the Scottish play *in situ* smacks of desperation. If ever a sky looked daggers, this is it.

I was quite looking forward to the drive, actually. Impossible to get lost, my esteemed colleague Malkie MacNeil told me, just follow the A82 all the way and enjoy the scenery, the mountains, best in the world, blah blah. So I left Glasgow reasonably bright and hopeful this morning after a dish of porridge, up along Loch Lomond, and the light has drained steadily away through Tarbet, Ardlui, Tyndrum, until I realise that it's eleven in the morning on the fifth of August and I've got to turn on the headlights. Storm clouds over Glen Coe. 'The cloud-capp'd towers, the gorgeous palaces.' Not really. More like a celestial housing estate.

All right, let's have something suitably gloomy in the way of music. Here we are. *Winterreise* with Dietrich

Fischer–Dieskau and his manly baritone. No finer example of the pathetic fallacy than Schubert's *Winterreise*. 'What's that when it's at home, Dr Beauman?' That is the reading of one's own emotion into external nature, child. I still cannot believe that I, confirmed commitment–phobe, have been cast as the rejected lover, ignominiously dumped like some soppy First–Year.

Nun ist die Welt so trübe, / Der Weg gehüllt in Schnee. My German may not be fluent, but it's become more than passable in the last year. You'd allow that, Angelika? Now the world is so bleak, the path shrouded in snow. *Schnee.*

It was immediate. As soon as we first clapped eyes on each other, et cetera. But, joking apart, it was. I was over in Munich to give my paper on 'Milton's *Comus*; the Masque Form as Debate and Celebration', mainly because I wanted to check out the painted rococo Cuvilliés-Theater – crimson, ivory and gold – on Residenzstrasse. I needed it for my chapter on European Court Theatre, for the book that now bears your name as dedicatee.

You were in charge of that conference, Head of Arts Admin for all the participating institutions that week. Once it was over we went back to your flat in Cologne. Jens was staying with his grandmother as luck would have it. Beautiful Angelika, with your fierce pale eagle eyes and beaming smile. I remember capering round your bed like a satyr after you'd given me the first of your ecological curtain lectures. I was quoting *Comus* at you to shut you up:

Wherefore did Nature pour her bounties forth
With such a full and unwithdrawing hand,
Covering the earth with odours, fruits and flocks,
Thronging the seas with spawn innumerable,
But all to please and sate the curious taste?

I was proud and stout and gleeful in the presence of
your angularity. It felt like a challenge. Heaping you with
good things became part of that. I filled your austere
kitchen with delicacies, though that wasn't easy as you are
of course vegan.

'Enough is enough,' you said, pushing me away.

'You can never have enough,' I laughed. 'Didn't you
know that?'

'Not so. I have.'

Ich will den Boden küssen, / *Durchdringen Eis und Schnee* /
Mit meinen heissen Tränen. *Schnee* again. I want to kiss the
ground, to pierce the ice and snow with my hot tears.
Yes, well. Romanticism was your besetting sin, Angelika;
your quasi-mystical accusatory ecospeak about the planet.
Whereas my line is, if it's going to happen, it's going to
happen – I don't see how anything mankind does can
impose change on overwhelming natural phenomena like
hurricanes and tsunamis. We resemble those frail figures
in a painting by Caspar David Friedrich, dwarfed by the
immensity of nature. You took me to see his great painting
Das Eismeer in the Hamburger Kunsthalle, jagged ice floes
in a seascape beyond hope; and you used it as a jumping-
off point to harangue me about the collapse of the Larsen
B ice shelf. My clever intense passionate Angelika, so
quick to imagine the worst, and so capable of anguish;

you wept like a red-eyed banshee when you gave me the push.

An ominous cloudscape, this, great weightless barricades of cumulonimbus blocking the light. I can't see another car or any sign of humanity. Once out of this miserable valley, I'll stop for petrol in Ballachulish. Then it's on up past Loch Linnhe, Loch Lochy, Loch Oich, Loch Ness, and I'll be there. Inverness. What's done is done. Halfway through the week there's a day trip planned to Cawdor Castle, where Duncan doubtless shakes his gory locks on mugs and mousemats all over the gift shop.

So then I applied for a peripatetic fellowship at the University of Cologne, and got it. I brushed up my Schiller. I wrote a well-received paper on Gotthold Lessing's *Minna von Barnhelm* and gave a seminar on Ödön von Horváth, the wandering playwright who all his life was terrified of being struck by lightning and then, during a Parisian thunderstorm, took shelter beneath a tree on the Champs-Elysées and was killed by a falling branch. Let that be a warning to you, Angelika: you can worry too much.

We were very happy, you and me and Jens. He's unusually thoughtful and scrupulous, that boy; like his mother. They had their annual day of atonement at his school while I was over, when the children are instructed to consider the guilt of their militaristic forefathers in the last century. That was the night he had an asthma attack and we ended up in Casualty. Cue copious lectures from you on air quality, of course.

And here's the rain, driving against the windscreen with a violence fit to crack it. It's almost comic, this journey, the menace of those massed clouds, the grey-green gloom.

Nor do I have a residual belief that rain is in any way cleansing or purgative. No, no. As you so painstakingly taught me, Angelika, our sins of pollution lock into the clouds and come down as acid rain. Hence *Waldsterben*, or forest death; and from *Waldsterben* you would effortlessly segue into flash floods, storm surge, wildfire, drought, and on to carbon capture. You were not the only one. You and your friends discussed these things for hours, organising petitions, marching here and there. Your activism made my English students look like solipsistic children, their political concerns stretching with some effort to top-up fees and back down again to the price of hair straighteners.

You were in a constant state of alarm. I wanted you to talk about me, about you and me, but the apocalyptic zeitgeist intruded.

Darling, shall we go for a swim? No, my love, for the oceans have warmed up and turned acidic. All plankton is doomed and, by association, all fish and other swimmers. Sweetheart, what can I do to melt your heart? Nothing, for you are indifferent to the ice albedo feedback; you are unconcerned that the planet's shield of snow, which reflects heat back into space, is defrosting. That our world grows dangerously green and brown, absorbing more heat than ever before, leaves you cold.

My own dear heart, let's make a happy future for ourselves, for you and me and Jens. How can that be when the world is melting and you don't care? How can we be *gemütlich* together in the knowledge that the twin poles of the world are dissolving, that permafrost is no longer permanent and will unloose vast clouds of methane gas to extinguish us all?

You did love me. You told me so. *Ich liebe dich.*

Then came your ultimatum. We couldn't go on seeing each other like this. Yes, you loved my flying visits, you loved being with me. But no, you could not bear it that our love was sustained at the expense of the future. By making it dependent on cut-price flights we were doing the single worst possible thing in our power as private individuals to harm the planet.

'Love Miles,' I countered, morally righteous, fighting fire with fire.

'Selfish miles,' you retorted: 'We are destroying other people's lives when we do this.' Very truthful and severe you are, Angelika; very hard on yourself as well as others.

Time for a change of CD. More Schubert lieder, I think, but let's drop Fischer-Dieskau. He's a tad heavy-hearted for Scotland, a bit of a dampener where it's already damp enough. Ah, Gérard Souzay, he's my man. Rather an eccentric choice, but my father used to listen to him and I cottoned on to what he admired. A great voice, fresh, rich, essentially baritonal but keener on beauty than usual. Let's skip *Der Jüngling und der Tod*, though. OK, here comes the Erlking. There's a boy here, too, riding on horseback through the night with his father, holding close to his father. Oh, it's a brilliant micro-opera, this song, one voice singing four parts – narrator, father, boy, and the lethal wheedling Erlking. I'd forgotten how boldly elliptical it is, and how infectious the boy's terror – '*Mein Vater, mein Vater, und hörest du nicht,/ Was Erlenkönig mir leise verspricht?*' My father, my father, and don't you hear/ The Erlking whispering promises to me? But his father can't hear anything, can't see anything, only the wind and the trees.

I used to start laughing uncontrollably at this point, which annoyed *my* father, who was trying to listen; but it appealed to my puerile sense of humour – *Vater* as farter.

> *Mein Vater, mein Vater, jetzt fasst er mich an!*
> *Erlkönig hat mir ein Leids getan!*

My father, my father, now he is taking hold of me! The Erlking has hurt me! And by the time the father has reached home, the boy lies dead in his arms. *Tot.*

Listen, Angelika. You make my blood boil. What possible difference can it make whether I get on a plane or not? The plane will take off regardless. Why don't you concentrate your energies on all those herds of farting cattle, eh? All those cows and sheep farting and belching. Then after that you could get the rainforests under control! The blazing forests! You don't want me.

It's stopped raining at last. I can see ahead again, the air is clearer now. A truly theatrical spectacle, this sky, with its constant changes of scene. I couldn't do it in the end. I wanted tenure, sure, but I was being asked to give up too much. The world. The world well lost? No. No, no, not even for you, Angelika.

In September I'm attending a weekend conference on Performance Art at the University of Uppsala in Sweden. I'm not going by coach. There's a seminar on *Sturm und Drang* in Tokyo this autumn, as well as my Cardiff-based sister's wedding party in Seville. After that there's an invitation to the Sydney Festival to promote my new book, and the usual theatre conference at Berkeley in spring. All paid for, of course, except the return ticket to Seville, which cost me precisely £11 – just about manageable even on an academic's meagre stipend.

You used to have to join the Foreign Office if you wanted to travel on anything like this scale. Now everybody's at it. The budget airlines arrived and life changed overnight. Sorry, but it's true. The world's our sweet shop. We've got used to it, we want it; there's no going back.

The downside is, I lost my love. She followed through. And how. She caused us both enormous pain. Ah, come on! For all I know, she's got back together with that little dramaturg from Bremen, the one with the tiny hands and feet. So?

Look at those schmaltzy sunbeams backlighting the big grey cloud. Perfect scenery for the arrival of a *deus ex machina*. 'What's that when it's at home, Dr Beauman?' A far-fetched plot device to make everything all right again, my dear. There's Ballachulish in the distance. A painted god in a cardboard chariot. An unlikely happy ending, in other words.

Geography Boy

They were up very early against the heat, paniers packed and off on their bikes towards Angers before anybody else at the youth hostel was awake. It felt like the beginning of the world, with the fresh damp smell of the hedgerows and the faint reveille from a cockerel several fields away, although it was in fact the last day of their holiday. Six weeks ago they had met at a party, in the summer term of their second year. Neither of them had ever felt this strongly before about anyone.

Adele was reading history and had chosen the End of the World module rather than the History of Human Rights as her special dissertation subject. It was because of this that she had suggested adding Angers to their itinerary, after reading the guidebook's rapt account of the apocalyptic tapestries there.

'It's the largest wall-hanging ever to be woven in Europe,' she had quoted from the guidebook the other night in Chinon. 'Six huge tapestry panels, each with fourteen scenes displayed on two levels, like a sort of double-decker cartoon full of monsters and catastrophes.'

'Can't wait,' Brendan had said, chivalrously. His subject was geography, and he was aware that he had probably dragged her round one too many troglodyte caves that day. Amazing, though, the way those caves had been created by chance from quarrying for the local tufa stone with which to build the white chateaux of the Loire. The damp ones were now used for mushroom cultivation, their guide had informed them, while the rest were being lived in, or snapped up by Parisians as *résidences secondaires*. 'I'd like to live in a cave with you,' he had wanted to say to Adele, but hadn't been quite brave enough.

They were bowling along between fields of ripe corn, and he felt like singing or shouting. Sometimes in the last week, when they had been swooping down a hill in the forests near Chinon, he had shouted aloud into the air rushing past him in sheer exhilaration. Then there was the long stiff climb up the next one, moving the piston legs, ignoring the keen sensation in the front thigh muscles of being flooded with boiling water, Adele panting alongside him, and the reward at the top, as their hearts gradually stopped pounding and they gloated once again over the sweet swooping downward stretch ahead.

On they cycled as the sun climbed higher and the day grew hotter. Sweat was flying from their faces now and inside their clothes it was trickling down their bodies as they pistoned forward. There were few cars – perhaps one every ten minutes or so – although evidence of their existence was displayed at intervals along the way, flattened hedgehogs, little birds and mice. Once, by a low orchard of strictly serried apple trees, there had been a great silver serpent, half a metre long, flattened in mid-zigzag.

'Chateau,' he called as they rounded a bend in the road. There it was, white against the green, another one, the twenty-seventh this holiday, set in an illuminated meadow of grass and flowers with the shining river beyond. These chateaux were like the ones in fairy-tales, she had said earlier in the holiday, the sort where Sleeping Beauty might be found. You're my sleeping beauty, he had told her, but she had rejected that particular princess as a bad role model – too passive – and had told him it was Little Red Riding Hood who was now recommended to girls, for her ingenuity and resourcefulness. He had tried to make her promise to join him in his activism next term; it's no longer a case of crying wolf, he'd told her, the end of the world really is nigh. Too late, she had replied; it's too late.

'Money's won,' she'd shrugged. 'It's obvious.'

'But the worst thing we can do now is nothing,' he'd cried.

At this she had shrugged again and returned to her book.

'Baguette stop?' he called to her now after an hour or so on the road. The sun was already strong in a bold blue sky sparsely plumed with cirrus clouds.

'*D'accord.*'

They set their bikes against a wall at the edge of a field of sunflowers, in the shade of one of a line of whispering silver-green poplars planted three generations ago. There were armies of these sunflowers round here, great thick stalks as tall as a man, dinner-plate faces turning heavily in the direction of the sun. The thing was, Brendan had faith in the world's adaptive powers whereas Adele didn't, it seemed.

While he unstrapped the water-bottles, she took out some bread and fruit saved from the night before. She started to clean the peaches by rubbing off their down with the hem of her T-shirt, then paused to watch as he drank, his head flung back, his eyes closed.

'Last day,' he scowled, wiping his mouth with the back of his hand. 'I wish it wasn't.'

'Can you remember all the days in order? Where was it we cycled first, after Tours?'

She went up and wound her arms round his damp waist, inhaling his heat and the grassy smell of sweat drying.

'It was that Plantagenet place, the abbey with the painted king and queen on top of their tombs,' he said, tucking her head beneath his chin. 'Fontevraud. The queen was Eleanor of Aquitaine.'

'Yes. And their son was on his tomb beside them, Richard the Lionheart. Remember? The Crusades. Crushing the infidel.'

'I'll crush you,' he said foolishly, twisting her arms behind her back.

She was pressed close to his chest, her ear against the thump of his heart.

They were testing each other on this holiday, competitive and protective and teasing. It was neck and neck so far. She didn't yet know if she had met her match. Sometimes she suspected not, and this made her feel like crying. Anyway, how can we promise to stay together when we don't know how we'll change? thought Adele. Look at my parents. Look at anyone. Brendan was thinking, I want her in my bed and at my side now and for good. We belong together, it's a fact, not a choice.

She pulled away and started to eat a peach.

'You've got juice on your chin,' he said, watching as she ate.

'No!' she flared at him, laughing.

'No what?'

'Just no.'

'How did you know what I was going to say?'

'It's too hot,' she said, blushing.

He pulled himself up to sit on the wall where the bicycles rested; with a broad smile he held his arms out to her.

He had begun to look fierce and brick-brown with sun-damage, she thought, like some sort of wild man or wandering minstrel. One evening she had told him what she knew about troubadours and courtly love in the Middle Ages, about their songs and code of courtesy and chivalric belief that desire was in itself ennobling; all that. He had listened intently, before seizing an imaginary lute and capering to and fro and warbling rubbish, until she, cracked into unwilling laughter, had run about trying to swat him as he dodged and skipped around her.

'It's what the French call *bronzer-idiot*,' she said now, rubbing a fingerful of suncream into his forehead, his cheeks, his chin and neck. He took her hand and turned it, kissing inside the wrist, then pulled her round so that she was leaning back, an elbow on each of his knees. He undid the clip holding up her sweat-damp hair, and twisted it slowly, held it away from her head.

'No wonder you're so hot, with all this hair,' he murmured. 'Hothead.'

She closed her eyes, ensnared by thoughts of the night before.

'We're making good time,' said Brendan after a while, glancing at his watch and at the sky. 'We'll be there soon after midday at this rate.'

Once at Angers, they found a shady patch of grass by the Maine, beneath the chateau, where they could lie and eat their *supermarché* picnic. They had bought cherries, a small soot-coated goat's cheese and some cold beer.

'It's not one of the fairy-tale ones, is it?' said Adele, looking up at the massive black-striped circular towers.

'More of a fortress than a chateau,' said Brendan, following her gaze and taking a swig of beer. He rolled the bottle over his brow and then along the inside of her arm.

'Angers, city of Cointreau. Chateau built between 1229 and 1240. Famous for Apocalypse tapestries,' said Adele, frowning over the guidebook. 'They say famous, but I've never heard of them. Not like the Bayeux Tapestry. Do you want to know what it says about them?'

'In a nutshell,' said Brendan. He was rifling through the bag of cherries.

'Oof, let's see. In a nutshell. Well, they were commissioned by the Duke of Anjou, not long after the Black Death. He used them to show off, bringing them out for jousts and troubadour events and that sort of thing. Then they were given to Angers Cathedral, which had trouble displaying them because they were so enormous.'

He smoothed her hair back gently and hung twin cherries over her ears.

'Look, I've made you earrings!'

'Thank you. Then came the French Revolution, and

religion was out of the window. Bits of the tapestries were chopped off and used for rubbing down horses, or as bed canopies, or to clear up after building work.'

'Would you pass me another beer?'

'Won't you be too sleepy then to go round the chateau?'

'I'll be fine,' he said. 'Weird to think of the French as revolutionaries. They take their cats for walks on leads! Remember that woman in Saumur?'

'Then in the nineteenth century there was a craze on the Middle Ages,' she continued. 'They rescued the tapestries and washed them in the Maine, which did their plant-based pigments no good at all. That's why the trees and grass are blue. And in the twentieth century they restored them and built a special long gallery in the chateau grounds to house them.'

'Do you know, your ears are perfect. Very rare, perfect ears,' murmured Brendan. 'Come here, we need a siesta.'

Adele lay in the crook of his arm with her head on his shoulder.

'You look like that king on his tomb in Fontevraud,' she murmured to his profile. 'Calm and complete.'

'You're my queen,' he breathed, before falling asleep. She lay moving gently to the rise and fall of his chest.

They were in a long dimly lit gallery, and had the place almost to themselves. Dawdling along, every now and then one of them would hold the other back to examine a detail, the grapey clusters of a cloud or the leaf-shaped flames of hell.

'The guidebook was right, see, all the grass and trees and foliage are blue,' said Brendan. 'Look at the shapes of the leaves! That's an oak, that's a vine leaf. Look at the detail.'

'And these must be the Four Horsemen of the Apocalypse,' said Adele. 'Yes, see, there's Famine on that black horse there. And look, look at this skeleton grinning as he trots past the blue jaws of hell, that's Death on his pale horse.'

'Nice,' said Brendan, peering at the fine-stitched skull.

'Look! Seven angels with seven trumpets, heralding seven different disasters, just like in Revelations.'

'Revelations?'

'It's the book that got tacked onto the end of the New Testament. It nearly didn't get in at all. It's raving. I had to read it for my dissertation last term, remember?'

'Oh, yes. The End of the World. Of course.'

'Full of stuff about the Whore of Babylon and the Anti-Christ and seven-headed monsters,' she sniffed. 'Seven was supposed to be some sort of magic number. Apocalyptic talk always comes from nutters, and they always quote Revelations. It's like a rule. Basically, they want a purge, a wipe-out, they justify it with the Bible, then they say everything afterwards will be purified and perfect for the survivors. Nee-naw nee-naw.'

'I want you on board next term, Adele. You've got to join my pressure group. There's no way you're going to get out of it.'

'Oh, not that again, Brendan.'

'Sorry,' he said, hurt.

'No, I'm sorry,' she said, and gently butted her forehead against his arm.

There was a pause.

'So,' he continued, almost reluctantly, 'so, up till now everyone involved in any of this end-of-the-world stuff has been raving mad and nothing but trouble. That's what you're saying. But now, now that it really does look like it's about to be all over, we can't seem to get a grip at all. Is that it?'

'If you like,' she sighed.

'Kiss me.'

She paused and did as he asked, slowly, thoughtfully, then took a step away from him.

'Come on,' she said, taking his hand and pulling him along to the next panel. 'It's a big tapestry. Look at this shipwreck, it's amazing. See, the floods have come. Look at the faces on the drowning men, their mouths are open, you can see their little teeth.'

'Floods! I could use this next term. I wonder if they've got a postcard of it. It's brilliant! Sorry. Sorry. But you're right; look at the expressions on those faces!'

'I suppose I did rather cover the same material,' she said, relenting for a moment. 'Floods, drought, storms, all that. "The Environment, Human Activity and the End of the World." Only two of us chose it; they nearly didn't run it. The module on human rights was way more popular.'

'That's what pisses me off about students,' declared Brendan. 'So fucking short-sighted. We want to travel, basically.'

'Give it a rest, Brendan!' she said, losing her temper. 'Can't we talk about something else?'

She marched on ahead of him. He stood and ground his teeth and took a deep breath.

No, he wanted to say, no we bloody well can't; you've

got to listen to me; you don't get it, do you. He swallowed his exasperation and made an effort to do as she asked.

'That's the star Wormwood,' she said when he caught up with her at the next panel.

'I thought wormwood was some sort of bitter plant,' he said curtly.

'It's a star that streams blood,' she read from the guide-book, 'and pollutes the skies and oceans.'

'Wormwood,' muttered Brendan, drawn in despite himself. 'Wow!'

'Moving on past the Eagle of Misfortune, we get to the locusts swarming up from hell. Ha. They're enormous. They really are quite scary.'

'Locusts! The insects are winning. You won't be so cocky when we've all got malaria.'

'Brendan.'

'It's all right for the middle-aged ones, the ones in charge now,' he burst out, unable to contain himself, 'but they're deliberately not looking into the time when it'll be our turn. Because by that time they'll be dead or past it, so it won't be their problem.'

'Look,' she said in a stony voice. 'Here's the fall of Babylon and its ramparts tumbling down.'

'The fall of Babylon. It's still not too late, not quite, but we've got to act *now*. How *can* you be so defeatist, Adele?'

'Oh, Brendan,' she groaned. 'You've got a one-track mind.'

'A one-track mind,' he muttered, drawing her to him, then slid his fingers down inside her shorts and grabbed a spiteful handful.

She gasped.

'We're on CCTV,' she hissed, wriggling out of his grip.

'You look like an angry bushbaby,' he hissed back.

She stalked on a few metres ahead, and even her pale legs looked indignant in the gloom.

'Sorry,' he whispered when he had caught up with her. He did not feel sorry; he felt angry and cruel.

'A plague of frogs,' she snapped, staring ahead. 'You'll like the next one, I bet. Armageddon.'

Despite himself he was peering closely at the forces of hell, the scimitars and swords and charging horsemen, the blade-shaped flames in the sky.

'So that's Armageddon,' he said. 'Not exactly convincing, though, is it. A bit tame.'

'You'd prefer the real thing,' she said, furious. 'You'd rather be cycling round the battlefields of Normandy.'

'I bet they thought *that* was Armageddon at the time,' he said. 'But it wasn't.'

'Yes, you liked that Musée des Blindés in Saumur,' she added nastily. 'The tank museum.'

'It wasn't actually that interesting. It was quite disappointing really. Though there was an FT 17 Renault from 1917.'

She had stayed outside and watched the bikes while he went round the museum in the company of what looked mainly like ex-army types and their tired wives. She had been able to hear the taped military music, brashly jaunty and tear-jerking, male voices swinging along in enthusiastic company, drum rolls and crude trumpet voluntaries.

'It happens, war,' said Brendan. 'It's major. It's part of life.'

'I do know that, geography boy.'

'Though if we get a proper global treaty on this, it could mean the end of war altogether. You'd like that, wouldn't you?'

'Huh. I don't think *that's* going to happen.'

'What? The global treaty? Or the end of war?'

'Both. Neither. Look, Brendan, I'm sure you're right about it all, the climate stuff, but the thing is, the world doesn't want to cut back. In fact the world thinks it's *wrong* to cut back. Can't you see that? What the world wants is economic growth. Increased productivity. The world won't listen to a word you say. You know that.'

'Even if it means the end of the world?'

'Yup. Even if it means that.'

'But . . .'

'Look. Last one. The New Jerusalem. Happy ending. Time to go.'

'Wait, Adele,' he cajoled, taking her hand. 'Look. Look, it's a lovely white chateau! Circular towers and crenellations and lancet windows. Your favourite sort!' She stood, head averted, her hand rigid in his. 'All the flowers and fruit trees are back in action – I bet they're organic – and it's floating between land and sky,' he crooned.

He caught a flicker of a smile at the corner of her mouth.

'Sorry,' he whispered, and this time he really did feel something, a stirring, though it wasn't exactly remorse.

She gave his fingers a faint squeeze. Hand in hand, blinking, they emerged into the late-afternoon sunlight.

For their last night they had put euros aside for a meal in a proper restaurant. The rest of the holiday it had been peaches and tomatoes, a baguette and some cheese, and evening picnics on park benches or under trees until the dark drove them back to whichever hostel they were staying in.

Now they sat in unaccustomed formality across the table from each other with a candle between them casting a glow. On the wall beside their table was a machine-stitched hanging of a medieval hunting scene.

'A bit feeble, isn't it, after the real thing,' said Brendan, as they examined its pastel stags and undifferentiated trees. 'I can't believe we're going home tomorrow. Who will I talk to without you there?' He grabbed her hand and gave it a hasty kiss.

What still surprised them both was the ease with which they had spoken to each other from the start, and how they had not run out of things to talk about even though they had been together exclusively now for ten days without a break. In fact it felt as if they had only just started. It was as if all this was only the beginning of a much longer conversation between them.

'I'm going to have to apply for another loan when I get back,' said Brendan. 'I really hope I can get a decent amount of work this August. September.'

'Snap,' said Adele. 'Eighteen thousand. More than, probably, by the end of Finals.'

'Worth it, though, if you get a decent degree. A 2:1. A First, even.'

'As long as it's not a 2:2.'

'No, nobody wants a Desmond. Of course, we're rich compared to most of the world.'

'I do know that,' she said. You're not my conscience, she

did not need to add. There had been several dangerous semi-submerged rocks, she reminded herself, in the broadly halcyon sea of this holiday. His tendency to lecture made her want to turn on her heel and walk away.

'Sorry,' he said, touching her hand again. 'Stop me when I do that.'

'Thanks,' she smiled. 'I will.'

It delighted her, their fluidity, how open and interested in each other they were, checking and clashing and counter-balancing. By this process they had been leading each other into unanticipated fields of fresh thought and feeling. She still thought him misguided, though, if he imagined he could change anything about the future.

'*Onglet à l'échalote*. That's steak, isn't it?' said Brendan uncertainly, studying the menu. '*Civet de marcassin*. Wild boar casserole. I might have the steak.'

'I thought meat was as bad as coal. Especially steak,' said Adele, who called herself a pescatarian. '*Barbue*. What's *barbue*? Oh, brill. What's brill?'

'There aren't exactly plenty more fish in the sea, either.'

'We could have the vegetable soup.'

'Yes. Cheaper, too,' he said, brightening. 'Then the *tian de courgettes*, whatever a *tian* is.'

'And they've got profiteroles. My favourite. I'm going to have profiteroles if I have room. Funny, that monster in the tapestry this afternoon made me think of profiteroles.'

'What monster?'

'The Beast of the Sea.' She thought back to the weird tapestry creature and its long thick stalky neck supporting the pyramid-cluster of multiple lions' heads. Each of these seven round faces had worn a nasty smile of its own.

'Like a *croquembouche*,' she added.

'A *croquembouche*?'

'My aunt had one when she got married, instead of a wedding cake. It's a pyramid of profiteroles stuck together with caramel.'

We could have a *croquembouche* when we get married, Brendan caught himself thinking, and turned red. It wasn't that he wanted her to agree with him all the time, in fact he positively relished most of the differences between them; but when that afternoon it had come to the one thing he was most passionate about and she had refused to listen, he hadn't been able to help himself falling into a pit of anger.

'I've got something of a monster in me,' he said now. 'I can't believe I was like that with you at the end there, in the gallery. The beer at lunch didn't help, but that's no excuse. Anger. That's my monster.'

Just then their food arrived, and for some minutes there was no more talk, only chewing and swallowing and appreciative little noises.

'My monster is melancholy,' she admitted after a while.

'That's not a monster.'

'Yes it is. It really is. I've got to fight it.'

'I'll help you.'

'All right. For example. I can't see any future.'

'We could live in a cave,' he grinned. 'Like those trog-lodytes in Chinon.'

'Nobody our age will ever be able to afford a cave, even.'

'A tent, then. We're bound to be allowed to pitch our tent in some old person's back garden. We don't need much, we could grow stuff, grow our own food . . .'

'Not lemons,' she said, 'or bananas.'

'No, not them, obviously. But we could grow all the stuff the monks were growing in that garden at Villandry, remember, all those cabbages and lettuces and courgettes? We could make *tians* every night! You're so beautiful. When I look at you I know I could do anything.'

'That's why I haven't been wanting to listen to your plans, Brendan. The trouble is, I don't think they're going to work. I wish I'd chosen Human Rights for my special subject; all that reading I did for the End of the World was just too much.'

'I know, I know,' he said. 'But think! Those guys who stitched that tapestry back there, it must have looked the same to them – they must have thought the world hadn't got long, what with the Black Death, and famine, and the clergy threatening them with plagues of monsters. And that was eight hundred years ago.'

'True.'

'Also, I feel happier than I ever have in my life.'

'Do you?' she said, and smiled a watery smile. 'Why?'

'I'm with you,' he shrugged.

Outside was warm and darkly velvet. They started the walk back to the hostel at a languorous pace, under a star-packed sky. He stopped to kiss her, and their tongues tasted of the wine they had drunk at dinner, the light strawberry-red Chinon.

'I wish this wasn't the last night,' she murmured into

his shoulder. She felt a lurch of concern at the thought of him alone, his sudden scowls misunderstood by others, his sanguine sunny breadth ignored or wasted.

'But we're not over just because the holiday is,' he said.

'I thought last night when we were, um, you know, that I didn't want that ever to be over. But I knew it would be. Same with the meal just now, while I was enjoying it I knew that would be over in a little while, too.'

'And one day we're all going to die!' he said. 'But not yet. Just because we're going to die one day doesn't spoil being alive, does it?'

'Everything's always got to be over in the end.'

'You're like Pandora. You need to look on the bright side. Think outside the box, Pandora!'

'That's great, coming from you. You're the one who's going round setting end-dates.' She pulled away. 'Sorry. Not that again. Look, there's the Plough, and there's Orion with three stars in his belt.'

I'm not a gloom-and-doom merchant, Adele, he wanted to say; you know I'm not; in fact, I'm a sight more of an optimist than you are.

He doesn't need to convince me, she thought. I know what he's saying. I just think it's hopeless and we're the last generation. The last but one, to be more accurate. Our children will be the last. That's my considered opinion as an historian, is it? Yes, it is.

'What I think,' he said carefully, 'what I think is, if you really want something to happen, to change, then that definitely improves the chances of it actually coming true.'

'Sounds reasonable. I can see the sense in that. Yes.'

'Good. So . . .'

'I can't promise anything,' she responded, with equal care. 'Or rather, I can. I promise I won't close my ears again. That was stupid of me this afternoon. I'm sorry.'

'That's good enough for me,' he murmured. He wrapped his arms round her again, and poked the tip of his tongue into first one of her ears and then the other. She closed her eyes and sighed.

'Listen,' he whispered, his breath rustling in her hair. 'I know what I want, Adele.'

Something had shifted in his voice, in the temperature of the microclimate that enveloped them, and it roused her to pull away and hold him at arm's length.

'No,' she said. 'Don't say it.'

She put her hand up to his mouth to stop the words coming out.

'Why not?' he spluttered, after a struggle.

'It's too soon,' she said. 'It might not be true.'

'Can I say it in French?'

'No.'

'Then I'll think it instead,' he said, holding her hard. 'I'll dream it at night and I'll think it in the day.'

She was twisting and turning, trying to struggle out of his arms. He enjoyed these tussles more than she did, she realised; he liked a challenge. She looked up frowning into his delighted face.

'Why are you smiling?'

'I can smile, can't I? There isn't any law against smiling, is there?'

He ran several steps ahead of her and skipped around playing air guitar.

'I'm a troubadour!' he sang. 'I'm a troubadour!'

She ran after him, caught between laughter and protest. 'Look at the stars!' he yelled. 'Hello, Wormwood! Come in, Wormwood, are you receiving me? OK, the universe is huge, we don't matter, all that . . . So what?'

'It's no use,' she panted, lunging at him and missing.

'So what,' he shouted, running ahead of her. 'So what so what so what! You can't stop me saying it! I'm going to say it!'

'Don't!' she called, running after him. 'Don't say it! Kiss me, though.'

'I'll do that,' he said, lifting her in the air and letting her slide slowly down the front of his body. 'I'll do more than that.'

He lifted her again and whirled her in his arms until they were both dizzy. Breathing hard, exhilarated, they leaned into a mutual embrace, this time for balance as much as anything. Then they stood in the fathomless dark and stared saucer-eyed beyond the stratosphere into the night, as troupes of boisterous planets wheeled across the blackness all around them.

Charm for a Friend with a Lump

First let me take a piece of chalk and draw a circle round you, so you're safe. There. Now I'll stand guard, keeping a weather eye open for anything threatening, and we can catch up with each other while we wait.

Have a glance through this garden catalogue if you would. I need your help in choosing what to plant this spring. I thought the little yellow Peacevine tomatoes, so sweet and sharp, along with Gardener's Delight and Tiger Toms; but there's a lot to be said for Marmande too.

I'll have a word with the powers-that-be. The Health Czar. Ban parabens. I'll keep away the spotted snakes with double tongue, I'll be like Cobweb and Mustardseed in the play; I'll make sure the beetles black approach not near. By naming the bad things I'll haul them up into the light and shrivel their power over you. Hence, malignant tumour, hence; carcinoma, come not here.

Then I thought I'd try those stripy round courgettes this year, Ronds de Nice. You have to pick them as soon as they reach the size of tennis balls, you mustn't let them get any bigger than that or they won't be worth eating. They'll swell and grow as big as footballs if you let them. As for fruit, what do you think of Conference pears? Or, the catalogue recommends the Invincible, a very hardy variety which crops heavily and blooms twice a year.

Let's not even start on those predictable but useless paths which lead to nowhere. If only I hadn't smoked at fifteen, if only there hadn't been that betrayal, if only I hadn't spent so much time putting up with the insupportable – whyever did I think endurance was a virtue? Didn't I *want* to stay alive? If only I hadn't sipped wine, or drunk water from plastic bottles. If only I hadn't gone jogging the day Chernobyl exploded. Oh, give it a rest! We live in the world as it is, we all have to breathe its contagious fogs. It's wrong of them to claim it must somehow be our own fault when our health is under attack.

Let's get back to the catalogue. Help me choose some soft fruit. If I had more space I might try gooseberries again now there's this new cultivar that cheats American blight. But it's probably wiser to add to the existing black-currant patch; here's a new one, Titania, 'large fruit and good flavour. Crops very heavily over a long period. Good resistance to mildew and rust.'

We're advised to build up an arsenal of elixirs if we want to strengthen our own resistance. We're told we ought to call in light boxes, amulets, echinacea drops and oily fish, we should fix on organic free-range grass-fed meat, Japanese green tea and a daily dose of turmeric. And if we're really serious about protecting ourselves we must avoid dry-cleaners, getting fat, aluminium, insecticides; shun trans fats as the devil's food; forswear polystyrene cups. We've got to fight shy of white bread, a sedentary lifestyle, perfume and anger, if we truly want to save ourselves. And even if we tick off every item on the list, there's absolutely no guarantee that it'll lengthen our span by a single day.

On your last birthday, with your natural dislike of being reminded of the passing years, we skirted round the subject for a while. I asked what you'd be doing to celebrate. You scoffed. You said you'd rather forget about it. Do you remember? Then I reached down into myself and managed to say, 'You *should* celebrate, your birthday *should* be celebrated, because the world's a better place with you in it.' May you continue to pile on the years, but with more pleasure from now on. In time may you embrace fallen arches and age spots; decades from now may your joints creak and your ears hiss, may your crow's feet laugh back into the mirror at your quivering dewlaps.

Nobody in their right mind looks at an old oak tree growing in strength and richness and thinks, You'll be dead soon. They just admire and draw strength from its example. May you keep your hair on and your eyebrows in place. May you never have to wear a hat indoors. May you and your other half tuck two centuries under your belts between you and then, like the old couple in the tale, when some kind god in disguise grants you a wish, may you go together, hand in hand, in an instant.

I'm willing you to be well. Do you hear me? If there does happen to be some disorder in your blood I'm like Canute – I'll stay here by you and turn the tide. You're my persona grata.

And if they find that some weed or canker has gained hold after all – Japanese knotweed, it might be, that ruthless invader and ignorer of boundaries – well, then, we'll deal with it. There are powerful new weed-killers these days, and they work. Doctors are like gardeners in the way they know how to distinguish between healthy growth and uncontrollable proliferation. There's a fine line, and what I am casting a spell for is that nothing inside you has stepped over it.

In my spell we are dreaming our way forward through the year into the green and white of May, and on into the deep green lily-ponds of June. The lushness of June, its new heat and subdued glitter of excitement at dusk, its scent and roses, that's what we'll aim for. I do love roses, their scent and beauty, particularly my Souvenir du Dr Jamain and the thorny pink eglantine beside the vegetable patch.

We'll have a party there this Midsummer's Eve, up by the tomato plants and ranks of cos lettuce, just the two of us. Let's write it in our diaries now. I can't spare you. You're indispensable! We'll have a party, and pledge your health by moonlight on the one night of the year when plants consumed or seeded have magical powers.

There is a great deal of talk about the benefits of mistletoe extract and so on, but I'm not convinced. You can spend a lot of time and energy chasing magic potions, when you might be better occupied weaving your own spells over the future. En route, sleep will help. Everyone has their own private walled garden at night where they can prune their troubles and dream change into some sort of shape. That's what I'm trying to say, a dream can be a transformer, as well as providing a margin or grassy bank where you can rest while the outside world goes on. Active dreaming, which is what I would prescribe, can be a powerful form of enchantment.

You're not out of the woods yet, that's clear; but a little while from now I want you to walk out of the woods and into the June garden. Leave the black bats hanging upside down; they'll stay asleep. While we wait for summer, let's choose to be patient and hopeful. And soon, not really long from now at all, I aim to smile at you and say, Come into the garden, friend of my heart.

The Festival of the Immortals

The Daniel Defoe event had just been cancelled, and as a consequence of this the queue for the tea tent was stretching halfway round the meadow. Towards the back, shivering slightly this damp October morning, were two women who looked to be somewhere in the early November of their lives.

'Excuse me, but are you going to the next talk?' one of them asked the other, waving a festival brochure at a late lost wasp.

'Who, me?' replied the woman. 'Yes. Yes, I am. It's Charlotte Brontë reading from *Villette*, I believe.'

'Hmm, I hope they keep the actual reading element to a minimum,' said the first, wrinkling her nose. 'Don't you? I can read *Villette* any time.'

'Good to hear it in her own voice, though,' suggested the other.

'Oh I don't know,' said the first. 'I think that can be overdone. Some curiosity value, of course, but half the time an actor would read it better. No, I want to know what she's *like*. That difficult father. Terribly short-sighted. Extremely short full stop. The life must shed light on the work, don't you think. What's the matter, have I got a smudge on my face or something?'

'It's not . . . ?' said the other, gazing at her wide-eyed. 'It's not Viv Armstrong, is it?'

'Yes,' said Viv Armstrong, for that was indeed her name. 'But I'm afraid I don't . . .'

'Phyllis!' beamed the other. 'Phyllis Goodwin. The ATS, remember? Bryanston Square? Staining our legs brown with cold tea and drawing on the seams with an eyebrow pencil?'

'Fuzzy!' exclaimed Viv at last. 'Fuzzy Goodwin!'

'Nobody's called me that for over fifty years,' said Phyllis. 'It was when you wrinkled your nose in that particular way, that's when I knew it was you.'

The rest of their time in the queue flew by. Before they knew it they were carrying tea and carrot cake over to a table beneath the rustling amber branches of an ancient beech tree.

'I'm seventy-eight and I'm still walking up volcanoes,' Viv continued, as they settled themselves. 'I don't get to the top any more but I still go up them. I'm off to Guatemala next week.'

Eager, impulsive, slapdash, Phyllis remembered. Rule-breaking. Artless. Full of energy. In some ways, of course, she must have changed, but just now she appeared exactly, comically, as she always had been, in her essence if not in her flesh. Although even here, physically, her smile was the same, the set of her shoulders, the sharpness of nose and eyes.

'The first time I saw you, we were in the canteen,' said Phyllis. 'You were reading *The Waves* and I thought, Ah, a kindred spirit. I was carrying a steamed treacle pudding and I sat down beside you.'

That's right, thought Viv, Fuzzy had had a sweet tooth – look at the size she was now. She'd had long yellow hair, too, just like Veronica Lake, but now it was short and white.

'I still do dip into *The Waves* every so often,' she said aloud. 'It's as good as having a house by the sea, don't you think? Especially as you get older. Oh, I wonder if she's on later, Virginia, I'd love to go to one of her readings.'

Viv knew many writers intimately thanks to modern biographers, but she was only really on first-name terms with members of the Bloomsbury Group.

'Unfortunately not,' said Phyllis. 'That's a cast-iron rule of this festival, a writer can only appear if they're out of copyright, and Virginia isn't out of it for another five years.'

'But she must be, surely,' said Viv. 'Isn't copyright fifty years?'

'Well, it was, until recently,' said Phyllis. 'And Virginia *was* out of it by the early Nineties, I happen to know because I was at one of her readings here. Oh, she was wonderful. What a talker! She kept the whole marquee in stitches – spellbound – rocking with laughter. But then they changed the copyright law, something to do with the EU, and now it's life plus seventy years, and she went back in again. So she won't be allowed to return until 2011 at the earliest. Very galling as we might not still be here by then.'

'Oh, I don't know,' said Viv. 'Aren't you being rather gloomy? Seventy-eight isn't that old.'

'It is quite old, though,' said Phyllis doubtfully.

'Well, I suppose so. But it's not *old* old,' said Viv. 'It's not ninety. Come on, now, Fuzzy, we've got some catching up to do.'

In the next few minutes they attempted to condense the last half-century into digestible morsels for each other. Viv had put in a year at teacher-training college, then found teaching posts through Gabbitas-Thring, while Phyllis had taken a secretarial course at Pitman's College in Bloomsbury followed by a cost accounting job at the Kodak factory where she lived, totting up columns of figures in a large ledger at a slanting desk. At some point between the Olympics being held at Wembley and the year of the Festival of Britain, they had met their respective husbands.

'All this is such outside stuff, though,' said Phyllis obscurely. She was supposed to be writing her memoirs, spurred on by a local Life-writing course, but had been dismayed at her attempts so far, so matter-of-fact and chirpy and boring.

They ploughed on. Viv had settled just inside the M25, before it was there, of course, while Phyllis lived just outside it. They'd had three children each, and now had seven grandchildren between them.

'Two girls and a boy,' said Viv. 'One's in computers, one's a physiotherapist and one has yet to find his feet. He's forty-eight.'

'Oh,' said Phyllis. 'Well, I had the other combination, two boys and a girl. Ned's an animal-feed operator but his real love is Heavy Metal, much good it's done him. Peter's an accountant – no, I keep forgetting, they don't call them accountants any more. They're financial consultants now.'

'Like refuse collectors. "My old man's a dustman."

Remember that?' said Viv. 'Then there was "My old man said 'Follow the van, and don't dilly dally on the way'." My mother used to sing that. I divorced *my* old man, by the way, sometime back in the Seventies.'

'I'm sorry,' said Phyllis.

'Don't be silly,' said Viv. 'I've realised I'm a natural chopper and changer. Or rather, I start off enthusiastic and then spot the feet of clay. It's a regular pattern. I did eventually find the love of my life, when I was in my sixties, but he died. What about your daughter, though? Didn't you mention a daughter?'

'Yes,' said Phyllis, blinking. 'Sarah. She went into the book business. In fact, she's the one who dreamt up the idea behind this festival, and now she runs it. Artistic Director of the Festival of Immortals, that's her title.'

'Good Lord,' said Viv. 'The opportunities there are for girls these days!'

'It's a full-time year-round job as you can imagine,' said Phyllis, gaining confidence. 'She spent months this year trying to persuade Shakespeare to run a workshop but the most she could get him to do was half-promise to give a masterclass in the sonnet. He's supposed to be arriving by helicopter at four this afternoon but it's always touch and go with him, she says, it's impossible to pin him down.'

'Good Lord,' said Viv again, and listened enthralled as Phyllis told her anecdotes from previous years, the time Rabbie Burns had kept an adoring female audience waiting forty minutes and had eventually been tracked down to the stationery cupboard deep in congress or whatever he called it with Sarah's young assistant Sophie. Then there was the awful day Sarah had introduced a reading as being from *The Floss on the Mill* and George Eliot had looked so reproachful, even more so than usual, but Sarah did tend to reverse her words when flustered, it wasn't intentional. Every year Alexander Pope roared up in a fantastic high-powered low-slung sportscar, always a new one, always the latest model. Everybody looked forward to that. Jane Austen could be very sarcastic in interviews if you asked her a question she didn't like, she'd said something very rude to Sarah last year, very cutting, when Sarah had questioned her on what effect she thought being fostered by a wet-nurse had had on her. Because of course that was what people were interested in now, that sort of detail, there was no getting away from it.

Last year had been really fascinating, if a bit morbid; they'd taken illness as their theme – Fanny Burney on the mastectomy she'd undergone without anaesthetic, Emily Brontë giving a riveting description of the time she was bitten by a rabid dog and how she'd gone straight back home and heated up a fire-iron and used it herself to cauterise her arm. Emily had been very good in the big round-table discussion, too, the one called 'TB and Me', very frank. People had got the wrong idea about her, Sarah said, she wasn't unfriendly, just rather shy; she was lovely when you got to know her.

'They've done well, our children, when you think of it,' commented Viv. 'But then, there was no reason for them not to. First generation university.'

Phyllis had tried to describe in her memoir how angry and sad she had been at having to leave school at fourteen; how she'd just missed the 1944 Education Act with its free secondary schooling for everyone. Books had been beyond her parents' budget, but with the advent of paperbacks as she reached her teens she had become a reader. Why couldn't she find a way to make this sound interesting?

'Penny for your thoughts, Fuzzy,' said Viv.

'Viv,' said Phyllis, 'would you mind not calling me that? I never did like that name and it's one of the things I'm pleased to have left in the past.'

'Oh!' said Viv. 'Right you are.'

'Because names do label you,' said Phyllis. 'I mean, Phyllis certainly dates me.'

'I was called Violet until I left home,' confessed Viv. 'Then I changed to Viv and started a new life.'

'I always assumed Viv was short for Vivien,' said Phyllis. 'Like Vivien Leigh. I saw *Gone with the Wind* five times. Such a shame about her and Laurence Olivier.'

'Laurence Olivier as Heathcliff!' exclaimed Viv. 'Mr Darcy. Henry V. *Henry V!* That was my first proper Shakespeare, that film.'

'Mine too,' confessed Phyllis. 'Then later I was reading "The Whitsun Weddings" – I'd been married myself for a while – and I came to the last verse and there it was, that shower of arrows fired by the English bowmen, just like in the film. The arrows were the new lives of the young married couples on the train and it made me cry, it made me really depressed, that poem.'

'Not what you'd call a family man, Philip Larkin,' said Viv.

'Not really,' said Phyllis. 'You know, thinking about it, the only time I stopped reading altogether was when they were babies. Three under five. I couldn't do that again.'

'I *did* keep reading,' said Viv. 'But there were quite a few accidents. And I was always a Smash potato sort of house-wife, if I'm honest.'

'I wish I had been,' said Phyllis enviously.

She cast her mind back to all that: the hours standing over the twin tub, the hundred ways with mince, nagging the children to clean out the guinea-pig cage, collecting her repeat prescription for Valium. That time too she had tried to record in her memoir, but it had been even more impossible to describe than the days of her girlhood.

'It's not in the books we've read, is it, how things have been for us,' said Viv. 'There's only Mrs Ramsay, really, and she's hardly typical.'

'I've been bound by domestic ties,' said Phyllis, 'but I'm still a feminist.'

'Are you?' said Viv, impressed.

'Well, I do think women should have the vote so yes, I suppose I am. Because a lot of people don't really, underneath, think women should have the vote, you know.'

'I had noticed,' said Viv.

'It's taken me so long to see how the world works that I think I should be allowed extra time,' said Phyllis.

At this point she decided to confide in Viv about her struggles in Life writing. For instance, all she could remember about her grandmother was that she was famous for having once thrown a snowball into a fried-fish shop; but was that the sort of thing that was worth remembering? Another problem was, just as you didn't talk about yourself in the same way you talked about others, so you couldn't *write* about yourself from the outside either. Not really. Which reminded her, there had been such a fascinating event here last year, Sarah had been interviewing Thomas

Hardy and it had come out that he'd written his own biography, in the third person, and got his wife Florence to pretend that *she'd* written it! He'd made her promise to bring it out as her own work after he'd died. The audience had been quite indignant, but, as he told Sarah, he didn't want to be summed up by anybody else, he didn't want to be cut and dried and skewered on a spit. How would *you* like it, he'd asked Sarah and she'd had to agree she wouldn't. This year she, Sarah, had taken care to give him a less contentious subject altogether – he was appearing tomorrow with Coleridge and Katherine Mansfield at an event called 'The Notebook Habit'.

'Yes,' said Viv, 'I've got a ticket for that.'

This whole business of misrepresentation was one of Sarah's main bugbears at the Festival, Phyllis continued. She found it very difficult knowing how to handle the hecklers. Ottoline Morrell, for example, turned up at any event where D.H. Lawrence was appearing, carrying on about *Women in Love*, how she wasn't Hermione Roddice, how she'd never have thrown a paperweight at anyone, how dare he and all the rest of it. Sarah had had to organise discreet security guards because of incidents like that. The thing was, people minded about posterity. They minded about how they would be remembered.

'Not me,' said Viv.

'Really?' said Phyllis.

'I'm more than what's happened to me or where I've been,' said Viv. 'I know that and I don't care what other people think. I can't be read like a book. And I'm not dead yet, so I can't be summed up or sum myself up. Things might change.'

'Goodness,' said Phyllis, amazed.

'Call no man happy until he is dead,' shrugged Viv, glancing at her watch. 'And now it's time for Charlotte Brontë. I had planned to question her about those missing letters to Constantin Heger, but I don't want Sarah's security guards after me.'

The two women started to get up, brushing cake crumbs from their skirts and assembling bags and brochures.

'Look, there's Sarah now,' said Phyllis, pointing towards the marquee.

Linking arms, they began to make their way across the meadow to where the next queue was forming.

'And look, that must be Charlotte Brontë with her, in the bonnet,' Viv indicated. 'See, I was right! She *is* short.'

THE HISTORY OF VINTAGE

The famous American publisher Alfred A. Knopf (1892–1984) founded Vintage Books in the United States in 1954 as a paperback home for the authors published by his company. Vintage was launched in the United Kingdom in 1990 and works independently from the American imprint although both are part of the international publishing group, Random House.

Vintage in the United Kingdom was initially created to publish paperback editions of books acquired by the prestigious hardback imprints in the Random House Group such as Jonathan Cape, Chatto & Windus, Hutchinson and later William Heinemann, Secker & Warburg and The Harvill Press. There are many Booker and Nobel Prize-winning authors on the Vintage list and the imprint publishes a huge variety of fiction and non-fiction. Over the years Vintage has expanded and the list now includes great authors of the past – who are published under the Vintage Classics imprint – as well as many of the most influential authors of the present.

For a full list of the books Vintage publishes, please visit our website
www.vintage-books.co.uk

For book details and other information about the classic authors we publish, please visit the Vintage Classics website
www.vintage-classics.info

www.vintage-classics.info